A few hours later the parachutists became part of the Northern Landing Force. No one knew what that meant or where the convoy would bring them, but an air of excitement and fear filled the LCI as the big landing craft slid out into the Slot and zigzagged past the Russell Islands.

The late afternoon crawled nervously by, filled with scuttlebutt. Everyone had an idea where the landing would be, and no two ideas matched. Old letters were pulled out of packs and reread while some Marines wrote home, each wondering if it would be the last letter he would ever write.

At 0600 the convoy hove to off Barakoma as the tiny intercom blasted the captain's order, "Stand by the landing party."

Jessie's stomach knotted. He jumped out of his rack. The faces around him looked terrified. Others had a dull resigned stare as if they had already accepted the inevitable.

"All hands on deck!"

"You heard it! Saddle up!" Gunny O'Cleary barked. "First Platoon! You leave anything and it's history! Ain't no lookin' back now, Marines!"

Also by Johnnie M. Clark
*Published by Ballantine Books:*

GUNS UP!

SEMPER FIDELIS

# THE OLD CORPS

Johnnie M. Clark

BALLANTINE BOOKS • NEW YORK

Library of Congress Catalog Card Number: 90-91842

ISBN 0-345-35815-5

Manufactured in the United States of America

First Edition: November 1990

*Any officer can get by on his sergeants. To be a sergeant you have to know your stuff. I'd rather be an outstanding sergeant than just another officer.*

—Gunnery Sergeant Daniel Daly,
two-time Medal of Honor winner

# Acknowledgments

Bob Wyatt, Pam and Ernie. Thanks for believing in me. To my old Gunnery Sergeant, Alpha Company, First Battalion, 5th Marine Regiment, An Hoa Valley, 1968. Thanks to the one and only Para-Marine Regiment. Special thanks to Mr. Joe Pagac, an old Para-Marine and my new friend. Joe provided me with a wealth of information, documentation, photographs, and even souvenirs from Vella Lavella to Iwo Jima. More importantly Joe provided memories, and every Marine knows that memories can be painful. Thanks to two old Mustangs, Tom Lynch and Rudy Moffler. Thanks Kat. I want to acknowledge an outstanding book entitled *The Spearhead: The World War II History of The 5th Marine Division,* by Howard M. Conner, copyright 1950. Thanks to St. Petersburg Junior College for a place to work. To Haslams for a place to enjoy the work, and to all of my Tae Kwon Do students for prayers and encouragement. To Shawn and Bonnie and Nancy, thanks for everything.

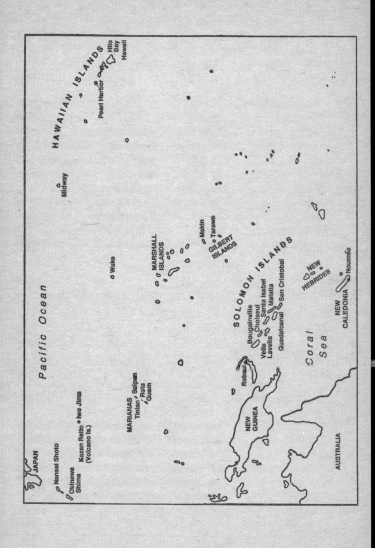

JAPAN

Nansei Shoto

Okinawa
Shima

Kazan Retto ° Iwo Jima
(Volcano Is.)

*Pacific Ocean*

MARIANAS
Tinian ⸴ Saipan
⸴ Rota
⸴ Guam

Wake

MARSHALL
ISLANDS

Makin
Tarawa
GILBERT
ISLANDS

Midway

HAWAIIAN ISLANDS

Pearl Harbor
Hilo
Bay
Hawaii

NEW
GUINEA

Rabaul

SOLOMON ISLANDS

Bougainville
Choiseul
Vella ⸴ Santa Isabel
Lavella ⸴ Malaita
Guadalcanal ⸴ San Cristobal

NEW
HEBRIDES

NEW
CALEDONIA ⸴ Nouméa

*Coral
Sea*

AUSTRALIA

# PROLOGUE

**THEY LOOKED, STRAINING** to see through the gray rising mist of the fetid jungle floor. The familiar clapping sound of a single chopper reverberated off fog-shrouded mountains and snaked through deep valleys until it seemed to be coming from every direction. Seventeen Marines in a small, tense perimeter gripped their weapons. One, a kid with deep-set eyes and a long nose, chewed nervously at his bottom lip, then spit beyond the flash suppressor of his M14 rifle.

"That friggin' chopper's gonna bring 'em down on us, Barry."

"Could be, Moose, could be."

"Every gook in the mountains is gonna know right where we are, bro."

"And you know why?" Moose spit again.

"The Mouth told me we was waitin' on that old gunny."

"There it is, bro. We're gonna get every swinging one blown off, and why? Waitin' on some old fossil. The clown must be a real bird if he's still a gunny after—"

Moose's comments were cut off, and his voice turned into a painful wheeze as he gasped for air and clawed to remove the pincerlike grip of another Marine, a huge Indian, from around his throat.

"Gunnery Sergeant Slate has more time in the bush than you've got in the chow line, maggot."

"I'm sorry, Chief," Moose managed.

The big Indian corporal released the pale Marine with a shove that lifted his chin.

"You will address Gunny Slate as sir, PFC." Swift Eagle's tone was businesslike. No hint of emotion showed in his piercing black eyes.

1

"All right, all right, Chief! Chill out, man. Let's do the peace pipe, bro."

The Indian turned away and moved silently back to the center of the perimeter with Lieutenant Neader, Doc Rice, and Mouth, the radioman.

Barry and Moose exchanged puzzled glances, then turned their attention back to the thick jungle that surrounded the small clearing.

"Throw out the smoke, Mouth," Lieutenant Neader said.

Mouth the radioman pulled the pin on a smoke grenade and tossed it a few feet away. Swirls of green rose up through the morning mist.

"There he is!" A voice from the far side of the perimeter carried across the clearing.

"This is Alpha One."

"We got a cold LZ, but there's heat nearby."

A moment later the belly of the twin-rotor CH-46 Sea Stallion hovered over the small clearing. It lowered quickly, and the back ramp dropped. Someone started tossing out cases of C-rations as fast as he could. A salty-looking Marine ran down the ramp with two cases of C-rations under one arm and a pump shotgun under the other. He looked about six feet tall, medium build. He wore a big, floppy NVA pack and one of the new Army flak jackets that all Marines coveted. His boots were worn thin on the bottom, and there was no hint that any part of them had ever been black; they were molded to his feet like well-worn moccasins. He wore a special cartridge belt filled with shotgun shells and had two more bandoliers of shotgun shells crisscrossing his chest. He stopped beyond the chopper ramp, dropped the C-rations, and signaled a thumbs-up to the pilot. Accelerating rotors whined. The CH-46 lifted off, nose first and then the tail, until she was level. The chopper swung out beyond the perimeter and climbed away.

"Gunny Slate!" Lieutenant Neader called as he ran forward with his hand out. The lieutenant smiled. He was lean, clean-cut, and handsome, a real billboard Marine.

"Lieutenant," Gunnery Sergeant Slate said as he grabbed the young officer's hand and gave it one quick strong shake. The gunny removed his helmet and scratched the top of his head. He wore the white sidewall jarhead haircut, but even as tight and high as it was, it didn't hide the telltale snow on top. His eyes were steel-gray and all business. His face was lean and tan and ruggedly good-looking, with a square jaw carved out of granite.

"I'm honored to have you with us, Gunny."

"Thank you, sir. I'll try not to get in the way."

"The skipper told me you requested First Platoon. I know a little about the special friendship you had with Corporal Swift Eagle's father at Iwo and the frozen Chosen. . . ." The young lieutenant hesitated as if he were unsure how to say what he wanted to say.

"It won't affect my performance, Lieutenant," Slate reassured him matter-of-factly.

Lieutenant Neader nodded. He looked relieved. Insulting a living legend would be a lousy way to start off an already miserable day.

Corporal Swift Eagle walked to a stop behind the lieutenant.

Neader turned. "Gunny, this is Corporal Swift Eagle."

The old man smiled, and his teeth looked whiter than normal against his darkly tanned face.

Swift Eagle's spine straightened, and his shoulders rolled back as he extended his hand. "It's an honor, sir."

Slate shook Swift Eagle's hand firmly and looked him in the eye. "I named you, son, at the base of Bagana."

"Bagana?"

"It was an active volcano on Bougainville. Japs had us pinned down pretty good. I kept watch while your dad read the letter telling us you'd been born. You owe me, Marine."

The big stone face looked puzzled for a moment then opened his eyes wide in recognition.

"Yes, sir. You saved my father's life on Iwo Jima. . . ."

"No, son, not that. Your daddy was gonna name you Walking Skunk!"

A grin cracked across the Indian's granite face. Lieutenant Neader laughed out loud, then quickly covered his mouth to keep the noise down.

"We better saddle up, Gunny," Neader said.

"I'm with you, Lieutenant," Gunnery Sergeant Slate said with a nod.

Lieutenant Neader knelt down on one knee, pulled a grid map from inside his flak jacket, and unfolded it on the ground. "Here's where we are now, Gunny."

"So what do we got here, about five to nine clicks to the Laotian border?"

"About that. We're supposed to set in here by nightfall." Lieutenant Neader pointed to a spot on the map along the Laotian border.

"Saddle up, Mouth! Pass the word," Swift Eagle called.

A minute later the staggered column of eighteen men pushed through the tangled jungle growth that surrounded the clearing, waded across a meandering stream, up a rock-strewn hill, down the other side, and then climbed steadily into the Thua Thien mountains. The copper sun rose high into the hot blue sky, and by noon the temperature was 105. One thirty-minute break in a quick perimeter for chow, then the tiny column started up the long hot hump again. Three hours later the platoon stumbled onto a steep mountain trail and staggered up it like a group of overburdened donkeys, under packs that grew heavier with each step. Gunny Slate paused and lifted his eyes from the ground. He looked past a chunky M79 man and Corporal Swift Eagle and Lieutenant Neader to the point man fifty meters up the narrow path. Suddenly the old salt's steely eyes locked onto a branch hanging ten feet above the point man's head.

"Halt!" Slate called, trying not to shout out their presence to every NVA in the area. The point man paused and glanced over his shoulder. Each man in the column dropped instinctively to one knee and searched the heavy woods on both sides of the winding trail, with his weapon following his gaze.

Lieutenant Neader looked back. "What's up?"

Gunny Slate moved past the M79 man, who was flicking his safety on and off nervously, and squatted beside the lieutenant and Swift Eagle. Mouth the radio man looked on from behind. Slate waved the point man back down the trail.

"Look just above where the point man stopped," Slate said.

"Yeah, what? In the trees?"

"See that big branch that stretches straight over the trail?"

"I see it." Swift Eagle sounded irritated.

"What?" Lieutenant Neader asked impatiently.

"I should have seen that," Swift Eagle said, shaking his head in disgust.

"Look, Lieutenant." Slate drew a line in the dirt by Lieutenant Neader's boots. "That's the branch going straight over the trail."

"Yeah."

Slate drew three lines sticking up from the first line. "See those three smaller branches all the same length sticking straight up toward the sky?"

"Yeah."

"See the middle one?"

"Yeah."

"It doesn't have any leaves. I can't make it out for certain from here, but I'll bet some peaches and pound cake that middle branch is tied on by a vine."

The young point man squatted beside the lieutenant. "What's up, Lieutenant?"

"Gunny Slate here just saved your life, Marine. He spotted a marker right over your head. Trail's booby-trapped."

"Wooh. Hey, thanks."

"Next time we hit a slop chute, you owe me a beer."

"I'll bag you the whole bar, Gunny!"

Slate smiled as he turned to look back down the column. "Pass the word to look for some sign of a trail goin' off from this one."

Helmets turned as the word was passed down the column. A moment later a tall, thin black Marine rushed forward carrying an M60 over one shoulder.

Lieutenant Neader stood up. "What you got, Sally?"

"Got some Ho Chi Minh sandal tracks back here leading around the side of the mountain."

"Let's see 'em," Lieutenant Neader said.

Gunnery Sergeant Slate and Corporal Swift Eagle followed. Halfway down the column, Sally stopped and pointed down to the side of the trail. The gunny knelt quickly to study the tire tracks of an NVA sandal print.

"This track ain't five minutes old, Lieutenant. Look, the dust still holds on the edges."

Lieutenant Neader waved the point man back down the trail. "Try to follow those prints, Cooper. He's not far ahead. Be ready to fire."

The column peeled back around and headed after Cooper, the point man. The brush was tangled and thick for a hundred meters, then Cooper found another trail. He stopped and waved Swift Eagle forward. The gunny followed.

Cooper knelt down with his M16 ready. "Look at this, Chief," he whispered excitedly. "Look at all the sandal prints. Must be a friggin' gook interstate!"

The trail was three to four feet wide and was covered with fresh sandal prints. Two small bicycle-size tire prints ran parallel about two feet apart down the trail. Lieutenant Neader moved forward and knelt beside Corporal Swift Eagle.

"We got a lot of gooks here, sir," Swift Eagle mumbled quietly. "But the tracks don't run deep enough for an ammo cart or any heavy weapon."

Gunnery Sergeant Slate nudged the wide-eyed point man. "Look on that side of the trail. See if you can find some commo wire," he said calmly.

"Yeah, Gunny, I got some blue funk right here," Cooper said as he lifted two strands of heavy blue communication wire four feet off the edge of the trail with the barrel of his M16.

"Nice call, Gunny," Lieutenant Neader said. "How'd you know?"

"I didn't. It's just that the Japs on Bougainville used to use a little cart for layin' commo wire, and it made tracks like these."

Slate moved over to the wire and gave a light tug until a long stretch of it pulled out of the brush and dirt that camouflaged it. It ran parallel to the trail. He studied the two strands carefully.

Fingering the wire, Lieutenant Neader looked cautiously up and then down the mountain trail.

"What do you think, Gunny?"

"This is heavy gauge. I'd say we found a lot of gooks. Get that radioman up here, Chief."

Swift Eagle turned to Cooper.

"Get back there and pass the word for Mouth to get up here."

A few moments later Mouth pushed through the brush and onto the trail. His eyes always seemed to be in a state of surprise, open wide with brows arching toward his receding red hairline.

"What's up? What's happenin'?" Mouth asked excitedly.

"Get down here beside me, Marine," Gunny Slate snapped.

Mouth jumped over beside the gunny and took his radio pack straps off. Within two minutes the gunny had stripped the commo wire with his K-bar, wired two clips into the field phone, and tapped into the enemy communication wire.

"It's hot wire all right, Lieutenant," Slate said after a moment of listening in. He handed the phone to Lieutenant Neader.

"Man, they're jabbering away," Neader said. "Sounds like a party line, no pun intended."

"I think it is, of sorts," Slate said.

"You speak this lingo, Gunny?"

"Just a tad, but I caught enough to know at least that this is a battalion staging area."

Suddenly two shots from the rear of the column brought every Marine to a firing position. Then silence. A moment later the word came up the column.

"Pssst. Blaine said a Charlie walked right up to within ten meters of him. He missed him."

Lieutenant Neader shook his head and looked around. "Cooper."

"Yes, sir."

"Take the point. Let's move up a ways and see what we got."

Cooper headed off up the winding mountain trail. The platoon followed in a staggered column.

Gunny Slate quick-stepped up to the lieutenant. "This might be a good spot to put out some flank guards, Jim."

"Sounds good, Gunny. Pass the word back for Morse and Kelly to take the flanks about twenty meters off the trail line."

The word drifted back down the column, and the two Marine flank guards split off the jungle trail. Too wide, Slate thought as he watched Cooper round a bend out of sight about fifty meters ahead.

Suddenly Cooper gave a shout. "Gooks!"

An automatic burst of M16 fire was quickly answered by the louder cracks of Russian AK-47s. The shooting stopped. Swift Eagle and Gunny Slate ran forward as Lieutenant Neader motioned the platoon down. The big Indian corporal reached the bend in the trail first. Cooper lay writhing in pain on the side of the trail, clutching his right knee with his left hand while holding his M16 with his right. Thick crimson blood gushed between his knuckles. Ten meters farther on, a khaki-clad NVA soldier lay sprawled facedown in the center of the trail. An AK-47 assault rifle lay in the dirt beside him. Swift Eagle ran to Cooper and squatted.

"Move your hand!" Swift Eagle barked as he yanked Cooper's hand away from the shattered knee. A bullet had blown away the entire kneecap. White splinters of bone stuck through a bloody hole in his jungle trousers.

Cooper grimaced and lay back. "How bad, Chief?"

"You like running track?"

"No."

"Good."

"Throw him over your shoulder, Corporal!" Gunny Slate yelled.

"Aye, aye, Gunny," Swift Eagle said calmly.

Slate pointed at small round tree stumps scattered in the woods. "Look over there, Chief."

"They're cuttin' trees," Swift Eagle said as he picked Cooper up in a fireman's carry as if he were a rag doll.

"Yeah, see how they're all about the same size?"

"Spread out. You couldn't see trees missing from above."

"Affirmative. We better dee-dee-maw out of here. We walked into a big nest."

"How many did you see, Cooper?" Swift Eagle asked.

"Three, Chief." Cooper's voice cracked. Big tears filled his eyes.

They moved back to the column. Lieutenant Neader had the men fall off to the left side of the trail. Swift Eagle laid Cooper down beside Lieutenant Neader.

"Corpsman up."

"Corpsman up."

"Corpsman up."

The word was whispered down the column, and Doc Rice ran forward. He dropped his medical pack, grabbed bandages, and quickly stuck Cooper in the thigh with a shot of morphine. Helmets snapped around as a warning echoed up the column.

"Gooks comin' up the trail!"

Gunny Slate grabbed Cooper by his pack straps and

pulled him into the brush to the side of the trail while Doc Rice fumbled to stop the bleeding. Suddenly four pith-helmeted NVA soldiers appeared around a bend. They jab-bered casually as they walked along with their rifles slung.

"Who's walking Tail-End Charlie?" Lieutenant Neader whispered toward Corporal Swift Eagle as he shifted to aim back down the trail.

"Think Blaine's still got it."

A series of single-shot blasts from an M16 reverberated through the rugged mountains. A moment later cracking AK-47's echoed through the thickly wooded forest. A Viet-namese soldier began shouting. Three more Vietnamese sol-diers appeared fifteen meters up-trail, rounding the bend where Cooper had been hit. Gunny Slate lifted himself off his stomach, sprinted onto the trail, and opened fire with his pump shotgun. His first blast ripped open a gaping hole in the chest of the lead NVA. The man blew backward, knocking down the soldier behind him. Pumping and firing as he ran, Slate charged the lone Vietnamese still standing. His second shot blew the face off the third NVA, who had tried to raise his rifle to a firing position. Slate pumped and blasted until the three enemy soldiers stopped moving.

A burst of AK fire kicked up dirt around Slate's feet. He turned. PFC Blaine and the machine gun team were shoot-ing it out with the remaining NVA at the rear of the column. Another burst of enemy fire smacked through the leaves just above Slate's head.

"Get down, Gunny!" Swift Eagle shouted as he opened up at the muzzle flashes in the brush across the trail, twenty meters down the wooded slope of the mountain.

Slate hit the ground and rolled back toward Swift Eagle. The woods erupted with gunfire. Green tracers streaked from the thick brush at two angles, crisscrossing over the trail. Both enemy machine guns shot high. Bullets smacked through the leaves above the Marine line like corn popping.

"Pull back!" Lieutenant Neader shouted as he grabbed radioman Mouth's pack and yanked hard. Mouth fired one last round with his M16, then began to move backward on his stomach. Suddenly his helmet twirled violently on his head, and he screamed. Blood ran down the side of his face.

"Form a perimeter!" Lieutenant Neader shouted over the gunfire.

"Corpsman up!" Swift Eagle yelled.

Lieutenant Neader looked left. "Chief! Get the Sixty on—" The young lieutenant's command was cut short by a bullet striking his right shoulder. The impact rolled him onto his back. A second round exploded bone chips and blood from his right hip. He screamed through gritted teeth, closed his eyes, and lay still.

"Jim!" Swift Eagle shouted, scrambling to the lieutenant.

"Get into a perimeter! Now!" Slate screamed above the cracking gunfire. He jumped to his feet and sprinted back down the trail. "Get into a perimeter! Move it! Move it!"

When he got all the way back to PFC David Blaine, the Tail-End Charlie, he found Blaine lying at the side of the trail, curled up in a fetal position and clutching his rifle. Slate dived for the cover of a fallen tree ten meters downhill from Blaine on the same side of the trail.

"Get that friggin' weapon working, Marine!"

Blaine lifted his head enough to look for the gunny. His freckled face was ashen. He touched his buttock and held up his hand for Slate to see. His hand was red with blood.

"Lay still, son. I'm coming!"

Slate scrambled back uphill on his hands and knees. Bullets thudded into the ground close by and whined off trees and rocks. Fire seemed to come from every direction. He moved in beside Blaine, slung his shotgun over one shoulder, and cradled the freckle-faced Marine in both arms.

"Grab your weapon, Marine!"

Blaine reached for his M16. Slate struggled to his feet, shifted Blaine's weight, and started back up the trail. A .30-caliber machine gun opened fire from behind. Green tracer rounds streamed past on the right, and Slate broke left and into the brush.

"Gunny! This way!" Sally shouted. He was waving from behind a tree fifteen meters uphill.

Slate shifted Blaine's weight in his arms again and climbed up the forty-five-degree incline to Sally's machine gun position.

"Where's the CP?" Slate barked.

"Over here, Gunny!" Corporal Swift Eagle shouted, and waved from another fifteen meters farther up.

"I'm comin' to you."

Slate climbed uphill again. The steady incoming fire

seemed to lessen, but sporadic bursts still cracked through leaves and branches.

"Corpsman up!" the gunny bellowed as he neared the Chief's position.

Doc Rice rushed down and grabbed Blaine's boots. "Bring him over here to this level spot, Gunny."

"Chief!" Slate called.

Corporal Swift Eagle looked up from checking the radioman's pulse.

"Bring him over here, beside Mouth," Swift Eagle said.

Slate and Doc Rice laid Blaine down on his side and rolled him gently onto his stomach. Blaine's utilities were soaked with blood. Doc Rice pulled out his K-bar and slit open the seat of Blaine's trousers.

"Looks like you got an AK round clean through both cheeks. You'll live, Marine. Lay still while I check Lieutenant Neader."

"Where's the radio, Doc?"

"Right here, Gunny." Doc Rice shoved the radio toward Slate with his boot while he pressed with both hands on Lieutenant Neader's stomach wound.

Slate turned to Swift Eagle.

"Get on the phone to Alpha One. Tell em' we need medevacs on top of 660. Hot LZ."

Swift Eagle grabbed the field phone and pulled out the antennae on the radio.

"Alpha One, Alpha One, this is Alpha Three, over."

The corpsman turned away from Lieutenant Neader. "Hey, Gunny," he said, wiping at tears running down his dirty face. His lip quivered, and he seemed unable to finish his sentence.

"What is it, Doc?"

The young corpsman looked dumbly down at the handsome, pale face of Lieutenant Neader. He picked up the lieutenant's pack, pulled out a poncho, and spread it over the lieutenant's body.

Swift Eagle dropped the field phone. "Medevacs are on the way, Gunny. Alpha One said they're sending in a Chinook to pull us out."

A neck-cringing sizzle sound pushed every man onto his stomach.

"Incoming!"

A B-40 rocket exploded into a huge 200-foot-tall mahogany tree just inside the perimeter below the CP. The mighty tree snapped in half from the white explosion. Sally opened fire with the M60, spraying streams of orange tracers through the green woods below. AK rifle fire opened up from positions along the trail. Bullets cracked through branches and thudded into the earth all around.

"They're movin' in!" a Marine yelled back.

"Hey, we're catching fire from over here!" another man shouted from the opposite side of the makeshift perimeter.

Gunny Slate slapped Swift Eagle on the helmet. "We can't defend this position, Corporal. Let's get these wounded and the lieutenant's body back up to the other trail. I'll take the point and bring us to the top."

"Aye, aye, sir," Swift Eagle replied quickly, and turned away to shout the word to the perimeter.

"Stand by to saddle up!" The Indian's booming voice broke through the deafening chaos.

"Chief, what's that gunner's name?"

"Sally."

The gunny turned and yelled downhill. "Hey, Sally!"

"Yo!"

"Who's on your right down there?"

"Polock."

"Hey, Polock!"

"Yeah!"

"Pull back and follow my lead. Gun team!"

"Yo!"

"Pass the word to the position on your left to follow you out of there."

"There it is, bro!"

Slate spun around quickly, laid his shotgun on the ground, and picked up the dead lieutenant. He threw him over his left shoulder. Blood ran down the back of his neck. It felt warm and sticky.

"Doc, hand me my pump."

The corpsman rushed over and picked up the gunny's pump shotgun. He handed it to the old salt and stared at him like he wasn't sure what to do next.

"Well, move it, boy! Pick up Mouth the radioman!"

"Yes, sir."

"Corporal Swift Eagle!"

"Yes, sir."

"Get a man to carry this other wounded Marine, and you stay here until every man on the perimeter files around into the column. Lay down cover fire for our retreat for three minutes. Just three! You got that?"

"Yes, sir."

"Move out!"

The gunny led the way back up to the original trail. A murderous fusillade of high-pitched cracks from AK-47s roared from the woods below. The sound of an M16 answered, and Gunnery Sergeant Slate knew that his godson was still alive as he stepped up onto the ground of the original trail. The way was clear for thirty meters downhill, at which point the trail veered right. He could see no farther. He looked back up to where he had first spotted the booby trap. The gunny turned to motion the rest of the column up.

A sudden burst of AK fire knocked Slate to his knees. He dropped the lieutenant's body and flattened out as an M16 behind him opened fire. He rolled off into the brush and prepared to fire, but there was no target. He felt for blood but couldn't find a wound. He breathed deep and hard and squeezed his weapon to keep his hands from shaking. Behind him, a big Marine with an oval face and a droopy mustache was squatting on one knee, still aiming down the trail.

"Get him, Polock?" Sally called from five meters back.

"No. Slimy little turd ran away." He looked at the gunny. "How bad you hit, Gunny?"

"I'm okay; the bullets must have hit the lieutenant's body."

"Can't cut it much closer, Gunny."

"There it is, Marine. Okay, come up onto the trail."

"Here I come." Polock stepped up onto the trail and flattened out on his stomach, aiming at the bend thirty meters downhill.

"Guns up!" Gunny Slate barked.

Sally and his chubby-faced A gunner hustled onto the trail and set up the M60 on its bipod legs. Four NVA soldiers ran into view from around the bend thirty meters downhill, firing as they came. Sally opened up, raking the onrushing NVA with orange tracers. Polock and the chubby A gunner fired single-shot while the gunny pumped out five shotgun blasts. The onrushing NVA jerked like men having seizures, then crumpled to the ground. The Marines ceased fire. Another AK opened fire from down the trail, but his aim was high, and the bullets thudded into the mountainside.

"Well, don't look like we're goin' down, boys."

Polock looked over at the old salt. "We can't go up-trail, Gunny! You said it was booby-trapped!" A hint of panic rang clearly in the big Marine's voice.

"I'll clear it first. You give me cover, and when I give the word for you and the gun team to move out, you bring him." Gunny Slate pointed at the lieutenant's body lying on the side of the trail, still wrapped in a poncho.

"I ain't packin' no stiff up that trail under fire."

Gunny Slate pushed up onto his knees and popped Polock in the helmet with the butt of his shotgun. The old salt's steel-gray eyes swelled with rage. Polock stared at him, frightened as a kid waiting for his father's belt.

"You tryin' to disgrace my Marine Corps, boy! I'll give you a size ten enema if you ever suggest leaving a brother behind! Is that clear, Marine?" Slate's roar caused the young Marine's eyes to blink.

"Yes, sir, Gunny!"

Slate stood and yelled back at the column. "Move out! Stay fifteen meters back."

He stopped ten feet from the overhanging branches that marked the booby trap and studied every inch of the ground below. He turned. "Can't see a thing," he mumbled. He dropped to one knee, shoved in six rounds of buckshot, then fired into the trail ahead. Nothing. He pumped and fired again, this time aiming farther up-trail, and again hit only dirt and rocks. He pumped and fired a third time. A sharp blast exploded dirt and rocks into the air over a twenty-meter radius. The gunny moved forward, forcing himself to take each frightening step. He pumped and fired again into the trail ahead. Behind him, the M60 machine gun opened up with a 20 round burst. Slate twirled around in time to see two NVA disappear into the brush near the bend. Another wave of crackling AK fire erupted from the woods below. A single M16 answered.

"Swift Eagle," Slate mumbled as he turned back up-trail.

He continued to move forward, firing as he walked. His battle-aged eyes strained to spot any sign of more booby traps. To his left, jutting out of the mountainside, was a large triangular boulder. Just beneath it lay a small triangular rock. Slate backed up ten paces and opened fire, spraying buckshot up the trail. A white flash blinded him. He felt himself tumbling in pain through the warm air.

An irritating flapping noise nagged at Slate's ear. He forced open one eye, then the other. He blinked to clear away the fuzz. A dark green poncho stiff with dried blood flapped against the dead face of Lieutenant Jim Neader. Slate heard himself sigh. Even in death the young Marine was a good-looking man.

"Hey, the gunny's awake," a voice shouted over the prop wash of the helicopter blowing through the open gun port.

Doc Rice wiped away a tear and looked at the gunny. "Lieutenant's dead."

Slate nodded. "Ain't no better way to live or die, son. He died like a Marine."

"Gunny."

Slate rolled his head to the right and came face to face with Corporal Swift Eagle. The big Indian's straight black eyebrows pinched together as if he were under great strain.

"Good to see ya, son," Slate said quietly.

Swift Eagle's brow eased. "You feel all right?"

The old salt grimaced and looked down at his bloody trousers. "Feel like a mine shaft just fell on me."

"You got a few shards in you, but I don't guess it's the first time." The Indian's face came close to making a grin.

"Let's just say magnets are drawn to me. Did everyone get out okay?"

"Yes, sir. Piece of cake after you cleared the trail of mines."

"Good."

"You ought to look into having that MOS changed, Gunny." A hint of sarcasm came through the corporal's tone.

"You think?"

"Yes, sir. I hear the Army uses machines for minesweeping."

The old man smiled and closed his eyes.

"Hey, Gunny!" Mouth the radioman yelled from the other side of Swift Eagle.

Slate opened his eyes. "Yeah."

"The pilot said they're dropping the wounded off on the USS *Sanctuary.*"

"That right?"

Swift Eagle looked over at Slate. "Funny. I've been in the Corps four years this April, and I've never been on ship. Matter of fact, I've never been on ship in my life."

"You ain't missed nothing, boy. I been on more than I care to remember. God, I hate boats!"

"Bet you can't even remember the first ship you boarded, can ya, Gunny?"

"Sure do, Corporal. We didn't like it much, either. Para-Marines, you know. We planned on flying into combat."

"I remember Dad's old Para-Marine song."

"Yep. That song was sort of my introduction to the Corps," Slate mused. "That was the Old Corps."

# CHAPTER ONE

JESSIE SLATE DROPPED HIS SCHOOLBOOKS AND turned on the Philco. He gently removed an old magazine from the bottom drawer of a maplewood desk, then slumped down on the couch and flipped open the December 1937 issue of *Life* magazine for the thousandth time as he waited for the tubes on the Philco to grow warm. The pages were tattered, and the photo of the Japanese ambassador was beginning to yellow. He read the headline again.

## A TERRIBLE BLUNDER PUTS JAPAN'S AMBASSADOR ON THE ANXIOUS SEAT
Early Sunday afternoon, December 12, on the Yangtze River 27 miles above Nanking, Japanese Navy warplanes swooped down and bombed the U.S. Navy gunboat *Panay* as she was carrying American Embassy officials and other refugees away from the Chinese capital.

The silky rhythm of Cole Porter's "In the Still of the Night" began to come through clear on the Philco. Jessie continued to read.

The ship was abandoned at 2:05 P.M. An hour and three-quarters later she sank, and over her hulk the muddy waters of China's greatest river again rushed on, undisturbed, to the Yellow Sea. But the repercussions of that bombing boomed around the world and will send Japanese and American officials flying for many a day to come.

\*     \*     \*

17

Ten thousand miles away in Washington it sent Hirosi Saito, Japan's ambassador to the United States, scurrying to a hard horsehair sofa outside Secretary of State Hull's office. The Japanese are proud and dignified people, and the Japanese ambassador is the personal representative of a ruler whom 69 million people regard as divine. But as he perched anxiously on the seat, submitting to an American ordeal by candid camera, Ambassador Saito looked neither dignified nor divine. He protested that the bombing was "completely accidental," calling it a "terrible blunder" as he waited to offer his country's humblest apologies to Secretary Hull and to receive the sternest reception a foreign diplomat had had from a secretary of state since 1917.

Jessie stared at the photo on the opposite page for a long moment before reading the words below it.

UNIVERSAL CAMERAMAN DOCUMENTS AMERICAN HISTORY: THE *PANAY* INCIDENT
The flag-draped coffin above is that of an American seaman, Paul R. Valenga, being lifted from a launch to the deck of the cruiser *Augusta* in Shanghai Harbor. Valenga was one of three Americans killed when the little gunboat *Panay* was bombed in the Yangtze River by Japanese airplanes on December 12.
   The picture above is one frame from a remarkable film which reached U.S. theaters on December 30. It was so remarkable that four destroyers convoyed it from Shanghai to Manila, lest Japan try to seize the ship which carried it.
   The film establishes two disputed points. It proves that the *Panay* was prominently displaying three large American flags. And it proves that the "poor visibility" on which Japan blamed the attack was in fact bright sunlight. The film is a record of such courage and heroism on the part of Navy officers and seamen that audiences broke into repeated applause. The international incident has brought America to the brink of war.

Jessie flipped to page 30 as an advertisement for Aqua Velva began its irritating jingle. No matter how many times he read the captions under the series of photos on page 30, an overwhelming sense of pride would push a lump into his throat and tears into his eyes. The photos were numbered with brief captions. It was the fourth that most interested him.

The last boatload of refugees come aboard the *Panay* under the watchful eyes of U.S. Marine Sergeants James Slate and Michael O'Cleary. (Sergeant Slate, one of three Americans killed when the USS *Panay* was bombed one hour later, was posthumously awarded the Silver Star for heroism.)

"Jessie!"

"I'm in here, Mom."

"Turn the Philco off and get me some more blackberries from the cellar, son."

"Come here, Mom. There's news from Wake Island!"

Jean Slate's pretty face flushed red as she hurried into the tiny living room. She wiped her hands on her bright red Christmas apron and brushed a strand of long dark hair from her eyes.

"They were saying what to do in case of a blackout if they bomb us."

"Oh, my Lord! Can it be as bad as that, Jessie?"

"I got Dad's 03 all oiled and ready. I'll shoot the first Jap that steps into Kanawah Valley."

"Shhh!" Jean Slate wagged her finger at Jessie as she leaned closer to the big Philco.

And now from the Pacific. Three Jap warships sunk in day's battle as Wake Island Marines rout attackers. With the United States Army and Navy striking back yesterday at Japan for the surprise attack on Pearl Harbor, the war news was no longer of disaster but of victory. This is the emerging story. A 29,000-ton Japanese battleship, *Haruna,* sunk. A light Jap cruiser, sunk. Jap destroyer, sunk. And severe damage to another Nippon battleship of the Kongo class. A detachment of U.S. Marines has beaten back one invasion and is expecting another at any moment. Wake is still holding firm!

At 9:42 P.M. last night, Los Angeles received an alert
signal flashed by the Fourth Interceptor Command,
and because it was misunderstood by the fire department, part of the city, including San Pedro, was
plunged into darkness for thirty minutes. . . .


"Turn it off, Jessie. We got work to do before Thelma and
Leefee get here." Jean Slate's voice quivered as she spoke.

Jessie turned off the Philco and hugged her.

"Don't worry, Mom." He could feel her tremble and
knew without looking that she was biting her lip to keep
from crying. He liked that about his mother. She'd rather
bleed than cry.

She pulled away and began to twist her apron nervously,
anticipating what Jessie would say next.

"If I wait till I'm eighteen, those coward Japs will probably already give up the fight, Mom. I'll miss everything."

"I don't want to talk about it anymore, Jessie. Now go
to the cellar and get those blackberries or we'll miss the
troop train for sure."

The drive to the Charleston terminal in Leefee Brubaker's
new DeSoto was only about fifteen miles up the valley, but
the chattering women made it feel a lot longer. Leefee's husband, Dan, was in charge of the rubber drive for Kanawah
Valley, and she seemed to have more stories about rubber
than anyone could keep up with. Thelma Monroe was a history teacher at Kanawah Valley High with Jessie's mom.
She was a huge woman with a giant bosom, which she would
sometimes rest on her desk during class. She had a daughter
named Janet who made Jessie sweat just to look at her.
Thelma twisted to look back at Jessie from the front seat.
She smiled. Her cheeks were fat and red.

"Janet says that you played a whale of a game for
Kanawah County High the other night, Jessie. I'll tell you,
Jean, every pretty girl in the valley seems to have their eye
on that boy of yours."

Jessie felt his face flush red.

"I know, Thelma. If he wasn't so shy, he could be a regular Valentino." Jean Slate pointed at the gas gauge. "Did
you hear what Washington is about to do with gas?"

"I heard something about rationing on the radio yesterday," Leefee said.

Good ol' Mom, Jessie thought. She knew that Thelma embarrassed the heck out of him, so she always found a way to change the subject.

"They're serious, Leefee. Automobiles, bicycles, fuel oil, gasoline, kerosene, shoes, stoves, tires, typewriters, sugar, meats, butter, fat, oil, coffee, and canned foods."

"Really?" Thelma asked, as if she had lost her breath. "Well if it's going to help our boys whip Hitler and those horrible little Japs, then Roosevelt can ration everything I own. I forgot to tell you what old Mrs. Mills told me yesterday. You know Mrs. Mills. She's the old lady that lives down the road from me. She said that there's a little flag with a blue star hanging in the window of the Barnes house."

"Oh, no!" Leefee said, covering her mouth with one hand.

"Yes. They said his ship went down in the Atlantic."

No one spoke much after that until Leefee pulled into the parking area near the terminal. The day was overcast, but the snow on the ground was beginning to melt.

"I sure hope Mrs. Parker is here with the coffee. Those boys drink more coffee than anything I've ever seen," Thelma said as she walked toward the trunk.

Leefee opened the trunk, leaned down, and gently brought up a large cardboard box.

"Here, Jessie. Now, be real careful; there's a two-layer yellow cake in there with a pie on top of it."

"Yes, ma'am. You going to play the piano, Mrs. Brubaker?"

"I probably will, Jessie, until one of those soldiers asks for some swing music."

A faraway whistle signaled the approaching train. Jessie hustled into the cold, cavernous terminal. Some of the ladies had already set up the tables and were busy putting out cups and plates.

Ten minutes later the troop train pulled in amid clouds of steam and the whoosh of powerful brakes. Conductors shouted out departure times as hundreds of soldiers and sailors unloaded. It didn't take any of them long to discover the free cakes, pies, and coffee that were set up on tables surrounding the old piano inside the terminal.

"Jessie, keep that coffee coming," Jean Slate called back to her son as she cut another slice of blackberry pie.

"Got another batch cooking, Mom."

"Excuse me, ma'am," a young freckle-faced sailor said as he squeezed between two soldiers waiting for coffee at the table where Jessie stood.

"Yes, sailor," Thelma answered.

"Anybody know how to play that piano?"

"Excuse me, squid. Me and my mates here were just about to take care of that."

The sailor turned into the broad and rugged face of a very wide and very strong-looking man. His uniform looked different from those of the others. It fit better, and there didn't seem to be a thread out of place. His trousers were bloused into tall boots that shone like glass. An instant later ten more men in the same uniforms shoved an aisle through the mob of servicemen and sprang over the tables with ease. Jessie leaned close to the scowling sailor.

"Who are those guys?"

"A bunch of lugheads."

"Are they soldiers?"

"They're Para-Marines. I don't like 'em much, but I got a feeling Tojo's gonna like 'em even less."

Suddenly the broad-faced Marine started banging out the tune of "Glory, Glory, Hallelujah!" The ten Para-Marines burst into verse after verse of what somebody said was the "Paratroopers' Song." It was the very last verse, though, that Jessie instantly knew he would never forget.

There was blood upon the risers, there was blood upon the chute,
It was blood that came a tricklin' from the paratrooper's boots;
they picked him up still in his chute, and poured him from his boots—
And he ain't gonna jump no more!

When the song ended, everyone in the room applauded and laughed and jeered. Then the piano player began playing the "Marines' Hymn," and the room full of sailors and soldiers began to boo. Jessie, singing along with the Marines, thought of his dad. He had never wanted to be part of something so badly in his life. They stood above the crowd, he thought, as he scanned the room full of uniforms and faces until he came to his mother's face. Her eyes were filled with tears. She smiled at Jessie in a way that left him feeling empty and alone. He had never seen such an odd expression in her eyes.

An hour later the coffee, cake, and pie were all gone, and so were the boys going off to war. The Para-Marine song played in Jessie's head. He hummed it and the "Marine Hymn" all through the cleanup and all the way to the car.

"Gives you a warm feeling to see those boys laugh and sing," Leefee mumbled as she wheeled the big DeSoto away from the terminal.

Thelma chuckled. "Yes, they were something, weren't they!"

"And, my Lord, what a terrible song that was," Leefee said with a laugh.

"Be careful what you say about my son's song, Leefee," Jean said with a serious tone.

"Your son's song?"

Jessie's spine straightened in the backseat as he stared at the back of his mother's head. She turned and looked into her boy's eyes with the same strange smile he had seen in the terminal.

"Yes, my son's song. He'll be joining the Marines soon."

Thelma and Leefee gasped out loud.

Jessie leaned forward and kissed his mother's cheek. A single tear trickled down her soft face.

# CHAPTER TWO

*Camp Gillespie, San Diego, July 1942*

THE PAIN, AGONY, AND OUTRIGHT TERROR OF THIR-
teen torturous weeks on Parris Island were still fresh in Jessie's memory as he snapped to attention along with the
thousand other Marines who were present and tried to ignore the sweat that stung his eyes. A stiff-looking major in
twelve-inch jumping boots, flying helmet with chin strap,
and coverall jumping suit stood on a platform with a bullhorn, staring down at the large formation. He raised the
bullhorn.

"At ease, Marines! Thank you for volunteering. Your
country thanks you, and your Corps thanks you. About
three out of one hundred Marines will earn their wings.
Don't let that bother you! You are already the best fighting
men in the world. You're Marines! Now, listen up and listen
good as Gunnery Sergeant O'Cleary reads out the requirements for the First Para-Marine Regiment!"

The major turned and handed the bullhorn to a rugged,
thick-necked old gunnery sergeant dressed the same way,
with an unlit cigar in one corner of his mouth. The gunnery
sergeant exchanged a salute with the major and faced the
formation.

"Now hear this! I'm here to tell you volunteers what it's
going to take to be in this lashup. If you don't fit any of these
requirements, I want you to fall out and form up a formation on the back side of this platform!" He shifted his cigar
from one side of his mouth to the other and held out a clipboard to read from.

"Now hear this! You will be unmarried! You will be between the ages of eighteen and thirty-two, have completed
recruit training at Parris Island or San Diego! You will be

athletic! Well proportioned! Weigh from 135 to 190 pounds and be between sixty-six and seventy-three inches in height." As the gunnery sergeant read on, the huge formation of Marines began to shrink until nearly a fourth of the original group was forming up on the other side of the platform.

"The only exceptions to these requirements will be some officers and specific NCOs. In addition to these requirements, you will pass a physical examination and modified flight examination in visual acuity, binocular vision, depth perception, and equilibrium facilities, and a flight ear examination. Prior injuries! If you have ever had a broken bone, you may not qualify. You will run a minimum of eight miles each morning. You will never walk. You will double-time to the head, you will double-time to chow, you will double-time to classes, you will double-time each and every time you are required to move. Right after this little run you will prepare to stand down for a full junk-on-the-gunk inspection. The 782 gear that you have been issued had better be in top shape. Platoon NCOs will make sure that each man has a full field marching pack for the run. Do it!"

A few minutes later the run began with the ruddy old gunnery sergeant leading the column. His pace was strong and steady, and five miles later Jessie was beginning to wonder if he had what it was going to take to make the lashup. The run finally ended in front of a row of large tents. The number of potential Para-Marines had shrunk still further.

"Stand down for inspection in twenty minutes!"

Exactly twenty minutes later Jessie stood at attention in front of his cot, along with a squad's worth of other Marines ready for inspection. The old gunny entered the tent like the commandant himself.

"Now hear this! You will have laid out in the proper order these items! Pack, including haversack, knapsack, and belt suspenders, a cartridge belt, a bayonet with scabbard unsheathed. Combination cleaning tool, brush and thong, an oiler, and an oil and thong case. BAR men will have their kit containing spare parts and accessories. Leather and web gun slings. Mess gear, consisting of a meat can with cover and knife, fork, and spoon. Canteen and cup with cover! First aid packet and pouch. A poncho. A shelter half with a pole, five pins, and a guy line. Steel helmet with fiber lining. Gas mask. Entrenching tool, pick and mattock, or machete! Any of this equipment missing will send you out of this outfit!"

With that final threat the old man began inspection by shouting into the face of each fatigued Marine: "Name! Rank! Serial number!" When he reached Jessie, he seemed to pause for a moment to study the young Marine's face, then shouted.

"Name! Rank! Serial number!"

"Slate! Private!"

"Slate?"

"Yes, sir, Gunny."

The old salt squinted as he leaned closer to Jessie's face. "Was your daddy a Marine, boy?" he asked as if he were angry.

"Yes, sir."

"Jim Slate?"

"Yes, sir."

The gunnery sergeant nodded. "I'll be on your tail every minute, Marine. You got big shoes to fill. You foul up my Marine Corps, I'll make you wish you were a dogface!"

"Aye, aye, Gunny!" Jessie barked defiantly.

And so began the toughest six weeks any of the men had ever experienced. Nonstop training in everything from jujitsu to swimming through burning oil to packing one's own parachute. Knife fighting, practice falls, training jumps from platforms, jumps from a 250-foot tower, more knife fighting, calisthenics and more calisthenics, judo, and more jumps and falls than the average ape would do in a lifetime, and then finally the first parachute drop from the big DC-5. Anyone injured was sent back to start over or was cut from the program.

Graduation day finally came, though the six weeks had felt like six years. So much had happened since Jessie had joined the Marines that it was hard to keep up. The war news had gone from bad to good to bad again. Over 70,000 British troops had surrendered to the Japs in Singapore. Bataan had fallen to the Japs in April. Corregidor had surrendered to the Japs in May. The U.S. Navy had won a big victory at some place called Midway, and it had lifted the spirits of the whole country, but as Jessie and the men around him were about to finally get those coveted wings, the Marines of the First Marine Division were barely hanging on to some island named Guadalcanal. It was America's first offensive, and it was up to the Corps to prove that the Jap was no superman. Every single survivor of the Para-Marine training seemed anxious to get into the fight. As the number of candidates had dwindled, some faces and names had become more familiar. The handful of survivors from the original thousand-odd applicants could now fit inside a couple of small tents.

The skipper was First Lieutenant Pierce. He was a tall, lean inconspicuous man with a baby's bright eyes who looked more like an overworked bookkeeper than a leader of Marines. He was a Mustang, having earned his commission for bravery in Haiti in 1934, or so the scuttlebutt said. The NCOs looked to be as good and tough as Marine NCOs were supposed to be. The gunny was the kind of man a Marine would follow all the way to Tokyo. He had been a hero in the Great War, and he'd fought in Nicaragua, Haiti, the Philippines, and China. Sergeant Rim was an attack-dog sort of man with a horseshoe-shaped shrapnel scar on his right cheek that turned blue when he got mad, which was often. He had served with the gunny and Lieutenant Pierce since Nicaragua. The corporal was a decent Joe named Phil DiCicca from Suffern, New York. He seemed smart and had had two years of college chemistry at Rutgers, where he had worked as a soda jerk on campus. He was always playing jazz music on a Victrola. Scuttlebutt said he had a kid he hadn't seen in three years. He was thirty years old and divorced and had served with the gunny in China. The gunny said that DiCicca had made corporal faster than anyone he'd ever known.

The new Para-Marines were a rough bunch. If one went by looks alone, a Mexican Marine named Lopez would be the main man. He was an ugly, barrel-chested twenty-eight-year-old with a pitted greasy complexion, menacing dark eyes, black hair growing out of a wide flat nose, and a hostile attitude toward everyone. Lopez had been an unsuccessful criminal, or so said the scuttlebutt. There was a big, strong handsome Louisiana boy named Christopher Diez LaBeau. LaBeau was nineteen years old and built like Tarzan. It had become apparent to everyone, including the bayonet and K-bar knife instructors, that the kid with the cornflower-blue

eyes and the matinee-idol looks could outmuscle a bear. He
was proud of his southern heritage and seemed constantly
on the verge of strangling another southern boy from Wil-
more, Kentucky, named Charlie Rose. Chris thought that
Rose was a living insult to the South, but Rose was Jessie's
favorite character out of all the survivors. Rose was eighteen
and had a funny habit of giving people gifts like extra soap
or writing paper even if they hated him. He was short and
square with blond hair and wide-open bright green eyes that
seemed to be in a permanent state of surprise.

The bookworm of the squad was Private Benjamin B.
Oglethorpe. Why he joined the Marine Corps or how he
made it through Para-Marine training was a complete mystery to everyone. He was twenty-nine years old, about five
foot eleven, and 170 pounds, with funny round reading
glasses, red hair, and big freckles. He had been a librarian
in Connecticut before the war and seemed perfectly suited
for such a job. Jack Ellinwood was another quiet Marine
from Saint Petersburg, Florida. He was tall and lean, very
strong, and the most agreeable person Jessie had ever met.
He agreed with everyone about everything. He had been a
salesman at Sears on December 7 and a Marine on December 8.

Private Aldo Perelli was the talker of the group. He could
spread scuttlebutt faster than the squad could digest it. Perelli was from Brooklyn, where he bragged that he had
worked for the second biggest bookie in New York. He had
sold used cars, too. He had a good head for baseball trivia,
especially the Dodgers, and he argued constantly with Private Joseph Stukowski, who was from Newark. Stukowski
had played some B League ball there before finally going
into a Single A farm team in the Yankee organization. It
was brief; he evidently had gotten into a fistfight and had
been cut from the team. He had just made the Padres in the
Pacific Coast League when Pearl Harbor was bombed.

The ceremony was short. Lieutenant Pierce pinned the
curled silver wings on the final man, a short fireplug of a
Marine named Ronnie Garland, then stepped back and exchanged a sharp salute. Lieutenant Pierce walked to the
front of the row of Marines standing at attention.

"Congratulations, men! You are part of the finest group
of Marines in history, and we're going to prove it by kicking

some Jap butts all the way to Tokyo and taking a leak on the emperor's grave.

"Now, I'd like to give you men time to go into San Diego and celebrate, but we got our orders to report to Camp Elliot by 1400 hours. Get back to your tents and get saddled up!"

The men groaned. More training. Advance infantry training at Camp Elliot was easy compared to what the Para-Marines had just been through, but still it was no cakewalk, and when the final day at Elliot was over and the word came down that the entire replacement battalion was to saddle up and prepare to ship out, no one was sad to hear it.

# CHAPTER THREE

**A** CONVOY OF DEUCE-N-HALF TRUCKS FILLED WITH
Marines rumbled through the bustling, sailor-packed streets
of San Diego. No one seemed to notice. It wasn't the first
convoy, and it wouldn't be the last. Private First Class Jessie
Slate leaned out over the tailgate and tried to inhale every
sight, sound, and scent of his last night in America. The convoy rushed past the huge aircraft factories and the familiar
drive-ins, bowling alleys, and cocktail lounges. Joseph Stukowski removed his helmet, scratched at his short blond
hair, and pointed at the bright green fence of the San Diego
Padres ballpark.

"That's where I'd be playing if it wasn't for those scummy
little Japs."

Perelli's dark eyes blinked. He held his banana-shaped
nose and gave a scoffing wave. "Stukowski, they don't play
baseball there."

"Is that so, Perelli?"

"Sure," Perelli said with a nasal twang. "You wanna see
real baseball, you got to go see the Brooklyn Dodgers. Any
green boot knows that."

"Right now, Perelli, I'd even play for those bums," Stu
said solemnly.

"If we don't win this war, there ain't gonna be no more
baseball, Mac."

Jessie couldn't see who had made the last statement, but
no one was about to argue the point, at least no one in that
truck full of Para-Marines.

One by one the convoy trucks slowed and turned into the
waterfront area. Jessie gawked at the world of giant gray
ships filled with the clamor of winches, shouting dock-

workers in their denim overalls, huge piles of equipment, and long lines of helmeted Marines carrying seabags, packs, and rifles. His truck stopped with a jerk.

"All right! Move it, Marines! Move it! Move it! Move it!" Gunnery Sergeant O'Cleary shouted as he ordered the men from the trucks.

"Platoon leaders! Form 'em up!"

"First Platoon, over here!"

"Get the lead out, Marines!"

"First squad all present and accounted for, sir!"

"Second squad all present and accounted for, sir!"

Within moments chaos turned into order as the men quickly formed into two long lines facing the gangway of a big gray troopship. The damp air was thick with the smell of fish and diesel oil. A stern-faced second lieutenant shouted off names from an embarkation roster. With each name came a quick "Aye-aye, sir!" from somewhere in the long lines. He finished the list of names and turned angrily toward the surly old gunnery sergeant standing close by.

"What kind of garbage is this, mister?"

"What's your question, Lieutenant?" the old man said clearly.

"I wanna know why these prima donnas rate the prime area on this ship. Closest to the only freshwater shower and the chow hall!"

The old gunny pointed at the red and blue patch with a white parachute and five white stars on his shoulder. "First Para-Marine Regiment, Lieutenant. Elite of the Corps, temporarily attached to the First Replacement Battalion."

The lieutenant's face turned crimson, but he said no more. A surge of pride sent goose bumps down Jessie Slate's spine as he felt himself stand just a little straighter. How he admired Gunny O'Cleary, a Marine's Marine. Dad would probably be a gunnery sergeant by now, he thought with a melancholy gaze down at his treasured twelve-inch-high Para-Marine boots.

"Yeah, tell him where to stow that horse manure, Gunny," a Marine with a country twang as clear and homey as a cow pasture said loudly from behind Jessie.

"That's all I needed, Rose!" an angry voice shouted.

Jessie looked over his shoulder just as scar-faced Sergeant Rim grabbed the arm of Charlie Rose.

"I told you, Rose! You run that mouth of yours and Marines die on the line! I'm takin' that stripe, and you got head duty, mister, till we reach Tokyo!"

"That was my fault, Sergeant," Jessie blurted. "I asked the PFC if he had any spare writing gear."

The horseshoe-shaped scar on Sergeant Rim's face seemed to get deeper as he stepped closer. He stood face to face with Jessie. Jessie's stomach tightened, and for an instant he wished that he'd kept his mouth shut.

"You're lying, Slate, but I'm gonna let it pass. If your buddy here gets somebody killed with that big mouth of his, it's on your head, too. That clear, Marine?"

"Aye, aye, Sergeant."

The sergeant turned and walked back down the long line of Marines.

Gunnery Sergeant O'Cleary yelled from the gangway. "Hoist those seabags! Prepare to board! Get 'em saddled up, Sergeant Rim."

The lieutenant checked off names from an embarkation roster as the Para-Marines filed up the gangway.

Troopships were usually freighters, old tubs that were drafted and supposedly redesigned, but it was hard to believe that someone with competence had actually sat down and drawn up the idea for putting men inside them. This one was named the *Barkley*. The *Barkley* had four holds, each two decks deep. Officer country was somewhere in the middle, and to no one's surprise, the living quarters for the officers were closer to human standards, at least according to scuttlebutt. The only freshwater shower was in the bottom aft deck, along with the head area.

Jessie stepped onto the deck and followed the men in front of him as they filed into a narrow hatchway. It was a clumsy journey. Nearly every man stumbled at least once under the weight of seabags, packs, and rifles as they worked their way down ladders and squeezed through narrow passageways crammed with boxes of equipment. By the time they finally reached the compartment, the true nature of what the journey would be like was obvious.

Each hold was sectioned off in compartments, and each compartment was crammed with rows of canvas cots that hung from the ceiling in tiers of five. Between rows there was a narrow aisle that could be negotiated only by turning sideways while balancing one's gear on one's head. Pipes of every size and temperature ran along the bulkheads and the ceiling.

"Good Gawd almighty!" Charlie Rose griped. "Sardines ain't packed this close."

"I want the first squad right here!" Sergeant Rim shouted, pointing at two stacks of canvas bunks separated by a tiny aisle.

"This looks like a plumbing warehouse," Jack Ellinwood said from somewhere behind Jessie.

Jessie looked at Charlie. "Mind if I take the top?"

"Shucks no, boy. Guess I'll take the one under you. Thanks for saving my butt with the sarge. I owe ya, Jessie."

"Forget it. Just don't burp or roll over; you'll shove me through the roof."

Charlie grinned and took off his helmet. He had blond hair and a square face.

"Guess I'll squeeze in here," a tall Marine with a pale white face said as he turned sideways to move past Jessie and Charlie. It was Oglethorpe.

"I think you got the wrong squad, sailor," Jessie said sarcastically.

"You was supposed to be on that ocean liner, weren't you, Oglethorpe?" Charlie Rose asked.

"Powers beyond my control have seen fit to place me here." He took off his helmet and scratched his head.

"Move it, you slackers! You're blocking the aisle!" Sergeant Rim shouted.

Jessie climbed up the ladder of makeshift bunks and flattened himself out on top. He stared at the gray ceiling a foot away and tried to keep his mind off the butterflies in his stomach.

"Now hear this!" A tinny loudspeaker began blaring orders throughout the transport ship. "All cooks and messmen lay below to the galley! Guard watches report . . ."

"Another pleasant night with Uncle Sam's orphans," Oglethorpe groaned.

"Sweepers! Man your brooms!"

A few minutes later Corporal DiCicca shouted and pointed as he rushed through the crowded quarters. "Volunteers for a cleanup detail! You, you, and you!" He pointed at Jessie.

Three hours later Jessie climbed into his bunk again. He was almost thankful for the work detail, which had kept his mind off the journey ahead. A rush of air swished through the rusty ventilator and into his right ear, but it did little to make the crowded compartment any less stifling. He closed his eyes and tried to remember home and his mom's soft pretty face. A nudge on his backside opened Jessie's eyes.

"Hey, Slate."

"Yeah, Charlie."

"What you thinking 'bout?"

"My mom."

"She still teaching English in Charleston?"

"Yeah."

"South Carolina?" Oglethorpe asked from the cot below Charlie Rose.

"West by-God Virginia."

"How'd you end up in Charleston?"

"We moved to the capital after Dad died. Mom had a chance to teach English at Kanawah County High."

"I thought you once told me she worked in an armament factory, Slate," Oglethorpe remarked.

"She does some cleanup work at night. She wanted to help the war effort."

"She sounds like a strong woman," Oglethorpe said sincerely.

"Course she is," Charlie Rose said matter-of-factly. "She's a country girl. There ain't a weak woman ever come out of the mountains of Kentucky, West Virginia, or Tennessee. Strong as tree-climbing cows."

"Nooo!" A Cajun war cry shrilled from the bottom cot. The dark-complected LaBeau stood up in the narrow aisle and stared at Charlie Rose in disbelief. "A tree-climbing cow?" LaBeau repeated quietly, pinching the bridge of his nose as if a sudden headache had struck.

"Yep," Charlie said.

"You know something, Rose?" LaBeau said, leaning closer. "I think some Yankee family brought you to the South just to give southerners a bad image."

"Now, I can take abuse, boy, but when you start callin' a man a Yankee, you're slanderin' a man's mother."

LaBeau pinched the bridge of his nose again, shook his head, and crawled back into the stack of flattened Marines.

Jessie laughed, then closed his eyes.

The ship shuddered as a huge engine rumbled to life. Jessie's gray eyes popped open. A rush of hot, foul-smelling air whooshed from the rusty vent a few feet from his face.

"Hey, we're movin'," a nervous voice mumbled from somewhere in the cramped compartment.

Jessie sat up quickly, banged his head against an overhead pipe, then climbed down from his rack. He made his way to the upper deck. It was dusk. Half the battalion lined the guardrail to watch the ships cast off their moorings and slide out into San Diego Harbor. There they turned west to form convoy lines and nosed down the channel past North Island and Point Loma. Jessie watched as the lights of San Diego faded.

"Won't be seeing that for a while," Charlie Rose said quietly from Jessie's left.

He turned to Charlie Rose just as the first lurch from a sea of ground swells began rocking the transport.

"Rides like a mean three-legged pony," Charlie Rose said, grabbing a railing for balance.

"Good grief!" LaBeau shook his head in disgust and moved toward the bow of the ship.

"You don't look so good, Charlie. You okay?" Jessie asked.

Charlie Rose leaned over the railing and began to retch.

"Better get those sea legs under you, Marine. There's a deep-water war out there."

Jessie looked back over his shoulder and into the shadowy outline of Gunnery Sergeant O'Cleary. The old salt walked to the railing with something in his hand.

Charlie Rose straightened up. He seemed to be feeling better.

"You ever get seasick, Gunny?" Jessie asked.

"Not if I stay away from the slop chute."

Charlie nodded toward a shoe box in the gunny's hands. "What you got there, Gunny?"

"One of my dolls."

"One of your what?" Jessie asked.

"My dolls. Here, look, this is a beauty." He removed the box lid.

"It *is* a doll!" Charlie squeaked.

The doll was dressed in a long-sleeved green Victorian dress.

"Ain't she a beauty, men?" Gunny O'Cleary asked proudly.

"Yeah. Real . . . real nice, Gunny," Jessie stammered.

"Prettier than a heifer in heat, Gunny," Charlie Rose said.

"This one's from the early 1800s. Some people call 'em China-head dolls."

"She don't look Chinese," Charlie Rose said.

"She isn't. See the face? It's made out of porcelain. Like glass. They break easy. Not many around that are this old. And look here; see how bands of hair loop under the exposed ears?"

"Yep," Charlie Rose said as if he had not missed a single detail.

"That's like Queen Victoria. See? That helps date this doll. I have one that's older."

"You mean you got more . . . dolls?" Charlie Rose asked.

O'Cleary pulled a chewed-up half cigar out of his shirt pocket, stuck it in a comfortable corner of his mouth, and winked proudly at Charlie Rose. "That's affirmative, Marine."

"That's an odd thing to collect, Gunny," Jessie said, being careful to sound respectful.

"Started collecting down in Haiti back in '27 with old Gunnery Sergeant Jeremiah Polk. A fine Marine. We had been together since Belleau Wood."

"Belleau Wood! Were you with my dad back then, Gunny?" Jessie exclaimed.

The gunny's graying eyebrows lifted. "Jim Slate and me and old Gunny Polk drank our share of fine French wine together. Everybody knew everybody in the Old Corps. See, boys, the Old Corps was sort of like a club. Shoot, we only had about two brigadiers back then."

"In the whole Corps, Gunny?" Charlie Rose asked.

"Well, you know the dog-faced Army was always trying to get the Corps disbanded, but we was always cheaper and better when the fightin' had to be done. Congress didn't mind keeping us as long as we were small and problems kept popping up, like Haiti and Nicaragua and the Philippines. The Army brass couldn't get rid of us."

"You were there, too, Gunny?" Charlie Rose asked.

O'Cleary nodded. "So me and old Jeremiah was chasing Sandino through the thickest God-awful—" The old salt paused and looked up. "No offense intended, Lord. So we was ambushing and being ambushed in the worst possible place to fight a decent war you could ever imagine."

"Jungle, Gunny?" Jessie asked.

"Thick as the starch on a DI's neck, son."

"How in tarnation does a man start collecting dolls in a jungle war?" Charlie Rose asked.

O'Cleary pushed up on the bill of his soft cover cap and looked out across the moonlit ocean. The gunny's mood seemed to grow somber. He cleared his throat.

"Well, we got mail call one day, and I got word that I was a new daddy. My little girl Evelyn Jane was born."

"I didn't know you had a girl, Gunny," Charlie Rose said.

"We chased a band of Sandino's men up into some real rugged mountains. Followed 'em right into a base camp where they even had women and kids. A fight started up, and we licked 'em pretty good. It ends up that some of these women and kids had been kidnapped and were being held in the camp and used as slave labor, so when we killed a platoon's worth of these no-goods, the women and kids loved us. This one little darlin' found out I just had a baby girl born, so she made me a doll for my Evelyn Jane."

"And you've been collecting them for Evelyn Jane ever since?"

Gunny O'Cleary put the lid on the box and turned away from the rail. He pulled his used cigar from his mouth.

"You boys better get below soon. You want to get used to sleeping aboard ship so you don't end up tired and sick all the way there." He walked away before Jessie or Charlie could ask where "there" was.

Jessie and Charlie stayed on deck until the ground swells grew. Many of the young faces began to turn pale, and the chatter on deck died away as the convoy put out to sea. For some reason Jessie didn't feel sick. The sailors seemed to get a big kick out of all the sick hard-core Marines.

By the second day out scuttlebutt had the convoy heading

toward every Jap stronghold from Guadalcanal to Tokyo.
The worst rumors were the ones about wolf packs of submarines that were wiping out entire convoys. Every man on
board was afraid of being trapped below the waterline. The
small Italian PFC from Brooklyn, Aldo Perelli, was a scuttlebutt specialist. Each unit seemed to have a Perelli. He
found a new rumor with every trip to the head, and he har-
vested them greedily as if each had special value.

"Now hear this, Marines," Aldo said as he squatted between two tiers of canvas racks.

"Listen up! Perelli heard a new one," Stukowski bellowed
as he leaned out of a middle cot.

Aldo looked around to make sure that he had every ear
before speaking. "I got this from a guy in the Third."

"Get serious, Perelli," the burly Mexican named Lopez
scoffed. "They'd feed you anything. They hate us for making the extra fifty bucks."

"No, really, this is on the level. We're heading for New
Guinea."

"Where the crap is New Guinea?"

The next day unit commanders announced the destination. New Caledonia. After that Aldo stayed quiet for a couple of days, but then he came up with the best scuttlebutt
anyone had heard so far.

"Now hear this, Marines."

"What happened to New Guinea, Perelli?" Lopez
quipped.

"Yeah, man, you ain't hit one right yet," LaBeau
growled.

"I got this one right, jarhead, and you're gonna want to
kiss my feet."

"You make more noise than a cow pissin' off a flat rock,
Perelli," Charlie Rose grumbled into the canvas above him.

"I hear ya, hick, but you're gonna be whistlin' a different
tune. I need two men to go with me."

"Get on out of here, Perelli."

"You don't like women in Kentucky?" Perelli finished
his sentence slowly, then gazed nonchalantly at the faces
gawking out of the ten canvas racks. Lopez rolled out of
his rack and squatted in front of Perelli so that they were
face to face.

The burly Mexican always looked menacing, but now he looked *intensely* menacing. "Out with it, Perelli."

Perelli grinned. "Dames. W-O-M-E-N. Remember? They smell good and make you crazy. You do remember, don't you, men?" Perelli grinned at the stunned faces around him. He laughed at Jessie. "Well, most of you remember. Slate's gotta be a virgin."

"Stuff it in your ditty bag, Perelli!" Jessie snapped.

"Quit blowin' wind, boy, and say somethin'," Charlie Rose snarled, and threw a wadded-up piece of paper at Perelli.

"I don't know where they are yet, but they're on board, all right. Nurses. Some civilian, some Army."

"Why?" LaBeau asked.

"They're on their way to a forward hospital."

"Where?"

"New Zealand, Australia, or Hawaii—no one knows for sure."

"Maybe New Caledonia's got a hospital," Ellinwood said.

"I didn't see any women boarding the ship," Stukowski said accusingly.

"Of course not, dope. They didn't want a thousand Marines jumpin' out of their skivvies—you know what I mean."

"You got bull comin' out of your ears, Perelli," Charlie said.

"All right, hick! You and the virgin meet this guy for me Thursday night."

"Where?" Jessie asked.

"On deck, by the 37-millimeter at half-past taps."

"Why ain't you meetin' him?" Charlie Rose asked.

"I got mess duty for the next three nights."

"Who is this guy?" Jessie asked.

"Big blond mortarman from the Third. He's got a map, but it's gonna cost some greenbacks. Don't pay a dime till you're sure."

"I'd never trust no Rear Echelon Pull," Lopez said.

Jessie looked down at Charlie's suspicious face leaning out of the rack below, then glanced at the hungry stares across the tiny aisle.

"What ya think, Slate?" Charlie Rose asked.

Jessie frowned. It sounded stupid to him, but he knew he had to go. He couldn't look like a coward in front of everybody.

"I'll go if you're going, Charlie Rose."

Perelli laughed. "Don't worry, kid, you just find 'em, and the men will show you how they work." The squad laughed along with Perelli. For an instant Jessie thought about jumping down on Perelli with both boots, but he didn't. He decided to keep from getting seasick by closing his eyes.

The next seventy-two hours were spent trying to avoid work parties. Most days were spent chipping paint, cleaning the heads, swabbing the deck, doing mess duty or guard watches, or wasting time on some other backbreaking Marine Corps way of avoiding boredom. At night the poker games started up, though they were strictly forbidden by the officers. Some men cleaned gear, while others wrote letters and waited for taps.

From the moment Perelli had mentioned women, the first squad had found new reason for hope. Everyone agreed to keep the news secret. Each man took an oath of silence, and Lopez threatened Perelli with castration if he breathed a word. Lopez had a good deal of prison time behind him; he was mean, and the consensus among the men was that he would indeed castrate Perelli and in all likelihood enjoy doing it.

Jessie felt the poke of a fist in his spine. He rolled onto his right side and looked down at Charlie Rose beneath him.

"What time is it?" Charlie Rose asked.

"About ten minutes later than the last time you asked."

"I don't think the kid's the right man for the job," Lopez mumbled from the bottom cot across the aisle.

Stukowski rolled onto his side and frowned at Jessie from the cot straight across the aisle. "Yeah, kid. There's two out in the bottom of the ninth, DiMaggio's up to bat. Don't botch this."

The mission was growing in importance, and Jessie could feel the pressure of responsibility.

"He's too young for this," another voice from below added.

Jessie felt his face flush with anger.

Stukowski chuckled and looked down at Lopez with an evil grin.

"I remember my first time, but Lopez, you're too ugly to have ever had a woman."

"I can't even remember my first one," Lopez said as if he were bored.

An hour later the first note of taps over the loudspeaker brought instant silence to the first squad. Anticipation was as thick as the sea air above. The next few minutes passed with agonizing slowness.

"Time," someone whispered.

"Saddle up," Charlie Rose said with a nudge.

Jessie climbed down behind Charlie Rose.

"Good luck," Stukowski whispered, and signaled thumbs-up.

Jessie's stomach tightened, and he wondered if the Marines in the first wave on the Canal had had butterflies as bad.

"Don't blow it, kid," Lopez warned.

For whatever reason, no one stopped or questioned Jessie and Charlie as they made their way to the upper deck. It was clumsy going through the dark passageways and stairways that led to the deck of the *Barkley*. The night was warm, and the stars looked bigger and brighter than Jessie could ever remember. A half moon bathed the *Barkley* in blue. There were more men on deck than Jessie had thought there would be. Most were swabbies.

Charlie Rose stopped and turned to Jessie. "Remember, anybody asks what we're doin' here—"

"I know, I know. Seasick."

Charlie Rose nodded and headed for the 37-mm gun that sat on the port side of the bow deck. He stopped again and whispered over his shoulder, "I see somebody standing by the 37."

"Let's go."

The moonlight outlined a swabbie hat on the man near the 37-mm gun. Jessie's hopes sagged.

"That's not our man, Charlie."

"Yeah, it's a swab jockey."

"What now?"

"Ain't nothing to do but wait."

Charlie Rose was right. They waited for over an hour. The big blond Marine didn't show.

\* \* \*

The next few days dragged by one minute at a time. The officers did what they could to change the dull routine. They made the men exercise topside every day and even arranged a boxing match between the Para-Marines and the division Marines, but a storm blew in and it had to be postponed. That night half the Marines on board made at least one puke call to the railing on deck. If there was anything worse than being seasick, Jessie prayed that he would never find out what it was as he climbed back into his rack after a trip to the rail. He flattened out on the canvas bunk and tried to think of home or anything that would stop the spinning.

"Jessie," Charlie Rose whispered, and poked Jessie in the back.

"I'm sick."

"Jessie."

"Can't talk, too sick."

The *Barkley* rolled hard to port from the force of a huge wave. Jessie covered his mouth and swallowed back the bile. He rolled to his right and climbed down. He scrambled up to the top deck and rushed to the railing, just in time. The bad thing about being seasick was that even after one threw up, one didn't feel any better. The ship didn't stop moving just because one's guts turned inside out. Jessie belched again, but there didn't seem to be anything left in his stomach. The rain stopped, but the waves rolled into the convoy as if they would never end. He lifted his head and noticed for the first time that Charlie Rose was beside him.

"You sick, too?" Jessie asked.

"Not yet." Charlie's eyes opened wide. "I gotta tell ya, boy!"

"What's up?"

"I found the big blond guy in the Third. Perelli was tellin' the truth!"

"You're joking."

"No, boy. Women! We meet the guy tonight after taps, in the head. He's got a map. His name's Duffy Johnson. Big guy."

"Women?"

"Women! Don't tell anybody till we find 'em."

"Right."

Jessie wasn't sure why. Maybe it was just the challenge or the mystery of it all, but his stomach started feeling a little better after that. By the time taps played, he felt like jogging around the ship and banging on bulkheads until he found a woman. With so many of the men sick, no one questioned Jessie and Charlie as they made their way to the head. Unbelievably, the big blond guy was there. Jessie tried to hide his excitement, but he knew he had a stupid grin on his face when Charlie Rose introduced him.

"Jessie, this is Corporal Duffy Johnson."

Jessie shook hands with the big Marine, and Duffy squeezed his hand until it turned white. Jessie smiled, but he hated jerks who shook hands like that.

"You got the map?" Charlie Rose asked.

Duffy pulled a folded-up piece of paper out of his trousers pocket and held it up beside his big round face.

"You got the money?"

"I wanna see it first," Jessie said.

"Bullcrap, Gyrene! You see it and you know where they are."

Jessie looked at Charlie Rose. Charlie Rose shrugged.

"Okay, I guess," Jessie said.

"It's good with me, Jessie," Charlie Rose said.

"This is costin' you guys two Hamiltons."

Charlie whistled. Duffy Johnson turned his big head, spit, and held out his palm. "Don't give me the depression routine. The eagle crapped before we boarded, so I know you got the greenbacks."

"The eagle crapped, boy, but that don't mean he had diarrhea."

"Save it for the chaplain. I know you Para-Marines draw an extra fifty, so don't tell me you ain't got it."

Jessie dug into his pocket and handed Charlie Rose a ten-dollar bill. Charlie Rose pulled out another ten and handed both bills to Duffy. Jessie snatched the map out of the big man's hand. He unfolded it with Charlie Rose hanging on his shoulder.

"Nice doin' business with you, Para-Marines," Duffy said sarcastically as he walked out of the head.

The map drawing of the *Barkley* gave a detailed view of each level of the ship, with special details of the officers' area amidships. There were two decks of cabins with eight cabin doors on each deck, four on the starboard and four on the port.

"That's it! Upper deck, port side, third door from the stairway." Charlie pointed at a door marked with an X.

"We got it," Jessie mumbled, staring wide-eyed at the X like a kid looking at a new bike.

Charlie Rose nudged Jessie with an elbow. "You ready?"

"Now?" Jessie suddenly felt stiff, weak, and nervous.

"Yeah, now, boy."

Rose headed for the door. Jessie followed. He felt as if he were in a daze. They moved through tiny passageways and up noisy metal ladders until Rose finally paused to study the map under a dim green light on a bulkhead by a stairway.

"Up these stairs; it's the third door." Rose looked at Jessie and smiled. "You ready for a beachhead, Marine?"

"Yeah, I'm ready, but we're making too much noise."

Rose gave a nod and hustled up the stairs, with Jessie right behind. The stairway led to a narrow corridor with the bulkhead on the right and four cabin doors on the left. The doors were varnished wood. A dim green light barely illuminated the corridor.

Charlie Rose tiptoed past the first two doors and stopped in front of the third. He turned to Jessie. Charlie's square face scrunched up as if he were suddenly perplexed.

"What if they won't let us in?"

"What if they do let us in?" Jessie whispered.

Charlie's square face seemed to go from worried to confused to angry.

"What bull you talkin', Slate?"

"If they're nurses they'll be officers," Jessie said. "Then what?"

"Keep yer dad-blamed voice down, boy!"

"We're going to the brig for sure, Charlie Rose." Jessie looked at the door. His stomach churned into a knot.

"You call yerself a Marine?" Charlie Rose whispered, and gave Jessie a light shove toward the cabin door.

That did it. Charlie Rose was right. Any real Marine would go gung ho through that door. He bit his lower lip and stepped up to the door. He could hear voices inside. Someone laughed. Jessie took a deep breath, grabbed the doorknob, and turned it. It was open. He shoved through the door as his mind raced to find an opening line.

"Hello, ladies."

Two steps into the cabin Jessie froze stiff—so stiff that he barely moved when Charlie Rose plowed into his back. He tried to speak, but the words wouldn't form.

Six stone-faced officers stared at Jessie like a firing squad ready to shoot. They were sitting around a small table. Each held a hand of cards. There was money in the center of the table. The small room was lit by a single light bulb swinging on a cord above the table. Jessie felt Charlie Rose snap to attention beside him. At least he wouldn't hang alone.

Forty-five minutes later every muscle in his body ached to relax. He was sure that even POWs could not legally be grilled to that extent. First one officer and then another took turns shouting out any question that came into their minds.

"What is the nomenclature of the M1 Garand rifle, Marine?" a squat-looking division captain shouted into Charlie's face.

"They're Para-Marines, Tom," a familiar-looking lieutenant said sarcastically.

"So what, Lieutenant Pomper?"

"They don't carry the Garand like every other Marine in the Corps." The lieutenant stepped in front of Jessie and leaned close enough for Jessie to smell the beer on his breath. "Do you, PFC?"

"No, sir. Our rifle is the Johnson rifle, sir."

"You prima donnas think you're better than other Marines, don't you, PFC?" Three firm knocks on the cabin door seemed to go unnoticed. Jessie heard the door open behind him as he shouted out his answer.

"We are the First Para-Marine Regiment, sir!"

"Think you're top of line, PFC?" Lieutenant Pomper asked sarcastically.

"You bet your . . . I mean, yes, sir!"

Lieutenant Pomper's face turned pale with anger. He took a step back and opened his eyes wide with rage.

"Excuse me, sirs." The low, strong voice of Gunny O'Cleary had never sounded better.

"What is it, Gunnery Sergeant?" the squat captain snapped.

"Two of my men weren't in their racks, Captain. I think I found 'em, sir."

"You in the habit of entering officers' quarters without notice, Gunnery Sergeant?"

"No, sir, Captain. I clearly knocked, sir, and thought I heard an answer."

"What are your men doing out of their compartment, Gunny?" Lieutenant Pomper barked.

"Can't say for sure, Lieutenant, but there's been a shipload of barfin' going on above deck, sir."

"Wait outside, Sergeant," the captain ordered.

"Aye, aye, sir." Gunny O'Cleary saluted and did an about-face.

The instant the door closed, the captain motioned the other officers into one corner of the tiny room. Jessie kept his eyes straight ahead as the officers huddled and whispered. Gray wisps of cigarette smoke rose from three butt-filled ashtrays on the table, forming a blue cloud around the swinging light bulb. Lieutenant Pomper's high-pitched voice was louder than those of the other officers.

"That's what we should do, sir," Pomper said with a laugh that brought on chuckles from the others.

The officers broke up and walked toward Jessie and Charlie Rose with their arms folded in front of them as if a decision had been made. The captain stepped in front of Jessie and stood grinning for a moment before he spoke.

"So you men say that a division Marine sold you this map?" He held the folded map in front of Jessie's eyes.

"Yes, sir," they answered in unison.

"Duffy's map."

"Sir?"

"Somebody printed 'Duffy's Map' right down in this bottom corner here. Is that the man's name?"

"Can't remember, sir," Jessie said.

"How about you, Marine?"

"I ain't much on remembering names, sir," Charlie Rose said.

"Lieutenant Pomper here happens to have a Marine under his command named Corporal Duffy Johnson. Since we don't know who's lying and because we're curious to see a real Para-Marine in action, we have come up with a way of clearing your honor. Instead of busting you both and throwing you into a brig until you both turn gray"—The captain poked a finger into Jessie's chest—"PFC Slate will fight Corporal Johnson in the ring on deck at 0900 hours tomorrow. Is that clear?"

"Aye, aye, sir!"

"Don't ever let me see you two in officer country again! Dismissed!"

"Aye, aye, sir!"

The cabin door had not fully closed behind them when the gunny's angry bellow greeted them.

"Attention!"

Gunny O'Cleary leaned forward, staring at the two as if he were seeing them for the first time.

"Out having some fun tonight, Marines?" His voice was low and calm. "Think you're back on the block with the old gang, cutting a rug down at the bowling alley, maybe taking in a moving picture with your broad?" He smiled the smile that every man in the outfit dreaded.

The gunny looked at his watch.

"You men better hurry along. You're running out of time."

"For what, Gunny?" Charlie Rose asked. Jessie wanted to ram Charlie Rose with an elbow for asking such a stupid question.

"You will have every crap bowl on this ship clean enough for the skipper to brush his teeth in! After that you will swab the decks until I am tired. You will have a full-dress inspection at 0400 hours, at which time if I even smell Cosmoline on your weapons or find any form of matter not intended to be on any and all Marine Corps equipment, you will spit-shine every pair of boondockers on board the USS *Barkley*! Do I make myself clear, Marines?"

"Aye, aye, Gunny!"

"Move it! Now!"

From that moment until the first harsh notes of reveille at 0400 hours the two Marines moved like madmen on a mission of life and death. Each time one of them stopped to rest for a moment, the gunny would mysteriously appear with an angry shout. "Move it! Move it! Move it!" At exactly 0400 hours the gunny marched into the compartment with a look on his face that had the waking men stepping aside like matadors dodging an angry bull.

"Ready for inspection, sir!" Charlie Rose snapped to attention.

"Ready for inspection, sir!" Jessie echoed.

Lopez rubbed the sleep from his eyes as he rolled out of

his canvas bunk. He whistled low, like artillery getting closer. "You two eight balls must have stepped in it this time!"

"Shut up, Marine!" Gunny O'Cleary snapped. "Get squared away and get your lazy butt into formation on deck!"

"Aye, aye, Gunny." Lopez and the others hurried into their utilities and left.

"PFCs Slate and Rose!"

"Sir!"

"Put your hands straight out, palms down."

The two Marines held out their arms with palms down. For a moment Jessie thought that the gunny was checking their fingernails. He tried to remember if he had cleaned them, but fatigue was setting in and his thinking was fuzzy. The gunny grabbed Jessie's rifle, gave it a quick inspection, then laid it on the back of Jessie's outstretched fingers. He quickly did the same to Charlie Rose.

"You will hold that position until the inspection is complete. The first Marine to drop his weapon fails inspection."

The Johnson automatic rifle weighed 8.9 pounds. After ten minutes it felt like eight tons. Jessie began to tremble. He bit at his bottom lip and tried to get his mind off the pain, but the trembling in his arms was getting worse. Beads of sweat dripped from his eyebrows and into his eyes, stinging them with salt. He glanced at Charlie Rose on his left. If only Charlie Rose would drop his rifle first—but even if he did, it might not help. Finally the gunnery sergeant cleared his throat as if to signal that a change was coming. The muscles in Jessie's neck and back began to spasm, and he grimaced from the pain but held on.

"Let your weapons down."

Jessie dropped to his knees, allowing the rifle to lie across his thighs. He quivered for moment, then stood to attention.

"Stow this gear away and be on deck for PT in five minutes!"

The calisthenics lasted for two hours and matched any torture that Jessie could remember from boot camp. The swab jockeys on deck loved seeing what they had missed by being sailors instead of Marines, but, even through the occasional laughter, respect for the maniacs who stormed beaches was always there.

"Give me thirty more Marine Corps push-ups!"

"I said Marine Corps push-ups, Rose! Get your squatty body flat, mister! Your chest did not touch my hand, PFC! Add five for both of you!"

And so it went until the old gunny had the two young Marines swooning with exhaustion. O'Cleary looked at his watch, then stood at parade rest in front of the gasping PFCs.

"It is now 0850 hours, gentlemen. You have until 0900 hours to crap, shower, and shave and be back on deck with brooms and mops!"

"0900, Gunny?" Charlie Rose asked.

"You deaf, PFC?"

"No sir, Gunny, but PFC Slate has a big scrap at 0900."

Jessie felt his mouth drop slightly open. How could he have completely forgotten?

"What are you babbling about, Rose?" Gunny O'Cleary demanded.

"Lieutenant Pomper and those officers last night said that Jessie had to fight that big scumbag that sold us the map!"

"What map?"

"That's how we got into this, Gunny," Charlie Rose claimed.

"He's telling you the truth, Gunny," Jessie said.

"All right, at ease. Let's hear the whole story."

Charlie Rose sighed with fatigue as he put his hands behind his back and stood at parade rest.

"Tell him, Charlie," Jessie said.

"This bigmouth monster from the Third sold us this map for twenty greenbacks."

"Map of what?"

"A map to where the women were being kept, Gunny," Jessie blurted.

"You boot-brain idiots." Gunny looked at the deck and shook his head in obvious disgust.

"He set us up, didn't he, Gunny?" Jessie asked, already knowing the answer.

"No women on board, Gunny?" Charlie Rose asked as if he were pleading.

The crow's-feet around the old man's eyes deepened as his smile turned into a full laugh. He kept laughing and stomping his right boot for a minute or two, then just grinned at the two PFCs and shook his head.

"Your reconnaissance is off, lads! There's women, all right, and they're aboard that ship just ahead of us." The gunny pointed and laughed again. "Now, what's this about a fight?"

"It's that Lieutenant Pomper, Gunny," Jessie said.

"Yeah," Charlie Rose snapped. "That sister to a jackass has it in for the Para-Marines. He's the one that set up this fight with this Duffy Johnson."

"Why in God's Marine Corps didn't one of you idiots tell me this before now?"

"You didn't let us do much talking, Gunny," Jessie said.

The old man scratched at the back of his neck. "Well, you sure ain't in no shape to get in that ring now."

"Boy, you can say that again, Gunny. I don't think I can lift my arms."

"Get on down and get a shower. I'll see what I can do, but I can't promise anything."

Charlie Rose took a deep breath and sighed. "Get him out of it, Gunny. If he feels like me, he couldn't lick his granny right now."

"Go get that shower."

Jessie and Charlie Rose did an about-face and headed for the hatchway leading below.

"Slate!" Gunny called.

Jessie stopped and looked back.

"You any good? Do you know how to box?"

"Never done it before."

The gunny grinned and shook his head.

The shower did little to revive Jessie. The walk back to his compartment felt like the end of an all-night forced march. Each step was an effort. By the time Jessie reached his cot, there was no doubt in his mind that if the gunny couldn't at least change the time of the fight, he was in for a beating.

"Hey, Slate! Now hear this." PFC Perelli leaned his head over the edge of his cot. "Big fight! It's us against the division Marines."

Jessie's heart sank into his stomach.

Lopez rolled out of his cot and stood up.

"That's right?"

"Yeah, 0900 on the aft deck."

Benjamin B. Oglethorpe climbed out of his cot and stretched. He looked over at Aldo Perelli. "Who's the Joe representing the First?"

Perelli shrugged his shoulders and poked Jack Ellinwood above him. "Ellinwood, you hear who's fighting for us?"

Jack Ellinwood put down his Ellery Queen paperback and stood up slowly. The tall soft-spoken Marine rubbed his chin thoughtfully. "I don't remember Sergeant Rim mentioning the name."

Jessie closed his eyes and leaned against the stack of canvas cots on his right. He blinked to keep from falling asleep and yawned so wide that it hurt his jaw.

"Slate."

Jessie turned. "Yeah, Gunny?"

"Sorry, Slate. They won't change it. Be on deck in five. Just do the best you can, son."

"Aye, aye, Gunny." The gunny turned and walked through the hatchway as the questions started flying from every man in the squad.

The sun was already warm when Jessie came through the starboard hatchway. The morning was clear, and the sea air was sweet and fresh. The convoy of gray ships stretched for miles in both directions under a cloudless blue sky. War seemed far removed from the peaceful scene. The calm sea made the deck sway only slightly as Jessie walked aft. A makeshift boxing ring with mats for a floor and two strands of heavy rope tied to four two-by-fours standing in buckets of sand was set up in the middle of hundreds of noisy Marines. Jessie paused for a moment. Maybe it was all a dream.

"Hurry up, Slate," Sergeant Rim said, prodding Jessie's back.

Jessie moved toward the boisterous crowd in a daze of fatigue.

"Gunny O'Cleary will be your cornerman, Slate," Sergeant Rim shouted over the jeers and cheers of the shirtless mob.

"Gang way, gang way!" O'Cleary yelled as Jessie stepped through, around, and over sitting Marines until he reached the ring.

"This corner, Slate!" Gunny O'Cleary shouted, and waved Jessie to the far corner.

As Jessie climbed through the ropes and walked over to the gunny, Marines from the rest of the replacement battalion shouted insults and Para-Marines cheered. Duffy Johnson stood in the opposite corner, pounding his gloves together and smiling confidently. Jessie glanced out to sea as a speedy destroyer weaved by off the starboard side. He wished he were on it.

"Look, Slate." Gunny O'Cleary shoved a hard rubber mouth guard into Jessie's mouth. "Try to stay away from him. See if he gets tired."

"He'll never get as tired as me, Gunny," Jessie grumbled through his mouth guard.

"He's got a good thirty pounds on you, but you're solid muscle, Slate. I'm bettin' you're stronger than that big jackass."

Lieutenant Pomper climbed through the ropes with a grin that grated on Jessie's nerves. Pomper held up his hands for quiet, then announced that he would be the referee. He introduced both men to the cheers of their units, then motioned them to the center of the ring.

"You men know the rules. No hitting below the belt or kicking or any of that. Shake hands and come out fighting."

Jessie touched gloves and walked back to his corner wondering what it felt like to get hit in the face with a boxing glove. His fear made him remember meeting the bully of Kanawah County High after school. His name was Davy Yard. He'd never been so scared as that time, but after it had started, all the fear had disappeared and he had beaten the crap out of Davy Yard.

Someone cracked the side of a metal bucket with a big galley spoon, and the fight began.

Burning ammonia stung deep into Jessie's sinuses. He jerked away from the smell and opened his eyes. Bright overhead lights forced them closed again.

"Hey, you okay, Marine? You hear me?"

Jessie opened his left eye slowly. A throbbing headache forced the eye shut.

"You're in the dispensary, Marine."

Jessie opened his left eye again. The tan face of a young

Navy corpsman stared down at him through the bright white lights.

"You did all right for a minute, but, boy, you caught a left hook that would have put Joe Louis on the canvas. You boxed much?"

"Not till today," Jessie groaned.

"What'd you expect, Mac? That guy was heavyweight Golden Gloves champ from Oklahoma."

Jessie opened his eyes wide, then closed them and took a deep breath to control the anger swelling up inside him. The corpsman kicked angrily at something metal.

"You never boxed before, Marine? Good grief!" he yelled before Jessie could answer. "I put seven bucks on you."

"Why'd you do that?" Jessie asked.

"He had you by twenty-five pounds, easy. Right?"

"At least."

"I figured the Para-Marines must have put you in there as a ringer. You know, just to clean up on the odds. Didn't make sense any other way."

"How's he doin', Doc?" a gruff voice asked from the open hatchway behind the corpsman. Gunny O'Cleary stepped into the dispensary with his soft cover in his hand and a grin on his rugged face.

"He'll live, Gunny."

Jessie touched the goose egg above his right eye and grimaced. "Why didn't somebody tell me that big ape was a Golden Gloves champ?"

The gunny chuckled as he maneuvered a chewed-up cigar to one corner of his mouth. "Wouldn't have helped any, Slate."

Jessie sat up too quickly. He winced from a sharp pain in his head and neck. The corpsman tried to push him back down.

"Stay down, Marine."

Jessie shoved his hand away and glared at Gunny O'Cleary. "I let the whole outfit down, didn't I? I embarrassed every Para-Marine on this ship."

The old man grinned. "No, you did not, PFC Slate. You showed courage in the face of overwhelming odds. Proud of you, son. Jim would have been proud, too. Never had a chance to tell you that I heard your reply to that butter-bar Lieutenant Pomper last night in the officers' cabin. Couldn't have said it better myself, Marine." Gunny O'Cleary turned and walked through the hatchway and out of the dispensary without another word.

Jessie sat still for a few moments staring at the hatchway and repeating in his mind what the gunny had said. A warm feeling of pride slowly grew until he no longer felt the lump that impaired the vision in his right eye. There wasn't a more squared-away Marine in the Corps than Gunny O'Cleary. Jessie grinned contentedly. He'd take a dozen beatings to gain the gunny's respect.

An hour later Jessie was released from sick bay with a two-day light-duty slip. The good feeling the gunny had left him with vanished the moment he entered the compartment hatchway.

"If it ain't Max Schmeling," Lopez shouted.

"Way to go, slugger," someone else yelled.

"You made the elite of the Corps look like a bunch of GIs!" fireplug Ronnie Garland shouted at the top of his lungs.

Charlie Rose rolled out of his cot with fists clenched. "Stuff it where the sun don't shine, Garland! I done told y'all what happened. Ain't one of you Gyrenes coulda done a dang bit better if you'd been put on the end of the gunny's boot like we was."

"It's all right, Charlie Rose. I don't blame 'em. I let the outfit down."

"Shame you couldn't use one of them judo throws they taught us at Elliot," Stukwoski said.

Jessie said nothing more. He climbed into his cot, stared at the ceiling, and listened to the clacking of dice from the never-ending game of craps being played nearby. He tried not to think of the fight, but it was no use. His anger and embarrassment grew and grew until he slammed his fist into the ceiling. He closed his eyes and thought about Sergeant Mitchell, the hand-to-hand combat instructor at Camp Elliot. Mitchell was an expert at that oriental stuff. He could put the biggest Marine in the camp on his butt with a kick or a throw. Jessie felt the poke of a finger on his shoulder. He looked left.

"Yeah, Oglethorpe?"

"Jessie, I firmly believe in revenge."

"You do?"

Oglethorpe pushed his glasses back against the bridge of his long, thin nose. "Yes, I do. If you keep attentive, your opportunity will present itself." Benjamin Oglethorpe turned away and climbed back into his cot.

Jessie leaned back and smiled. Benjamin Oglethorpe was an odd fellow but likable. Revenge did sound like a good idea, but what kind of revenge? Punching an officer like Pomper would probably get him shot, and punching Johnson would probably break his hand. Jessie closed his eyes. He would wait for his chance.

Three days passed, three days of constant work details: chipping paint, scrubbing the decks, cleaning the head, standing inspection, and anything else the noncoms could think of to relieve the boredom. Through it all Jessie waited for his chance, but with each passing day, it seemed less likely to appear. Then, early one afternoon, Jessie stared at the ceiling and pinched his nose as the noisy air vent burped out another foul-smelling rush of hot air.

Charlie Rose groaned. "I tell you right now, that there air vent was made in Japan."

"Think so, Rose?" Stukowski asked with a chuckle.

"Yes, sir, it was, or I'm a-milking somebody's horse."

"No! No, no, no!" LaBeau sounded like a man receiving terrible news. He rolled out of the rack, stood up, and stared at the good-natured Charlie Rose like a scientist studying an unknown specimen. His cornflower-blue eyes pinched together. Finally he pushed his hand through his short black hair, shivered slightly, and crawled back into his cot, mumbling something about the Confederacy.

"Jessie," Oglethorpe said, poking him in the shoulder.

"Hi, Oglethorpe. What's up?"

Benjamin Oglethorpe looked at his watch. "It is precisely 1830 hours."

"That's nice to know."

"Corporal Johnson has just finished eating along with Bravo Company, who will now be making their way to the head area."

"How do you know that?"

"I am extremely observant. I have observed that many of the men of Able Company make a head call after chow to avoid making the long walk back to the head area later on, when many of the passageways are dark."

"That is very observant, Oglethorpe. Now, why should I care?"

"Revenge."

The edges of Benjamin Oglethorpe's pale, thin lips lifted slowly into an unmistakably evil grin; his eyelids lowered until he seemed to be peeking out of little slits.

Charlie Rose poked his head out of the stack of cots. "That boy has a plan or I'm the left foot of a black and brown sow."

"Ohhh nooo!" LaBeau sounded as if he were in serious pain. Jessie leaned out of the top rack and looked down as the big Cajun leaned out, looking up.

"You all right, Chris?" Jessie asked.

"What the crap does the left foot of a black and brown sow mean? It means nothing! I tell y'all, Rose is a Yankee implant sent to disgrace the South. He's an idiot! Nothin' he says makes any sense. He's crazy! His mother and father were probably crazy!"

Charlie Rose leaned out of his cot and frowned. "You know now, Chris, I ain't one to complain, but I don't think it's right for you to be calling such a good friend a name like Yankee. Here, Chris." Charlie Rose dropped a pack of cigarettes to Chris.

Chris LaBeau caught the cigarettes and stared at them. "What's this?" he asked.

"Lucky Strikes. That's your brand, ain't it? I traded a swab jockey a couple packs of Chelseas for it."

"What?"

"I know it looks different with the red circle on the front instead of the green one, but that's cuz they're using something in that green dye for the war effort."

Openmouthed, LaBeau stared up at Charlie Rose.

Oglethorpe cleared his throat before breaking the silence. "We must shove off now if the event is to take place."

Jessie rolled out of his cot and climbed down.

"I'm with you, boys," Charlie Rose said as he rolled out of his cot and followed the other two out of the compartment. Jessie didn't look back, but he had a feeling that LaBeau was still staring at the spot where Charlie Rose had been.

The main head area was below deck aft. Oglethorpe paused in the narrow passageway leading to the head area and glanced back at Jessie and Charlie Rose. He pushed his round glasses back against the bridge of his thin, straight nose.

"Now, there are certain aspects of this plan that must fall into place in order for it to work," Oglethorpe cautioned. "One aspect is the position of the target; we can only hope that he shows up and deposits himself in the appropriate area."

"What in the world—" Jessie began.

Oglethorpe held up his right hand. "If only one target shows up, then we will just have to settle for one. Both of you follow me and sit directly across from me at the top of the trough. Put a newspaper in front of your face so that Johnson or Pomper do not recognize you when they show up. Clear?"

Charlie Rose saluted. "Aye, aye, boy."

"God, I hope we don't end up in the brig," Jessie moaned.

"A defeatist attitude will only hinder our efforts, PFC Slate," Oglethorpe cautioned. "A just man must stand tall and balance the scales of justice whenever and wherever an imbalance exists. A just man must be willing to risk imprisonment or any and all punishment if need be. I, gentlemen, am such a man." With that, Oglethorpe drew back his shoulders, did a sharp about-face, and marched into the head.

For a moment Jessie felt obligated to salute.

"Charlie Rose, there goes a noble human being."

"I think the boy's leaning just a tad to starboard."

"Obviously, but we can't let him hit the beach alone."

"Yep."

The smell of lye soap was strong enough to make one's eyes water inside one's head, and if the lye didn't, then the normal stink of urine and crap would. Funny thing about being a Marine: odors that would make a civilian barf seemed hardly worth complaining about in the madness of a military environment crammed with three to four thousand Marines.

The same engineers who had created the sleeping quarters had also created the toilet system. It was probably the best way to accommodate such large numbers of men, but it had the privacy of a pig trough, which was exactly what it was modeled after. The head was a long, narrow compart-

ment about twenty-five feet long and ten feet wide. Two gal-
vanized metal troughs ran along each wall, with fifteen
makeshift toilet seats fitted and spaced about a foot and half
apart on each trough. The troughs were angled down toward the back of the ship so that a steady stream of salt
water allowed the refuse to float downstream and into the
ocean. The head also served as sort of a library. There were
always out-of-date newspapers and magazines lying about
and usually pinups of Gene Tierney or Betty Grable stuck
to the bulkhead.

The head was about half-full, with around fifteen men
spaced evenly on both troughs. Most were reading newspapers or old copies of *Collier's* or *Life.* Oglethorpe had carefully placed himself two toilet seats down from the very
peak of the port-side trough and was pretending to read a
newspaper. Jessie and Charlie Rose strolled to the starboard
side but didn't sit yet.

Oglethorpe frowned and whispered across the aisle. "Pick
up a paper before they come in so you'll be ready."

Jessie and Charlie Rose did so immediately. The wait was
on. Benjamin had poked out a small hole in his paper,
through which he could observe the entrance to the head
while pretending to read. Jessie and Charlie Rose did the
same.

Five minutes passed. No sign of Pomper or Johnson.
Charlie hummed to the tune of "Accentuate the Positive"
and tapped his foot restlessly. He lowered his newspaper.

"You sure about this plan, Oglethorpe?"

"Justice rarely comes quickly, Charlie Rose. Be patient.
If the enemy sits on this side, I want you two to move dis-
creetly to these two seats beside me."

As if on cue, big Duffy Johnson walked into the head.
Charlie Rose yanked up his newspaper. Duffy unbuttoned
his trousers and sat down near the end of the port-side
trough. He picked up a newspaper, leaned forward, elbows
on knees, and seemed to concentrate intently on the paper.
Jessie and Charlie Rose casually moved across the aisle and
sat beside Oglethorpe. Oglethorpe put his newspaper down
and produced a stiff piece of cardboard about the size of a
shoe-box top from inside his shirt. He leaned out on his
knees to see past three other Marines who were sitting between himself and Duffy on the far end. Duffy continued

to read, oblivious to anything around him. Oglethorpe sat up straight and proceeded to wedge the piece of cardboard down into the trough, constructing a makeshift dam. He then turned to Jessie and Charlie Rose.

"Now would be an appropriate time to relieve yourselves."

Jessie and Charlie Rose exchanged puzzled glances, then looked at Oglethorpe as if they were both concerned for his mental well-being.

Oglethorpe seemed to sense their apprehension. "Have faith, gentlemen. Justice is at hand."

Jessie and Charlie Rose relieved themselves. The cardboard dam worked. Once the procedure was completed, Oglethorpe stood up and buttoned his trousers.

"Stand by for action."

Jessie and Charlie Rose stood up and buttoned their trousers as Oglethorpe pulled a box of wooden matches from his breast pocket. He put one match in his teeth and emptied the rest into a small square of toilet paper, which he laid on top of the dammed-up refuse. He made a final observation of Johnson's position, then signaled thumbs-up.

"Fire in the hole, men."

He removed the match between his teeth, struck it, and lit the toilet paper all around the refuse. He glanced down at Duffy Johnson, who was still engrossed in his newspaper, then lifted the dam.

"Retreat," Oglethorpe muttered as he walked casually out of the head with Jessie and Charlie Rose following, both now biting at their bottom lips to fight back the screams of laughter swelling up inside as they fully realized the magnificence of Oglethorpe's revenge. Jessie paused at the hatchway to look back. The tiny fire on the raft of excrement grew larger as it floated downstream toward Duffy. The points of flame were well above toilet-seat level when Jessie decided that total retreat might be a good move.

Approximately half the ship's four-thousand-man complement claimed to have heard Duffy Johnson's bloodcurdling scream. There was even some fear that Jap submarines might have been alerted. A ship's corpsman reported that Duffy had suffered first-degree burns on his buttocks and that all pubic hair had been singed off his groin area and testicles. One other Marine had been slightly burned.

Oglethorpe was sincerely sorry that an innocent man had been caught in the line of fire, so to speak, but he explained it in biblical terms: "The rain falls upon the just and the unjust alike."

# CHAPTER FOUR

THE LEAD SHIPS OF THE LONG GRAY CONVOY MADE their first landfall two weeks after the submarine nets had closed behind them across the San Diego channel. After so much time of nothing but vast, empty blue South Pacific, a rumor of land spread through the ship like a gasoline fire. Within minutes, shirtless young men with longing stares crowded the deck. They were the kind of stares the men usually reserved for young women. New Caledonia was a radiant emerald on the shimmering horizon. Just the sight of it seemed to settle queasy stomachs.

A group of smaller islands were scattered around the big island, but New Caledonia, at nearly eight thousand square miles, was by far the largest. It was a territory of France, situated 875 miles east of Australia, and a vital supply link to Australia. The population was mostly French and Melanesian. With the influx of Allied military personnel, the population of twelve thousand had grown to nearly thirty thousand. The capital city of Nouméa, also the largest on the banana-shaped island, was situated on the eastern tip. Though it looked tiny from the decks of the huge ships anchored around it, the sight of even so small a city lifted everyone's spirits. At least, no one aboard the *Barkley* was sad when the loudspeaker blared "Prepare to disembark!"

A quick truck ride from the harbor on a narrow dirt road skirted the edge of the city and ended at the foothills of a long mountain range. Tired brakes squealed as the trucks came to a stop.

"Get out of those trucks! Move it! Move it! We ain't got all day!" Sergeant Rim shouted to the men from the trucks.

They hurried into a quick formation, facing a large camp

61

of brown pyramidal tents that formed a square nestled in
a vast stand of tall pine trees. Two Quonset storage huts
were positioned like gateposts on each side of the road leading into the camp. A few huts of wood and grass sat on the
outer edges of the encampment. A hand-painted sign over
the front door of one Quonset hut said "Com Shack." Over
the door of the other was a sign that said "Camp St. Louis
HQ."

The replacement battalion was quickly marched into the
tent area and split into four companies, which were each
in turn split into four platoons and then further into six-man
fire teams, before the men were assigned to tents. By nightfall the camp was organized except for the chow hall. Boxes
of C-rations were issued. Rain began to pelt the roof of the
tent with the last notes of taps. Jessie fell into a dreamless
sleep. For the first time in two weeks the world did not move
with the rolling waves.

Reveille at 0500 sounded no better on solid land than it
had on board ship. Noncoms shouted into tents around the
camp. The tent flap was pulled back, and the gray morning
light filled the tent, along with Corporal DiCicca's high-
pitched voice.

"Reveille! Get out of the rack! This ain't no country
club!"

Jessie rubbed the sleep from his eyes and listened. "No
rain, thank God," he mumbled to himself. He sat up and
swung his legs over the edge of the cot, lowering his feet
to the hard dirt floor. Mud squashed between his toes.
Somebody nearby cursed as he, too, discovered the mud.

"Formation on the road in five!" The tent flap closed with
a slap.

Five minutes later the First Replacement Battalion stood
in two long columns on the dirt road that led through the
middle of the camp. They were marched to a clearing on
the eastern fringe of the square city of tents and told to sit
on rows of tattered sandbags facing a small wooden platform. "Tenshun!" someone shouted. The men stood as a
square-jawed lieutenant colonel mounted the platform and
quickly saluted his captive audience.

"As you were, men."

The battalion of replacements sat back down on their
soggy sandbags.

"I'm Lieutenant Colonel Silk. We will be in Nouméa for approximately one month or until ordered elsewhere. During that time most of you will remain with your specific platoon or company. Raiders with the raider detachment, Para-Marines with Para-Marine detachment, artillery, engineers, and so on. Platoon and company commanders will see that no replacement unit does less than a six-mile march in full pack every single day that we remain at Camp St. Louis!"

Charlie Rose nudged Jessie with an elbow. "That means the raiders will march fifteen and we'll—"

"Yeah, twenty miles for sure," Jessie moaned.

"Now, every Marine here listen to this and listen good! Some of you may be fortunate enough to get liberty in Nouméa. If that happens, you will be representing your country and your Corps. Act accordingly or pay the price. No fighting in the slop chutes! Even with the Army! Nouméa is the capital city of New Caledonia. New Caledonia is a French territory under French law. The principal language is French; however, the population is international. There are nearly 1,500 Japanese residents on the island. Most have been here for a decade or more and have no contact with Tokyo, but if you think for one minute Tojo doesn't have spies in Nouméa, then you better think again. You get drunk and run your mouth in the wrong place at the wrong time and you may as well stick a Jap bayonet in another leatherneck's back. Now, some of you will be used for special working parties, and others will be given various assignments as needs arise."

Colonel Silk pulled a piece of yellow paper from his trousers pocket and unfolded it. He pulled out a pair of glasses from his breast pocket, put them on, and began to read from the paper.

"Listen up! The raider replacements are to provide a working party for the galley. They need ten men. The Para-Marines will provide three volunteers to work with a specialized communications detachment. Artillery will provide . . ."

Charlie Rose shot an elbow into Jessie's ribs. "Let's volunteer for that communication detail, fellas!"

"Volunteer? An ugly and often dangerous verb," Oglethorpe submitted.

"I bet it's some Rear Echelon Pull duty."

"I don't know, Charlie Rose."

"Guess we'll just be trying to outmarch them raiders again."

Jessie and Oglethorpe exchanged glances.

"Volunteer," Jessie mumbled.

Oglethorpe shrugged his shoulders in resignation. Jessie pinched the bridge of his nose as if he'd been hit by a headache. Charlie Rose slapped his hands together and spit.

After the lieutenant colonel left the platform, the battalion was dismissed, and Jessie followed Charlie Rose and Oglethorpe over to Lieutenant Pierce, who was speaking to Gunny O'Cleary.

"We want to volunteer, sir," Charlie Rose said as he came to attention and saluted.

Lieutenant Pierce seemed surprised.

"That's fine, men. Are you each high school grads?"

"Yes, sir."

"Have each of you ever studied a foreign language?"

"Numerous languages, sir," Oglethorpe said smugly.

"Does Latin count, Lieutenant?" Jessie asked.

"Yes."

"I had an old history teacher who made us learn some Choctaw Indian."

"That's great. You three report to the com shack."

The three saluted, did an about-face, and headed for the com shack Quonset hut at the entrance to Camp St. Louis.

"Hold up a minute there, men."

They stopped and waited for Gunnery Sergeant O'Cleary, who ambled up to the three young Marines like a cowboy who'd been on a horse all day.

"Good morning, Gunny," Jessie said.

"I hear some scuttlebutt that says Lieutenant Pomper is just a bit put out right now." The gunny wore a sly expression, as if he knew more than he was saying.

"Why's that, Gunny?" Jessie asked.

O'Cleary scratched at his chin and scrunched up his rugged face. "Well, I understand he got up to go to the head last night, and he put on his boondockers without no socks and discovered that somebody had just about filled his boots with crap."

Charlie Rose slapped his forehead. "Oh, my Gawd!"

"I heard he stayed up half the night soaking his feet," Gunny continued. "Had to deep-six his boondockers."

Jessie and Charlie Rose looked at each other for a moment, then both slowly turned to stare at Oglethorpe. Oglethorpe kept his eyes attentively on the gunny, nodding politely, head tilted slightly, with all the innocence of an altar boy.

"Imagine that," Oglethorpe said in a ponderous tone.

"Don't suppose you men would know anything about this phantom crapper?"

"No, I for one have absolutely no information concerning this subject, Gunny," Benjamin Oglethorpe said.

Charlie Rose and Jessie shrugged in agreement. The gunny walked away mumbling something no one could make out.

Charlie Rose slapped Oglethorpe on the back and whispered, "Oglethorpe, you should get the Bronze Star for this, boy."

"Phantom crapper," Jessie muttered as he bit the inside of his lip to keep from laughing.

Oglethorpe shrugged.

They walked down the dirt road and through the tall trees and tents until they reached the two Quonset huts at the entrance to Camp St. Louis. They stood still in front of the com shack staring at the front door, each waiting for the others to go in first.

Jessie's stomach growled. For some reason he felt as though he'd been there before. Impossible, he thought, then smiled, remembering how he had once stood in front of Principal Kubler's office awaiting prosecution for playing "Boogie Woogie Bugle Boy of Company B" over the school intercom.

Charlie Rose nudged him. "After you, boy."

Jessie scratched at his neck, checked his military alignment, stepped up, and slapped three times hard above the door with his palm, the way he'd been taught in boot camp. He opened the door as he removed his overseas cap.

"PFCs Slate, Oglethorpe, and Rose reporting, sir!"

"Advance, Marines," an unfamiliar voice answered quickly.

They stepped into a tiny office packed full with green filing cabinets. A cane board wall with a gray curtain door no more than six feet from the front door separated the office from the rest of the Quonset hut. To their left, a tan corporal sat behind a cluttered metal desk studying the contents of a manila folder.

"Close the hatch behind you," he said without looking away from the open folder.

Charlie Rose pulled the door closed.

"We were told to report to the com shack for a communication detail, Corporal," Jessie said.

"You wouldn't by a hound's chance know what this detail is, would ya, Corporal?" Charlie Rose asked.

The corporal looked up, glanced across the three faces in front of his desk, and gave them the kind of smug grin that made Jessie dislike him on the spot.

"You volunteered, Mac."

"For what?"

"Consider yourselves cowboys," the corporal said with a snicker.

"What?"

"You'll see."

"Dad-gum Remington Raiders," Charlie Rose grumbled under his breath.

The corporal's blue eyes opened wide, and his jaw tightened. He glared at Charlie Rose for a long moment, then relaxed and grinned. He gave his typewriter a couple of pats, smiled, and leaned back.

"Me and this Remington will still be around, PFC, 'when the lights go on all over the world.'" He sang the words to the popular song, then laughed.

"Yes, Semper fi to you, too, Corporal," Oglethorpe scoffed.

Jessie screwed up his face and shivered. "You know, I used to like that song."

"Tenshun!" the corporal shouted, and stood up as Lieutenant Pomper pushed through the gray curtain door.

"At ease. Now listen up, you three. I understand as Para-Marines you had some basic training in all areas of Marine Corps ground operations and tactics."

The three stood stiffly, gazing at Second Lieutenant Pomper in a state of shock.

"Yes, sir," Jessie finally forced out the answer.

"So you are basically familiar with the TBY radio, setting

it up, laying the com wire, various code calls and equipment limitations?"

No one answered. The three glanced at each other, waiting for somebody to speak.

"Do you or don't you?" Pomper snapped impatiently.

"Well, Lieutenant." Charlie Rose rubbed his chin. "We was taught just enough to call for help if the radioman gets hisself killed."

Pomper sighed and shook his head.

"You three are now under my command. From this minute until we weigh anchor, you will have one objective and only one. The Nips started up a nasty little business on Wake, and they did it again on Guadalcanal. They patch into our com wire, and some of those riceballs speak better English than you three." He gave Charlie Rose a look of disgust. "We think they might even know some code words. We have American Indians doing the talking now. Navajos. So the Nips have no idea what they're hearing."

Charlie Rose slapped his thigh. "Shoot fire, Lieutenant! That's 'bout the best idea I ever heard."

"We lost some Navajos on the Canal. If we lose any more, it could jeopardize the success of our next operation. I'm teaming each of you men up with one of our Indians. You will be reserve radio teams. I hope you'll never be needed, but you will be ready if called upon. That means you will spend every waking minute with your partner. Is that clear, Marines?"

"Yes, sir," Benjamin Oglethorpe answered quickly.

"I mean *every minute of every day*, mister. You will eat with your Navajo partner. You will sleep in the cot closest to his. You will go to the head together. You will go on liberty together. You're gonna think you married a squaw before you ship out of this camp. Now, go get your gear and meet me here in front of the com shack in ten minutes! Dismissed!"

Packing every item he owned in ten minutes would have been impossible for Jessie eight months earlier, but not now. Packing and moving at any ridiculous hour for any stupid reason was just part of the routine of the Corps.

Ten minutes later the three PFCs were standing in front of the com shack with packs, helmets, rifles, and seabags. Lieutenant Pomper came out of the com shack checking his

watch. The three Marines lowered their seabags and saluted. Pomper returned a casual wave, walking past the men
without making eye contact with any of them.

"This way. Move it!"

Jessie glanced at Oglethorpe and showed his teeth like an
angry dog.

"Phantom crapper," Jessie muttered under his breath.

Benjamin Oglethorpe grinned sheepishly and threw his
seabag over his shoulder.

Lieutenant Pomper led them back into the tent area. He
stopped in front of a row of four-man pyramidal tents and
opened the flap to the first one.

"Private Broken Wing!"

"Yo. Yeah . . . yes'ir," a sleepy-sounding voice stuttered
out an answer.

Pomper looked back at Slate and grinned. "You, Slate,
over here." He motioned Jessie forward as they entered the
tent.

"Good luck, boy," Charlie Rose said.

"Yes. See you later, Slate."

Jessie pulled back the tent flap, ducked down, and
stepped inside. From the moment he lifted his gaze off the
dirt floor, he felt as though he had fallen into the bottomless
black of two of the most unfriendly eyes he'd ever seen. The
pupils were surrounded by dull white amid a road map of
bloodshot lines. They were angry black eyes. Jessie stood
still, almost hypnotized.

"Slate, this is your home," Lieutenant Pomper said.
"This is Private Broken Wing."

The piercing eyes shifted to Lieutenant Pomper. "Request a transfer, Lieutenant!" Broken Wing snapped.

"Request denied, Marine. You have your orders, mister!
If I so much as see one of you making a head call without
the other, I'll make you two the sorriest Marines that ever
wore the uniform. Is that clear?"

"Aye, aye, sir," Jessie said slowly, still watching the Indian.

Broken Wing said nothing. He stood staring at Pomper
until the lieutenant looked uncomfortable. Pomper turned
away and pushed through the tent flap.

"That earbanger's a real sweetheart, ain't he?" Jessie said
with a nervous smile.

Broken Wing sat down on his cot, then lay back, using his pack as a pillow. He closed his eyes and crossed his boots.

"Yeah," Jessie said, looking around the tent, "he's a real sweetheart."

Broken Wing said nothing. There were four dusty cots, two on each side of the canvas pyramid. Jessie moved to the cot opposite Broken Wing and dropped his seabag.

"Guess I'll bunk over here if that's all right with you."

The dark-skinned Marine said nothing. Jessie dropped his pack and rifle on the cot, took off his helmet, and sat down. He wasn't sure, but he couldn't remember ever seeing an Indian before except in books or a Tom Mix moving picture. His skin really is sort of red, Jessie thought, but I wouldn't really call it red skin. More like a dark, sunburned tan. His utilities were faded, but not from a sea washing behind a transport, Jessie guessed. The guy was a veteran, and it showed all the way down to his worn-out boondockers. He looked to be about five foot nine and 150 or 160 pounds. His nose was prominent but not huge; it didn't look as big as the Indian's nose on the nickel but was sort of the same shape. His acne-scarred cheekbones were high on his broad, brooding face, and with his eyes closed he looked almost oriental. His short, straight hair was black as coal with white sidewalls above the ears. Jessie suddenly had an urge to write his mom. She loved to read about faraway places and odd characters. She'd love to hear about Private Broken Wing, Jessie thought, but he didn't know enough about the man yet. Jessie cleared his throat and decided to try again.

"Have you seen much action, Private Wing, or, uh, is it Private Broken, or . . ." Jessie paused, took a breath, and tried again. "I apologize for my ignorance, but I've never met an Indian before, and I don't know if you guys have first names or is it all one name?"

"Keep your ballast to yourself, boot. I'm trying to sleep," Broken Wing growled without opening his eyes.

"Hey, look, Mac, I'd rather be shootin' the breeze with Ginger Rogers—"

The Indian sat up fast. Jessie flinched, then readied himself for a fight. Broken Wing's cheeks ballooned out like he'd been shot full of air, and his eyes opened wide with a shocked straight-ahead stare. He slapped both hands over his mouth, stood up, and bolted out of the tent.

Jessie walked over to the tent flap and looked out. Five feet away, the strange, angry Indian was bent over with hands on knees and vomiting up a waterfall of pinkish liquid. Jessie watched until Broken Wing's gagging dry heaves made him feel queasy, too. He closed the tent flap and stowed his gear beside his cot. Jessie plopped down with a depressed sigh and wondered how in the world he had gotten mixed up with Lieutenant Pomper again. He slammed his helmet to the deck. Pomper's angry shout brought Jessie to his feet.

"Get your red rear end over to the com shack, Broken Wing! On the double! And bring Slate. I better not see one of you without the other from now till we ship out. Is that clear, Marine?"

Jessie moved to the tent flap and peeked out. Broken Wing stood up straight, then slowly began leaning to starboard.

"I mean it, Private," Pomper said through clenched teeth. "If I catch you two more than a rifle's length apart, I'll have you two burning crappers for the rest of this war."

"Aye, aye, Lieutenant." Broken Wing's tone was closer to insubordination than Jessie would have ever dared.

"Now, move it!" Pomper barked, and walked away.

Broken Wing stood still for a moment, then began a slow, circular counterclockwise sway from the waist up like a top ready to fall. Jessie stepped out of the tent, trying not to grin. He knew it was probably a mistake as he rushed forward to help balance the Indian before Broken Wing fell into a puddle of his own vomit.

"Let me give you a hand, Mac." Jessie put Broken Wing's arm around his shoulder and tried to tug him toward the tent.

Broken Wing slapped Jessie's hand away and stumbled to one knee. "Leave me alone."

"You got it, Mac. I'd like nothin' better, but we're together like it or not, and I sure as crap ain't doing brig time because of you. I came here to fight Japs, not Indians!"

Broken Wing struggled to his feet and staggered back into the tent. Jessie started for the tent just as Broken Wing came back out. The Indian looked better. The waxiness of his face when he was vomiting had vanished, and the whites of his eyes were clear instead of road-map red.

"Come on, boot, let's get on with it," Broken Wing mumbled as he walked toward the dirt road.

Jessie shook his head, sighed, and decided not to try to figure it out. He retrieved his helmet and followed Broken Wing to the com shack, staying far enough back to keep from having to speak.

Oglethorpe and Charlie Rose were waiting in front of the com shack when Jessie and Broken Wing arrived. They stood talking to two other Indian Marines.

Charlie Rose waved. "Hey, Jessie."

"What's the scuttlebutt, Charlie Rose?" Jessie asked.

"Better ask old Perelli that. This here's Gray Cloud, my partner." Charlie Rose turned to the tall Indian beside him.

"Nice to meet you, Gray Cloud," Jessie said, extending his hand.

The thin Indian Marine shook Jessie's hand. He smiled, but it looked uncomfortable for him.

"Hello, Jessie."

Oglethorpe tapped Jessie on the shoulder. "And PFC Slate, this is my partner, PFC Sam Hill."

"Sam Hill?" Jessie asked with a grin as he turned to shake hands with a heavyset man.

"Sam Hill," he repeated with a nod. "Guess what my father said when this came out of the chute?" Sam pointed at his own face. His mournful eyes had dark pouches under them. His large oval face was scarred by acne, and though he was quick to smile, he looked sad.

"I like that name, Sam."

Pomper came out of the com shack with his helmet on.

"Listen up. Your routine will not vary from day to day after this. Reveille at 0400. Language class with your partner in a private cubicle inside the com shack from 0500 to 0800. A ten-mile march with full pack, rifle, TBY radio, and com wire into the local boondocks for a little OJT. Now saddle up and meet me at the supply tent in five minutes. Move it!"

The long march was hard. Camp St. Louis sat at the foot of a large forested mountain. It was part of a long mountain range that rose to 5,400 feet in some places. The forest was mostly kauri pine trees, considered the most valuable lum-

ber in the South Pacific. The long ridges were interrupted
in places by plunging valleys thick with nearly impassable
jungle and large inland plateaus. New Caledonia was perfect
by Marine Corps standards. Though it was supposed to only
be about 250 miles long and an average of thirty miles wide,
it had nearly every kind of terrain. Second Lieutenant Pomper led the way, and although it was obviously his plan to
march the six Marines into exhaustion, he soon looked to
be suffering the most, even though he didn't carry a pack
or a rifle. The Navajos seemed to hate Pomper as much as
Oglethorpe, Rose, and Jessie did, but they weren't much at
chitchat. Jessie did manage to find out that they were Para-
Marines, too, and had been attached to the First Marine Division on Guadalcanal along with a detachment of Marine
raiders.

The march cleared the forest-covered mountain, went
down the other side, and proceeded into a valley of dense
jungle, finally stopping on a small inland plateau that was
fairly clear of growth. They set up the TBYs in a big trian-
gle, running com wire between each, and practiced sending
and receiving various codes, first in English and then in
Navajo.

The Navajo language was tough. It became immediately
apparent that this would be anything but slack duty. The
same Navajo word spoken with four different inflections had
four different meanings. It seemed impossible that the Japs
could ever figure out the strange tongue-twisting half-
guttural, half-nasal sounds.

Three hours later the order came to saddle up. The march
back seemed shorter but no less tiring. By the time they finally reached the top of the mountain, even Camp St. Louis
was a welcome site. Two miles beyond the camp, Nouméa
was as beautiful and inviting as a coastal town in southern
France.

Pomper looked over his shoulder as the tiny column plodded downhill behind him. "When you get in camp, you got
one hour to rest and chow down. Be at the com shack at
1730 hours for code and language instruction."

"He's joshin'. Ain't he?" Charlie Rose asked from behind
Jessie.

He was not. At 1730 the six tired Marines entered the

com shack like prisoners reporting for a rock-breaking detail.

"We gettin' liberty tonight, sir?" Charlie Rose asked.

"I'll tell you when you get liberty, PFC," Pomper snapped as he led the men by teams to closet-sized cubicles partitioned by ropes and green wool Marine Corps blankets. Each tiny room had two folding metal chairs, with a pencil and notepad on each chair. Pomper grinned as he pulled back the blanket door to the last cubicle.

"And this is your classroom, Marines. You will sit facing each other. On the pad is a list of words that PFC Slate must learn to translate verbally into Navajo. You have two hours."

Jessie stooped under the rope and sat down. A sullen-faced Broken Wing followed as Pomper closed the curtain door. Broken Wing sat down and scribbled something on the notepad.

"*Tkele-ch-gi,*" he mumbled.

"What's that mean?"

The Indian didn't answer.

"If you're cussing me out, do it on the up and up like a man!"

"No cuss words in Navajo."

"There ain't? How do you tell somebody to go to you know where?"

"Go the way of the cursed to the land of the devil with no return."

"Sure is the long way around. No easier way than that?"

Broken Wing's expression showed no change, just a dull stare. Jessie waited for a response as long as he could, then blurted out the question that could wait no longer.

"What's your problem, Marine? You act like you've got it in for me, and you don't know me from Adam."

"I did not join the Corps to baby-sit an all-American boy," Broken Wing said calmly, showing no hint of anger.

"You're strange, Mac," Jessie replied just as calmly.

"Let us do the job and be done."

"That's fine by me, but you know our orders. If Pomper catches us more than a bayonet apart for the next few weeks, we're seein' brig time for sure."

"So what? Every Marine does brig time, boot."

"I'm here to kill Japs. I'm not doing brig time. Not while a swell bunch of Marines do my fighting for me."

"You should be writing Roosevelt's speeches."

"I mean it. I'm sticking to you like stink on a Jap."

The Indian's shoulders sagged as if he had resigned himself to the reality of the situation. He looked down at the pad.

"The Navajo word for 'mortar' is 'gun that squats.' "

Two hours later the long day ended. The walk back to the tent was dark and quiet. Most of the camp was in Nouméa on liberty, but right then the only thing on Jessie's mind was sleep and lots of it. Broken Wing pulled back the tent flap and lit a match. He bent down by his cot and produced a small kerosene lantern.

"Where'd you get that?" Jessie asked as he plopped down on his cot.

Broken Wing didn't answer. He pulled a small pocket-knife from his trousers pocket, opened it, knelt down on both knees, and began drawing on the hard dirt floor beside his cot with the tip of the blade. Jessie leaned closer but still could not make out exactly what it was the Indian was working on in the dim light. It looked sort of like a bird. Broken Wing stood up, put the knife away, and quickly took off all his clothes, including his skivvies. He sat cross-legged on his cot with his hands resting on his feet and his eyes closed. He began a quiet melodic chant that lasted a full ten minutes, then suddenly stopped. He leaned over and pulled a long bamboo smoking pipe from under his cot, lit it, and took a long, slow puff.

"You trying to suck a basketball through that thing?"

Broken Wing did not answer.

He smoked for five minutes while staring straight ahead toward the rear of the tent. The smoke smelled awful, more like burning weeds than tobacco, but Jessie remained quiet, sensing that this was a private ritual that the Indian was allowing him to witness. Finally Broken Wing snuffed out the pipe with his thumb, stuffed it back under his cot, stood up, and began putting on his dress khakis.

"What are you doing?" Jessie asked.

"Going to drink firewater."

"What? You can't go to Nouméa!"

"Why?" Broken Wing asked dryly.

"We didn't get liberty."

"Don't want liberty, just want firewater."

"That's AWOL!"

Broken Wing continued to dress.

"Come on, Broken Wing, don't do it."

Broken Wing put his low-top boondockers under his cot and pulled out his twelve-inch jump boots. He put one on and tied the laces halfway up.

"We have a direct order to stay together!" Jessie shouted, then covered his mouth for fear of being heard by the wrong person.

Broken Wing tied his other shoelace, sat up, and looked at Jessie. "I'm goin' for firewater. You coming or not?"

"I'm not much on drinking."

Broken Wing stared suspiciously at Jessie for a moment. "New Caledonia is a French territory. Lots of French women, and they never seen Marines much."

"I don't think we should."

The Indian glared at Jessie. "A virgin boot Para-Marine that don't drink. Howlin' wind god!"

Jessie felt his face flush. "No way. I'm not goin' AWOL for you or anyone else. You go out of this tent and I go straight to Pomper."

"You earbanger! You'd turn in a brother Marine?"

"Brother Marine! You've treated me like a Jap from the first moment you laid eyes on me. I owe you nothin', mister."

Broken Wing yanked off his barracks cover and slapped it onto his cot. He stared angrily at the ground, breathing loudly through his nose for a minute. Then he pulled off his boots, reached under his cot, and came up with a canteen. He leaned back, opened it up, and began to drink. The smell of strong whiskey hit Jessie's nostrils with a rush that opened his eyes a bit wider.

At 0400 the next morning the tinny sound of reveille began another grueling day. Only one thing was different from the previous day. Second Lieutenant Pomper made his typist corporal take the six Para-Marines on the long march instead of going himself. Scuttlebutt was that he'd found a dame in Nouméa.

The routine finally changed on the fifth day. Pomper met the tired Marines as they entered camp after the daily march. He was an irritating sight, standing in front of the com shack with his arms folded like an angry parent, but none of the men was scared of him.

"All right, drop your gear and listen up."

No one did. Each man stood slouching under the weight of the TBYs and packs and batteries and rifles.

"It is against my better judgment, but starting today you will no longer have the evening classes. Each day after the field exercise, which should end at—" Pomper checked his watch "—1700 hours, you will have liberty in Nouméa."

"Eeeee-yiii!" Charlie Rose shouted, and jumped off the ground.

Pomper pulled a piece of paper from his breast pocket. "We'll see how long you keep your liberty privileges. You will be in the rack at 2400 hours or all liberty ceases. Your orders to stay with your partner twenty-four hours a day include time on liberty. Your partner is also your date. Is that clear?"

"Yes, sir," Oglethorpe said. No one else spoke.

"I said, 'Is that clear?' " Pomper shouted.

"Aye, aye, sir," the six Para-Marines mumbled together.

"I'll be in Nouméa, too. I better not find any one of you without your partner. If I do, liberty will be canceled for the duration on New Caledonia. That better be understood, Marines."

Pomper glared hard at the six faces. The men remained unimpressed. He looked more like an accountant than a Marine.

"You will see Allied troops from New Zealand and Australia, possibly some British or even French. You get into a fight, your liberty is finished. The currency here is French francs. Exchange your money at the HQ on the way out. The last liberty truck leaves camp at 1730. Now, I expect you men to show your gratitude by exhibiting proper Marine Corps behavior at all times. Dismissed." Pomper saluted. The men straightened to attention and replied as he did an about-face and strolled away.

Oglethorpe's Navajo partner, Sam Hill, grunted and spit at the ground. Charlie Rose pointed at Sam with his thumb and winked.

"I'm with ya, Sam."

"I'm still glad we got liberty," Jessie said.

"It sure ain't because of that pig's rear end!" Charlie Rose shouted. "It was Gunny O'Cleary's doin'."

"I wonder," Oglethorpe said thoughtfully.

"How do you know?" Jessie asked.

"Aldo Perelli gave me the scuttlebutt yesterday at chow. He said the gunny reamed Pomper out for not giving us no slack."

"Perelli's scuttlebutt ain't worth the price of a bad shoe shine," Jessie said.

"True. But I think he's right this time."

In spite of the fact that the information had come from "Know Nothing" Perelli, Jessie chose to believe it. Just the thought of old Gunny O'Cleary reaming out Pomper made the two-mile trip to Nouméa a pleasant one. The coastal dirt road made for a bumpy ride in the back of the big liberty truck, but no landscape could be more picturesque. The scenery was like a bright new painting filled with a hundred hues of green sweeping across plains and into the island mountains on the right. To the left were the dazzling crystal-blue waters of the Coral Sea. He wondered if his dad had ever been there.

They drove past a village of six thatch-roofed dwellings clustered around a large square carpet of well-manicured grass. Two dark-skinned native men wearing wraparound floral-print skirts waved and smiled from the village green. The Marines waved back. Perelli shouted some stupid crack about liking their dresses, but the natives continued to wave, seemingly oblivious to his insult.

The coastal road led through the busy dock area. Huge American warships lay at anchor in the nearly landlocked harbor. The smell of fish permeated the wharves. Just beyond the wharves the tranquil sun glistened off of the corrugated-iron roofs of clean white French colonial cottages.

"Any of you guys hear Tokyo Rose last night?" a stout-looking sergeant with the skull-and-crossbones patch of a Marine raider asked.

"Sure didn't, Sarge," Charlie Rose said.

"Did she play 'In the Mood,' Sarge? Man, I love that song. She played it a few nights ago," a baby-faced Marine next to the tailgate asked.

"No. She was telling us how they beheaded nine of Carl-son's raiders that got left on Makin Island."

"Did she give their names? I heard her do that before," a big corporal asked.

"No. She was just taunting us. She wanted to know where all of the big tough U.S. Marines were hiding."

"She's about to find out," Jessie said quietly.

The sergeant gave Jessie a discreet thumbs-up as he glared at the countryside. "Semper fi, Marine."

No one spoke much after that. The coastal dirt road turned into a shady narrow cobblestone street lined with two- and three-story French colonial–style wooden build-ings topped by rusting metal roofs and fitted with shuttered windows. The truck rumbled through a busy market area where the street was suddenly crowded with housewives and farmers haggling, in French, with food merchants over the prices of everything from breadfruit and coconuts to squawking poultry. Fishermen pushed wooden wheelbar-rows filled with flopping fish to vendors.

There looked to be no average dress for Nouméans. Many native women wore missionary-inspired Mother Hubbards, while others were dressed in prewar Parisian fashions. New Zealand soldiers, their misshapen cowboy hats pinned up on one side, strolled past the smiling Japanese standing be-hind the counters of small shops.

The truck moved through the crowded marketplace, turned right down another shady narrow street, and stopped in front of a large well-kept park that looked to extend at least four blocks through the center of the city. It was bor-dered by palms and big tropical trees that exploded with bright red flowers like crimson umbrellas around the park. In the center of the park a group of native women in their colorful tent dresses shouted through a game of cricket be-side a turn-of-the-century bandstand.

The truck driver leaned out the window. "Disembark, Gyrenes! I'll pick you up here at 2400 hours. It's called Place des Cocotiers."

"Where they keep the easy women?" Charlie Rose yelled as he jumped from the tailgate.

"I ain't no tour guide, Marine, but you can reconnoiter the Avenue du Marechal Foch."

"What in tarnation is that?"

"A street, Mac. Better get used to it. This joint's all French."

Oglethorpe made a face like he had just bitten into a sour pickle. "Your pronunciation, PFC, has very little to do with the French language."

The driver frowned, gave a scoffing wave, and drove away.

"You speak French, Oglethorpe?" Jessie asked.

"Yes, a bit."

Charlie looked at Sam Hill. "I guess college is worth something."

Sam shrugged and scratched his rugged face. "Suppose."

"Where's your partner, Jessie?" Oglethorpe asked.

Jessie looked around. Broken Wing was gone.

"That blasted *Lobe-ca* is determined to get us busted!"

Jessie glanced at Sam Hill. The chunky Indian's mournful eyes looked even sadder than normal. He shook his head slowly.

"You called him a 'fish shell.' That is code for 'torpedo.' "

"Better find him, boy," Charlie Rose warned.

"He's right, Jessie," Oglethorpe agreed. "Pomper is bound to show up somewhere tonight."

"I know where Broken Wing will be," Gray Cloud said quietly.

"You do?" Jessie asked.

The tall thin Indian forced his uncomfortable smile. "The closest bar."

Jessie nodded. "Of course."

They walked on past the Place des Cocotiers until they reached an intersection where Sam Hill turned right. A street sign read Rue Auguste Brun. A block down Rue Auguste Brun the sidewalk on both sides of the narrow street was packed with American soldiers, Aucklanders, a few British soldiers and sailors, and U.S. Marines.

"I take it we're either in the red light district or we just missed a parade," Oglethorpe said to no one in particular.

"Firewater," Sam said as he turned right into a noisy open-door bar. Jessie, Oglethorpe, and Gray Cloud followed.

"Boogie Woogie Bugle Boy" by the Andrews Sisters blared from a jukebox at the far end of the bar. In front of the jukebox four couples did the jitterbug on a small dance floor surrounded by crowded tables.

"This place is hoppin'!" Jessie shouted.

Sam pointed through the blue cigarette haze. "Knew it," he said.

Standing at the far end of the long pinewood bar packed with half-drunken soldiers, sailors, and Marines sat the solemn Broken Wing, staring into the bottom of an empty glass.

Charlie Rose nudged Jessie. "There's your date, boy. Uglier'n sin, but he's all yours."

"Oglethorpe! Slate!"

Jessie searched the room for the familiar voice. Aldo Perelli stood up beside a table back near the dance floor and waved.

"Come have a drink with us," Perelli shouted.

Jessie looked over and saw that he was with Stu and Lopez.

"Okay by me."

Jessie glanced at Broken Wing, still leaning against the bar a few feet from Perelli's table. Their eyes met. The Indian frowned and turned away as the bartender filled his empty glass with whiskey. Jessie followed the others to Perelli's table. Lopez gave a nod, gulped down the end of a mug of beer, and puffed on a cigarette.

Perelli stood grinning with conceit as they neared the table. He held out his hand toward a pretty dark-haired girl in a flower-print dress.

"Gentlemen, meet Claudette."

Charlie Rose whistled.

"Nice to meet you, Claudette. *Parlez-vous français?*" Oglethorpe said.

The girl smiled, and her dark eyes brightened.

*"Oui, monsieur."*

Claudette pulled Oglethorpe into a chair beside her and began chattering like a Browning automatic in French. Oglethorpe managed a word now and then, but she was gushing like a broken dam.

"So sit down, men," Perelli said.

Jessie grabbed a couple of chairs and slid them toward Sam, Gray Cloud, and Charlie Rose.

"So what do you think of my chick?"

"Outstanding," Jessie said.

"Where'd you find her?" Charlie Rose asked.

"I met her a few nights ago watching a ladies' cricket match over in Place des Cocotiers."

"The big park?" Jessie asked.

"Yeah, Perelli thought it was the Brooklyn Bums playing an exhibition game!" Stukowski shouted, and laughed.

"Is that right, Stukowski? Well, maybe you didn't hear the lineup for the NL All-Star team."

"How could you know the lineup?"

"I got my sources. Hear 'em and weep, son. Four! Count 'em." Perelli held up four fingers and grinned. "Only team with more on the All Stars was the Cards with eight."

Stukowski dismissed the information with a scoffing wave and looked at Jessie. "Say, I heard you guys really got the shaft with that Lieutenant Pomper."

"You heard right," Sam Hill muttered sadly.

"This is the first night we got liberty," Jessie said.

"I think Pomper is one of those Nazi fifth columnists that Roosevelt's been warning us about," Charlie Rose said.

Perelli nodded toward the dance floor. "You see who's here?"

Jessie and the others looked at the dancers.

Charlie Rose slapped the table. "Good Gawd almighty!"

"Who ya talking about?" Gray Cloud asked.

"See that mountain with blond hair?" Charlie Rose asked.

"The corporal with the skinny woman?"

"That is Duffy Johnson, Golden Gloves heavyweight champ from Oklahoma."

"So?"

Charlie Rose slid back in his chair. "That mule's rear end stole twenty bucks from us."

"Calm down, Rose," Oglethorpe said soothingly.

"You start anything and our liberty will be over before the first drink," Jessie added.

Lopez gave a coarse laugh and looked at Sam. "He kicked Slate's virgin butt in front of half the division, too!"

Jessie gritted his teeth and tried to ignore Lopez. He knew that he had no chance in a fair fight with Duffy Johnson, but he ached for revenge.

"Unclench your fists, Jessie, and try to remember the satisfying odor of burning pubic hairs." Oglethorpe's voice seemed to come out of nowhere. Jessie pulled his angry glare from Johnson and tried to relax. Charlie Rose pounded the table.

"I came here to drink, boy!"

"Yes. Let us partake," Oglethorpe said.

Charlie Rose slapped down some New Caledonia francs and shoved them toward Jessie. Jessie grabbed the money and stood up.

"I must look like a waiter."

"This will probably be the first drink Slate ever bought," Perelli said with a chuckle.

"Your sister's a squid, Perelli," Jessie shot back, and headed for the bar.

"Whiskey and beer all around," Charlie Rose called.

Jessie stepped up to the bar, squeezing in between Broken Wing and a New Zealander. A harried, fat-faced dark-haired man with a droopy mustache rushed back and forth delivering drinks behind the bar.

"Bartender!"

*"Oui."*

"Give me eight beers and eight shots of whiskey."

The bartender nodded. Jessie turned to face Broken Wing on his right. The Indian was already glassy-eyed. He held a full shot glass in his left hand and half a mug of beer in his right.

"You drunk already?" Jessie asked.

Broken Wing threw back a shot and chased it down with a long gulp of beer, then slammed the empty whiskey glass on the pinewood bar.

The music stopped, and the dancers began heading back to their tables. Broken Wing staggered backward from the bar with his half-full mug. He smashed into a chunky Nouméan girl, knocking her back into none other than big Duffy Johnson. Duffy's moon-shaped face flushed red as he righted the girl.

"Square away, Marine!" Duffy barked at the back of Broken Wing.

The Indian regained his balance and faced Duffy.

"It figures," Duffy bellowed. "Useless redskin, as useless here as you are in Oklahoma!"

Broken Wing held out his mug and slowly poured the beer onto Duffy's spit-shined boots. Duffy stiffened in rage, then suddenly hit Broken Wing in the chest with both palms, sending the smaller Marine crashing against the bar.

Broken Wing tried to stand upright but staggered back and forth, looking for the guy who had pushed him. He squinted as he focused in on Jessie, then drew back his fist and threw a roundhouse right. Jessie ducked. Broken Wing spun halfway around, lost his balance, and dropped to his knees, facing the bar. Duffy stepped forward and grabbed Broken Wing by the back of his collar. He drew back his fist.

"Leave him alone, Johnson!" Jessie shouted, and yanked Duffy's grip away from Broken Wing's collar.

Duffy looked stunned. He stood staring at Jessie with his right fist drawn back ready to punch. A look of amused comprehension broke across the huge round face.

"I know you."

Jessie pulled the drunken Indian to his feet. Duffy grabbed Broken Wing by the front of his shirt and again drew his fist back.

An ear-splitting smack against the bartop rattled glasses. The patrons at the bar fell silent. Gunnery Sergeant O'Cleary shifted his soggy-looking cigar to the corner of his mouth as he lifted a long flat cricket bat from the bar top.

"You boys better save some of that energy for the Japs. I'm on my way for a cup of joe, Slate. Looks to me like your Navajo there could use a pot."

"Yeah, he could, Gunny."

Gunny O'Cleary handed the fat bartender the cricket bat. "Thanks for the use of your club."

"*Oui, monsieur.* Thank *you.*"

Duffy leaned close to Jessie. The big man's nostrils flared like an angry bull's and his green eyes narrowed.

"You tell your squaw here I'm gonna put him in sick bay soon, and if you get in my way, Slate, you go with him." Duffy spit at the floor beside Jessie's shoes and stomped off toward the door, practically dragging his Nouméan dance partner outside with him.

"Somebody has to kick his butt."

Jessie turned to face Charlie Rose. "Yeah, and soon, I hope."

"Jessie," Oglethorpe called from the table, and pointed toward the open door. "I just saw Pomper go by."

"That's just great," Jessie growled.

"You better get Wing sobered up, Slate," Gunny said.

Broken Wing's head and shoulders were lying on the bar top with his feet still on the floor.

"This drunken Indian's just about as big a pain as Pomper!"

"Yep, 'pears so, but scuttlebutt has it that this guy was all Marine on the island."

"He was on Guadalcanal?"

"I hear he got the Silver Star."

"He better be a good Marine in combat, cuz he sure ain't worth a—"

"Help Slate get him moving, Charlie," Gunny O'Cleary ordered.

They straightened Broken Wing up. Jessie put the Indian's limp left arm around his own neck and shoved a shoulder into his armpit.

"You got him?" Charlie Rose asked.

"Yeah. But where am I going with him?"

"Follow me." Gunny O'Cleary pointed with his thumb.

The walk was a lot like pushing a wheelbarrow full of coal without a wheel. Rue Auguste Brun was packed with people, mostly soldiers, but when they turned down the Avenue du Marechal Foch, it was nearly deserted. It was easy to see why. No bars. And it was a dead-end street. Most of the shops were either clothing boutiques or restaurants. Two blocks down was a small French café that could have passed for a private residence with its barn-red shutters on the white colonial-style house. LA RUE SANS ISSUE was printed in red on a white wooden plaque over the front screen door. To the right of the door was a large colonial window, squared into a dozen little windows by thin strips of wood. A small black and white sign hanging in the window read OUVERT. The shades were pulled down, the sun was almost gone, and the blackout curtain formed a closet-like foyer that kept light from escaping when the door was open.

"Is this it, Gunny?" Jessie asked.

The gunny paused and crossed his arms as if to admire the facade of the little place.

"La Rue sans Issue. This is it. Old Sergeant Polk told me the French don't have a translation for dead-end street."

"That what that says, Gunny?" Charlie Rose asked as he shifted the weight of Broken Wing's arm around his shoulder.

"No. It says, 'The Street without Exit.' "

"Dang funny way to talk," Charlie Rose said.

"Jeremiah's wife was French."

"Is this your old sidekick from Haiti and Nicaragua?" Jessie asked.

"And Belleau Wood."

"Belleau Wood?" Charlie Rose repeated in an awed tone.

"That's when old Jeremiah met the prettiest little French gal you ever saw in your life."

"How long has it been since you two chewed the fat, Gunny?" Charlie Rose asked.

"Too long, boys," the gunny said as he walked toward the front door.

"You haven't seen him yet, Gunny?" Jessie asked.

"This is the first chance I've had."

"I'll be getting back to the bar before Pomper catches me and Gray Cloud apart."

"Yeah. Go ahead, Charlie. I'll take care of Broken Wing."

A small bell rang as the door closed behind them. Broken Wing could walk, but only with Jessie's support.

"Now don't go pukin' your guts up inside this café."

Broken Wing grunted but didn't answer.

The café looked empty except for three American soldiers sitting at a table in a far corner. Three big ceiling fans kept the square room comfortable.

"Doggone it!"

"What's the matter, Gunny?"

"I left a package with that barkeep back at that slop chute."

"I'll drop Wing here and go get it for you, Gunny."

"No, you two stay. I'll be right back. If you see Jeremiah, don't tell him you're with me. I want to surprise the old leatherneck."

Jessie guided the drunken Indian into a chair, then sat himself down. There looked to be about ten round tables, each with a red and white checkered tablecloth and white cane-bottom chairs. Colorful island paintings hung on the white walls. As Jessie picked up a menu, a stunningly beautiful girl in a short white dress pushed through a single swinging door at the opposite end of the room. Jessie heard himself sigh out loud as she came toward him. She was a fantasy. Her hips swayed perfectly with each step, her long shimmering auburn hair flowed past her shoulders, and even at a distance her eyes were shockingly blue. Cool air from the fan above touched Jessie's open mouth. He closed it and blushed as the young woman stopped and smiled.

*"Qu'est-ce que vous voulez?"*

"Uhhh, well, ma'am, I don't speak French."

*"Parlez-vous Français?"* she said with a hint of amusement in her bright blue eyes.

"No, ma'am. Please forgive my ignorance. Could we have some black coffee?" Jessie pretended to drink from an invisible cup. "Coffee."

Her eyes widened.

*"Café au lait?"*

"Coffee?"

*"Oui, oui. Café au lait."*

Jessie grinned as much to himself as to the beautiful French girl. "Every word out of your mouth sounds delicious to me, ma'am."

She smiled and looked at Broken Wing. His head was lying on his right shoulder, and his eyes were half-open. The girl made a funny face.

*"Café."* She shook her head no. "No *au lait.*" She turned and walked away.

"That means no cream, PFC."

Jessie forced his eyes away from the hips of the departing beauty to see who was talking. A white-haired old man wearing tattered bib overalls walked past Jessie's table and sat near the blacked-out windows.

"Oh, thanks," Jessie said.

The old man gave him a nod and sat down. He had only one arm. The right sleeve of his plaid flannel shirt was pinned up at the shoulder. His leathery old face was hard and wrinkled more than it should have been, Jessie thought, but there was something kind about the old man's blue eyes.

"Looks like your friend there is leanin' hard to starboard," the man said with a chuckle.

Jessie laughed. "You sound like an American."

The old man gave a somber nod. "What are those wings for, Marine? And I know those trousers shouldn't be bloused in your boots like that."

Jessie glanced down at his boots and smiled. "I'm a Para-Marine. The First Para-Marine Regiment, and only an old Marine would know I'm not supposed to blouse my trouser legs."

"Sometimes it don't seem all that long ago, and sometimes it feels like another lifetime."

Jessie stood up and held out his hand. "An honor to meet you, sir. My name is PFC Slate."

The old man shook hands with his remaining left hand. He looked pleased.

"I'm Jeremiah Polk. Nice to meet you, PFC Slate." The old man looked at Broken Wing. "Looks like your mate won't be much conversation for a while. I'd be pleased to buy you a cup of coffee." He shoved a chair out from his table with his foot, revealing the crustiest-looking work boot Jessie had ever seen.

"Thank you, sir." Jessie pulled the chair to himself and sat down.

"Where you from, Slate?"

"Logan County, West Virginia."

"Mining country." It was a statement.

"Where you from, Mr. Polk?"

"Pittsburgh."

"How in the world did you end up here?"

The old man grinned and scratched at the two-day growth of gray beard on his leathery face. He pondered the question for a long time, almost as if he were not sure how he had ended up in Nouméa.

"Well," he finally said, "I managed a mine back in Pittsburgh after the Corps. To make a long story short, my wife died, and I wanted a change of scenery. I saw this ad for a job managing a nickel mine in New Caledonia. The pay was good, and you had to speak French. I spoke enough to get by because my wife had been French and she used to teach me. Anyway, that was goin' on ten years ago now." The old man's voice seemed to weaken, and his sad blue eyes revealed a hidden pain that touched Jessie's heart.

"Is there something wrong, Mr. Polk?"

"Nothin' I should be bothering you with, son. You got enough problems ahead of you without me tellin' you mine." The old man forced a grin and winked at the younger Marine.

"I'm a good listener, sir, and to tell ya the truth, I'd just as soon not think too much about what's ahead of me."

Jeremiah smiled and stared down somberly at the red and white checkered tablecloth. "You probably got yourself a point there, Marine. The good Lord's blessed me in a whole lot of ways in my life." He shook his head. "Funny how quick all the past blessings don't seem to count for much with us humans when the chips are down."

"*Café au lait,*" the stunningly beautiful waitress said with a smile as she placed Jessie's cup and saucer before him.

"Thank you, ma'am."

She turned and placed a cup of coffee on Broken Wing's table.

"No *au lait,*" she said with a grin, and Jessie's stomach fluttered with excitement.

Broken Wing's face was now on the table. His eyes were closed, and his arms were hanging so limply that his hands nearly touched the floor. He looked like a drunken ape, Jessie thought, then followed the auburn-haired beauty with his eyes until she pushed through the kitchen door at the back of the café.

"She's lovely," Jessie sighed.

"Prettiest girl in the South Pacific, son," the old man said matter-of-factly.

"I can sure believe that, Mr. Polk."

He faced Polk again. The old man seemed so sad, Jessie wondered if he should try to cheer him up by telling him about Gunny O'Cleary. Better wait, he thought. Let it be a surprise.

"What's wrong, Mr. Polk? Maybe if you talk about it . . ."

"No. I'm afraid talkin' won't help, son."

"You never know, sir."

Mr. Polk nodded. "Ever heard of Société le Nickel, Marine?"

"No, sir."

"I manage it. It's the largest nickel-mining company on New Caledonia. Anyways, to make a long story short, the war has really hurt us, and we're just a hair away from goin' under. We got a Russian freighter coming our way right now for a load of nickel that can keep this company afloat, but the nickel won't be on the dock."

"Why not?"

"Two of our three shafts ain't working."

"Cave-in?"

The old man shook his head in disgust. "The shaft-car motor's died on us. Anything else we might've overcome, but not that."

"Why?"

"There's only one man that might have helped us, and he's in Australia eight hundred miles away." Mr. Polk stared down at the floor and sighed.

"By any chance do you use the old Samson?"

Jeremiah Polk lifted his saddened gaze from the tabletop. An expression of utter surprise fell across his face. "Yes. How do you know about the Samson?"

"Does it start up at all?"

"Yeah, they'll start right up, then—"

"Then start clicking and quit."

Mr. Polk's eyes opened wider. "How in the world could you know that?"

"My grandpa died in the mines in Logan County, Mr. Polk. I ran the motor on his shaft almost every summer from the time I was twelve."

"You think you could fix it, son? This sure ain't the best-equipped island in the world."

"If it's what I think it is, I'll need a smooth steel pin about, well, I'll tell you exactly what fits: the firing pin from an old squirrel gun."

"I can find you something close to it."

"I'll need some tools."

"Got 'em sittin' right by the engine." The old man's eyes were suddenly as wide as a little boy's on Christmas morning.

Jessie looked over at the drunken Indian, then back to the old man. "This is gonna sound crazy, sir, but I can't go without that drunken sot laying there. We're under orders to stay together twenty-four hours a day."

"No one would know if we put him in the back room to sleep it off."

"I guess that's true. Would the café owner go along with it?"

"I can guarantee that. His future depends on it."

"What?" Jessie asked.

The old man forced a smile. "I own the place. She don't make many francs, but I wanna leave my kid something. God knows it won't be much if I don't get this shipment out."

"You have a kid?"

"Yep. She's everything in the world to me."

Jessie stood up and put on his barracks cover.

"Help me carry this useless character to the back room and let's get that pull motor fixed."

The old salt jumped to his feet with renewed energy.

They carried Broken Wing through the kitchen to a small back room with two bamboo chairs and a couch. They laid him on the couch. Mr. Polk ran upstairs and was back quickly with an old rifle in his hands. A new hope on his leathery face made Jessie feel good inside. "Here's your firing pin," he said.

"You live upstairs?" Jessie asked.

The old man handed him the rifle. "Me and Kate."

"We'll need two of these pins to fix both shaft motors. If that's what the problem is, I can't guarantee it."

"I got my truck out back. You meet me out front and we'll run by my friend's house on the way up to the mine. We'll find us another pin."

"Meet you out front. Do you think you should let your waitress know what this drunken Marine is doing here on your couch, sir?"

"I'll let her know, son."

Jessie gave a nod and headed for the front door. The beautiful girl in the short white dress was waiting on a table of four gawking British sailors. They could hardly be blamed, Jessie thought. If there was a sexier-looking woman on Earth, she had never passed his eyes. Jessie paused at the front door for one last gaze at the girl. He could tell her about Broken Wing in the back, he thought. No. He couldn't speak French. He would only come off looking stupid. "Who am I kidding?" Jessie mumbled as he pushed through the café door. "Half of the Allied forces have probably put the make on her by now. For sure every Marine that ever stepped into this place."

"Slate!" Gunny O'Cleary called from the end of the sidewalk leading to the front door as Jessie pushed through the blackout-curtain. He had a box and a bottle of whiskey under one arm.

"Yes, sir, Gunny."

"Where you going?"

"I'm meeting Mr. Polk out front, Gunny. It's a long story, but he needs some help with some mining equipment that I happen to know something about and—"

The squeaking brakes of an old '32 Ford truck stopped Jessie short. The door of the truck flew open, and the old man jumped out. His eyes were on Gunny O'Cleary. The two old salts stood grinning at each other for a long moment, then started to laugh and sing a French song that Jessie didn't recognize. The song turned into loud laughter. Gunnery Sergeant O'Cleary opened the bottle of whiskey, lifted it in a toast to Jeremiah, and threw back a gulp. He smacked his lips, walked over to his old friend, and handed the bottle to him.

"Viva la Devil Dogs!"

Jeremiah poured whiskey into his open mouth from a foot and a half away. The booze spattered his face and ran down his neck and chest. He straightened up and lifted the bottle in a toast.

"Viva la French Fortegeur!"

"Give me that bottle back before you go AWOL with it."

"Advance and board the truck, O'Cleary. Got a mission here, and I ain't got all dad-blamed night to do it."

"As you were, Gunny Polk. I got a package here for the girl, and I want to see her face when she opens it."

"You can do that later, Pat. Right now I need some help, and your PFC here has volunteered to give it a go."

"What's up?" O'Cleary asked with concern.

Jeremiah looked at Jessie. "I was gonna tell you this, PFC. I don't let other men do my fightin', and I'm not one to lead men into an ambush."

"Stop splashin' galley water, Sergeant Polk! Just lay the map on the deck," O'Cleary demanded.

The two old salts paused and grinned at each other. Jessie realized then that he was on the outside of an inside joke.

"Well, here's the scuttlebutt, Marines. Like I told your PFC, if I don't get these shaft motors working, I'll lose everything."

"He's got a Russian freighter on the way," Jessie said.

"What I didn't tell you, son, is that one of the reasons I haven't been able to get those motors fixed is because of a bunch of frogs that make me wonder why we saved their useless rear ends in the Great War."

O'Cleary stomped past Jeremiah and climbed into the open door of the truck. "By your leave, Gunny. Fill us in on the way!" he barked.

"This could get you busted, Pat. I don't want that."

"Saddle up, Slate," O'Cleary said, ignoring his old friend's warning.

"Aye, aye, Gunny."

Jessie climbed into the truck and slid over beside O'Cleary. Jeremiah stood outside.

"Saddle up, Gunny Polk!" O'Cleary shouted. "We got a reunion to take care of between me and you."

"Well, I'll tell you, Patrick, my plan was to try and sneak by these scumbags because two or three of us ain't gonna be enough troops."

"Just get in and start driving."

Jeremiah nodded and climbed in. He carefully placed the bottle and package under the seat. It took three tries to start the engine before they were finally on their way.

"Mr. Polk, why are these men trying to stop your mine?" Jessie asked.

"Money and politics, son. Somebody is paying this group to make sure that I fail. Somebody wants my job, and he can have it, too, but not yet."

"How about the gendarmes?" O'Cleary asked.

"Yeah," Jessie added, "what about the police?"

"Well, I tried but got nowhere. I got a sneakin' suspicion that the captain of the gendarmes might get a fatter wallet by ignoring me."

"How do they know when you go to the mine?" O'Cleary asked.

"There's only one road up to the mine, and it goes right by this slop chute called the Café des Mineurs. That's their hangout."

"They got a guard out front?" Jessie asked.

"They put up a barricade across the road."

O'Cleary pointed ahead. "Pull around the corner up here and park in front of the slop chute that I point to," he said.

Jeremiah turned left down Rue Auguste Brun. The street was still packed with soldiers, sailors, and Marines. Gunny O'Cleary pointed at the bar they had left earlier.

"Over there, Jeremiah."

"What are you up to, you old sea dog?" Jeremiah asked as he parked in front of the bar.

"You two mark time till I get back." O'Cleary jumped out of the truck and slammed the door.

Five minutes passed before Jessie spoke. "What do you think he's up to, Mr. Polk?"

Jeremiah pointed at the bar with a knowing grin. "He called out the Marines, son."

Jessie looked toward the bar. A squad's worth of scowling Marines in various stages of intoxication were following Gunny O'Cleary like an angry mob toward the truck. Gray Cloud and Sam Hill were at the front of the pack. Oglethorpe and Charlie Rose brought up the rear. In the middle were some division Marines whom Jessie didn't recognize.

"Climb in the back, Marines!" O'Cleary bellowed as he pulled the passenger door shut.

"What'd you tell those men, Patrick?" Jeremiah asked suspiciously.

"Nothin'. Let's move out."

"O'Cleary," Jeremiah said.

"Well, now, I ain't certain where it came from, but there was some scuttlebutt."

"What kind of scuttlebutt?"

O'Cleary shrugged. "Just loose rumors."

"Yeah?"

The Marines in the back of the old pickup pounded on the roof of the cab and began to shout impatiently.

"Come on, Gunny!"

"Move it!"

"We gonna screw around and let 'em get away!"

Jessie whistled. "Man, what did you tell 'em, Gunny? They want raw meat!"

O'Cleary pointed at himself. "Me?" he said indignantly.

"What did you tell them, Patrick?" Jeremiah asked calmly.

"Well, there was some scuttlebutt going around the bar about how the Marines on Wake Island were a bunch of boot-licking cowards."

"No wonder," Jessie said.

Every regiment in the Corps was hoping to be the outfit that avenged the heroic garrison of Marines on Wake Island.

"And you told these guys where to find the characters who said this."

"There was some mention about a slop chute outside of town, I believe."

Someone kicked the cab of the truck hard enough to rock it.

"Move out!"

"Let's go, Gunny!"

"Yeah! Hurry up before they get away!"

Jeremiah shook his head and grinned at O'Cleary as he pushed on the starter. "These Para-Marines, they any good?" he asked as they drove out of Nouméa.

O'Cleary lit a cigar and puffed on it three times. "Well, now, they're dang good, but it ain't like the Old Corps."

"I figured that, Sarge," Jeremiah said.

O'Cleary pointed his cigar at Jessie as if making a point. "Slate, you think you got it rough now—"

"You should have been in the Old Corps, boy!" Jeremiah finished O'Cleary's sentence with a sly wink.

O'Cleary shoved his cigar to the far corner of his mouth. "Gunny Polk, you remember Captain Tally?"

"That old guy that fought up a storm in Mexico?"

"Yes, sir," O'Cleary said. "Sixty-five if he was a day."

"O'Cleary's speaking the truth, son. Back in the twenties it weren't nothin' to see officers in their sixties. Of course, that was the Old Corps."

"Is that right, sir?" Jessie asked.

"Yeah, Slate," O'Cleary said. "There was very little as far as jobs went, and the Corps was small. It was like family."

Jeremiah nodded in agreement. "Sure. Everybody knew everybody. We only had a couple of brigadiers in the whole Corps."

"Remember that crazy major from Tennessee, Sarge?"

"Crazy McCully?"

"That's the one."

Jeremiah glanced at Jessie in the middle. "Now, that was a hard man, PFC. He was our CO at Belleau Wood, back in the Great War."

"Yeah, boot," O'Cleary added. "Now, back in the Old Corps we had us a war."

"Sarge, do you know whose boy this is here?" O'Cleary pointed a thumb at Jessie.

"Who?"

"This here's Jim Slate's boy."

Jeremiah Polk's eyes widened in disbelief. "Bulkhead Slate's boy?"

"The same."

"Well, I'll be darned."

"Gettin' old, ain't we, Sarge?"

"Remember when Slate brought in all of those Sandinistas that gave up?" Jeremiah asked.

"Like it was yesterday."

"We was gettin ready to move out, and we needed some information out of those boys, and they wasn't talkin'."

O'Cleary pointed at Jeremiah with his cigar. "And Major McCully lined seven of 'em up at attention."

"Remember, he had that bet with old Slate. Your daddy bet a month's pay that he could get 'em talking by just using his head."

"Yeah, that was really something to see."

The two old salts chuckled at the memory, then stopped talking.

"Well, what happened?" Jessie asked.

"He marched up to them one at a time," O'Cleary said, "and head-butted each one of those bandits just like a billy goat!"

"You could hear the heads pop together all over that compound," Jeremiah said. He released the steering wheel, pulled on the headlamps, and grabbed the wheel again.

O'Cleary scratched the back of his neck and leaned forward. "They started talking up a storm, didn't they, Sarge?" he said.

"Except for that one old boy, remember him?"

"Sure do. He kept grinning back at Slate after each head butt. Pretty soon they were both bleeding like pigs."

"Yeah, Slate must have head-butted that guy ten times before he dropped him."

"I've never heard that story," Jessie said.

"Your dad was a fine Marine, Jess."

"That he was," O'Cleary added.

"Good death, too."

"None finer. Died like a Marine."

Jeremiah slowed the truck to a stop. Five big yellow oil drums blocked the dirt road. He pulled up the emergency brake to keep from rolling back downhill. There were trees on the right side of the road and a small wood-frame café on the left. Bypassing the drums was impossible. The sun had set, but the three-quarter moon was so bright that even after Jeremiah turned off the headlamps, visibility was still good.

"This is it," Jeremiah said with a sigh.

The front door of the café opened. A yellow shaft of light fell across the dirt road, and two men walked out of the café. They stood staring at the truck full of Marines.

O'Cleary leaned out the open window. "Two of you Marines jump out. Get those barrels off my road!"

"Aye, aye, Gunny!" Charlie Rose shouted as he jumped, with Gray Cloud right behind him.

When they had rolled the drums off the road, Jeremiah released the brake and pulled up to the Café des Mineurs.

"Well, Sarge, how do you want to do this?" O'Cleary said.

Jeremiah bit his bottom lip and stared at the two men standing in front of the Café des Mineurs. "I'll tell you the truth, old friend. I'd like nothing better than to go in there and kick some tail, but I have to get those shaft motors running just as fast as possible or I'm gonna lose everything."

O'Cleary nodded. "Say no more. The youngsters can have all the fun. Besides, if Slate here goes and breaks his hand on some frog's jaw, we never will get them motors fixed."

"Wait a minute, Gunny," Jessie snapped. "If the guys are going into a fight, I'm going with them!"

"Jeremiah needs your help, Slate. Besides, how many men do you think they got in that slop chute, Sarge?"

Jeremiah scratched his chin. "About ten at the most, I'd say."

"There, Slate. We got how many? Eight Marines in the back of the truck. You think eight Marines can't handle ten Frenchmen?"

"Of course they can, Gunny, but—"

"No buts. We got a mission to complete."

"Aye, aye, Gunny," Jessie said reluctantly.

O'Cleary got out of the truck and pointed at the café.

"Go in there and remember Wake Island!" he growled to the Marines in the back of the pickup.

The truck emptied in a flash.

"We'll be back to pick you up. We got some business up the road here," the gunny shouted. The angry mob of Marines pushed the two men standing by the café door back inside.

Gunny O'Cleary got back into the cab of the old Ford and smiled when something made of glass shattered and someone hollered in French. Jeremiah threw the truck into gear and pulled away.

Three hours later Jessie had one of the shaft pull motors humming like a new Packard, but there wasn't enough time to fix the second one. Jeremiah found it so hard to control his joy that Jessie's back was sore from all his congratulatory slaps.

"I'll try to get to that other motor next time, sir."

"That'll be fine, son," the old salt said, and slapped him again.

The drive back off the mountain to the Café des Mineurs was short and silent. No one knew what to expect as they neared the café.

Jessie tried to wipe the windshield clean to get a better look ahead. A group of seven men stood at attention in front of the café. Sitting comfortably in chairs facing them were the Marines, each of whom held a glass or bottle in his hand and waved it like an orchestra conductor.

"What in the world's going on, O'Cleary?" Jeremiah asked in disbelief.

"Your guess is as good as mine, Sarge."

The drunken chords of the "Marines' Hymn" became clear as the truck approached the café.

"You hear what I hear?" Jessie asked.

No one spoke. Jeremiah stopped the truck on the road behind the seven standing men. The singing stopped as Gunny O'Cleary, Jessie, and Jeremiah got out.

"Hey, Gunny!" Gray Cloud shouted, and waved a whiskey bottle.

Charlie Rose stood up on a cane chair, took a drink from a beer bottle, and shouted. "Listen up, Gunny! We taught 'em real good!" Charlie shot a baleful look at the row of battered and bleeding men standing before him. "Ready! Lopez?"

Lopez and another Marine staggered behind the Frenchmen. Lopez booted a fat, bearded one in the seat of the pants.

"Bass is ready!" Lopez shouted.

The division Marine smacked a tall, thin Frenchman in the back of the head. "Soprano, ready!" he shouted.

"Stand by, Gunny!" Charlie Rose bellowed as he stepped down from his cane chair. Benjamin B. Oglethorpe stepped up onto the cane chair and bowed.

"Ah, crap!" Lopez yelled. "I wanted to be the conductor this time."

"Hush, Lopez," Charlie Rose said.

Oglethorpe bowed again. "The Wake Island Seven-Man Quartet will now sing the 'Marines' Hymn.' " He lifted his hands.

"From the halls of Montezuma—"

"Belay that!"

"Belay that order!" Gunny O'Cleary barked.

Charlie Rose jumped up and down. "But, by golly, Gunny, they sing real purty!"

"Saddle up! We got to make that liberty truck back to camp. Move it! On the double!"

Jeremiah smiled. "Well, they ain't the Old Corps," he said to O'Cleary.

"They ain't professionals."

"But I think they might just do all right, O'Cleary."

# CHAPTER FIVE

THE NEXT DAY WAS A COPY OF ALL THE OTHERS EX-
cept for a two-hour addition to the curriculum—recognition, operation, and nomenclature of Japanese pistols, rifles,
and heavy and light machine guns. Six men at a time were
thrown into craterlike holes while various Japanese weapons were fired just overhead. Slowly but surely the NCO
combat veterans made sure that each boot Marine inched
closer to an understanding of what it would take to survive.
Half the time Jessie couldn't tell if he was scared or excited.

By the time the day was over, Jessie wanted to skip liberty
call and sleep. He fell back on his cot and closed his eyes.

"Broken Wing, can we just stay in camp tonight? I'm
beat."

"No."

"Aren't you tired?"

"Thirsty."

"Well, I'm not moving."

"What about the auburn-haired beauty with big tom-
toms?"

Jessie sat up.

"Wasn't she something?"

"Yes. Pray to wind god that girl has the vision of a desert
bat."

"Bats are blind."

"Your only hope."

"Ha, ha, ha. What do you know, a sense of humor. Broken Wing, I don't think you even got to see her. You
couldn't see your own hand when we put you on that
couch."

"I saw her. Beautiful tom-toms."

"Will you quit talking tom-toms!"

"You don't like tom-toms?"

"No! I mean, of course I love tom-toms! I mean . . . okay, let's go on liberty. It couldn't possibly be more tiring than a conversation with you."

Five minutes later Jessie sat on the truck bench facing Perelli, who sat between Jack Ellinwood and Charlie Rose.

"Youz guys hear the latest 'butt?" Perelli's dark eyes flashed with his news.

"By Gawd, lift them boondockers, Marines," Charlie Rose scoffed. "It's 'bout to get deeper than the Coral Sea."

"Now, that's more like it, Rose. That analogy makes sense," Chris LaBeau said.

"Hey, stifle it, cornbread," Perelli snapped, pretending to be insulted.

"All right," Lopez growled, "let's hear it, Perelli."

Perelli frowned as if his feelings were hurt. "I don't think you guys appreciate all the trouble I go to to get the inside dope on the brass."

"Out with it, Perelli, before I squeeze your neck," Lopez said.

Perelli held up both hands. "All right, calm down." He leaned forward and cupped a hand confidentially around one side of his mouth. "We weigh anchor tomorrow night."

"Where?"

"Destination unknown, but I'm working on that, too."

The ride into town that night was eerie. Talk was at a minimum. The brakes of the truck squealed to a stop in front of the old turn-of-the-century bandstand in Place de Cocotiers.

Jessie jumped out of the truck behind Charlie Rose and Sam Hill. He turned to look for Broken Wing. "Not again," he moaned.

"How's he disappear like that, Sam?" Charlie Rose asked.

"Same question Custer asked," Sam said with a sly smile.

Two hours later Jessie found Broken Wing halfway under a table in a smoke-filled bar. Charlie Rose and Sam helped Jessie get Broken Wing to the door of La Rue sans Issue café, then they headed back to the slop chutes. The old Marine, Mr. Polk, was there waiting for Jessie at the same table.

His blue eyes opened wide with the eagerness of a young man.

"It's good to see you, Jessie."

"Good to see you, sir."

"I'd have been here sooner, but he got away from me again," Jessie said as he struggled to lower his drunken partner into a chair.

The jingle of the small bell hanging over the door turned Jessie's head. Lieutenant Pomper pushed through the blackout curtain with his barracks cover in his hand and an irritating smirk on his face. Jessie frowned, then faked a half smile and nodded hello.

"What are you two doing here? Lose your way to the slop chute?" Pomper asked.

"Just grabbing a cup of joe, Lieutenant."

"Look's like he'll need more than a cup," Pomper said as he turned and scouted the room. He spotted the beautiful auburn-haired waitress, and a huge grin spread across his face. Pomper waved. She smiled and waved back. *"J'avais peur que tu n'étais pas ici ce soir,"* Pomper rattled off as if the language were his own.

Jessie clenched both his fists and turned to the old man. "Mr. Polk, she doesn't like that earbanger, does she?"

The old man scratched at his gray whiskers and shrugged as if he knew more than he was saying.

"What's that look mean?" Jessie demanded.

"Well, son, he's one up on ya cuz he speaks the lingo."

Jessie felt his face flush red. Mr. Polk chuckled.

"It ain't funny! That's the jackass that will send me to the brig if he sees me more than a rifle's distance from this drunken Indian. That means I can't fix your other pull motor till he's gone."

"That lieutenant never takes his eyes off her from the second he gets here till the second he leaves. He ain't gonna pay no attention to you two or anybody else while she's in the same building."

"I can't take that chance, Mr. Polk."

"Well, let's just bring your buddy with us."

"How?"

"We can throw him in the back of the truck and let him sleep it off up at the mine while we fix the motor. He sure ain't gonna know the difference."

Broken Wing sat bent forward in a chair with his face on the table and his eyes shut. Across the room Lieutenant Pomper, now sitting at a table with the beautiful waitress, spit out French like a native.

"The jerk!" Jessie mumbled aloud.

"What's that?" the old man said with a knowing snicker.

Jessie turned away from the painful scene and glared at the old man. "She works for you, right?"

"That's right."

"Well, are you in a habit of letting your waitress sit around with any scumbag that comes in here? Isn't that bad for business?"

The old man glanced across the room, then turned a serious scowl toward Jessie. "You could be right, son. That young lieutenant got to the beachhead a while back. He was here with the American Expeditionary Force that first showed up April of last year. He's been writing my waitress, and now he's back."

"What could she possibly see in a jackass like that?"

"Oh, don't ever do that, son! God help the man that does."

"Do what?"

"Never try to figure why they do what they do; just accept it as God's will in your life. Be it pain or joy, just see it as a sailor views the weather."

Jessie's shoulders sagged. "Crap, it doesn't matter. I'll probably ship out tomorrow."

"I don't think so, son."

"Why?"

"Pat was in here today."

"Gunny O'Cleary?"

"Yes. He said he thought your outfit would be here at least another week."

Jessie straightened up. He looked at the beautiful girl and felt better. "That's great. Do you think I can meet her, Mr. Polk?"

"I'll see what I can do, son."

"Say, do you think we'll have any more trouble out of those miners up at the shaft?"

"No, I don't. I got a crew up there working right now, and the word is out: Don't bother that old Marine anymore unless you like to sing."

Jessie laughed out loud as he and Jeremiah each got under an arm of Broken Wing. They carried him outside and lay him in the back of the old man's truck. By the time Broken Wing was able to sit up, Jessie had the number two pull motor humming. Typically, the Indian never asked why or how he had ended up in the back of a truck parked on top of a mountain looking down a nickel-mining shaft. Jessie refused to volunteer the information even after they got back to Camp St. Louis and inwardly hoped that the mystery was driving the stubborn Indian crazy.

The next day proved Perelli's scuttlebutt wrong once again. The day of training was as brutal as ever, but as always the men forgot about the aches, pains, and fatigue the moment they climbed aboard the liberty truck. Jessie managed to stay with Broken Wing this time, though it was like holding on to an eel. He followed him to a bar creatively named Nouméa Bar and waited the usual two hours before the Indian began his leaning tower routine. Then Jessie led the half-conscious Navajo to La Rue sans Issue café.

Jessie pushed through the blackout curtain and found himself face to face with old Jeremiah. The old man laughed out loud. He put a shoulder under the arm of the limp Broken Wing.

"Good to see ya, Jessie. Let's get your friend to the back couch."

"Thanks, Mr. Polk."

"Sorry, gentlemen," Jeremiah called toward a table of New Zealand soldiers. "We'll be havin' a private party now. We're closing up for the night. Just leave the bill unpaid. It's on the house."

"Thank you, sir!" a New Zealand corporal shouted with a friendly wave as they stood to leave.

"You're having a party, Jeremiah?" Jessie said. "Here, let me take Broken Wing somewhere else to sleep it off."

"Nonsense, Marine. You're a guest of honor, and he is, too, if he ever wakes up. I'm treating you two to the best whiskey this side of Ireland!"

Broken Wing slowly lifted his chin from his chest, and his head continued back until his closed eyes stared at the ceiling. With his mouth hanging open, he looked like a blind seal searching for food.

"You said whiskey? Party? Free whiskey?"

Jessie burst out laughing until tears filled his gray eyes. Jeremiah doubled over laughing.

"You started the party without me?"

Jessie's laughter fell silent. He wiped at the tears with his free shoulder and stared at the auburn-haired waitress like a man in a trance as she walked toward them.

"What will you have?" she asked clearly with just a hint of an island accent in her voice.

English? English! She spoke perfect English! "You speaked! I mean, you spoked!" Jessie paused and cleared his throat. "You speak English?"

The beautiful girl laughed. "I'm sorry, Jessie. It's Dad's idea to have me pretend to only speak French."

"Well, she couldn't get any work done at all with the Marines firing on her every five minutes," Mr. Polk complained.

"You mean she's your daughter?"

"Where's the free firewater?" Broken Wing asked with one eye open.

"You mean you've understood . . ." Jessie could feel the warmth of blood rushing to his embarrassed face.

She winked and smiled and shrugged her shoulders.

Broken Wing turned and looked at Jessie through one bleary dark eye. "You redder than me."

Jessie's blush deepened. "Shut up and drink some whiskey," he growled.

The girl's smile covered Jessie with goose bumps.

Jessie gave a tight-lipped grin. "I'm really sorry, ma'am. Nice to meet you."

"Is everything ready, Kate?" Jeremiah said with a wink at his daughter.

"The galley's ready, Pop. Why don't you gentlemen have a seat while I bring out the meal." She looked at the sagging Indian and made a funny face. "Can you prop up your friend long enough to eat?"

"He's more of a responsibility than a friend, but I'll try."

Kate laughed and headed for the kitchen. Jessie stared after her with the half-conscious Indian drooping over his shoulder.

"What kind of music you Marines like?" Jeremiah asked.

Jessie gathered his dignity together, guided Broken Wing toward a nearby table, and dropped him into a chair.

"Whatever you like, sir."

"How about 'All God's Chillun Got Rhythm'?"

"Sounds great!" Jessie said. "But isn't Gunny O'Cleary coming, sir?"

"He was by earlier; said he had to get back to camp early."

Jeremiah dropped in a nickel and came back to the table just as Kate backed through the swinging door of the kitchen with a large plate of appetizers. The meal began. It was a meal suited to royalty. Jessie was not exactly sure what some of the exotic island delicacies were, but they were delicious. Even Broken Wing was awakened by the wonderful spicy aromas rising up from the dark red soup and mixing with the blackened swordfish. Two hours later the feast was over. The three men loosened their belts and leaned back contentedly as Kate served white wine.

"I can't tell you how much I appreciate this, Miss Polk," Jessie said as Kate poured wine into his glass from a tall decanter. "I've never tasted a better meal in my life," he said as he kicked Broken Wing in the shin under the table.

"Oh, yes, the meal was very good," Broken Wing mumbled.

"It's we who are grateful, lad," Jeremiah said firmly.

"We are, Jessie," Kate added with a knee-weakening smile. "I could never repay what you did for Dad. I've never seen him as distressed and hopeless as he was over not being able to meet this shipment."

"We would have lost everything," Jeremiah said. "But I think we're gonna make it now. The mines are working. No reason we can't."

"Glad I could help, sir. I don't have too many talents. It was real lucky I had the one you needed."

"Luck had nothing to do with it, lad. It was one of the clearest answers to prayer I've ever had in my life. Do you know the Lord, Jessie?"

"No, I don't have much to do with religion. My dad always said that if you do right by everybody, that's all that counted."

"That's the biggest lie Satan ever manufactured, Jessie. God says that the very best a man can do is like dirty rags at the foot of Christ and He ain't lettin' no dirty rags into paradise."

"What God do you worship?" Broken Wing asked. His bleary eyes seemed to be clearing up.

"There is only one God. Acts 4:12 puts it as plain as the Marine handbook: 'Neither is there salvation in any other; for there is none name under heaven given among men whereby we must be saved.' "

"And this one name is Jesus Christ, correct?" Broken Wing asked.

"That's affirmative."

"But to sacrifice your son? This the deed of a god?"

"Yes. Think about that. Do you have children?"

Broken Wing smiled. "Wife might be pregnant."

"Wow. Really?" Jessie asked.

"If you have a child, then you will see," Jeremiah said.

"See what?" Broken Wing asked.

"There could be no greater proof of God's love for us. He told us he'd send a sacrificial lamb to cover our sins. The lamb of God."

Broken Wing stared hard at the old Marine without speaking.

Jessie wanted to say something to break the uncomfortable silence, but he couldn't think of anything. It was Kate who finally came to the rescue. While she was obviously in complete agreement with her father, she seemed to realize instinctively that the conversation had gone as far as it could for the time being.

"Would you like to dance, Jessie?" she asked.

"Well, I'll give it a try."

Kate stood up and led Jessie to the jukebox. She dropped in a nickel and pushed two buttons. She turned to Jessie, put both arms around him, and began to sway slowly, staring up at him.

"I love this song," she said.

The rich voice of Bing Crosby began the melancholy song "I'll Be Seeing You."

For the next nine liberty days Jessie spent every free minute with Kate. It felt like they had been friends for his entire life. Just seeing her filled him with more joy than anything he had ever experienced. Seeing her at the end of each day consumed his every thought.

The short ride from Camp St. Louis to Nouméa felt

longer each time. Jessie stared out at the troopships sitting silently in Nouméa Harbor as the slow-moving truck crawled toward the town. He wondered when they would get the word. Part of him was anxious to finally see the shooting end of the war, but part of him could just as easily sit the war out in Nouméa. An uneasy feeling gnawed at his stomach.

"Good grief, I could run to Nouméa faster than this!" Jessie's loud complaint surprised even himself. He looked at the staring faces in the back of the truck and shrugged.

The blank stares turned to grins. LaBeau snickered and nudged Charlie Rose. "Your boy there's got somethin' more than coffee at that café."

Charlie Rose turned a suspicious eye toward Jessie. "You know, Slate, you're as nervous as a hound sittin' on a dead turkey."

"What?" LaBeau bellowed.

"Yep," Charlie Rose replied with his customary nod.

LaBeau turned his back to Charlie Rose.

Perelli leaned forward on the truck bench with a toothpick in his mouth. "You wanna hear the latest 'butt or not?"

He bobbed his head slightly as if the others were begging for his information.

"Please inform us, PFC Perelli," Oglethorpe said in a mocking monotone.

"Yeah. Okay. Sure, Professor. Since you're beggin', I'm gonna let you in on it."

Perelli sounded so serious that for a moment Jessie wondered if he was too stupid to realize that Oglethorpe was being sarcastic.

"In three days," Perelli said.

"What in three days?" LaBeau asked angrily.

"We ship out in three days. Straight from Gunny O'Cleary."

"The gunny said it?" LaBeau asked with new interest.

"Gunny don't sling no cow manure," Charlie Rose added thoughtfully.

"Shut up, Rose. Just shut up." LaBeau sounded like he was pleading.

Charlie Rose smacked his lips. "Yep."

Nouméa seemed busier than usual as the liberty truck rolled to a stop beside the big park. A large group of people

cheered a heated cricket match going on near the old bandstand. Most of the players were plump Nouméan women
wearing loose-fitting Mother Hubbards with lace trim and
floral prints. Jessie thought of Kate and sighed contentedly.
Thank God Kate didn't wear Mother Hubbards.

"You look like you just stepped in a perfumed cow
patty," Charlie Rose said.

"What?" Jessie said as he swallowed his fool grin.

"Shut up, Rose," Chris LaBeau groaned.

Sam Hill jumped from the truck and pointed down the
street. "Broken Wing just went around that corner."

Jessie jumped off behind him.

"Better go after him," Charlie Rose said.

"No," Jessie said, "not now. I'll find him later."

Oglethorpe slapped Jessie on the back. "Don't let Pomper
catch you, Jessie. He's just looking for a reason to kill our
liberty."

"I'll be careful."

The walk through Nouméa felt good. Rue Auguste Brun
was as busy as ever. Troops of various nationalities crowded
the sidewalks, pushing into and out of the narrow barroom
doors. Jessie's heart fluttered just enough to produce a few
goose bumps as he turned down the Avenue de Marechal
Foch. Marechal Foch seemed more crowded than normal
with Nouméans shopping in the boutiques.

Nouméan dress varied dramatically. Women wearing the
latest French fashions walked past others dressed in Mother
Hubbards, and men wearing stylish suits and fedoras mixed
freely with men wearing the native flowered wraparound
skirts. New Caledonia seemed like a pleasant place to live.
The people appeared so carefree. Jessie wondered if they realized just how tenuous their security really was. If the Marines couldn't hold Guadalcanal, it would open the South
Pacific door all the way to Australia. Back in California
there were blackouts, but right here under the Japs' noses
the Nouméans had the city lit up like a state fair.

He paused at the door of La Rue sans Issue and checked
his military alignment before entering. His tie was off center
with his belt buckle. He straightened it, removed his barracks cover, took a deep breath, and assaulted the door. He
pushed through the blackout curtain and quickly reconned
the café.

A group of British sailors sat chatting and drinking tea at the far end of the room. Four New Zealanders near the door stood up to leave. No one else was visible. Then the kitchen door pushed open, and every man in the café paused to stare. Kate smiled brightly and walked toward Jessie. Her short, tight skirt made the muscular curves of her body so pronounced that he had to force himself to swallow back the urge to groan out loud. Kate kissed him on the cheek. Her lips felt too soft to be real. Jessie dropped his barracks cover.

"Have a seat while I take care of these customers," she said.

Jessie picked up his hat and floated toward the nearest chair. He had a sudden need to look into a mirror. He wondered for a moment if he was as handsome as his mom had always said. She really likes me, he thought. It just didn't feel possible. Why me out of all the guys she could have? Nobody could be that lucky.

Before Kate could leave the cash register, the British sailors paid their bill and left. The café was empty. Kate locked the door. She came through the blackout curtain and went to the front window, lifted the shade, and turned the OPEN sign around. Jessie bit at the inside of his mouth to see if he was awake. It hurt. Kate dropped the shade and faced him. She looked suddenly very serious.

"Lieutenant Pomper was in just before you got here."

"He was?"

Kate walked slowly toward Jessie. She looked apprehensive. "Yes."

"I hate that jerk."

"Oh, Don is a nice person."

"He's a jerk! He's got a thing for you, doesn't he?"

"We were seeing each other, but I broke it off tonight. I told him that I wanted to spend time with you and I didn't want to be dishonest about it."

"You did?" Jessie couldn't believe he was having this conversation.

"Don said that your outfit might ship out this week."

"Yeah. That's what the scuttlebutt is."

Kate looked up at him. Her eyes grew misty, and it seemed hard for her to speak.

"I don't know how to say this, Jessie. I've never been this

way before. I've watched you come in each night, and I'm just so excited to see you."

"God, that's incredible!"

"Why do you say that?"

"I, I can't believe it."

"Do you feel the same, Jessie?"

Jessie's mouth felt as if someone had just stuffed it with cotton. He swallowed hard and glanced around the empty café. This was it. The doors were locked, and the prettiest girl he'd ever laid eyes on was practically offering herself to him. He pulled her close and kissed her lips. He felt for the button on the back of her skirt and fumbled with it until it broke off. Kate pulled back aghast and slapped him hard across the face.

"Get out!" she shouted, and pushed Jessie away. She grabbed up her skirt and ran sobbing through the swinging kitchen door.

Jessie felt paralyzed until the sound of a door slamming beyond the kitchen pulled him out of his trance. He ran to the kitchen door and pushed through. The kitchen was empty. On a counter was a small round chocolate cake. The words on the cake, written in white icing, stung more than the slap:

Thanks for the happiest 10 days of my life.
Love Kate.

Jessie ran into the back room. Empty. He opened the back door and stepped down to a narrow dirt alleyway. He searched both directions, but she was gone. His stomach twisted into a knot.

"Kate!" Jessie ran around the outside of the café until he ended up at the front door.

"Slate!"

"There he is!"

Jessie turned around to see the anxious faces of Sam Hill and Charlie Rose.

"What are you two doing here?"

"Lookin' for you, pal," Sam Hill said.

"You have to come with us, Jessie," Charlie said. "Your partner's hurt pretty bad."

"What?"

"We got to get him to sick bay, and if you two don't come through that guard shack together, we're all in for it," Charlie Rose said.

"He's right. Lieutenant Pomper was going on duty as officer of the day at 1800 hours," Sam said.

Jessie took one last futile look around for Kate, then followed Charlie Rose and Sam to a shady street corner a block past Rue Auguste Brun.

Benjamin B. Oglethorpe squatted beside Broken Wing, who sat slumping against the base of a large shade tree. Oglethorpe dabbed at the face of the half-conscious Indian with a blood-soaked handkerchief. Gray Cloud stood over them smoking a cigarette and mumbling to himself. Jessie ran across the cobblestone street ahead of Charlie Rose and Sam Hill.

"What happened?"

Gray Cloud looked at Jessie and grimaced. "Got beat up."

"Yes, he has been beaten very well," Oglethorpe added dryly as he dabbed at blood under Broken Wing's left eye.

"Somebody kicked him a few times when he was down," Gray Cloud said.

"How do you know that?" Jessie asked as he squatted beside Broken Wing.

"Look. Shoe polish and heel prints all over his shirt." Sam gave a grunt and shook his head.

"Perelli said he saw Duffy Johnson follow Broken Wing out of Nouméa Bar."

"Yep," Charlie Rose said. "Looks like his work."

"What shall we do with him?" Oglethorpe asked.

Charlie Rose groaned. "Here comes Johnny Law, Marines."

"What?" Jessie asked as he followed Charlie's stare to a jeep pulling up to the curb behind him.

The driver was a U.S. Army MP, and his companion was a Nouméan police officer in his tropical white uniform with a French gendarme hat. Twenty minutes later Jessie, Broken Wing, and the French policeman were sitting in the back of the jeep in front of the Camp St. Louis guard shack. The Army MP came out of the guard shack, followed by Gunny O'Cleary and Second Lieutenant Pomper, who was wearing a black and yellow OD arm band.

Jessie leaned closer to Broken Wing. "Wake up! Here comes O'Cleary with the officer of the day." Broken Wing's eyes remained closed, but he gave a grunt.

Jessie nudged him in the ribs with an elbow. "Did you hear me?"

Broken Wing groaned and winced. "Not the ribs! *Chay-ta-gahi-be-woldoni!*"

"Sorry. What's *chay-ta-gahi-be-woldoni* mean?"

"Get out of that jeep and stand at attention!" Gunny O'Cleary barked.

"I can, Gunny, but Broken Wing might need a ride to sick bay," Jessie said as he hopped out of the jeep.

"Aren't you two under orders to stay together?" Lieutenant Pomper asked.

"Yes, sir."

"Why ain't you beat up too, PFC?" the gunny shouted like he was getting madder.

"I . . . I . . ."

"Quit stuttering and give me an answer, Marine!"

"I didn't get involved, Gunny."

The old man's eyes widened as he stepped closer to the jeep and stared at Broken Wing's hands clutching at his ribs.

Lieutenant Pomper stepped closer to the jeep, looked at Broken Wing, then exchanged angry stares with Gunny O'Cleary.

Pomper and O'Cleary moved over to Jessie until both men were close enough to feel their breath when they spoke.

"This MP tells me this Marine appears to have been kicked a few times when he was down. Is that true, PFC Slate?"

"I, ah, it's hard to say, sir."

"You try real hard, mister!" Gunny O'Cleary's shout forced Jessie's eyes to blink.

"Well, sir, I didn't exactly . . ."

"Were you together or did you disobey orders, Marine?" Lieutenant Pomper barked.

"No, sir."

"That's brig time, PFC!" Pomper shouted.

"No sir, I mean, we were together, sir."

Gunny O'Cleary's brown eyes widened with rage. He shoved his face nose to nose with Jessie. "Are you telling

me that you stood watching while your Marine Corps partner was being kicked on the ground?"

"It's hard to say just how—"

"I bet it is, boy! And I mean boy! You ain't no Marine!
And God knows you ain't got no business calling yourself
a Para-Marine! The most elite fighting outfit on earth."

"Gunny, it's not—"

"Shut up, PFC!" Lieutenant Pomper bellowed.

Gunny O'Cleary turned away and spit at the ground in
disgust. "Lieutenant, unless this man can rectify the situation, I do not want him hitting the beach with my Marines."

"It ain't his fault, Gunny." Broken Wing's words were
raspy and strained.

"Shut up, Marine!" O'Cleary yelled. He glared at Jessie.
"I'll take Broken Wing to sick bay. Confine yourself to quarters, Slate."

"Aye, aye, Gunny."

Jessie faced Lieutenant Pomper and saluted sharply.
Pomper frowned and gave a wave of a salute in return.

Jessie's eyes were already open when the first shrill blast
of reveille broke through the dark, rainy September morning. He had begged Kate's forgiveness all night and flinched
awake as the echo of Gunny O'Cleary's accusation burned
in him.

He sat up and barely remembered Charlie Rose and Sam
Hill stopping by the tent the previous night. He remembered
telling them to go away.

"Reveille! Reveille! Get out of those tents, Marines!"
someone shouted as he jogged by just outside the tent.

"What are you jokers gonna do when it's a Jap air raid?
Sleep through it?"

Jessie sat up in his cot, fumbled for a matchbook under
the blanket he used for a pillow, and lit Broken Wing's small
lantern. He looked at the Indian's empty cot, and the
gunny's words burned in him again. He stiffened with rage.
He thought of Broken Wing and wanted to smash him for
being such a drunken jerk, but he knew in his heart the real
cause of his turmoil: Duffy Johnson. From the moment that
big slob had sold them the phony map, Jessie's life had been
under the boot heel of Lieutenant Pomper.

He dressed and headed for the morning formation. After

formation they marched to the chow hall and then back to the big open field for another formation. At the second formation the outfit split into various training squads for lectures and field exercises. The sun peeked through a constant drizzle as the colonel saluted and turned over command to the company commanders, who quickly turned command over to their individual training groups. Jessie stood at attention staring at Gunny O'Cleary and First Lieutenant Pierce as they exchanged salutes. This is it, Jessie thought. Act now or never face the gunny with pride again. Jessie stepped out of formation and marched up to O'Cleary and Lieutenant Pierce. He snapped to attention with a salute.

"Sir! Request permission to demonstrate hand-to-hand combat techniques, sir."

O'Cleary and Pierce looked startled for an instant, then Pierce's face tightened.

"What's this all about, Gunny?"

O'Cleary put his face in front of Jessie's and shouted, "You're out of formation, Marine!"

"Sir, I repeat! Request permission to demonstrate hand-to-hand combat with a fellow Marine, sir!"

The wrinkles around the gunny's brown eyes eased. Jessie sensed what he hoped was a hint of approval in the tough old Marine's demeanor.

"And just who would you need as partner to conduct this demonstration, PFC?"

"Corporal Duffy Johnson is the man I want, Gunny."

"Johnson." The gunny scratched at his chin and turned to Lieutenant Pierce.

"Absolutely not, O'Cleary," Lieutenant Pierce said.

"Could I speak to you for a moment, Lieutenant?" Gunny O'Cleary walked a few feet away, with Lieutenant Pierce following. They stopped and spoke quietly. Jessie couldn't hear. Lieutenant Pierce frowned and shook his head no. The gunny leaned closer to him and spoke again. Lieutenant Pierce's face and shoulders slumped. Gunnery Sergeant O'Cleary did an about-face and headed toward the next platoon. Jessie's heart began to pound so hard that his ears thumped with each beat. A minute later Gunny O'Cleary was back with the monstrous Duffy Johnson at his side.

"Corporal Johnson has volunteered to help PFC Slate demonstrate hand-to-hand combat, Lieutenant."

Johnson glared at Jessie. "Be my pleasure, Lieutenant."

Jessie stared hard at Johnson. "Did you inform the corporal that, unlike his usual choice of opponents, this one isn't too drunk to fight back?"

"All right, Second Platoon!" Gunny shouted. "Form a circle around here!"

"What are you doing, Gunny?" Lieutenant Pierce asked.

"No need for the other platoons to watch this demonstration, sir."

"Yes, I agree. I will be over at the com shack, Gunny, and will obviously know nothing about this training exercise. You can report to me there."

"Aye, aye, sir."

The platoon formed a standing circle around Jessie, Johnson, and Gunny O'Cleary. The gunny looked around to make sure that no one other than the platoon members could witness the demonstration, then turned to the two Marines, who were now facing each other in a staredown.

"Ready. Let the training begin!"

Jessie threw two fast hard punches into Duffy's big, round face, knocking the giant man back two steps. Dark red blood squirted from a deep split on the bridge of Duffy's flat nose and streamed down to his chin. A moment later the world turned black.


"You were markedly better than your first outing, Slate."

Jessie opened his eyes. The blurry image of Benjamin B. Oglethorpe stared back at him through round glasses.

"This here looks like a job for the phantom crapper." The familiar Kentucky twang came from behind Oglethorpe.

"Charlie Rose."

Jessie reconned the ward around him. The antiseptic smell told him he was in sick bay. The only other patient was unconscious in the bed beside him.

"Did better than last time, boy. Think you broke his nose."

"Where's your Navajos?"

"They threw us back in with the platoon again, all of us."

"You kidding?"

"He is correct," Oglethorpe said. "They are keeping us

in the first squad together so that if they need communication replacements, they will know exactly where both members of each team are located."

"That ain't all, boy. We got ourselves a war, and my innards feel like a swarm of grasshoppers."

Jessie looked at Charlie Rose, then turned a questioning stare toward Oglethorpe.

"Does he mean what I think he means?"

"Yes, as a matter of fact." Oglethorpe checked his watch. "We ship out for parts unknown in approximately forty-eight hours. Tonight is the last liberty call."

"And Gunny wants us to pack your gear."

"Yes, this is true. We have to go."

Charlie Rose gave Oglethorpe a tug toward the door. "C'mon, Oglethorpe, time's a-wasting, boy."

"One last bit of ominous news," Oglethorpe said. "Our tormentor has been permanently attached to the Para-Marines as a communications specialist."

"No! No! You're lying."

"Wish he was, but he ain't," Charlie Rose said.

"It should not be too large of a problem as long as we remain in the squad and Pomper stays with communications." Oglethorpe gave a final wave as he and Charlie Rose left the sick bay.

Jessie sat up. He winced from a sharp pain knifing through his rib cage. A snickering laugh came from the bed on Jessie's left. He turned gingerly.

Broken Wing's snicker swelled into an all-out belly laugh that caused him to hold tight to his own wounded ribs. For a moment Jessie was stunned to see the normally deadpan Indian actually laugh out loud. Then he wanted to know why.

"What's so funny?" Jessie snapped.

Broken Wing held tight to his rib cage with one hand and pointed at Jessie with the other. Tears of laughter ran down his face. He couldn't speak.

"You . . . you . . ." Broken Wing started laughing again.

"I didn't think you knew how to laugh," Jessie said as he lay back down.

"You look like a raccoon!"

"What?"

"You have two of the best shiners I ever saw!"

"Oh, real funny. Semper fi to you, too, jerkface."

Broken Wing stopped laughing.

"Listen, Slate." The Indian looked embarrassed.

"Yeah."

"Heard what you did. Thanks."

"You mean what I tried to do, don't you?"

Broken Wing laughed. "You look just like—"

"Yeah, I heard ya, a raccoon. Look, I hit that big jerk as much for me as I did for you. I hate that guy."

"Easy man to hate," Broken Wing said unemotionally as he propped himself up on one elbow.

"Sounds like we're really shipping out this time."

"Looks like."

"What's it like the first time, Broken Wing?"

"Make man rain in pants."

"What's the worst?"

"Shelling."

"Artillery?"

"Jap naval shelling on the island was worse. Guys cracked up. Loco in the brain."

"Guadalcanal is in the papers every day back home."

Broken Wing looked at Jessie with a dull stare.

"Where you from, Wing?"

"Window Rock, Arizona."

"That's a funny name for a town."

"Capital city of Navajo Nation. A reservation."

"I always wondered what a reservation was like."

*"Tkele-cho-gi."*

Jessie pointed an accusing finger at Broken Wing.

"You just called me a jackass!"

*"To-kus-dan."*

*"To-kus-dan? To-kus-dan?* Approximately!"

"Yes."

Jessie felt rather pleased with himself for understanding. "So you're married?"

Broken Wing nodded yes.

"She live on the reservation?" Jessie asked.

"Yes."

"What do you do in Window Rock?"

"My family makes silver jewelry and pottery. We raise some sheep. Farm a little."

"Can you make jewelry?"

"My people make the finest silver jewelry in America for many years."

"Wish I could give Kate some jewelry."

"She is very beautiful. My wife is beautiful also."

"Miss her a lot, I guess."

"Yes. She is fat with child."

"You found out for sure?"

"Yes."

"Wow, that's great! Congratulations. Does she write you much?"

"Yes. How about you? This girl at café? Anything special?"

Jessie grinned. The thought of Kate gave him goose bumps. Then last night flashed across his mind, and he frowned and groaned.

"What's the problem? Her father is good man. Very wise. But fathers are like chiefs."

"No, Mr. Polk's a swell man. He's an old Marine, for gosh sakes."

"Oh," Broken Wing said with a knowing nod. "So beautiful girl finds you stupid or ugly."

"She does not find me stupid! Or ugly!"

"For what reason do you turn her stomach?"

"Who the crap said I turn her stomach?"

"I would like to know why I turned someone's stomach."

"So would I, if I turned her stomach."

"You should ask her."

"I don't make her sick! Look, let's just drop it, okay?"

"Yes, you need to find out why you turn her stomach before you can speak of it."

"Are you always this hard to talk to?"

Broken Wing shrugged nonchalantly. "Don't know. Only talk when I'm sober."

"That sure ain't very often."

"Like drinkin' better than talkin'."

Jessie laughed, "That's obvious. How'd *you* ever get a wife?"

"Don't turn her stomach. You thirsty?"

"No!"

"I am going into Nouméa. Better go with me."

"Have you seen those two wire cages they put guys in over in the brig area?"

Broken Wing looked at his watch and sat up. "Twenty minutes till old Joe leaves." He indicated an Army nurse sitting at a desk at the far end of the small Quonset hut sick bay.

"Who's Joe?" Jessie asked.

"Liberty driver."

The middle-aged Army nurse with bleached-blond hair came over.

"Time for your walk, PFC Wing."

"Yes, ma'am. Him, too." Broken Wing pointed at Jessie.

The stocky nurse frowned. "Oh, I'm afraid it's too soon for him to be walking."

"He has to, ma'am. We ship out with the new sun. He will have to be ready when we hit that beach."

The woman had a kind face. She looked at Jessie with sincere concern. "I don't know."

"We are Para-Marines, ma'am. He could be making a five-thousand-foot jump within the next week. He better walk now. Orders."

The nurse helped Broken Wing out of bed, then considered Jessie. "Well, I guess so. It has stopped raining."

Before Jessie could object, Broken Wing pulled him to a sitting position. Ten minutes later they were back at their tent, tightening the fair-leather belts on their dress greens. The ride to Nouméa was a sore one. Most of the Marines in the truck were replacements for the raiders. No one asked why Jessie and Broken Wing looked so battered or why they groaned every time the truck hit a pothole.

The truck stopped in front of the park, and men jumped out.

"Let's get a drink," Broken Wing said.

"No way. We go see Kate first."

"I am thirsty."

"This is real important to me, Broken Wing. I mean, more important than anything. I have to see her."

"One drink first. Then you will not be nervous."

"I don't trust you."

"If you have a drink, you will be calm like a smooth pond. Maybe you will not turn her stomach."

"I don't turn anybody's stomach!" Jessie shouted.

"You see. You need to calm down."

"All right! Just one. One drink, Broken Wing. No more!"

Charlie Rose and Benjamin B. Oglethorpe walked into the bar after the first drink. Naturally, a few final toasts were in order. Two hours later Jessie stumbled through the blackout curtain of La Rue sans Issue like a man on the pitching deck of a transport in rough squalls. Broken Wing, Charlie Rose, and Oglethorpe staggered in single file behind him. Jessie heard people laughing in the café, but their faces were blurry.

"Jessie. Are you boys all right?"

"Mr. Polk?"

"Right here in front of ya, son. Looks like you've been in a good fight. Good golly, boy! Your breath could knock down a Jap bomber!"

"I have to talk to Kate, sir."

"I don't know what happened between you two, but it might be better, Jessie, if you came back another time."

"I have to."

"Dad."

Kate's soft voice sent adrenaline through Jessie like no voice ever had. She stepped in front of her father, balancing a tray loaded with cups of steaming tea on one hand. She gave Jessie a cold, angry look.

"Tell this drunken little boy to leave our café, Dad."

"Kate . . ."

"I have nothing to say to you, Jessie. Just the sight of you upsets me."

"Ah. Yes. He turns your stomach," Broken Wing mumbled.

"Shut up!" Jessie barked over his shoulder.

Kate turned away to serve three British sailors at a nearby table. For an instant Jessie ached with a surge of grief, of the kind that he usually felt when he thought about his father's flag-draped casket.

Jeremiah Polk laid a consoling hand on Jessie's shoulder. "I'm sorry, Jessie."

"I love her, Mr. Polk, and I'm shipping out tomorrow."

The old man's eyes widened. He scratched thoughtfully at his gray beard. He turned, walked over to the cash register, and jotted something down on a piece of paper. He folded it and tucked it inside the breast pocket of Jessie's dress green jacket.

"That's our address. You write to her, son."

"Thank you, sir," Jessie said quietly. He swallowed back a lump in his throat and blinked back his tears. He felt a tug on his sleeve.

"Come on. I will fix," the Indian said with a sly wink.

Jessie sighed and followed the three Marines back to the blackout curtain, where the Indian stopped.

"You wait here," Broken Wing said.

"Wait. What are you gonna do?"

"Make her forget that you turn her stomach."

"You stay out of this before you mess things up."

"Yes. Your success will be hard to beat."

Jessie's shoulders slumped, and he looked down at the hardwood floor. Broken Wing turned and walked back to Kate as she set down a tray of soup and coffee for two New Zealand officers.

When he tapped her on the back, she spun around quickly and threw him an angry glance, then threw an even angrier one toward Jessie, Charlie Rose, and Oglethorpe. Broken Wing leaned close to Kate and whispered something that took him a full thirty seconds. Kate's shoulders straightened. She arched back just slightly and looked suspiciously at him, then at Jessie, and then back at him again. He leaned forward once more and cupped his hand around his mouth so that whatever he was whispering wouldn't be overheard. Kate cocked her head and looked at Broken Wing in disbelief, then shook her head no and turned away. Broken Wing tapped her on the shoulder and whispered something at the back of her head. Then he did an about-face and walked back to Jessie and the others.

"What was that all about?" Oglethorpe asked.

"Follow me," Broken Wing said, and headed out of the café.

"Hold it!" Jessie yelled as the door of the café closed behind them.

"Why?" Broken Wing said.

"What did you say to her?"

"Not much."

"Not much!" Charlie Rose exclaimed.

"Not too much."

"Not too much! You talked to her for five minutes," Jessie said.

"I am thirsty."

"Out with it, Wing," Jessie said.

The broad-faced Indian checked his watch. "Bed check in thirty minutes."

"What?"

"Joe is probably waiting on us now."

"Who's Joe?" Charlie Rose asked.

Jessie pointed at Broken Wing. "His friend, a liberty driver. What's this about bed check?"

"Yes. We will be reported AWOL if we are not there in the sick bay."

"Crap! Why are you just now telling me this?"

"You two better shove off," Charlie Rose cautioned.

Broken Wing turned and walked briskly away.

"Yeah, right. See you guys later," Jessie said as he started after Wing.

The ride back to camp was awful. Jessie puked all over the tailgate of the truck, and though he was dying to know what Broken Wing had said to Kate, he felt too lousy to question him.

The bleached-blond Army nurse sat in a chair with her head lying on her arms on her desk top. She was snoring quietly as Jessie and Broken Wing tiptoed past her. A dim reading lamp on her desk was the only light. Jessie stripped down to his skivvies, climbed in bed, and pulled a sheet over himself. A moment later the front door by the nurse's desk creaked. A Marine with a clipboard walked in. Light from the dim lamp reflected off a silver captain's bar on the Marine's shoulder as he walked past Jessie's bed. He went down one row of beds and back up the other, checking the empty beds. On his way out, he smiled at the sleeping nurse, then left.

Jessie stared at the ceiling and thought of Kate. The room was spinning in harmony with Broken Wing's snoring. Jessie closed his eyes and swore that he would never drink again. Kate. God, did I ever blow it, Jessie thought. The front door of the Quonset hut creaked again.

A few moments later the piercing beam of a flashlight forced him to open one eye.

"Jessie, you got a visitor, boy."

"Charlie Rose?"

"Shhh. Keep quiet or we all go to the brig, boy."

"It's me," murmured a woman's voice.

Jessie blinked and sat up.

"Please forgive me, Jessie. I didn't know what you were going through. How could I?"

"Kate! What are you doing here dressed like that?" Jessie asked as he gave a panicked look toward the nurse's desk.

The old blonde was still asleep. Charlie Rose signaled a thumbs-up as he tiptoed past the sleeping nurse and out the creaking front door. Jessie looked at Kate and started to speak, but she put a hand over his mouth. She removed a barracks cover and allowed her long hair to fall around her shoulders.

"Someone might hear us, Jessie."

"The place is empty."

"Where did you get the uniform?"

"Benjamin Oglethorpe. He's back in town."

Kate removed the jacket.

Jessie stared like a man in a trance. "God, you're so beautiful," he whispered. "I didn't think I'd ever see you again."

Kate looked down at the floor like an embarrassed little girl. Jessie lifted the sheet, and she climbed into bed beside him. They kissed.

"Jessie."

"Yes."

"Jessie, it's hard to talk to you when you stare at me like that."

"Oh, sorry." He continued to stare.

"Why didn't you tell me?"

"Tell you?"

"I know it's too fast and crazy, Jessie, but I think about you all the time."

"Me, too. I can't dream without you being in it."

"I think we're in love."

"Wow. You do? I mean, I already knew that I was, but why me, Kate? Every guy on this island would kill to be with you."

"Jessie."

"Yeah?"

"Can I . . . I mean Broken Wing told me about your terrible . . . accident."

"He what? Accident?"

"Shhh, Jessie, you'll wake someone."

"Me and Broken Wing are the only patients. Don't worry about him; he's drunk."

"Don't be mad at Broken Wing, Jessie. If he hadn't told me the whole story, I wouldn't be here. I was terribly humiliated that night in the café."

"Oh, Kate, you have to forgive me. I—"

"No, it's you that must forgive me. You needed me, and I ran away from you. I'm sorry, Jessie."

"What?"

Kate closed her eyes and cut Jessie's question short with a kiss on the lips. He stared wide-eyed through the long wet kiss and tried to make sense of what was happening. Kate opened her eyes and pulled her lips away. A single tear glistened in the dim light like a tiny moon trickling down her face.

"Jessie, I want to ease your pain."

"Kate, I don't think . . ."

She kissed him quiet again.

"Listen, Kate—"

"No more talking, darling," she whispered, and pressed against him.

"I love you, Jessie. I hope God forgives me."

Kate kissed Jessie softly.

Jessie opened one eye and knew that he had been grinning foolishly in his sleep. Kate sat on the edge of the bed with the sheet around her. She was staring down at Jessie's midsection with a rather studious expression. Jessie felt funny in a nice sort of way.

"Jessie?" she whispered.

"Yeah, honey."

"I don't even see a scar," Kate commented.

"Scar?"

The door creaked. Charlie Rose peeked in and motioned a come-on wave toward Jessie and Kate. Kate waved back. Charlie closed the door quietly and stayed outside. Kate jumped up, dressed quickly, gave Jessie one last lingering kiss, and whispered, "I love you. I'll write you and I'll wait for only you."

"Kate, can we get married when I come back?"

Kate smiled and suddenly jumped on top of Jessie. The bedsprings squeaked. They kissed and embraced. Her face was wet with fresh tears. She rolled away and stood up. Jessie sat up watching silently as she gathered her boots, socks, and hat in her arms and tiptoed out of the sick bay.

Jessie felt he had just dreamed the best dream of his entire life. He fell back onto his pillow, fighting an urge to giggle out loud.

"Sure glad that's over." Broken Wing's raspy voice startled Jessie back into a sitting position.

The Indian's bare back was facing Jessie. A sheet was pulled up to his waist.

"You mean you listened?"

"Would rather hear the Lone Ranger."

"I oughta break your big Navajo nose!"

"Hey, you eight balls!" a Marine yelled from the far end of the Quonset hut. "If the dame's gone, keep it down! I want some shut-eye sometime tonight!"

"Yeah, Mac!" another voice bellowed.

"You better marry that broad, Marine."

Jessie felt his mouth drop open. Broken Wing rolled over to face Jessie's openmouthed stare. The Indian's face was expressionless as always, but his eyebrows lifted.

"Nice tom-toms, huh?"

"No wonder we put you guys on reservations."

"Thought you were gonna blow it."

"Blow it! Yeah! That's another thing. What the crap did you tell her?"

"You told Rose, Oglethorpe, and me everything in the bar. How you practically assaulted her, and about the cake she made you."

Jessie pinched the bridge of his nose. "Was I that drunk?"

"I told the girl you acted crazy because your family had died in a big fire and you just got the word."

Jessie moaned.

"Oh, no!"

"You owe me great thanks."

"She's going to think I'm completely insane."

"You are welcome."

"What else did you tell her?"

"Told of your shame."

"Shame?"

"Terrible accident."

"Accident?"

"Testicle got cut in half by propeller of plane on last jump at Camp Gillespie."

"You told her—"

"Any man with only one testicle—"

"You told her that?"

"Think you will see her again?"

"I want to marry her."

"Ah. If she ever meets your mother, just tell her your mother had a miraculous recovery."

"Why'd you tell her so many lies?"

"Smoke screen."

"What do you mean?"

"Give girl with great tom-toms so much to think about, she forgets that you turn her stomach."

"It's sort of scary."

"What's scary?"

"The strange way your mind works."

# CHAPTER SIX

IN LATE JULY 1943 THE MEN OF THE FIRST REPLACE-
ment Battalion filed up the ramp of the LST *Beaton*. Scuttlebutt said that the zigzagging convoy of big LSTs—
affectionately known as floating coffins because of their lack
of speed and the fact that one torpedo hit would roll them
over and sink them like lead—was heading for the Canal.
The parachutists were to be replacements for the First Parachute Battalion. For the first time any of the Marines could
remember, the scuttlebutt was right. The convoy plodded
up to the famous island battlefield on August 5. Gunny
O'Cleary called the anchorage Iron Bottom Bay because
there were forty-eight ships beneath the coral-blue waters
around Guadalcanal. Gunny rarely exaggerated. The
thought of thousands of dead men just beneath the tranquil
surface was so unsettling that some of the men got nervous
just looking at the water.

The first three days on the island were spent marching.
The skipper had put out the word that there would be no
doping off. Some fool found out that the Marine raiders had
set a record for the longest march in the shortest amount
of time. Naturally, the Para-Marines would have to beat
that time. On a Saturday morning, in full combat gear, the
Para-Marine replacement battalion saddled up at 0400 and
didn't stop until the record fell, halfway across the island.
There were supposed to be Jap snipers left on the island,
but no one saw anything but fetid jungle, strange white ants,
and green-eyed frogs. The march back ended on Sunday afternoon. The Marines had barely taken off their boondockers and fallen into the sack when Gunny O'Cleary began
to bellow.

"First Platoon! Get out of those racks, Marines!"

Jessie opened his eyes in disbelief. The cursing echoed around the camp of pyramidal tents like a ricochet.

"You will shut your Marine Corps mouths and be in formation for chapel service in ten minutes! Move it!"

Jessie sat up in his cot and swung his feet to the ground. He groaned from a sharp burning pain on the bottom of his right foot.

"Man, my foot is killing me."

Broken Wing yawned and scratched his head. "Hold it up."

Jessie lifted his foot so Wing could see the bottom.

"Trench foot. You been lacing your boots all the way up."

"What?"

"Better see Doc Kuipers."

Jessie laid his right foot on his left knee so that he could see the bottom. The skin was yellow and cracked and bleeding a little.

"That's what trench foot looks like?"

"Gets uglier."

Charlie Rose rubbed the back of his thick neck, stood up, and walked over to Jessie.

"Boy, that foot needs tendin' to."

"Really hurts."

"You sit still. I'll get Doc."

Charlie pulled on his boots and rushed out of the tent.

Gray Cloud grinned and shook his head as he laced up a boot. "Charlie Rose is the nicest character I've ever met."

"Yeah. Hope he don't get killed," Broken Wing said casually.

"Good grief!" Jessie exclaimed. "That's a strange thing to say."

"Nope."

"Yes, it is."

"Nicest guy on the Canal was the first to die."

Jessie started to argue the logic of Broken Wing's thinking but decided not to. Gray Cloud stared at Broken Wing, then looked down as if in deep thought.

Doc Kuipers poked his head through the tent flap. "Who's got the bum foot?"

"I do, Doc."

The little Navy corpsman came in with his medical pack in hand. He couldn't have weighed more than one twenty-five, and he was about five feet five inches tall. He had a thin face with high cheekbones and curly blond hair like Harpo Marx, only cut shorter.

"Foot's not too bad yet," he mumbled as he pulled a small jar of salve out of his pack.

"How'd you get to be a corpsman, Doc?" Jessie asked.

"The Krauts torpedoed my dad's freighter."

"Merchant Marine?" Gray Cloud asked.

Doc Kuiper spread a cool salve on the bottom of Jessie's foot with a flat stick. "Yeah. So I joined the Navy to kill Nazis, and they send me to the stinking Pacific to patch up jarheads."

The Marines laughed. Corporal DiCicca pulled open the tent flap and shouted, "Saddle up you eight balls! Form up by the CP!"

Ten minutes later the tired, grumbling platoon staggered into a formation and limped in columns of two down the same dusty road they had seen too much of already. The gunny turned off the dirt road and followed a narrow but well-worn path through a deep ravine, then up a snakelike ridge line scarred and burned by shelling. Here he stopped and turned around to face the platoon.

"This is Bloody Ridge. Back beyond that spread of jungle is Henderson Field. Beyond that is the beach and the ocean. From the top of this ridge"—He pointed back in the direction they had come—"back down that spread and all the way to the Lunga River, about three hundred yards, was what the raiders held. Over here on this spur of the ridge, is where the parachutists of First Battalion were. Your battalion, Marines! Some companies fought down to fifty men."

"Thanks for the good news," Lopez mumbled from somewhere behind Jessie.

The gunny's face turned stone-hard, and his eyes flamed with intensity. "The Japs started the attack to push the Marines off this island right here where you're standing. They hit the ridge with naval gunfire for about twenty minutes, then the foot soldiers struck. They came down the bank of the Lunga and overwhelmed the right flank. The next day the Japs hit again with so many planes that the Fifth Regiment couldn't get here to help, at least not as a unit, and when the Fifth Marine Regiment don't get there, then the world's almost at its end. It was right here where Colonel Edson told the Marines still standing that if they didn't hold, we'd lose Henderson Field and the rest of Guadalcanal."

"Sounds like some colonel," Lopez said with a chuckle.

"Stow that mouth, Marine, or I'll put my boot up your rear end till you taste leather!"

Every eye in the platoon was on Lopez. His already dark skin seemed to grow darker. He said nothing.

"That man won the Medal of Honor here. So did Captain Bailey and three others, and over a hundred Marines won the Navy Cross, and they didn't stop the Japs with their mouths. They did it like Marines, with blood, guts, bayonets, and good American lead. You will show proper respect, and you will honor them! Over six hundred of your brother Marines died on this island, and on this Lord's day you will pay your respects and only God almighty will be able to save the man who shows disrespect when we reach the cemetery."

With that the gunny did a sharp about-face and led the platoon on a mile march that ended in an open field with rows of white wooden crosses. Each grave was covered with a palm frond, and someone guessed that it was to keep the grave mounds from washing away during the heavy tropical downpours. Buddies had carved out small inscriptions on some of the crosses, simple words of homage like "A swell friend" or "He never griped" or "A brave Marine."

"Two lines! At parade rest! Remove those helmets! Every head bowed!"

It seemed like a long time before the gunny called the formation to attention. With helmets back on and rifles at right shoulder arms, the platoon gave a final salute to the fallen Marines and soldiers.

Gunny O'Cleary led the platoon back by way of one small detour. They followed a narrow trail that stopped at a large mound about twenty yards from the beach. On top of the mound was a sign, made from the bottom of an ammo box, stuck on a bomb-shattered tree stump. The sign read "Take a piss on Tojo's son." The Seabees had attached a large funnel to a big Navy shell casing and had stuck it into the grave site. General Tojo, the Japanese premier, stood for everything that every American hated. One by one every Marine in the platoon climbed on top of the mound and relieved himself on the grave of Tojo's son.

That night was like so many other tropical nights. A warm soft breeze slowly nudged puffy white clouds overhead until the luminescent moon quietly disappeared and the clouds turned thick and black. The wind grew chilly, and the first drops of rain began to smack against the top of the pyramidal tent. Soon the place was a quagmire. It felt sort of cozy lying on a cot and listening to the pounding rain. Broken Wing's tiny lantern was in the center of the four cots. It reminded Jessie of sitting around a camp fire with his mom and dad back in Logan County when he was eight years old.

"Hey, Slate."

Jessie pulled his eyes off the lantern. He came up on one elbow and looked over at Broken Wing. "Yeah?"

"Oglethorpe says that if we can get him the right stuff, he can make some firewater to take care of this terrible headache I got."

"You ain't got no headache, Wing," Charlie Rose exclaimed.

"How you know?"

"That feelin' yer feelin', they got a name that goes right with that."

"What would that be, Charlie Rose?" Sam Hill asked with the timing of a vaudeville team.

"Sober! Ain't that what they call it in West by-Gawd Virginia, Slate?"

Jessie slapped at a whining mosquito. "We got those bloodsuckers in here again. Somebody light up a Chelsea."

"I would rather get sucked dry than smell one more Chelsea cigarette!" Sam Hill yelled.

"I don't mind the bite, but I sure don't want malaria," Jessie said.

Sam Hill grinned.

"Don't worry about it, Slate, your skin's about as yellow as a Nip's already from all that Atabrine in you."

Jessie held out his arm to see the color in the dim lantern light.

"Man, those pills do make a person look sick."

"A corporal in the Second Platoon said they make you sterile."

"I'd dang sure rather look yellow than have the shakes for the rest of my life," Charlie Rose said.

"Hey, you hear something?" Sam asked with his big sad face looking even bigger in the flickering light of the lantern.

"Yeah," Charlie Rose said, frowning.

The shrill voice of a faraway Marine broke through the slapping sound of the rain on the tent canvas.

"Air raid!"

"Take cover!"

"Air raid!"

The tent quivered from the shock wave of the first five-hundred-pound bomb as it ripped a gaping hole in the jungle growth a hundred yards beyond the city of tents.

"Where's my pack?" Charlie Rose howled as he jumped to his feet.

The others sprinted out of the tent, barefoot and shirtless, grabbing their Johnson rifles as they scrambled blindly for the foxholes in a muddy clearing nearby. Another bomb crashed through the upper branches of nearby trees, then exploded with a heart-stopping thud. Jessie dived for a dark hole just ahead, then clenched his jaw, closed his eyes, and awaited the impact with the muddy ground. His face struck the icy water first, shocking his eyes open even wider. An instant later he emerged from the cold muddy bath, spitting water and gasping for air.

Silence swallowed up the echo of the two explosions. Only the fading drone of a single bomber was left. The rain ceased. The grumbling Marines pulled themselves out of their water-filled foxholes and trudged, shivering, back to their tents, where they found Charlie Rose still searching on all fours for his pack.

"What the crap, Rose!" Broken Wing barked.

"You stupid jarhead!" Jessie yelled. "You trying to get killed?"

"The Corps can get you another pack, Rose," Sam added in a tone of disdain.

Charlie Rose reached back under Jessie's cot. "Here it is. How'd it get over here?"

"You're nuts, Rose," Broken Wing said dryly.

Charlie pulled his pack out from under the cot and sat

in the dirt grinning his good-natured grin. "I know, fellas, but I had some presents in here fer y'all, and dadgum, I just knew they was gonna get blowed up before I could give 'em out."

Charlie Rose loosened the flap strap buckles on his pack and pulled out six small packages wrapped like Christmas presents in bright red and green paper.

"Who are they for?" Sam Hill asked as they all tried to shake off the mud and water before sitting on their cots.

"This one here is yours, Sam. I noticed how much trouble you have with your feet blisterin' up."

Sam tore the green paper off his present. "Socks! Two pair!"

"Fella told me they was good. Might last all the way to Japan."

Sam gave Charlie a pat on the head. "I won't forget this, my small snow-headed friend."

"Aw! You're welcome, Chief."

Charlie Rose handed Jessie a thin, square package wrapped in red paper. "This one here is for you, Jessie."

"Thanks, Charlie."

Jessie unwrapped the paper and stared in disbelief at a five-by-seven photograph of Kate standing in front of the café.

"What is it?" Sam asked.

"How did you . . ." Jessie paused and brought the black and white photograph closer to the light.

"Well, I figured you was in love with that pretty little Kate."

Broken Wing leaned closer to see. "Great tom-toms," he injected.

"When we got back to town and gave Professor Oglethorpe his uniform back, I asked Kate for the best picture she had. There's some good writing paper there, too, just to keep in touch with her."

"I can't tell you how much I appreciate this, Charlie Rose."

"Shucks, I'm the grateful one, fellas. I never had friends much. Our nearest neighbor was five miles up the holler, and well, shucks, I just plain like you fellas, so that's all there is to it. Let's don't make no big thing out of it."

"Don't like me, huh?" Broken Wing muttered dejectedly.

"Heck, yes, I do! Here, Wing." Charlie Rose fumbled through his pack and pulled out another red package about six inches tall and four inches wide.

"I like presents," the stone-faced Indian said as Charlie handed it to him.

Wing sniffed the air like a bloodhound and looked suspiciously at the package.

"Well, open it," Jessie said.

He tore the red paper away and held a pint bottle of Johnnie Walker Scotch above his head. He lowered the bottle, dropped to his knees beside his cot, and started drawing in the dirt with his finger.

"What's he doing?" Charlie Rose asked.

"Giving thanks to the wind god by drawing him a picture."

"Now, that's a new one on me," Charlie Rose said. "Old Sam here don't do that."

Sam shrugged his shoulders.

Jessie shook his head and grinned at Charlie. "Why did you wrap them like Christmas presents, Charlie?"

"Well, I was gonna try to keep 'em till Christmas, but I got the funniest darn feelin' I ain't gonna be here when Christmas comes."

Jessie balled up a piece of wrapping paper and hit Charlie in the head with it. "Don't talk like that. I'll bring you back if I have to drag you across the Pacific."

"Who are the other presents for?" Sam asked.

"Well, this one's for Lopez."

"Lopez! He hates everybody," Jessie said.

"No, now I don't think so."

"What is it?"

"Shavin' razor. He was tryin' to steal mine, so I figured he must need one."

"Who else?"

"I got scarves for old Cajun LaBeau and a book for Benjamin B. Oglethorpe."

"You drive LaBeau nuts. LaBeau wants you surveyed out of the Corps," Sam said.

"No, now I'm sure that ol' boy likes me a lot. Otherwise, he wouldn't be so interested in what I say."

Jessie and Sam Hill chuckled.

Jessie pointed to a green package the size of a shoe box.

"What's the big package there?"

"Oh, that one's real special. Matter of fact I want to give it to the gunny right now, but I'll hold off till Sergeant Rim's mail-away package comes in."

"What is it?"

"You'll see soon enough."

"We better get some shut-eye, fellas," Jessie said.

"Yep," Charlie Rose agreed.

And so it went on Guadalcanal. They called the single nightly bomber Louie the Louse for what exact reason Jessie was not sure, but Louie the Louse's obvious job was to harass American troops, and he did so every night without fail. Sometimes he actually hit something.

"Mail call!" The shout seemed to catch every man by surprise.

"Did he say mail call?" Charlie Rose asked as he pushed another shovelful of dirt into a sandbag.

Jessie's eyes opened wide. Kate's beautiful face flashed into his mind, and his heart pumped stronger against his chest.

"Yeah! I saw a plane land at Henderson Field about a half hour ago!"

"Mail call!"

Jessie dropped his E-tool, wiped sweat and dirt from his hands onto his trousers, and ran toward the platoon CP tent. A crowd of Marines were already circling Corporal Di-Cicca, who stood in the middle with a seabag stuffed full with packages and letters.

"Broken Wing!" DiCicca shouted.

"Here!"

DiCicca sailed an envelope toward the raised hand.

"Ellinwood!"

"Here."

"Sergeant Rim!"

"Yo."

"Slate!"

"Here!"

DiCicca flipped an envelope toward Jessie. Another Marine grabbed it out of the air and passed it back. Jessie snatched it from an outstretched hand and pushed his way back out of the crowd of chattering, shirtless Marines. He

checked the return address. It was from Kate. He found the
stump of a shattered coconut tree, sat down, leaned back,
and opened the letter.

Dearest Jessie,
This is the most difficult letter I have ever had to
write. I'm scared and confused and have no one to turn
to but you. I love you, and no matter what your decision might be after reading this, always remember that
I blame myself, not you. There is one other person in
my life whom I love and would rather die than hurt.
I think that you saw the very special relationship that
exists between my father and me.
I've been feeling sort of sick lately, so I went to our
doctor. He says that I'm pregnant. I'm not sad about
having our baby, darling. I love you, and part of me
is thrilled, but Jessie, this will hurt my father so deeply
that I honestly fear for his life. He had a mild heart
attack last June, just a few weeks before you came to
the island. Our doctor, Doc Guiet, thinks that this sort
of shock might be too much for Dad to bear so soon
after the heart attack.
Do not misunderstand the purpose of this letter, Jessie. Dad will forgive my sin because he will know that
the Lord has already forgiven me. We will find a way
to live with my disgrace. But if you really meant what
you said about wanting to marry me, and if there is
any way you could get back to Nouméa soon enough,
then there would be no reason to risk hurting my father. If you are not ready to make such a commitment,
then I need to know that soon.
I know that this letter must be a shock for you. I'm
in a bit of shock myself. Whatever your answer is, Jessie, I'll understand.

All my love,
Kate

Jessie's head fell back against the coconut stump. He
stared up into the hot blue Pacific sky with his mouth and
eyes open wide. Part of him wanted to jump off the ground
and start singing at the thought of marrying the most beau-

tiful woman he'd ever seen . . . but how? How could he possibly get back to New Caledonia? A baby! He sat up straight, his eyes looking toward the ocean but not seeing it.

"I'm a dad," he mumbled in disbelief. He fell back against the coconut stump with the empty gaze of a blind man.

"Trying to catch flies, Slate?"

Jessie closed his mouth. Broken Wing stood over him. "I'm a father," he mumbled numbly.

Charlie Rose walked up beside Broken Wing and frowned. "What's wrong with him?"

Broken Wing's brows pinched together as he examined Jessie suspiciously. "You been drinking!"

"No."

Broken Wing fell to his knees beside Jessie and sniffed like a hound dog on the trail. "Don't smell it."

"I haven't been drinking."

"You sure look funny, boy," Charlie Rose said accusingly.

Jessie handed Charlie Rose the letter. His eyes grew bigger with each line he read. Broken Wing snatched the letter out of Charlie's hand and read, muttering aloud in Navajo, sounding out the syllables.

"Well, one of you say something," Jessie said.

"No wonder you look drunk," Broken Wing said.

"What are you going to do, boy?" Charlie asked.

"I'm gonna have a baby."

"That's right," Charlie Rose said quietly as if he were unsure of the idea.

"Who's gonna be a dad?" a gruff voice asked from behind Jessie.

He turned to see the pitted face of Lopez looking down at him with his usual evil grin.

"I am," Jessie said.

Lopez laughed until he had to hold his hairy stomach. "You kill me, kid," he said, laughing and pointing. "You knock up your first one! You'd been better off hittin' the old clap shack, kid." Lopez chuckled.

"Well, what you gonna do, boy?" Charlie asked.

Lopez laughed his raspy, irritating laugh. "Tell her to get somebody to punch her real hard in the stomach!"

The men within hearing distance stared at him incredulously. Jessie clenched his fist, and his gray eyes narrowed.

"What kind of a person would kill a baby?"

Lopez looked pale. He glanced nervously at the faces of the squad, then back to Jessie. He gave a scoffing wave.

"Hey, I ain't that low, man! Just flappin' my gums. Can't anybody take a joke?"

Jessie turned away in disgust. "I have to get back to Nouméa," he said.

"Long swim," Broken Wing said.

Charlie Rose grinned. "Them Jap submarines will probably put a torpedo right up your butt."

"You read the letter. I can't let her be disgraced like that. Her father's a good Christian man. I have to get back!"

"Semper fi, Mac," Broken Wing said with a shrug.

"Well now, Wing, there might be one chance," Charlie said thoughtfully.

"The gunny," Broken Wing said.

"Yep."

"Yeah!" Jessie grabbed his letter from Broken Wing.

"Don't go gettin' your hopes up, boy."

"If anybody can help, the gunny can," Jessie said. "Know where he is?"

Broken Wing pointed back at the CP tent. Gunny O'Cleary was standing out front talking with Corporal DiCicca and Lieutenant Pierce.

"Forget something?" Broken Wing asked.

Jessie paused and faced the expressionless Indian. "What?"

"Old Gunny Polk is old Gunny O'Cleary's best friend."

"By golly," Charlie Rose said, "he's right, boy. You go spillin' the corn, and he might have you hung, and us, too, for helping you get her! Him and the gunny are close."

"He was my dad's friend, too."

"Something else," Broken Wing said.

"What else?" Jessie asked dejectedly.

"You get married to squaw, you are out of the Para-Marines."

"He's right, Jessie," Charlie Rose warned.

"Well, how can *you* be married, Broken Wing?"

"Lied."

"How can they not know?"

"Reservation marriage is not recorded on paper."

"Well, I'll lie, too!"

He turned away and walked over to the CP tent, trying to gather his words as he went. Lieutenant Pierce was on his way out as Jessie approached.

"Gunny, could I talk to you?"

"Wait a minute, Slate," Gunny O'Cleary said briskly. He turned to face Corporal DiCicca. "All right, you got what you need to know?"

"Fall out in battle gear at 0500."

"Affirmative. Now, go find Sergeant Rim and have him report to me now."

"Aye, aye, Gunny." DiCicca turned and headed toward the dirt road that led to Henderson Field.

Gunnery Sergeant O'Cleary faced Jessie. "What is it?"

"Well, uh, it's sort of embarrassing, Gunny."

"Out with it, Marine. I don't have time to chew pogey bait."

"Look, Gunny, I know how bad this is going to sound—"

"Sound off, Marine."

"Gunny, I have to get back to Nouméa."

"What are you flappin' your gums about, Slate?"

"I have to get back to New Caledonia, Gunny. You have to help me, just long enough to get a chaplain to marry us."

"What?" Lieutenant Pomper shouted as he came out of the CP tent. His face looked pale and angry. "I'll take care of this man, Gunnery Sergeant," he said through clenched teeth.

"Aye, aye, sir." O'Cleary saluted and walked away.

Pomper walked up to Jessie until their faces were inches apart. Jessie stiffened to attention. The lieutenant's dark eyes darted from one part of Jessie's face to another, then finally locked onto Jessie's eyes.

"Look, Lieutenant, I know you got a thing for Kate—"

"Shut up! You ain't going to Nouméa, Marine; you're going to combat." Pomper tried to smile. "You will be saddled up and standing in formation on the beach in ten minutes! Is that clear?" he shouted.

"Yes, sir!" Jessie said through clenched teeth. He saluted and held it until Pomper replied, then did a sharp about-face and jogged back to his tent.

The others were already packing their gear when Jessie pushed through the tent flap. Broken Wing finished tying his poncho onto his pack and looked up at Jessie.

"Gunny spared your life. He's a good man."

Someone entered the tent behind Jessie.

"You spoke too soon," Sam Hill mumbled under his breath.

Jessie turned and found himself six inches from the penetrating eyes of Gunny O'Cleary. The gunny glanced around the tent.

"You men leave us alone."

"Aye, aye, Gunny," the three said in unison. They dropped what they were doing and left the tent without another word spoken.

Jessie wanted desperately to go with the others. He stared into the old salt's hard eyes and knew that his explanation had better be good.

"Is Kate pregnant?"

"Yes, sir. We are getting married, sir."

"My first instinct is not good news for you, Slate."

"I know, sir. I wouldn't blame you if you decked me, sir, but I love her and she loves me."

"If you don't do right by her . . ."

Broken Wing stuck his broad face through the tent flap. "Gunny O'Cleary."

"What do you want?" O'Cleary snapped without taking his penetrating stare off Jessie.

"We are boarding in a minute, and the men have to see you right now, sir."

"In a minute."

"Aye, aye, sir." Broken Wing closed the flap.

The old salt stepped closer to Jessie. "Nouméa is out of the question, Slate. At least until this landing is over."

"Yes, sir," Jessie answered as he straightened to attention.

"Gunny Polk saved my life in the Great War. Kate is very . . . she means the world . . . belay that! You gonna do right, Marine."

"Yes, sir."

"See that you do, and you better not get killed till you do what's right!"

The old salt grunted, turned, and stepped outside. Jessie followed the gunny to where the first squad stood in a huddle. Most of the men were saddled up in full gear and ready to board.

"No way, stupid!" Lopez shouted.

"What do you know about it, Lopez?" LaBeau barked back.

Lopez pointed at a magazine that Jack Ellinwood and Gray Cloud were studying while Stukowski read over their shoulders.

"Right in that issue, LaBeau. These two French guys imported the heads from England, glass eyes from the Nazis—"

"Get the beans out of your brain, Lopez," LaBeau shouted. "They didn't have Nazis in 1867."

"Says the heads were made of English wax," Jack Ellinwood mumbled as he continued studying the magazine over Lopez's shoulder.

"Listen to this," Stukowski said. He began reading aloud. "In 1862 Monsieur Jumeau saw French kids playing with German-made dolls and decided to undertake—"

"What's all the skylarking out here!" Gunny O'Cleary shouted. "And who stole my *Hobbies* magazine?"

Oglethorpe stepped forward. "I purchased it by mail, Gunnery Sergeant."

"You?"

Charlie Rose nudged Corporal DiCicca as he stepped forward with a green package under his arm. "We got you a couple of presents here, Gunny." He handed the package to Gunny O'Cleary.

"Yeah, for the little girl," Lopez said.

Gunny O'Cleary looked at Lopez as if he had never seen him before. Lopez shrugged and snatched the *Hobbies* magazine away from Ellinwood.

"This is the one that the squad chipped in on," Corporal DiCicca said as he handed the gunny a parcel wrapped with string and newspaper.

"I got this one here from a little ol' shop in Nouméa," Charlie Rose said.

Corporal DiCicca pointed at the other package. "We ordered that one, Gunny."

"Yeah, all the way from Boston," big Stukowski said proudly.

"It's a Yankee doll, Gunny, but it looks nice," LaBeau said with a shrug.

"It's a German doll, actually. Probably made in Sonne-berg," Oglethorpe said matter-of-factly.

Gunny O'Cleary's eyes widened with a newfound excitement.

"Papier-mâché head?" he asked as he sat down in the dirt and began unwrapping.

The squad huddled around the gunny. Each man tried to get a good view of his face to catch the expression when he first saw the doll.

O'Cleary gently lifted the doll out of the box. "Goodness, Marines! What a great find!"

"Nineteenth century, right, Gunny?" Stukowski asked.

"Oh, yes. See this blue dress and lace shirt? That dates it. They're in perfect condition."

"Open the other one, Gunny," Jack Ellinwood said.

O'Cleary nodded and gently laid the first doll back in the box. He tore off the green paper and opened the box lid.

"It's French, all right."

"Think your girl will like 'em, Gunny?" Gray Cloud asked.

Gunnery Sergeant O'Cleary swallowed hard. The age lines around his eyes seemed to deepen as he gathered up the two boxes. He cleared his throat as he stood up.

"Thank you, men. I'm real grateful. Now, let's police up this area before we go aboard." With that, Gunny O'Cleary turned and walked away.

Corporal DiCicca grabbed up a piece of green wrapping paper. "Knock off the skylarking! You heard the sergeant: Let's get this area policed up."

"What do you think, Corporal?" Stukowski asked. "Think he liked 'em?"

Short and stocky Ronnie Garland shoved Stukowski from behind. "Sure he liked 'em, you dope!"

"Yeah," Lopez chimed in, "that old salt ain't gonna stand here and get all teary-eyed."

"He did start to look a little shaky, didn't he?" Ellinwood said with a smile.

"You better not let him hear you say that," Corporal Di-Cicca said.

"All right! Saddle up!"

A few hours later the parachutists became part of the Northern Landing Force. No one knew what that meant or where the convoy would bring them, but an air of excitement and fear filled the LCI as the big landing craft slid out into the Slot and zigzagged past the Russell Islands. A small sleek destroyer led the way, weaving back and forth like an impatient watchdog as the plodding convoy of twelve LCIs and three large LSTs tried to keep up. Three other destroyers guarded the flanks and rear, but every man on board those ships knew that nothing could stop a torpedo once it had been fired. Jessie felt sick but knew it wasn't the rocking of the boat that had caused it this time. Anxiety over Kate and her father mixed with curious thoughts of death and the long-awaited chance to avenge his father.

The late afternoon crawled nervously by, filled with scuttlebutt. Everyone had an idea where the landing would be, and no two ideas matched. Anxious crap games formed in every available corner of the ship. The rasping of whetstones and metal against metal was constant as Marines turned K-bar knives and bayonets into razors. Weapons were field-stripped and cleaned and stripped again. Old letters were pulled out of packs and reread while some Marines wrote home, each wondering if it would be the last letter he would ever write.

The hot windless day dissolved into a steamy sweat-soaked night. A brilliant moon appeared in the cloudless sky, lighting the way of the convoy as it sailed up the Slot toward an island target that was still unknown.

At 0600 the convoy hove to off Barakoma as the tinny intercom blasted the captain's order: "Stand by the landing party!"

Jessie's stomach knotted. He jumped out of his rack. The faces around him looked terrified. Others had a dull resigned stare, as if they had already accepted the inevitable.

The Klaxon sounded. Nervous Marines flinched.

"All hands on deck!"

"You heard it! Saddle up!" Gunny O'Cleary barked. "First Platoon! You leave anything and it's history! Ain't no lookin' back now, Marines!"

Just over two hundred Marines moved above deck. Jessie's heart pounded with adrenaline as he scanned the ocean around him. Off the starboard bow, Navy destroyers had set up a defensive screen in the shape of a half-moon. Inside the half-moon sat the three big LSTs.

"Goin' in," Broken Wing mumbled.

Jessie followed Wing's stare to a small green mountainous island straight ahead. The mountain peaks were shrouded by puffy early morning clouds. The high-pitched drone of fighter planes pulled every eye skyward.

"Those are ours, men!" Lieutenant Pierce shouted. "From Munda airfield! First Platoon gather 'round!"

Lieutenant Pierce dropped one knee to the metal planking and unfolded a map from a transparent protective plastic cover. The men huddled around.

"This little jewel up ahead is the island of Vella Lavella."

"You sure those planes are ours, sir?" a nervous voice asked.

"Yeah, for now, but you can bet the Nips are on their way. If you end up in the water, drop your pack and canteens!"

The lieutenant pointed at the southeast tip of the gourd-shaped island on the map. "This is Barakoma. After the beach is secured, the Para-Marines and the Army 2nd BN 35th Infantry will make a two-pronged attack inland. See this grid area here? That's our objective."

"For an airstrip?" Gunny asked.

"Probably, Gunny."

A squadron of black corsairs roared by overhead.

"God! This is great!" Jessie was so startled by his own outburst that for an instant he looked around to see if someone else had said it.

"Great?" a voice grumbled from the packed-in Marines.

"Yeah, Semper fi, Randolph," another Marine chimed in.

"Hey, fellas, we got Randolph Scott over here!"

Jessie reddened and tried to shrink down. The ship's intercom crackled.

"Stand by the landing party!"

Jessie shivered as a rush of adrenaline shot through his system. He felt himself tremble and wondered if he was scared or just excited.

It seemed to take forever for the first of the big landing craft to finally slide up onto a narrow two-hundred-foot stretch of white sand that bordered the green jungle coastline of Vella Lavella. The deck of the LCI vibrated as the ship's engines shifted into reverse to keep the bow from lodging too deeply into the soft sandy beach.

Lieutenant Pierce tugged nervously at his ear as he searched the morning sky.

"Your men ready, Gunny?"

"Yes, sir."

"How soon do you think the Nips will be here?"

Gunny O'Cleary pulled his unlit cigar out of his mouth and glanced seaward. The destroyers were forming a defensive screen about a mile out.

"Hard to say, sir. If their planes are coming from Rabaul . . ."

"That's the guess at HQ."

"Well, that's about 380 miles northeast."

Pierce tugged on his ear. "Of course, if they spotted us coming up the Slot last night . . ."

"I think they would have hit us about an hour ago if they had, Lieutenant."

"You're probably right."

A crackle over the ship's intercom preceded the command.

"Prepare to disembark!"

"Move it! First Platoon! Down the port-side gangway! Come on! This ain't no Sunday walk with your girl!"

Each LCI had two gangways, port and starboard, for unloading troops, but it was still painfully slow for everyone involved. All eyes searched the sky for incoming planes. Within minutes after the landing, the narrow stretch of white sand was cluttered with the tools of war. Sergeant Rim jumped onto the beach just ahead of Lieutenant Pierce. Pierce pointed inland and shouted, "Move it! Set up a defensive line around the beachhead!"

Sergeant Rim twirled around and barked at the men already on the beach. "You heard the word! Move it!" The beach echoed with voices.

"We got three LCIs hung up on a coral reef!" someone on the beach shouted.

"As soon as you get a bulldozer off that LST, tell the Seabees to bulldoze up a coral ramp to those LCIs."

"We got that wire laid over to the 35th, Jeff!"

"Go tell the old man."

"Get those 90-mm guns set up!"

"The Fourth Defense Battalion's got sixteen .50-caliber and sixteen .30's ready to go!"

"The 40-mm's and the eight 20-mm's are being dug in now."

"Lieutenant Pierce!"

"Yes, sir."

"Take your platoon out to those LCIs and help get 'em unloaded before the Japs find out we're here!"

"Aye, aye, sir."

"They're sitting ducks out on those bloody reefs! Who in God's Marine Corps reconned this landing site?"

Gunny O'Cleary kicked at a piece of coral. "Friggin' Army, sir."

"Might be right, Gunny."

For an hour and a half most of the First Battalion formed a human conveyor belt unloading supplies from ship to shore. Three big LSTs beached and began to unload quickly. As the last of the twelve LCIs retracted from the beach and the coral reef thirty yards offshore, the blue morning sky just beyond the convoy suddenly erupted into a series of frantic dogfights. Aircraft spotters from vantage points farther up the beach began to shout.

"Air raid! Air raid!"

Six Japanese Betty bombers and eleven fighters broke through the American combat air patrol. The Marines unloading the ships dropped everything and ran for the cover of the jungle. Jessie and Charlie Rose stopped at the jungle's edge and stood staring into the sky, mesmerized. Jap planes grew larger, and the red rising sun painted on their wings became clearly visible. Men on the beach scrambled for cover as the big Marine Corps 90-mm antiaircraft guns opened fire. Black puffs from the 90's began appearing all around the incoming bombers. A Jap Zero roared in low with a strafing run.

Jessie's vision blurred as his helmet twisted on his head from a hard angry slap.

"Get down, boot!" Gunny O'Cleary screamed as he ran toward a fallen coconut tree.

Jessie instinctively followed. He dived over the tree and took aim at the sky. Charlie Rose dived behind a tree ten feet to Jessie's left.

Another banana-yellow Japanese fighter screamed in at treetop level. Jessie and every other man on the beach opened fire, but the plane didn't fall.

"This rifle's no good! I hit that plane, Gunny!"

"I hear ya, kid," the old salt said sarcastically.

"I did!"

"The Johnson's a fine weapon, Marine. You just thank God you aren't stuck with a Reising gun. You hit that Zero in the right spot 'n' she'll drop like a fat woman on ice."

"Air raid!"

Two more fighters banked in toward the beach. A ripping explosion erupted from the shoreline, spraying water, sand, and coral in a fifty-meter radius. An enemy plane dived straight down at one of the retiring LCIs. A fifty-pound bomb exploded just aft of the fleeing landing craft. The destroyers opened fire from the distance, and their antiaircraft tracers filled the blue sky like crisscrossing shooting stars. Still the planes came on. The beach erupted with every available weapon firing at three dive-bombers that had fallen into a screaming descent toward the nearly defenseless LCIs. A .50-caliber machine gun opened fire from a clump of coconut palms twenty yards to Jessie's right.

"Look out!" someone screamed from a 40-mm gun crew ten yards to Jessie's left. The gun swung and opened fire at a Jap Zero closing in fast. The Jap plane released a bomb and pulled out of the dive two hundred feet above the ship. The bomb exploded fifteen yards off the starboard side. Shrapnel clanged off the hull. A bluejacket on the bridge tumbled to the main deck like a limp doll.

Jessie opened fire with his Johnson automatic, but again, all the weapons on the beach seemed useless against bombers and fighters.

"Zekes! From the south! Zekes!"

Jessie turned his head as the wind from a roaring fighter plane slapped against his sweaty face. A fighter plane ripped by in a silver blur, both guns blazing. The .50-caliber on Jessie's right opened up. An earthshaking explosion covered Jessie and Gunny O'Cleary with sand and debris. Jessie lifted his face from the sand and looked right. The .50-caliber was silent. Two Marines lay sprawled outside the shallow machine gun emplacement. One body was jammed between two burning palm trees. It had no head. An eerie silence engulfed the beach, interrupted only by the crackling of burning fires. Patches of black smoke floated out to sea.

The enemy planes grew smaller and smaller until they were specks on the horizon.

"Corpsman!" a man shouted from somewhere down the beach.

The silence was broken. The beach suddenly blossomed with activity. Officers and sergeants began shouting.

"Move it! Move it!" Gunny O'Cleary's angry bellow brought Jessie to his feet. He brushed his hand across his face and spit out the gritty sand between his teeth.

"We got three LSTs to unload before they come back!"

"Gunny!" Lieutenant Pomper shouted as he ran toward them.

"Yes, sir!"

"Get your men ready. The LSTs are coming in with the rest of our gear. If we don't get some antiaircraft weapons set up, they'll be sittin' ducks out there!"

"So will we, Lieutenant," Gunny said.

Pomper stepped up to Jessie and shoved him toward the beach.

"What are you lookin' at, Slate? Get your butt out there and unload those LSTs."

Jessie stiffened and for an instant thought of decking the jerk, but the thought evaporated as quickly as it had developed. He turned and jogged back onto the beach. Within twenty minutes the first LST had nosed up to the shore. The big barn doors opened, and the ramp fell with a heavy splash. A company's worth of men again formed a human conveyor belt and began unloading. A few moments later the other two LSTs motored up to the beach.

"Get those 90's off first! We need the truck-mounted guns off now!"

Within the first half hour the vehicles were ashore, antiaircraft and truck-mounted guns were in position and manned, and the unloading and dispersal of bulk cargo were well under way. The destroyer screen, hull down on the horizon, bobbed up and down in the gentle swell. Jessie grabbed hold of a box of supplies and passed it on to the man beside him.

"Good to see ya, boy!" Charlie Rose took the box and passed it on.

"Charlie! God, was that a thrill!" Jessie yelled into the sky.

Charlie Rose paused, and two other Marines to his left leaned out of the line to see who was the madman making such a statement.

"I been worried 'bout ya, boy. I know I was right now."

"Where's Broken Wing?"

"He's back down the line."

"Anybody in First Platoon get hit?"

"Don't think so."

Small-arms fire erupted from the jungle-covered mountains to the north.

"Somebody's found 'em," a voice mumbled from down the line.

"Who's over there?" Jessie asked.

"I think that's where the New Zealand troops are supposed to be," a big blond Marine said.

"Zekes! We got Zekes attacking the destroyer screen!"

"All hands, man your guns!" The order blared from the LST's intercom as the Klaxon blasted out the warning.

Sailors rushed to their antiaircraft guns on the deck of the LST then relaxed to watch the show as the Jap planes dived and bombed and climbed into the bright blue sky, then dived again. Marines unloading the LSTs glanced curiously out to sea with every lull in the passing of supplies. It was like watching a newsreel back at the Victory moving picture house, Jessie thought.

Suddenly the buzzing flies over the destroyers seemed to gather into one group. They winged out east of the convoy. Almost immediately, twenty Zekes covering fifteen dive-bombers climbed and headed directly out of the sun for the beaches. Two big 90-mm guns opened fire at nearly the same instant from the jungle behind the beach. The gun crews aboard the three LSTs opened fire with a heavy and continuous barrage at the incoming Japanese planes. The heavy rattle of the 40-mm guns mixed with the automatic chatter of the .50-caliber and .30-caliber machine guns. Red tracer fire streaked out to meet the oncoming planes. A dark brown dive-bomber burst into flames and spiraled into the sea, but the others continued to bore in on the frantic men scattering over the beach.

"Incoming mail!" somebody shouted.

Men scrambled for shallow foxholes. Officers and noncoms screamed out commands as they shoved and waved

their troops to disperse from exposed positions. Jessie
dropped a box of C-rations into the surf and pushed Charlie
Rose as he ran past him.

"Charlie! This way!"

They ran for the cover of the fallen tree that had pro-
tected Jessie before.

Jessie struggled to unsling his rifle as he ran. His boondockers felt like lead weights in the sucking sand. He dived
over the fallen coconut tree and popped back up with his
rifle ready just as the first Zeke swept down over the beach
with guns blazing. Charlie dived over the fallen tree to Jessie's right. At the same moment Corporal DiCicca jumped
for cover to Jessie's left. Incoming bullets thudded into the
sand and whined off coconut trees.

"Hey, Phil!" Jessie shouted at Corporal DiCicca, and
pointed at an incoming plane.

The three Marines aimed and fired, but the dive-bomber
was already pulling up and away. The 40-mm gun opened
fire from their left. A ripping explosion covered Jessie, Di-
Cicca, and Charlie Rose with sand and palm fronds. Then
shrapnel smacked through the jungle behind them, and the
40-mm went silent. Spitting sand, Jessie peeked over the
fallen tree to see the damage. The three men of the gun crew
were lying near the big gun. One writhed in agony as blood
streamed from a large gash in his throat. He cried for someone to stop the bleeding. The other two lay side by side, motionless.

"Corpsman!" DiCicca shouted.

Little Doc Kuipers sprinted past them and slid in beside
the writhing Marine like a runner stealing second base. The
high-pitched whine of a dive-bomber's engine straining to
pull out of a dive turned Jessie's attention back to the sea
just as the deck of the LST 167 exploded in flames from a
five-hundred-pound bomb blast amidships. Four Zekes
climbed high above the beach, then lazily banked out over
the water, one at a time, perfectly spaced. The first one
swept in low toward the burning LST as men jumped over-
board. Jessie sprang to his feet and ran toward the 40-mm
gun.

"Phil! Charlie!"

"You know how to fire a 40-millimeter?" DiCicca yelled.

"No!"

Jessie dropped his rifle beside the big antiaircraft gun and climbed into the gunner's seat while DiCicca pulled a dead Marine out of the elevation seat, then jumped in and began cranking the barrel toward the sky above the LST. The lead Jap plane sent a hail of machine gun fire across the stern of the burning LST.

"Charlie! Shove in one of those big clips!" Jessie hollered as he took aim through a long, round sight attached to a metal bar that crossed the barrel near the base. The second Zeke of the four-plane formation swept down for a strafing run on the crippled LST. Jessie opened fire. He missed. A third Zeke dropped down low over the water and sent a stream of machine gun fire across the bow of the burning ship, then banked right, showing its belly for just an instant before climbing away. Jessie caught the underbelly in the cross hairs of the 40-mm sight and opened fire. The *boom, boom, boom* of the big gun vibrated through Jessie from his helmet to his boots. A yellow flash of fire exploded from the belly of the Zeke. The Jap plane climbed, then seemed to stall; smoke plumed from a fire underneath the cockpit. Suddenly the plane tumbled into the sea like a wounded dove.

"You hit him! You hit him!" Phil screamed.

"A hit! A hit!" Charlie Rose echoed.

Another Zeke swooped down on the burning LST. Phil cranked the 40-mm to the left. Jessie fired and missed. Suddenly ammunition on board the LST exploded, sending a shock wave of burning fuel and debris across the smoke-covered beach. Clouds of black acrid smoke hovered over the embattled landing party. Jessie coughed and gagged.

"There's our guys!" Phil shouted, and pointed into the sky over the convoy.

Two squadrons of twin-tailed P-38 Lightning fighter planes from Munda airfield began an attack on the enemy planes. A minute later a squadron of sixteen Army P-40's joined the battle, and within minutes the retreating Japs were swept from the sky in a running battle that finally disappeared in the eastern horizon. Someone slapped Jessie hard on the back. He spun in the gunner's chair.

Phil DiCicca's teeth looked white as chalk against his dark tan. "Great shootin', Slate!" he shouted.

"Thanks, Corporal."

"Where's Doc Kuipers and the wounded guys?" DiCicca asked as he looked around the area.

Charlie Rose pointed down the beach. "Him and Big Stu carried 'em down to where they're setting up the field med."

Corporal DiCicca nodded his approval. "That little corpsman is all right."

"Where in tarnation did you learn to shoot a 40-mm, boy?" Charlie Rose howled.

"Never learned," Jessie said, smiling.

"All right, the show's over!" Gunny O'Cleary bellowed.

Lieutenant Pomper ran by the 40-mm, then stopped when he saw Jessie.

"Saddle up! Let's get that ship unloaded!"

"Lieutenant!" Corporal DiCicca called.

"Let's get these men moving, Corporal."

"PFC Slate knocked down that Zeke, Lieutenant!"

"Get the wounded down to the field med, then get your men over there and form up a supply line before that ship blows up!"

"Aye, aye, sir."

Pomper turned and jogged toward another group of Marines. Phil turned to Jessie and shook his head.

"Pomper is one class-A jerk."

"Funny how everybody agrees on that," Jessie said.

"Slate!" Chris LaBeau shouted as he jogged up to the 40-mm gun emplacement.

"What's up, Chris?"

"Hey, did you shoot that Zeke down?"

"Well, I pulled the trigger, but Phil here and Charlie Rose helped man the gun."

"Hey, Phil, he ought to get a medal for that," LaBeau said.

"I agree, and I'm going to see the skipper about it after we get things settled."

Jessie waved them off. "Aw, come on, you guys."

The scuttlebutt had it that thirty-two men had been killed, but no one from the First Platoon had been lost. By nightfall the LCIs and LSTs had 4,600 troops and 2,300 pounds of supplies ashore. A defense line was formed around the beachhead, two men to a position. No one slept. Every bush took on the shape of a Jap soldier, and every sound seemed to tingle on the skin and race up the spine.

Jessie stared wide-eyed into the jungle night from his foxhole and played out every moment of that unbelievable day
over and over again, but it still did not feel real.

Broken Wing's chin rested on the stock of his Johnson
rifle. His eyes remained fixed on the jungle straight ahead.

"Wing," Jessie whispered.

"What?"

"This was the most exciting day of my life. I loved it. You
think I'm crazy?"

Broken Wing's eyes shifted so that he was looking suspiciously at Jessie out of the corner of his left eye, but his head
didn't move. "How did we ever lose war to white man?"

"Psst! Lollipop!" a voice whispered from Jessie's left.

"Licorice!" Jessie replied.

A moment later Gunny O'Cleary emerged from the darkness in a hunched-over run. He dropped onto his stomach
beside their shallow foxhole.

"Everything okay?"

"Yeah, Gunny. So far."

"You did real good today, Slate."

A rush of goose bumps and pride straightened Jessie's
spine.

"Thanks, Gunny. Gunny?"

"Yeah."

Jessie swallowed back a nervous lump in his throat, then
blurted out his question. "I have to get back to Nouméa.
Is there any way? Is there anything you can do?"

Gunny O'Cleary grimaced and rubbed the back of his
neck. "I'll see what I can do, but I don't think there's much
chance, Slate."

"I have to!"

"You better pray about it, son."

Jessie stared at the old salt in the blue-gray light of the
quarter moon and tried to think of a response but couldn't.
The gunny pushed up onto his knees and called to the next
position.

"Lollipop!"

A moment later a whispered reply came out of the darkness to Jessie's right.

"Licorice."

The gunny looked back at Jessie again. "Keep your mind

on business, Slate. And keep your ear sharp. The Japs have a real problem pronouncing the letter L."

"Perelli said most of 'em already pulled out by ship over to Kolombangara."

"Well, he was almost right this time. The Japs abandoned Kolombangara cuz we got 'em stranded there by taking Vella Lavella."

"What do you think?"

"Most of 'em were pulled off by ship, but there's bound to be some left."

He stood to a crouch and moved toward the next position. Jessie stared after him for a minute, then turned back to the dark jungle in front of him. Praying had never entered his mind. He wouldn't be sure how to go about it even if he wanted to. He tried to picture Kate as the restless night drifted by.

The first streaks of sunlight reached into the vast Pacific sky. Jessie felt a sense of relief at the sound of mess kits clinking together along the line. Soon the smell of coffee drifted by.

"Hey, how 'bout a spot of that joe," Jessie called out.

"Semper fi, Mac," fireplug Garland called back.

"Thanks for nothing, Garland." Jessie pulled a C-ration box out of his pack. He opened a can and dumped out three hardtack biscuits, two pieces of hard candy, one lump of sugar, and soluble coffee.

"Hey, boy, how 'bout some company?"

Jessie looked up to see the smiling face of Charlie Rose.

"Have a sit, Charlie."

"You hear all that thunder last night?"

"Thunder?" Jessie asked.

Broken Wing shook his head in disgust. "His mind on tom-toms."

Charlie Rose smiled.

"Weren't thunder, boy. Big shoot-out last night."

"Really?"

"Yep. That's the 'butt, anyway. Our swabbies ran into a convoy headin' down the Slot toward us."

"Wow! I wonder . . ." Jessie stopped in midsentence. The sound of small-arms fire erupted from the south.

Charlie Rose whistled. "Somebody stepped in a pile of Nip!" he said.

A minute later a call echoed through the platoon. "First Platoon, parachutists! Saddle up!"

Jessie looked up at Charlie Rose. "This is it!"

"Jessie, if my time's up, will you write my mama back home and tell her something good?"

"That's no way to talk."

"Will ya? You're my best friend, and I wrote her all about you and that there beauty you got in Nouméa and everything there was to tell, so she'll know you, boy."

"Saddle up! Move it, Marines!" Sergeant Rim shouted as he ran by. His horseshoe-shaped scar had turned blue with the rush of blood to his head.

"What's up, Sarge?"

"Settin up a blockin' action for the New Zealanders. They found some Japs."

The platoon of Para-Marines pushed out through the thick jungle, then south for about four hundred yards toward the chatter of small-arms fire. Stray rounds smacked through the brush overhead as the platoon moved to cut off the Japanese escape route. The lead man paused and knelt down on one knee. Helmets began to turn as the word was passed back.

"Slate and Rose up."

"Slate and Rose up front."

Jessie turned to pass the word back to Charlie Rose, who was already hustling forward.

When they reached the front of the column, Lieutenant Pierce said something to Gunny O'Cleary, then stood up.

"I need runners. You two think you can remember the way back?"

"I think so, sir. The brush we beat down should show the way," Jessie said.

"That foot good enough to run, Slate?"

"I can do it, Gunny."

Lieutenant Pierce pointed. "I want you to go about three hundred yards back and then cut over to the beach so you can come up behind the New Zealanders, understand?"

Jessie blanched—the thought of just the two of them going back through the brush alone sounded crazy—but he didn't hesitate.

"Yes, sir."

"Yes, sir," Charlie Rose echoed.

"Good. Now, ask to speak to Colonel Tormey and tell him we have the blocking action set up fifty yards inland from the beach, which should be the Japs' route of escape if his men move forward. You got it?"

"Yes, sir."

"All right. Move out."

They turned and jogged back past the crouching column of Marines. The gunfire coming from the New Zealand positions seemed to be growing in intensity. Jessie recognized the steady rattle of a Jap Nambu machine gun; he'd heard it plenty during weapons training on New Caledonia. Their progress through the hot jungle brush was agonizingly slow. Finally, Jessie paused and turned back to Charlie Rose.

"Think we're behind the New Zealand line?"

"We got to be by now."

"All right. Let's head in toward the beach."

"Lead the way."

The jungle vegetation grew less dense as the ground grew sandier, until finally all that grew were tall, lean coconut palms. The ground was covered with rotting coconuts.

"Is that them down the beach there?" Charlie asked.

About fifty yards down the beach, men were moving back and forth carrying crates from a large tent.

"Got to be," Jessie said as he started running toward the tent.

Halfway there Jessie and Charlie Rose were shouted to a stop.

"Halt! Who goes there?" a deep voice bellowed from behind a small bunker of fallen coconut trees.

"We're Americans! Marines!" Charlie Rose shouted back.

"We got a message for Colonel Tormey!"

"You'll find him in the tent up ahead, mate! If he's still alive."

Jessie and Charlie exchanged nervous glances.

"How many Japs did you run into?" Jessie asked.

"Just a couple of stragglers. The main group is long gone."

"Thanks," Jessie said.

They ran past what appeared to be a supply tent. New

Zealand soldiers, wearing shorts, no shirts, and old World War I helmets, hustled in and out with crates of ammunition and C-rations. Another twenty yards away, a second tent nestled in a stand of coconut palms. There was a red cross on the roof of the tent. They ran up, and Jessie peeked in. There were two rows of cots, all but three of which were empty. A thin, long-faced medic looked up from an unconscious man with a blood-soaked bandage around his head. As he wiped sweat from his sunburned face, the medic noticed Jessie.

"What do you want, Yank?"

"I have a message for Colonel Tormey."

The medic looked down at the unconscious man. "This is Colonel Tormey. He's pretty bad off. We got a PBY coming in for him in a jiff. If we can get him to Nouméa in time, he might . . ." The medic's voice trailed off.

"Who's in command?"

"Honestly don't know, mate." He turned toward another medic working on a wounded man near the back of the tent. "Hey, Jim, you handle it a bit while I run the Yank over to HQ."

The other man gave a nod.

The medic came outside, where Charlie Rose was waiting.

"Let's jog on over there, mates."

"I'll follow, but running is getting harder every minute."

"Been runnin' a ways, have you?"

"It's not the distance so much. It's this trench foot I got."

"Yes, nasty stuff, that. Better let me take a look before you set off."

"I been tellin' the boy it's gettin worse," Charlie Rose said. He scrunched up his nose. "Stinks like tarnation, too!"

"HQ is this way, gentlemen," the medic said as he started off down a well-trodden path that led through the coconut grove. Jessie started hobbling along behind him. The medic glanced over his shoulder after a few steps and stopped.

"Say, Yanks, you both look a bit worn. Why don't you sit still, and I'll see what's what."

Jessie looked at Charlie Rose. "Sounds good to me. It feels like I'm walking on a nail."

"We'll just have a sit right over here in the shade."

"Right. Be back in a jiff, and I'll take a look at that foot."

The medic jogged away. Jessie and Charlie Rose sat under a coconut palm and leaned against the trunk.

"Jessie?"

"Yeah."

"You hear where that PBY is taking that wounded colonel?"

"Base hospital back at the Canal, I guess."

"Nope."

"New Hebrides?"

"Nope. Nouméa."

Jessie sat up straight and grimaced.

"What are you thinkin', boy?"

"I'm thinking I'd give anything in this world to be on that plane when it takes off."

Charlie grinned. "Then you're gonna be on that plane, boy!"

"Real funny, Charlie."

Charlie Rose removed his helmet and scratched the back of his neck. "You can't let the kid be born without a name, Jessie. It ain't right."

Jessie slammed his helmet to the ground. "You don't think I know that? My insides are rotting out over it!"

"I know, boy. I been watching. That's why you got to get on that PBY."

Jessie forced a smile and gave Charlie a pat on the shoulder. "Shoot, Charlie Rose, you can't just walk away from the war. I mean, look at all the trouble everybody went to just to get us here."

"If you was wounded, you could get on that plane." Charlie Rose's words were slow and deliberate.

"That's a fact."

Jessie faced Charlie.

Charlie scratched the back of his head. "Well, there is one chance."

"What?"

"Well . . ."

"Well what?"

"Well, if that there foot of yours is real bad, you just might get on that plane."

Jessie stared down at his boot for a moment.

"Let's see it. That cobber wants to see it, anyway."

Jessie shrugged and unstrapped his legging. He unlaced

his boot and pulled the boot and sock off. Skin on the instep of his foot was cracked and bleeding slightly. The infection was spreading over the bottom.

"Looks ugly, boy, but it ain't ugly enough."

Jessie's shoulders sagged.

"Yeah. You're right."

"Let's think," Charlie Rose said thoughtfully.

Jessie sat up straight with his bad left foot crossed over his right thigh.

"Jessie! You got any packs of that powdered mustard?"

"Yeah."

"Give me a pack."

Charlie Rose pulled a canteen off his cartridge belt and took the small brown pack of powdered mustard from Jessie. He picked up half of a coconut shell and poured in a little water from his canteen, then mixed in the powdered mustard.

"What are you doing?"

"Making pus."

Jessie laughed. "You're crazy, Charlie! I can't do that."

"Now, look here, Jessie, that foot of yours is a mess, boy. And you heard that cobber down the beach there. There ain't fifty Japs on this whole island."

"That's no different than deserting. I'd rather get killed than be called a deserter, Charlie."

"Of course it ain't desertin'! You're just having your foot tended to."

"I don't know, Charlie."

"Look here, Jessie. Vella Lavella is already secured. There's plenty of fightin' up ahead all the way to Tokyo. And you can't let a little baby come into this world a bastard. It ain't right."

Jessie looked at the mustard for what felt like a long time. "Think it'll work?"

"Nope."

"Why not? It looks just like pus."

"Yep, but that medic needs to think it's spreading up your leg and into the bloodstream or something bad like that."

Charlie smeared on the mustard with his K-bar knife.

Jessie flinched.

"Hurt?"

"Yeah."

"I'm going to nick it a bit more with the knife so it mixes with blood," Charlie Rose said.

Jessie gritted his teeth. Charlie Rose poked the foot with the tip of his blade until it bled.

"Looks darn near right," Charlie Rose said. "That is a sick-lookin' yellow color, ain't it?"

"Looks sick to me," Jessie said. "Give me that coconut beside you."

"Here," Charlie said. "My uncle used to date an old gal that got pimples about that color."

Jessie laughed. "Charlie Rose. I've never met anybody like you."

"I think right kindly of you, too, boy. You are my best dang friend in the whole dang world."

Jessie paused and looked the stocky Kentuckian in the eye. Charlie's face was as sincere as his words.

"Thank you, Charlie. I feel the same about you."

"Yep. I knew that."

Charlie took the partially rotted coconut and split it with his K-bar. He pulled Jessie's trouser leg up and poured the fermented juice onto Jessie's calf and foot, then spread it around with his hands.

"There. What do you think?"

"Looks awful."

Charlie Rose studied Jessie's calf carefully for a few moments, then gave an agreeable grunt. "The skin does look sort of yeller, don't it?"

Jessie pulled on his sock. "It hurts, too," he said as he laced up his boot.

"Looks like it."

"If I do get to Nouméa, I won't stay any longer than it takes a chaplain to marry us. I promise."

"Oh, I know that, boy. Don't you think I know you by now?"

The sound of boots running toward them turned Jessie's head. The medic and another New Zealander, carrying an M1 Garand, ran toward them. The second man was covered with dirt.

"That's the Yanks there, Captain," the medic said as he came to a stop in front of Jessie and Charlie Rose.

The two Marines jumped to their feet and began to salute.

"No, no, Yanks. Still too close to the shooting for a salute," the captain said with a smile.

"Yes, sir," Jessie said.

"What's the message?"

"The First Platoon of the Para-Marines have set up a blocking action about two hundred fifty yards southeast. Lieutenant Pierce says that should be the Japs' route of escape if you move forward on 'em, sir."

"That's fast. You boys didn't waste a bloody minute. This will be fine. Get these Jap stragglers cleaned out, and the island should be quite tidy."

"Plane coming in!" a man shouted from down the beach.

"That'll be the PBY, sir," the medic said.

Charlie nudged Jessie. Jessie swallowed back a lump in his throat and forced out the words, "Think you could look at this, Doc?"

"Oh, your foot. Yes, let me take a quick look."

Jessie stooped to unlace his legging and boot.

The captain squatted and began to draw with his finger in the sand. "All right, take this message back to your lieutenant, Marines. Most of the Nips pulled out by ship before we got here. This is just a delaying action. Here's the waterline along the beach. We shall move about fifty yards down. At that point the terrain turns into swamp, so they will probably break left and run right into your men here." He drew an X in the sand as he glanced at Jessie's foot. The captain frowned. "I say, Yank. That is a very bad foot you have there."

"Yes, sir."

The medic lifted Jessie's foot. "This man needs treatment, Captain. He might lose this foot if something isn't done soon."

"How does it feel, Marine?"

"It hurts, sir."

"Boy, it looks awful!" Charlie Rose sounded aghast. "Maybe you should put Jessie here on that PBY, too, sir."

"Medic."

"Yes, sir."

"If there's room on that PBY, we better put this man aboard."

Charlie coughed and held his chest as the captain turned to him.

"You'll have to go it alone, Yank, unless you'd like me to send one of my men back with you."

"No, sir, I'll be fine. We didn't see a sign of a Jap on the way over."

"Very good. Well, off with you, then. Godspeed. Just let your lieutenant know that your man here was evacuated back to a base hospital at Nouméa. Let him know that our medic deemed it appropriate."

"Yes, sir."

Charlie Rose knelt down beside Jessie and slapped him on the back. "I dang sure wish you good luck, Jessie. And Kate, too. You give her a big sloppy one for old Charlie Rose."

"I will, Charlie, and you tell Broken Wing and the guys I'll get back as quick as possible."

Charlie Rose stood up. He winked and gave Jessie a thumbs-up then turned and jogged away.

# CHAPTER SEVEN

THE COLONEL DIDN'T MAKE IT. HE DIED THREE hours outside of New Caledonia. When the PBY taxied to a stop at Tontura airstrip, about fifty miles from Nouméa, two military ambulances were waiting for the wounded New Zealanders, who were helped out of the plane first. The body of the colonel went next, and Jessie was the last to leave.

One ambulance was already pulling away when Jessie climbed down from the open hatch of the PBY. Two Army medics pushed a stretcher with the New Zealand colonel's body into the back of the ambulance and turned to Jessie as he limped toward them.

"Guess I'm riding with you," he said.

One of the medics, a tall, thin guy with glasses, looked at Jessie. "American?"

"Yes. First Para-Marine Regiment."

The medic raised his eyebrows. "Para-Marine. I heard about you guys."

The other medic, a short, fat kid with a bad complexion, scratched the back of his neck and closed one eye. "They don't put Marines in the 29th."

He tugged up on his wrinkled trousers. What a slob, Jessie thought. Marines in combat looked more squared away than those two Army clowns did in their dress khakis. Nevertheless, there was something about them he was beginning to like.

"Guess you're right about that, Arvis," the first medic said in a slow Down East accent.

"What are we going to do with him?"

"Better take him to that little Navy hospital in Nouméa."

"Yeah!" Jessie blurted. "That would be perfect!"

"Hop in front, Marine," the short fat guy said with a yellow-toothed grin.

"Yes, the fella in the back is real dead company," the tall, thin New Englander said with a chuckle.

"They call us Stan and Ollie," the fat guy said.

The tall, thin one nodded. "Yes, but our real names are Bobby and Arvis. I'm Bobby Alcorn. This is Arvis Rilly."

"I'm Jessie Slate," came the reply, along with a friendly grin.

The drive to the U.S. Army 29th General Hospital was longer than Jessie thought it would be. The 29th was ten miles outside Nouméa. It had over a thousand beds and five hundred personnel, but it was all Army. Arvis and Bobby dropped off the body of the New Zealand colonel and got permission to drive Jessie the ten miles to a small naval dispensary serving as a hospital for Marines just inside the city limits of Nouméa.

Jessie closed the door of the ambulance. "Thanks for the ride, fellas."

Arvis pointed at himself with his chubby finger. "Entirely our pleasure, Jessie."

"Look, I know you have to get back to the 29th, but do you think you could swing by La Rue sans Issue café?"

"What?" Bobby shouted.

"La Rue sans Issue?" Arvis asked.

"At the end of the Avenue du Marechal Foch?"

"Yeah, that's the place."

Arvis and Bobby looked at each other with openmouthed stares, then turned their stares back to Jessie. Arvis cleared his throat.

"Your wife to be works there?"

"She sure does! Her dad owns it. Her name is Kate."

"And your Kate, does she have long auburn hair?" Bobby asked.

"And a body like Jean Harlow?" Arvis added.

Jessie grinned. "Yep, that's her. You've seen her?"

Arvis rolled his eyes. Bobby moaned.

"We drive into Nouméa at least once or twice each week just to stare at her." Bobby said.

Arvis flipped on the siren switch. "We'll let her know

you're here, Jessie!" he yelled as they peeled away from the dispensary.

The thought of those two clowns wheeling up to the café with the siren blasting kept Jessie chuckling until the first needle full of penicillin was pumped into the arch of his right foot, which by now was so irritated from the dried mustard that it had actually gotten much worse. Next came what was to be a twice-a-day scrubbing with a stiff wire brush to remove dead skin and inflict pain. Jessie showered and shaved. A big Navy corpsman issued him a pair of blue hospital pajamas and a hospital bed at the very end of a long ward with two rows of occupied beds. Jessie maneuvered his bandaged foot so that the sheet wouldn't be tight around it, and he lay back with a sigh, but before his head hit the pillow, a loud howl echoed through the hospital ward. A series of shrill whistles issued from the nurses' station. Every Marine who could sit up in bed was up and whistling. Kate stood at the nurse's desk, wearing a light blue linen dress and white high heels. Jessie could feel his heart thump all the way to his throat.

"Wow!" a thin-faced Marine across the aisle groaned.

"Gang way!" a red-haired Marine said. "She's coming this way."

Kate's beautiful face blushed as she walked down the aisle of gawking men. Each step brought uncontrolled moans as she passed by. Her bright blue eyes searched the ward until she found Jessie. Their eyes locked, and for a moment it felt as if they were alone together.

The red-haired Marine in the bed to Jessie's right followed Kate's stare. "You lucky stiff," he said sadly.

Kate rushed toward Jessie. She sat on the bed beside him and kissed his eyes, nose, forehead, and face. The catcalls turned to groans and then boos, and somebody threw a pillow that went wide of the mark. Jessie giggled through a hundred kisses, and finally they quietly embraced.

"Think you'll like being Mrs. Slate?"

Kate loosened her hug on Jessie's broad shoulders and sat up straight. She brushed away tears and kissed him again. "More than anything in the world."

"How did you get here so quick?"

"Those funny ambulance drivers insisted on giving me a ride."

"Where's your dad?"

"He's up at the mine."

"Any more trouble with that shipment?"

"Oh, no. The Tonkinese workers are all back at the mine every day since you and your friends convinced the Frenchmen to leave Pop alone."

"That's good."

"What should we do first, Jessie? About getting married, I mean."

"I guess we need to contact the Camp St. Louis chaplain and whoever is the commanding officer."

"Gee, that's going to be difficult for me. Dad's truck is broken down."

"Are Bobby and Arvis still here?"

"Yes. They're parked outside waiting to give me a ride back to the café."

"Good! Those two would go AWOL just to get to stare at your legs a little more."

Kate blushed and put her palm over Jessie's eyes.

"I can see one thing for sure already, Mr. Slate, if I'm ever going to get you to look me in the eyes instead of the thighs, I'll have to watch what I wear."

"Oh, no you don't, Mrs. Slate. This is gonna be one marriage where the wife keeps looking pretty even after you say 'I do.' "

Kate smiled and kissed Jessie. "I promise."

"I love you," he whispered.

"I love you, too, Jessie."

"Look, I don't want you to go, honey, but if we're going to get all the paperwork done, we better get started right away. I won't get to stay here very long. As soon as this trench foot is cleared up, the Corps has plans for me."

"Is the foot very bad?"

"It'll be okay. Now, go grab Bobby and Arvis and tell 'em our problem."

Kate kissed Jessie again, said good-bye, and left the ward to a chorus of whistles and howls. Jessie fell back against his pillow with what he knew was the most contented grin in the entire South Pacific.

The base chaplain was an old Marine who had known Gunnery Sergeant Jeremiah Polk back in the Great War.

His name was Major Rex Lewis, and he went above and beyond the call of duty to take care of all the necessary paperwork. The legalities were no real problem, as Kate was an
American citizen, but time was the enemy. Each day, the
foot looked healthier and the war got closer. After nine
days, with the foot nearly healed and time running out,
Chaplain Lewis, Kate, and Jeremiah walked into the small
hospital ward together.

Kate cupped her hands around her mouth and shouted
to Jessie at the opposite end of the ward. "Hey, good lookin'!
Wanna get married today?"

Jessie's eyes opened wide. The other patients howled, and
Jessie ducked three flying pillows that were quickly followed
by a dozen good-natured insults.

"Well," Kate called across the room again. "Let's hear
it in front of witnesses!" She put her hands on her hips and
pretended to be impatient. The howling Marines quieted.

"Gee, I don't know, lady. You got any money?" Jessie
shouted.

Another barrage of pillows and insults came flying toward Jessie. He held up both hands in surrender.

"All right! All right! Let's get married!"

Jessie climbed out of bed and met Kate in the middle of
the long room. There they embraced and kissed to the
cheers and jeers of the others. Jessie pulled away from the
long passionate kiss and stared into his girl's blue eyes.

"Where are we going to get married?"

"How about right here?" Kate said with a mischievous
grin.

"You're crazy, Kate. You mean now? Here?"

"We just talked to your commanding officer and the doctor, and you're shipping out in forty-eight hours."

Jessie's lips tightened. "I knew it had to be soon."

Jessie turned and looked back at Jeremiah, Chaplain
Lewis, and Captain Rowles, the Navy doctor who had been
treating him.

"Mr. Polk, Chaplain Lewis, we would like to get married
right now."

"Right here," Kate added.

The chaplain's eyebrows lifted. Jeremiah scratched his
gray beard and smiled with approval. He turned to the Navy
doctor.

"Captain Rowles, is that okay by you?"

"Why not?"

"Rex?" Jeremiah asked.

The chaplain smiled at Jeremiah. "It is an honor to marry your daughter, Jeremiah."

A burly Marine with a bandage covering his left ear sat up in bed and shouted like a DI. "Hey, any of you monkeys in here got a set of dress blues that'll fit this guy?"

"Are you kiddin', Mac? Who'd have dress blues in their seabag?"

"I do," a sandy-haired Marine near the nurses' desk shouted.

"What are you doing with dress blues?" someone shouted.

"I wanted to wear 'em when we march through Tokyo, as if it's any of your business, Mac."

The burly Marine with the ear bandage climbed out of bed. "Come on, all you guys that walk. Get him pressed and dressed. Lets get this operation under way!"

Ten minutes later Jessie was escorted from the head by five pajama-clad Marines. The dress blues were tight but wearable, and the sparkle in Kate's eyes when she saw Jessie made him glad that he was wearing them.

"All right you men!" the Navy doctor shouted. "Let's form two lines for the bride to walk between so she can meet the groom with her father."

The pajama-clad Marines quickly formed two lines. The men who could stand were at attention, while the others sat up in their beds. Jessie and Chaplain Lewis stood at the far end of the ward while Jeremiah walked Kate down the aisle. Kate's tan skin looked even darker against her white cotton summer dress. Any bride in the most expensive wedding gown would look pale beside her, Jessie thought. Someone started humming the "Marines' Hymn." A moment later the entire room was humming along.

The vows were a blur. He hardly knew he was speaking as he repeated them. Then he found himself saying "I do" and kissing Kate. They turned and walked back down the aisle.

"By the way, Mrs. Slate, where are we going?"

Kate smiled and winked. "You'll see."

The traditional rice throwing was replaced by pillows and

laundry as Jessie and Kate made a dash past the nurses' station and out of the ward. In front of the hospital, the green Army ambulance was parked, covered with toilet paper. A string of C-ration cans was tied to the back. Bobby, the tall medic, stood at attention with the passenger door open. Arvis was at the wheel. Jessie laughed until his eyes teared.

"I don't believe this."

Kate ran for the ambulance, pulling Jessie by the hand. "Hurry up, honey! They have to get the car back to the Army hospital in an hour."

Kate and Jessie squeezed in next to Arvis. Bobby jumped in and slammed the door, and the Chevy station wagon squealed off, laying rubber for forty feet.

"Hey, watch it, Arvis!" Bobby whined.

"Don't worry about me, fellas. The foot's fine now," Jessie said.

"It ain't you I'm worried about," Bobby said.

"Where are we going?" Jessie asked.

"Dad's cabin, overlooking the harbor. Actually it's my cabin. I mean, I spend more time there than Dad ever has."

Bobby leaned out and reached past Jessie to tap Kate on the shoulder. "Excuse me, Kate," he said. "You said that you wanted us to pick you up at 0800 Thursday, right?"

"Right."

"Did you two bring any clothes for the next two days?" Arvis asked.

Kate stared straight ahead blushing silently.

The drive into the hills was quiet and beautiful. Near the rounded top of one steep hill Kate pointed Arvis onto a narrow dirt road that led back toward the ocean. At the end of the road was a small white wooden cabin that looked like a tiny church without a steeple. The front yard sloped downhill for twenty-five yards, then seemed to drop suddenly into the ocean beyond. The old lighthouse in the harbor below was clearly visible. Out back was a hand pump with a corrugated iron cover over it. Arvis pulled the ambulance up to the front of the house. The smell of freshly cut grass filled the air as the four got out of the car and stretched.

"This place looks like a painting, Kate," Jessie said.

"I agree," Arvis said.

"We better get back to the 29th before somebody finds out we're missing, Arvis," Bobby warned.

"I'll never be able to thank you guys for all of the help," Jessie said, and Kate gave them each a kiss in appreciation.

Bobby and Arvis got back into the ambulance and waved good-bye as they backed up and turned around.

"See ya Thursday!" Jessie shouted as they drove away.

Jessie opened one eye and nuzzled his face into a stale-smelling down pillow. Kate's lips felt cool and wet on his back. Jessie moaned.

"You have the cutest buns, Mr. Slate."

"Kate, let's always be like this."

"We might have to wear clothes sometime, honey."

"Not too often. No, I mean let's always touch and kiss. You know how old married people get, like the wife will only make love if the lights are out or they would never think of hugging and kissing in front of other people."

"It can never happen to us, Jessie."

Jessie rolled over onto his back and pulled Kate to him. They kissed and hugged. Jessie glanced around the small bedroom. A shelf ran around the entire room, about eighteen inches from the ceiling. The shelf was filled with dolls of every type and color.

"Do you collect dolls, Kate?"

"They're my babies. I love dolls. Pop O'Cleary sent me most of them."

"Gunny O'Cleary?"

"Yes."

"He sends dolls to you, too?"

"What do you mean, me, too?"

"I mean that he sends dolls to his daughter all the time. Matter of fact, half of the platoon are becoming experts on dolls."

"You mean you didn't know?"

"Know what?"

"Pop O'Cleary's daughter died of polio when he and Dad were fighting Sandino in Nicaragua."

"What? Really?"

"Yes. Dad said it nearly killed Pop O'Cleary."

"God, that's awful."

"Yes. And Mrs. O'Cleary got so sick after the little girl died that she just gave up."

"She's dead, too?"

"She died about six months later."

"So he's been sending the dolls to you all this time."

Kate nodded. "That's why he stayed in the Corps," she said. "It's the only family he had left."

"God, that's so sad. It's just hard to imagine. I mean, that old salt is leather and steel."

"Kiss me, Jessie. Promise me you won't die!" Kate began to cry.

"Die?"

"I hate this war."

"So do I, Kate."

"Don't go back. Let's just stay here until it's over."

"You know that you don't mean that, Kate. Even the thought of running out on guys like Charlie Rose and Gunny O'Cleary and that stupid Indian makes my blood run cold. I'd hate my own guts for the rest of my life, and you'd end up hating me, too."

"I know that you're right, but if I lose you, Jessie, I'll die."

"You won't lose me."

Jessie wiped away a tear and kissed her on the nose. She forced a smile.

"Have you thought of a name for your daughter?"

"My *son* will be named Sidney Mosedale Slate."

"Sidney Mosedale Slate?"

"Sounds distinguished, doesn't it?"

"You either dump that name right now or I put on clothes."

Jessie whistled. "Consider it officially dumped."

They laughed and hugged and cuddled until the last possible moment. And when that moment was finally upon them, they cried.

# CHAPTER EIGHT

Jessie and four other Marines returning to their units were put aboard a C-47 cargo plane bound for Henderson Field, Guadalcanal. They spent the night on the Canal, refueled, picked up some other stragglers rejoining various Army and Marine units on New Georgia and Vella Lavella, and flew out at 0600 the next morning. When the C-47 landed at Munda Point on New Georgia, a crusty old first sergeant climbed aboard and two Seabees jumped off. The first sergeant was big. Jessie scooted over to make room for the old man to sit on the floor of the plane beside him. The first sergeant nodded; dropped his pack, helmet, and M1 Garand; and sat back against the bulkhead beside Jessie. His head was shaved slick, and his big gray handlebar mustache was waxed. He glared at Jessie's boots.

"Are you a parachutist?" His voice was deep and strong like Gunnery Sergeant O'Cleary's.

"Yes, sir."

"You are a Marine first, PFC."

"Yes, sir."

"Then I suggest you unblouse those boots before somebody mistakes you for a soldier."

A freckle-faced Marine sitting against the opposite bulkhead snickered as Jessie pulled his trousers out of his boot tops.

"First Sergeant," the freckle-faced Marine said.

"Yes."

"What's up? Where do you think the next invasion will be?"

"Well, I'll tell you, Marine, that might be two or three different islands."

172

"What's your guess, sir?"

"I see it like this." The old salt sat up straight and pulled a grenade off his cartridge belt. He laid the grenade on the deck. "All right, this is Guadalcanal."

Jessie and most of the fifteen other soldiers and Marines huddled closer to hear him over the revving engines of the C-47.

"This is New Georgia and Vella Lavella," he said as he laid two more grenades in line with the first one. He pulled a few loose M1 rounds out of his pocket and spread them out facing the grenades.

"And let's say these are the rest of the Solomons—Isabel, Choiseul, and Bougainville. The water between 'em here is the Slot. Down here at the bottom is New Britain and the Jap stronghold, Rabaul. It sits on the shores of Simpson Harbor, the best anchorage in the South Pacific."

"Is that why the Japs made it their main base?" Jessie asked.

"That's part of it. It's 436 miles from Port Moresby on New Guinea and 570 miles from Guadalcanal. From Rabaul, the Japs controlled New Guinea, the Solomons, the Bismarck Archipelago, and the waters all around. Now the Japs are still in control of everything north of Vella Lavella to Rabaul. My guess is we bypass Bougainville and hit Rabaul."

"God! That sounds like a bad one, Sarge," the freckle-faced Marine said.

"Yeah, you can bet on it. Word is that it's going to be the deadliest beach landing so far. The raiders and Para-Marines will go in first, either as a decoy or as the spear-head."

By the time Jessie climbed out of the cargo bay of the big plane, he couldn't wait to spill the new scuttlebutt. He and four other Para-Marines from the Second Battalion who had been in the evac hospital on Guadalcanal jumped aboard a truck for a ride over to Ruravai, where most of the parachutists were deployed. Marines at the Barakoma airstrip told him that the island had been secured. The Japs had evacuated without much of a fight, but air raids came from Rabaul almost daily.

The truck ride over a dirt road through the jungle was exhilarating. The first stop was a small grass-hut village called Narowai that had become a fairly secure base for the Second Battalion.

A little farther up the road was Ruravai, where a group of dark-skinned children greeted the truck with waves and shouts. Just beyond the village the truck turned right onto a smaller road that led to the tent city of the First Battalion of the First Parachute Regiment. Two .30-caliber machine gun bunkers marked the entrance to the camp. The truck rolled to a stop in front of the largest tent, which was situated in the center of the camp.

"HQ!" the driver shouted.

Jessie grabbed his pack and rifle and jumped over the tailgate.

"Hey, Slate!" Big PFC Stukowski waved from a nearby sandbag bunker. He shoved his E-tool into the sandy ground, wiped sweat from his forehead, and started toward Jessie.

"Hey, Stu. How you been?"

"Wow, Slate, you got here just in time!"

"What's up?"

Stukowski didn't have a shirt on, and he looked even bigger and stronger than Jessie remembered. It was probably just the dark tan, Jessie thought. Stu smiled and put out his hand. Jessie shook it.

"Glad you're back."

"Thanks, Stu. So what's up?"

"Well, Perelli says we're breaking camp to shove off tomorrow for a big invasion."

"Crap, Stu! If Perelli says it, then we ain't got anything to worry about."

"I don't know, Slate. I got a letter from my dad about a week ago, and he says old Dugout Doug is pushin' real hard in the newspapers to get the First Marine Division to hit Rabaul."

"Well, I don't know about you, Stu, but I'm anxious to go kick some Jap butts."

Stukowski looked suddenly solemn. "Yeah, I figured you'd feel like that, Jessie. Eddie Jancovic and me were best pals from grade school all the way to triple-A ball in Newark. When he died at Pearl, that's when I joined the Corps."

"Why do you look so glum?"

"You report in yet, Marine?" Gunnery Sergeant O'Cleary barked from behind Jessie.

Jessie twirled around to face the old salt. "Not yet, Gunny. I just got here."

"Well, get in there and report in."

"Aye, aye, Gunny. Catch you later, Stu. Kate sends her love, Gunny, and you two owe me some congrats. I'm married!"

"Yeah, swell, Jessie." Stu sounded hesitant.

Gunny O'Cleary said nothing. Jessie knew something was wrong. He wanted to ask Stukowski about it, but the gunny didn't look exceptionally patient. Jessie pushed through the headquarters tent flap and found himself face to face with Second Lieutenant Pomper.

"Get tired of the slop chutes and pogey bait, Slate?" Pomper asked sarcastically.

Jessie smiled.

"Wipe that grin off your face, Marine! Stand at attention!"

"Yes, sir." Jessie straightened to attention.

Pomper looked over at Corporal Churutti, the company clerk. Churutti sat behind a desk made of grenade crates, typing with two fingers.

"Check Slate in, Corporal."

"Yes, sir."

"So how'd you manage to get evacuated to Nouméa, Slate?" Pomper asked angrily.

"My foot, sir. Bad case of trench foot."

"So your foot hurt, and you wanted to go home to Mommy. How's your little foot now, Slate? Were you able to walk to the slop chutes in Nouméa?"

Jessie grinned. "That foot's fine now, sir. Matter of fact, it got well enough for me to walk around town with Kate."

Lieutenant Pomper's eyes opened wide in rage, and his pale face flushed red as he stepped close enough for Jessie to smell his stale breath. He bit at his lower lip, and his eyes fumed, but he didn't speak. He spun around and faced Churutti.

"You got this slacker checked in yet?"

Corporal Churutti wrote something on a nearby chart and looked at Lieutenant Pomper. "Yes, sir."

"All right! Get out of here, Slate."

Jessie snapped off a crisp salute.

"I've had better, but she wasn't bad," Pomper said, half under his breath.

"What's that supposed to mean?" Jessie asked.

"It means that I hope it was worth it, Slate, since your buddy had to pick up the check."

"What are you talking about, Lieutenant?"

Pomper looked suddenly pleased. Jessie's stomach tightened. Something was wrong.

"You mean you don't know? Then I guess I'll have to be the one to tell you. When you flew off to see your skirt, your buddy paid for it with his life."

Jessie stared at Pomper, almost too stunned to speak.

"What?" he mumbled.

"Charlie Rose never got back to the platoon. You're dismissed, PFC. Get your useless butt out of my sight."

Jessie turned and walked out of the tent like a man walking in his sleep. He wanted to cry, but he felt too numb.

"What's wrong with you, Marine? You look pale." The gunny's voice seemed to come from far away.

"Charlie Rose is dead?"

The old salt's leathery face softened. "Sorry, Slate. Rose was a fine Marine. Every man here liked him."

"What happened, Gunny?"

"Don't know for sure. We guess he ran into some stray Japs bringing back that message the day you and him were sent out as runners."

Jessie felt his heart swell up to his throat. Tears ran down his cheeks. He stared straight ahead, seeing nothing. Someone was patting his shoulder. He thought of his mom and how she used to comfort him as a child with her gentle hugs and kisses on the cheek.

"You all right, son?" Gunny O'Cleary asked.

"It's all my fault, Gunny." Jessie stared straight ahead and tried to visualize Charlie Rose's happy smile.

"Come over here with me, Slate."

Gunny O'Cleary led Jessie out of hearing range of the HQ tent. He stopped about ten yards away from the HQ tent and faced Jessie.

"You're at war, Marine."

"It's my fault, Gunny."

"Shut up, Slate! It ain't your fault no more than it's mine. He ran into some stray Japs from the Battle of Vella Gulf. A bunch of 'em survived when their ships went down. They swam to shore and were just roaming the island. It was nobody's fault, son."

"I saw a chance to go back to New Caledonia and marry Kate, and I grabbed it."

"Ah, bull manure, Marine! I saw that foot of yours. It was a mess back on the Canal, and that's how come you got put aboard that PBY."

"God, I wish you were right, Gunny, but Kate begged me to get back to Nouméa any way I could, and that's what I did." Jessie's voice cracked. He paused and wiped away tears.

"Drop it, Slate. You lost your best friend. You hurt, and that's all there is to it."

Jessie looked Gunnery Sergeant O'Cleary square in the eyes. He swallowed back a lump in his throat and tried to steady his voice. "My foot . . ."

"Doc Kuipers told me that your foot needed treatment back at the Canal. Square yourself away, Marine."

"If I had been with Charlie Rose, he would still be alive."

Gunnery Sergeant O'Cleary laid his hand on Jessie's shoulder and looked around nervously, "Slate, you can't . . . look, son, it might be best if you go see the chaplain with me."

"There's no way to rationalize it, Gunny, no way to make it right. There's no forgiveness. Charlie Rose is dead."

"Stow that crap away, Marine! I'll decide what you do in my Marine Corps, mister."

"Yes, sir."

"Follow me."

"Yes, sir."

Gunny O'Cleary led Jessie to a tent just behind the HQ tent.

A sign painted on the bottom of an ammo crate said "Chaplain's Quarters."

"Wait here, PFC."

"Aye, aye, Gunny."

The old salt looked angry as he slapped the tent flap. "Chaplain Parker? Gunny O'Cleary to see you, sir."

"Come on in, you old sea dog."

O'Cleary pushed through the tent flap. Jessie could hear the chaplain and the gunny speaking in hushed voices, but he didn't really care what was being said. Nothing mattered now.

A few minutes later Gunnery Sergeant O'Cleary came back out. He motioned toward the tent. "Go on in, Slate. I'll wait out here for you."

"I don't need a preacher."

"Belay that, PFC!" O'Cleary barked. "Move it!"

Jessie started to speak, then thought better of it. He would hear what the chaplain had to say—not that it would do any good. Jessie pushed through the tent flap and looked around. Chaplain Parker was a big, strong man. He looked more like a blocking guard than a chaplain. He sat on a stack of C-ration crates, with another stack serving as his desk.

"Have a seat on the edge of my cot, PFC."

"Yes, sir." Jessie sat on the cot facing the chaplain across his makeshift desk.

"Gunnery Sergeant O'Cleary explained a little of what happened, but I would like to hear it from you."

Jessie felt a tear trickle down his left cheek. He swiped at it angrily.

"Nothing can help, Chaplain."

"Maybe not. Your name is Jessie, is it?"

"Yes, sir."

"Where you from, Jessie?"

"West Virginia."

"You don't sound like a West Virginian."

"My mom used to be an English teacher. She was strict about diction."

"Is that right? My mom was a teacher, too."

"I really don't feel like talking, Chaplain."

"Listen, Jessie, it might help just to talk it out and hear another person's view of the situation."

"The situation is this. I had a chance to get evacuated back to Nouméa to marry my girl, and I grabbed it, and it cost my buddy his life."

"You don't know that. And you don't know that it didn't just keep both of you from being killed."

"There's no way to justify what I did. There's no forgiveness for this. I deserve to die."

Chaplain Parker sighed and looked down at his C-ration desk. He looked back at Jessie with an almost pleased expression on his broad face.

"God's word tells us that the penalty for sin, any and all sin, is death. Jessie, God's word also tells us that no one on earth is perfect and sinless. Even Mary wasn't perfect and sinless. David, Moses, Paul, and everyone else except Jesus Christ himself was a sinner. We all deserve to die for our sins, but Christ paid that penalty for us, if we accept that free gift."

"Look, I'm not in the mood to hear a sermon, Chaplain Parker. There's no justifying what I've done."

"No way to justify it? Gunny O'Cleary explained the letter from your girl and how worried she was about her father. I guess your Navajo friend filled the gunny in on everything."

"So what?"

"I believe that your motives were honorable and compassionate. That certainly doesn't ease the loss of a friend, but you're wrong about forgiveness."

"Nothing can bring Charlie Rose back."

"I'll tell you this right up front, Jessie. You can't forgive yourself without accepting Christ's forgiveness first."

"I'm not much on religion, Chaplain."

"I'm not all that crazy about it myself sometimes. Sometimes the practice of religion takes the place of Jesus Christ, even with some preachers."

Jessie looked at the dirt floor. He wanted the chaplain to just shut up and leave him alone.

"You don't understand."

"Jessie, I could never, no human being could understand totally. Only Jesus Christ can feel and understand your pain and loss. Have you prayed?"

"No."

"Can we pray together about it, Jessie?"

"I don't want to now, Chaplain."

"Fine, I understand. But when you decide to talk to the Lord about it, do just that, Jessie."

"What do you mean?"

"I mean talk to Jesus from your heart. He told us how to pray and how not to. I've had Marines come in here thinking that a prayer is reading out of some pamphlet or repeating the Lord's Prayer a dozen times, as if God's hard of hearing."

"Yeah. My Navajo buddy does little chants."

"He told us not to pray like the heathen Gentiles, with meaningless repetition."

Jessie stood up.

"Is that all, Chaplain?"

Chaplain Parker smiled and stood up. He extended his hand. "Take care, Marine. Come back and talk to me any time you want."

Jessie shook the chaplain's big hand. "Thank you, sir."

"You need to pray about it and clear your mind of it, Jessie. You don't want to be going into the big invasion with anything other than your job on your mind."

"When are we shipping out?"

"You'll probably get the word within the next forty-eight hours."

"Have you heard where, Chaplain?"

Chaplain Parker shook his head no. "I'm sure that no one under the rank of colonel has heard yet."

"Well, thanks, Chaplain Parker."

Gunnery Sergeant O'Cleary was still waiting outside when Jessie came out. He gave Jessie a nod.

"Follow me. I'll show you where your squad is."

"Are the rest of the guys okay?"

"Yeah, ornery as ever."

"Gunny, is it true there's a big invasion on?"

"That's the scuttlebutt I hear."

"On this next operation I wanna be put where I can kill the most Japs."

Gunnery Sergeant O'Cleary gave Jessie a curious stare then nodded as if to say that he understood.

"Keep your marriage to Kate under wraps for a bit longer, Slate."

"Why?"

"You got put in for a medal. If you get corporal out of it, you can probably keep from getting mustered out of the Para-Marines."

"Thanks, Gunny."

Not much had changed with the platoon. Lopez was still nasty, and Broken Wing had found a new supply of jungle juice by trading various U.S. supplies to the villagers in return for Vella Lavella's finest homemade coconut and berry wine. The scuttlebutt was wrong as usual. Week followed week, and still no word came to ship out. Each mail call brought a stack of letters from Kate and Jessie's mom. Every thought of Kate and the baby brought on memories of Charlie Rose and Lieutenant Pomper's insinuation. He started to write a hundred times, but guilt and anger would bring on frustration, and finishing the letter became impossible. The Para-Marines used every minute to train and build defenses. Fifteen-mile marches started each day, followed by refresher courses on knife, bayonet, and hand-to-hand fighting. No matter how hard the Corps tried to reduce boredom, the men were bored. Finally the long-awaited word came, but any hopes of making their first combat jump faded as the Para-Marines were marched aboard the LSTs at Ruravai.

# CHAPTER NINE

THE BOUGAINVILLE BEACH WAS CLUTTERED WITH oil drums and supplies of every type. Debris from four destroyed landing craft littered the water's edge and gave bloody testimony to what the first wave must have gone through. The brown wing of a Jap Betty bomber dangled by jungle vines from two tall trees a hundred yards inland.

A squat-looking lieutenant colonel was speaking with the skipper. The crackling of small-arms fire echoed from the jungle beyond the muddy beach. The skipper turned back toward the long column of Marines just as the last few men stepped from the LCI's gangway ramps.

"Move out!"

"Lock and load!"

A few moments later, word sifted through the column that the right flank of the beachhead perimeter was holding off a counterattack by the Japanese. The column began to pick up the pace as they reached a soggy, narrow trail that ran under the dangling bomber wing. The sound of small-arms fire was joined by the muffled thumps of outgoing mail from nearby mortars. Five hundred yards into the jungle the narrow trail joined a wider one that came from the south. The column split into platoons. A disabled American light tank sat crippled from a land mine where the two trails met. A group of officers knelt in a huddle beside the tank studying two small maps while two PFCs tried to protect them from the downpour by holding a poncho over the huddle.

A shouting captain waved the column forward, pointing platoon leaders down the wider trail like a traffic cop. Each platoon pealed off the trail at twenty-yard intervals. Lieutenant Pierce led First Platoon right off the trail, pushing through the tangled terrain for another thirty yards. The rattle of a Jap Nambu machine gun resounded through the jungle ahead.

The column stopped. Each man knelt on one knee with his weapon ready, searching the gray, rain-laden jungle but seeing nothing. Broken Wing laid his rifle across his lap and sat cross-legged on the ground. Jessie nudged him in the back.

"What's up?" Jessie asked.

Broken Wing looked back at Jessie as if he were bored, then shrugged. A moment later the platoon moved out again, this time veering left.

Lieutenant Pierce filed back down the column, whispering orders as he went. "Three men to a position."

"Three men to a position, ten yards apart."

"Three men to a position."

"We digging in, Lieutenant?" Jack Ellinwood asked from behind Jessie.

"No. We're getting on line for an assault. We'll push across this muddy stream up ahead. We got the Japs trapped in a swamp on the other side."

Jessie's heart took a jump. He followed the line of helmets ahead. Gunny O'Cleary shoved each team into place.

"You three. There."

"You three. Right here. Come on, ladies, move it."

"Wing. You and Slate and Ellinwood. Right here."

Jessie hunched over and moved up beside Broken Wing. Ellinwood hustled up beside Jessie and dropped to his stomach. Jessie strained to see the stream, but the brush was too thick. No one spoke. Each man stared through the pouring rain, waiting for the first movement. Jessie thought of Kate and the baby and his mother. He thought of Charlie Rose and gripped his rifle tighter.

"Fix bayonets," a voice whispered from the brush on Jessie's right.

"Fix bayonets."

"Fix bayonets."

Jessie felt an elbow from Jack Ellinwood. Jack's eyes were open wide. They looked wild, like a frightened animal's.

"I'm going to die in this place," Jack said.

Jessie opened his mouth to speak, but the gunny's bellow stopped him short.

"Get off your cans, Marines! Let's rip some yellow bellies open!"

Jessie was up and moving forward through the brush. The terrain dropped suddenly, and the sweeping Marines stumbled down into a ten-foot-wide shallow, muddy stream. They waded across; the water was knee-deep. On the other side was a small span of solid ground covered by thick briers that ripped at each man's leggings. Somewhere on the left flank, heavy small-arms fire erupted like a thousand firecrackers. The advance slowed.

"Move it! Keep on line!" someone shouted from Jessie's right.

Jessie picked up the pace. He glanced toward Broken Wing on his left, then quickly snapped his eyes back to the tangled jungle ahead. They pushed forward thirty, forty, and finally a hundred yards until they reached the edge of a murky gray, fungus-laden swamp.

"Hold it up. Pass the word."

Jessie looked right. Jack Ellinwood held up his hand.

"Pass the word, hold up."

A minute later the word came to dig in. Firing on the left flank continued. Jessie, Jack, and Broken Wing dropped their packs, removed their E-tools, and began digging out a foxhole in the soggy earth. Corporal DiCicca stood up and ran toward them from a position on their right. He dropped to one knee behind Jack as Jack dug furiously into the muddy ground.

Jessie glanced at Phil. "What's up?"

"One of the units on our left flank ran into a nest of 'em, and they didn't keep up with the rest of the sweep."

"We stayin' put?" Broken Wing asked.

Corporal DiCicca stood up. "Yeah. We're trying to link up with them before it gets dark so we can keep the perimeter intact."

"Funny how we haven't run into a single Jap," Jack mused as he continued digging.

"We'll see 'em soon," Phil said.

"Too soon for me," Jack replied. He gave a slow gloomy shake of his head as he lifted out another spade of mud.

"Better get that hole deep, you guys. Gunny says we might get shelled tonight."

Twenty minutes later the large, square foxhole was finished, and the three wet Marines crouched in their respective corners, staring at each other, waiting for someone to speak. Jessie looked down at his mud-caked boondockers, then peered out of the hole toward the swamp. He wiped mud from his hands and rubbed them together in the rain.

"This hole's going to be filled up in another hour."

Jack wiped water from his blond eyebrows. "I'm cold and hungry."

"Guess we better eat before it gets dark," Jessie said.

"I'm thirsty," Broken Wing said.

"Well, if you can find booze out here, I'm gettin' drunk with you," Jessie said.

"Hey, the shooting stopped over there," Jack said.

The three sat shivering quietly for a moment, listening for gunfire. Only the constant slapping of rain against the jungle foliage could be heard. Boots squashing through the mud approached from the right flank. They sat up stiff with rifles ready. Gunny O'Cleary stopped and squatted beside the foxhole.

"You three better have a man on watch every second."

"What's up, Gunny?" Jessie asked.

"The left flank fell so far behind on the sweep that we broke off from 'em."

"Bet they're still back in that big patch of Konai grass, Gunny," Jack said.

"They pulled up even with us now to form the night perimeter, but the word is that a bunch of Nips slipped through the gap trying to break off contact with that part of the sweep."

"Yeah? And?" Jack asked, as if waiting for the rest of the sentence.

Gunny pulled his cigar out of his mouth and looked at Ellinwood with one eye closed. "We got Japs inside the perimeter, Marine. Now you can bet they're going to be probing for a way out tonight." Gunny O'Cleary stood up.

"We're ready, Gunny," Jessie said coldly.

"You people set up in a bad spot. You can't see the position on either side of you."

"Who's on our right, Gunny?" Jack asked.

"Stukowski, Perelli, and Lopez."

"How 'bout the left?"

"LaBeau, Oglethorpe, and Corporal DiCicca."

The old salt looked left, then right. He glanced up at the dark sky.

Broken Wing groaned. "Don't say it, Gunny, don't say move."

The gunny smacked his lips and shook his head. "Got to. I want three men to a position, but we can't have this big gap in the line tonight. One of you go dig a hole over there about where that clump of weeds is by that rotted stump."

"Just one of us?" Jessie asked.

"Yeah. Dig in there and take turns every couple of hours rotating back to this position. That way at least you can get a little shut-eye."

"Very little," Broken Wing growled.

"I'll let Perelli, Lopez, and Stu know what we've done. They're another ten yards on the other side of that stump."

The gunny stood and sloshed away. They chose straws to see who got to do some more digging, and Jessie lost. The ground was like mud soup, so that other than the problem of rain washing in the walls, it was easier to dig than most foxholes.

Corporal DiCicca rushed by as the last gray shafts of daylight faded. "Lana Turner," he whispered as he rushed past on the way to Perelli's position.

"What?"

"Call sign's Lana Turner."

A few minutes later DiCicca rushed back toward his own position. Two hours later Jessie's eyes were beginning to blur from constant staring into pitch-black jungle swamp. The miserable rain was finally beginning to slack off to a drizzle. The water had risen to his chest. From the chest down he felt warm, but his upper half was so cold that it was difficult to keep his teeth from chattering. The drizzle stopped. A quarter moon poked through thick black clouds, silhouetting every bush and limb. The eerie blue light played tricks on a man's mind. A rustling sound stiffened Jessie's spine. He aimed to the right.

"Halt."

"Joe DiMaggio," a voice whispered from the dark.

"Come on in."

Jack Ellinwood crawled toward Jessie on all fours. He stopped and flattened beside the foxhole.

"Go get some sleep, Jessie."

"Sounds good. Seen any movement?"

"I been sleeping while Broken Wing stood watch. Man, I sure had a great dream."

"Oh, yeah?"

"Yeah. Me and Cindy Marie were dancing right in front of Artie Shaw's band. They were playing 'Stardust.' Cindy Marie was so real, I could smell her perfume."

"I read in *Collier's* that Artie Shaw's leading a band in the Navy now."

"A squid? Well, I still like his sound."

"Have you got a photo of Cindy Marie?"

"Sure do."

"If it ever stops raining, let me see it."

"Sure, Jessie."

Jessie crawled out of the foxhole and shivered. "I'm freezing."

"Good grief," Jack grumbled as he slid into the hole with a splash.

"Yeah, don't fall asleep; you might drown."

Jessie crawled back toward the larger hole. The moon disappeared behind another bank of black clouds, stealing what little vision there had been. He felt his way like a blind man on his knees until his outstretched hand touched the pile of dirt and mud that marked the perimeter of the hole. He quickly rolled over the small bank of mud and slid down. He crouched down into a corner of the big foxhole, managed to sit, and pulled his knees into a fetal position in a useless effort to stay warm. A dim sliver of moonlight streaked through a break in the clouds. In the dim light, the dark forms of two men, each hunched over in opposite corners of the foxhole facing Jessie, became clear. Jessie blinked his eyes to make sure of what he was seeing.

"Hey, Broken Wing, I thought it was supposed to be just two guys in this hole."

"What?" Broken Wing whispered.

"Where'd we get another . . ." Jessie's question faded along with his voice.

Suddenly both dark forms in the opposite corners moved. The dim moonlight was blacked out by another rain cloud.

"Jessie!"

Furious scuffling erupted from the other end of the big foxhole. Jessie lifted his rifle and aimed at the two dark forms fighting each other.

"Shoot him!" Broken Wing shouted.

"Shoot who? I can't tell who's who!" Jessie screamed and stomped his boots as he poked the barrel end of his rifle into the scuffling twosome in front of him. Somebody rolled out of the hole.

"Shoot him! Fire!" Broken Wing yelled.

Frightened feet scampered away, splashing through the wet terrain. Jessie gripped his Johnson rifle, ready to fire, but he still couldn't see.

"Broken Wing?"

"I'm here."

"You all right?"

*"Beh-na-ali-tsoisi."*

"Slant-eyed?" Jessie whispered.

The moon peeked through another break in the clouds, and Jessie could see Broken Wing's face. He was not happy.

"Lana Turner," a voice whispered from the blackness.

"Gunny?"

"Affirmative."

"Come on in," Jessie whispered back.

A moment later Gunny O'Cleary slithered into the foxhole on his stomach. "What the crap's going on over here?" he demanded.

"God, Gunny, we had a Jap sitting right here in the hole with us," Broken Wing exclaimed.

"Keep your voice down or you're gonna have a bloody platoon of 'em in this hole with you. Where'd he go?"

"Where'd he go?" Broken Wing repeated.

"Yeah, where?"

"How the crap do I know?"

Gunny O'Cleary sat up and leaned close enough for his unlit cigar to touch Broken Wing on the nose.

"You're gettin' paid to kill 'em, boy, not to chase 'em away."

Broken Wing grunted and looked at Jessie. Jessie shrugged his shoulders.

"What stinks in this hole?" Gunny O'Cleary demanded.

"Not me," Jessie said as if he was offended.

The gunny looked at Broken Wing.

"What are you lookin' at me for?"

"Something does stink in here," Jessie said.

Broken Wing sniffed. "Yeah, it does, but it ain't me."

The gunny leaned toward the far corner. He sniffed. "You must have scared the crap right out of that Nip."

Broken Wing stood up fast.

"You mean he dumped right here in our hole?"

Gunny O'Cleary yanked the Indian's shirt. "Get down, Marine."

Broken Wing squatted. "Don't like spending the night in a Nip's outhouse."

"Shut up and stay alert! There's bound to be more of 'em."

The gunny climbed out of the hole and disappeared toward the next position. Broken Wing shoveled out the offending corner.

No one slept. Two hours later Broken Wing relieved Ellinwood. Jessie stared wide-eyed into the black drizzle until the first gray shafts of sunlight filtered through the rain-laden sky. The clank of a canteen against a rifle was the first sound. It was quickly joined by the rustle of packs and the opening of C-ration cans. Jessie huddled in a corner of the big foxhole and stared at Ellinwood.

"That Jap could have killed us both. All he had to do was blast away. I had my rifle between my legs, and so did Broken Wing."

"Guess I better go check on Broken Wing."

"Yeah, he was pretty shook up when he relieved me last night."

"The good Lord sure saved you guys last night."

Jessie started to reply but wasn't sure what to say. He thought about Chaplain Parker as he climbed out of the hole. Every muscle ached, and his waterlogged skin began to itch. Broken Wing was kneeling beside his foxhole, drawing something in the mud with his K-bar knife.

"What's up, Wing?" Jessie asked.

"Prayer and gift to wind god."

"For saving our butts last night?"

Broken Wing nodded and continued drawing some sort of four-legged animal.

"Maybe you should give this one to the rain god. Seems like he's the only one who lives on Bougainville."

Broken Wing looked up at Jessie with an expression that was not one of amusement.

"Wonder why you weren't born with a sense of humor," Jessie said.

"I have a good sense of humor. I was called the funny one in my family."

Jessie stared down at the stone-faced Indian for a long moment then lost it. He laughed until his eyes got misty.

Soon the word to move out echoed around the perimeter.

"On line!"

They swept forward cautiously with bayonets fixed. Twenty yards inside the swamp, the crack of a sniper round brought Jessie to his knees.

"Keep moving!" Sergeant Rim bellowed from somewhere along the line.

Jessie stood up and rushed forward. Broken Wing was five yards to his left. Ellinwood was about eight yards away and moving forward. Ten yards on the other side of Ellinwood, Lopez dropped to one knee and aimed up into a tall, thin tree with a clump of large green leaves at the top. He opened fire. Stukowski ran over beside him and fired into the same tree. Suddenly bullets smacked into the mud around Stukowski's boots. Jessie looked up. A muzzle flash spit from the top of a nearby coconut palm. Jessie rammed the rifle butt into his shoulder and took aim, but before he could pull the trigger, Ellinwood had already emptied a clip into the top of the tree. A Jap rifle tumbled down end over end and splashed into the swamp below. Lopez opened fire again into the top of the tree. The limp leg of a dead Jap dropped out of the leaves and dangled back and forth.

"Listen up!" Gunny O'Cleary shouted as the firing stopped. "Pass the word. The first Japs will tie themselves to the back side of trees so they can pick us off after we go by."

"Keep it moving forward," Lieutenant Pierce shouted.

Jessie moved forward slowly. He kept his eyes up, studying each tree for the slightest rustle of a branch. A sudden blast of machine gun fire brought the platoon to their stomachs. Red tracer rounds shot out of the murky swamp from two directions, crisscrossing ten yards in front of Broken Wing and Jessie, then sweeping back and forth down the Marine line of attack. The single cracks of rifle fire joined in as the swamp erupted in gunfire.

"Can you see the machine guns?" Broken Wing shouted from behind a fallen tree.

Jessie lifted his head enough to look at Broken Wing and wiped the muddy swamp water from his eyes.

"I can't see anything!"

A burst from a Nambu machine gun sent a row of small muddy geysers ripping past Jessie's face. Another stream of red tracers shot from the gray swamp. Broken Wing buried his face in the muddy water as chunks of the fallen tree that was protecting him splintered away.

"You all right?" Jessie shouted.

Broken Wing lifted his face from the water and spit. "Yeah, where did that one fire from?"

"There's at least two of 'em!"

"Over there," Ellinwood shouted, and pointed. "That one fired from straight out here in front of me."

"Where?" Jessie asked.

Jack peeked up over a decaying tree stump and pointed. "See that dark clump of stuff between those two skinny trees about thirty-five yards straight out?"

"Got it!" Jessie yelled. "I'll open up on it, and you see if we catch fire from the other one."

"Right!"

Jessie fired four quick shots into the dark brush. The rattle of automatic fire filled the swamp as two enemy machine guns returned fire. Jessie flattened his body into the muck until only his pack was above water. He could hear bullets ripping all around. He gritted his teeth so tightly that his jaw hurt.

"Jessie!" Broken Wing screamed.

Jessie pulled his face out of the fungus-laden water and looked to his right as Broken Wing parried away the bayonet thrust of a screaming Japanese soldier. The splashing of someone charging forward turned Jessie's attention straight ahead. Five yards away a wild-eyed Japanese ran at Jessie with his rifle on his hip and his bayonet fixėd. Jessie struggled to his knees and lifted his rifle.

Three quick shots rang out from Jessie's left. The Jap soldier jerked violently and dropped his rifle. His eyes rolled back. He sank to his knees and splashed facedown into the ankle-deep water. Jessie felt his thighs grow suddenly warm. He knew that he had wet his pants. Jessie felt himself begin to breathe again. He looked left to thank Ellinwood. A Jap stood over Jack, plunging a bayonet into his back over and over. Jessie fired his remaining six rounds into the Japanese soldier. His rifle was empty. The Jap fell back dead. Jessie charged toward the fallen Jap now lying across Jack Ellinwood's boots. He heard himself screaming as he ran, struggling to lift his boots from the sucking swamp water. The Jap's hand twitched as Jessie reached him. Jessie screamed again and drove his bayonet into the man's chest so deeply that he couldn't pull it out. He stomped the Jap with his boot and yanked his rifle back to free the bayonet, then twirled around to face front.

The swamp was alive with enemy soldiers. A bullet shattered the stock of his rifle and sent a vibration through his arms that numbed both of them all the way to the elbow. Jessie caught a movement from the corner of his eye. He parried a thrusting bayonet down and away, and as he sucked in his stomach to avoid the long steel blade, he snapped the shattered butt of his rifle down across the left cheekbone of an openmouthed Japanese soldier. The Jap's cheekbone and jaw cracked like a brittle tree limb, and he fell face first into the swamp. He quickly pushed himself up onto all fours, but it was too late. Jessie drove his bayonet through the man's right kidney and out his stomach. The Jap made a belching sound and flattened out on top of his rifle, his face under water. Jessie dropped to his knees and fumbled for rounds to load into his Johnson rifle.

Broken Wing was wrestling nearby in the muck with a Jap. A second Jap was closing in on them, shouting "Banzai!" As soon as Jessie was finished loading, he opened fire on the charging Jap. His first two shots missed, but the third round ripped the man's neck open. Blood gushed from the wound, forcing the Jap to drop his rifle and clutch desperately at his throat with both hands. Jessie fired again, and the Jap fell forward. Broken Wing and the other Jap rolled to a stop. Broken Wing, on top, pulled his K-bar knife and stabbed into the man's ribs, then ripped the blade across his stomach until he went limp. He pulled the knife out and stabbed down hard one last time as Jessie ran toward him. Broken Wing rolled off the dead Japanese and grabbed his rifle.

"There!" Broken Wing shouted.

Jessie turned in time to see Lopez fend off a bayonet thrust and wrestle a Jap to the ground while two more screaming attackers closed in on him. Jessie and Broken Wing opened fire at the same time. One Jap stumbled forward, then collapsed. The other reached Lopez, who was already on the ground fighting for his life. Suddenly, as if from nowhere, Benjamin Oglethorpe's thin body sprang up from the swamp. He hit the charging man's head with the butt end of his rifle like Lou Gehrig putting one over the center field fence. The man's face splattered with a smack as loud as a rifle shot, and he slammed backward over a fallen branch. His head dangled limply. Lopez screamed. The man on top of him was biting into his neck. Lieutenant Pierce ran up, put his .45-caliber pistol into the Jap's side, and fired. A small explosion of blood erupted as the bullet went clean through.

"Stu!" Oglethorpe shouted.

Stukowski gave a violent snapping twist to a Jap's neck, then rolled off him and collapsed.

"Get up, Marines!" Lieutenant Pierce yelled, and waved the men forward.

"Move it! Move it!" Sergeant Rim screamed at the top of his lungs, and ran forward into the swamp on Jessie and Broken Wing's right.

Jessie stood up and quickly shoved in another nine rounds. Broken Wing did the same. They exchanged a glance. Broken Wing looked almost as calm as—for just an instant—Jessie felt. He wondered if their minds had snapped. How else could he explain it. He began to move forward, deeper into the swamp. Two Jap soldiers sprang from behind nearby brush and ran back toward their own lines. The powerful automatic burst of a BAR blew them off their feet. Garland shook his BAR, yelped, and signaled a thumbs-up to Jessie as his A gunner, Cliff Houston, fumbled to reload the BAR. Suddenly the enemy machine guns opened fire. Their tracers merged on the BAR team. Ronnie dropped facedown. Cliff spun around and fell beside Ronnie.

"Corpsman! Corpsman up!" Jessie shouted.

A stream of machine gun fire raked past Jessie and Broken Wing. They dropped to their stomachs. The enemy fire was high.

"Get that BAR working!" someone shouted from behind.

Jessie pushed to his feet and ran in a full-out hunched-over sprint toward the fallen BAR team. He could hear enemy rifles open fire as he dived in beside them.

"Ronnie!" Jessie shouted as he rolled Garland off the Browning automatic.

Blood so dark that it looked almost blue flowed from a bullet hole just above Ronnie's heart. Ronnie's face was ashen and lifeless. Jessie looked over at Cliff. His helmet lay beside him. The back of his head had been shot away. Jessie belched up a mouthful of bile and spit it into the swamp water. He grabbed the BAR and stripped Cliff's body of ammo. Broken Wing splashed in beside him, breathing hard.

"Here!" Jessie tossed Broken Wing the extra clips for the BAR.

"Both dead?"

"Yeah! God, I'm scared, Wing."

The faint thump of mortar rounds leaving the tubes echoed through the swamp. An instant later the first mortar round exploded in the top of a tall tree above the Marine line. A second round exploded twenty yards behind Jessie and Broken Wing. Then the muffled explosions of mortar rounds hitting the swamp erupted all around the Marine line. Someone screamed from the far left.

"Corpsman!"

"Pull back!" Lieutenant Pierce shouted.

Jessie gathered the weapons while Broken Wing grabbed hold of the two dead Marines by the backs of their collars.

"Ready!" Broken Wing yelled, and began dragging the two dead Marines back.

"Let's go!"

Jessie walked backward firing from the hip to cover Broken Wing. Lieutenant Pierce ran along bellowing orders and shoving men into position.

"Form up here! Line up here!"

The Jap machine guns and mortars stopped. Another group of screaming enemy soldiers emerged from the swamp fifty yards away and charged forward. Gunnery Sergeant O'Cleary walked past the line of Marines as if he were taking a stroll in the park.

"Here they come, ladies!" he bellowed. "First one of you that gets Maggie's drawers on this rifle range is gonna get out of my Marine Corps! You are supposed to be the best riflemen in the world! That's why you get the big money!"

"Take that breath!"

"Relax! Squeeze! Don't pull!"

"Fire!"

Jessie laid on the trigger of the Browning automatic rifle. The instant one twenty-round clip was gone, Broken Wing ripped it out and shoved in another. Rain sizzled off the long, hot barrel. From somewhere on Jessie's left the chatter of a .30-caliber machine gun opened up on the staggering line of Japanese soldiers. Tracers skipped off the slimy green water, through and around trees, and into the enemy line. Japanese began to fall. Their charge slowed as the Marines unleashed a withering barrage of automatic fire. The rumbling of a big engine sounded close. The whoosh of cannon fire caused Jessie to jerk around. A big Sherman tank behind him rocked on its tracks. A blast of fire spit from the turret cannon. The tank crushed through the tangled brush before it with ease. The tank's first shot sent a spray of mud and shrapnel into the Jap line. Two men fell backward. The second round exploded with fire and sparks as a geyser of mud spit out of the swamp in front of the charging Japanese. The "Banzai" screams ceased. The line of skirmishers broke ranks, turned, and ran back into the swamp.

The big Sherman churned past the Marine line and came to a stop. A young boyish-looking turret gunner poked his head out of an open hatch.

"Where we going?" he yelled as he lifted his goggles back onto his forehead.

Lieutenant Pierce ran forward.

"Follow me! I'll point out the gun bunkers. You put 'em with their ancestors."

"Aye, aye, Lieutenant!"

"Get 'em moving, Gunny!"

"Move out!" Gunny O'Cleary shouted from the far left.

Broken Wing stuck two rifles into the mud beside the bodies of Garland and Houston and placed a helmet on the butt end of one rifle to mark the spot for the corpsman.

"Lieutenant's gonna get himself killed," Jessie said.

"What's Pierce doing?" Broken Wing asked.

"He's gonna point out the gun bunkers for the tank."

A squad of Marines on the right flank opened fire into the tops of three nearby trees that grew in a tight row. A rifle tumbled from the top of one. A hail of small-arms fire shot from the swamp ahead. Lieutenant Pierce twirled like a top and fell to his knees fifteen yards ahead of the tank. He clutched at his left bicep and grimaced.

"Corpsman!" someone on the left flank shouted.

"Corpsman!" another man called out.

Lieutenant Pierce picked up his rifle and motioned the tank to keep following. He staggered deeper into the murky swamp, heading for the dark spot that had to be a bunker between two thin trees standing straight ahead.

"Where's it at?" the turret gunner shouted down at Lieutenant Pierce.

The lieutenant looked back over his shoulder. "Keep your eyes open. I'll draw their fire!"

Pierce jogged toward the dark spot between the two trees about twenty-five yards ahead and at a thirty-degree angle to the left of the tank. Suddenly a muzzle flashed fire from the spot. Red tracers streaked past the lieutenant, and like a puppet being yanked back by a string, he was blown off his feet. Jessie opened fire on the enemy bunker. The enemy tracers swept toward him. Broken Wing splashed to the ground. Jessie dropped beside him and tried to tuck his head under his helmet like a turtle as bullets sang into water and thudded into the mud all around them. A loud whoosh from the tank lifted Jessie's eyes from the mud. The Jap bunker exploded in flames. Coconut logs blew into the air. The tank fired again. The blast sent more fire and wood into the air.

Another machine gun opened fire on the advancing Marines. The big Sherman's turret swiveled, and the tank rocked as fire shot from the cannon. A ripping explosion silenced the second Jap machine gun.

"Charge!" somebody screamed out like a madman.

Suddenly everyone was running forward. Jessie could

hear his boots splashing and felt his heart pounding, as if he were running through a dream. Broken Wing screamed out a piercing war cry. Small khaki-clad men rose from the jungle ahead and began to run away. Marine fire cut them down as fast they jumped up, and suddenly it was over. There was no return fire. Marines stood staring at each other as if they couldn't believe what had happened. The swamp was deathly still.

"Form a perimeter!"

"Corpsman! We got wounded over here!"

"DiCicca! Get a squad and pile up those dead Nips. Take no chances. If they need another round, plug 'em!"

Sergeant Rim motioned Jessie to follow. He led him through groin-level water to a decaying tree stump.

"You and Wing set the BAR up here. It's about the best field of fire we're gonna get in this stinkin' swamp."

Jessie laid the BAR across the top of the stump, dropped to his knees, and stared down at the water. Broken Wing sat down next to him. Rain slapped into a patch of green algae floating by like a raft on the black water.

"I feel weird, like this isn't really happening," Jessie said.

Broken Wing didn't speak. Jessie followed the Indian's gaze. He was staring at Jessie's hands. They were clenched in tight fists and pressed against his chest. They were smeared with blood and algae and mud. His sleeves were stained red up to the elbows.

"You get hit?"

Jessie unclenched his fist and felt his forearms. "No."

"Good."

They sat staring into the swamp for the next four hours. Jessie wanted to talk, but each time he tried, there just didn't seem to be anything worth saying. Visions of Jack Ellinwood writhing under a bayonet flashed over and over through Jessie's mind until he made a noise and blinked his eyes to clear his mind.

The splashing of boots coming close from inside the perimeter didn't cause Jessie or Broken Wing to turn around. They both stared straight ahead as if in a trance.

"All right, listen up."

Jessie turned slowly around. Corporal DiCicca's dark eyes looked bloodshot with fatigue and tears. The corporal squatted down, pulled a Chelsea cigarette from behind his ear, and lit up. He inhaled deeply, slowly, like a man taking his final breath.

"Get ready to saddle up."

"Who'd we lose, Phil?" Jessie asked.

"Lieutenant Pierce is dead."

"And Garland and Cliff," Broken Wing said solemnly.

"Ellinwood. Stukowski got cut by a bayonet pretty good, but he'll live."

"Where we going?" Broken Wing asked.

"Long-range patrol. Gunny says a bunch of raiders got into a big fight on the Piva Trail."

"What's that?"

"Seems like there's only a couple of trails that are big enough for anybody to move on. They cross each other or something. Anyway, we're going to sweep around the big fight and cut off the Jap retreat up in the mountains."

Jessie spit into the black swamp water. "Least we'll be on solid ground."

"Rains anymore, rain god gonna drown," Broken Wing said.

"As long as I'm on solid ground, let it rain."

"Can't rain forever," Broken Wing said.

"That ain't what I hear," DiCicca said as he stood up.

"We getting a new lieutenant?" Jessie asked.

"Pomper temporarily," Corporal DiCicca said in a tone of disgust.

Jessie groaned and pinched the bridge of his nose. "That jackass isn't even a Para-Marine! He couldn't hold Lieutenant Pierce's cartridge belt."

"I don't like him, either, but he's still a Marine. Gunny says they're putting Lieutenant Pierce up for a medal."

"Good. Sure was a gutsy thing he did back there."

"Let me go pass the word. We'll be moving out in a little bit."

"How many Japs they got stacked up?" Broken Wing asked.

"Forty-two so far."

"Old Lopez is grabbing up souvenirs. Looks like he's opening a friggin' pawnshop. You get anything?"

"No," Jessie said.

Broken Wing grunted and produced a small tuft of hair he had tucked in his cartridge belt.

"My God!" Jessie exclaimed.

DiCicca pointed in wide-eyed disbelief.

"He scalped a Nip!"

"Not whole scalp," Broken Wing said as he tucked the hair back in his belt.

"You mean you guys still do that, Chief?" DiCicca asked.

"It is for squaw dance."

"What's that?" Jessie asked.

"Keep enemy spirit from causing sickness."

Phil and Jessie exchanged incredulous expressions. Phil walked away whistling the eerie music to the popular Sunday afternoon radio mystery *The Shadow*.

A few minutes later a fresh platoon of Marines from the Third Division moved up to replace the undermanned platoon of parachutists. Lieutenant Pomper led the platoon back the way they had come. The dead Marines had been carried back to a makeshift graveyard near the beach at Empress August Bay. The dead Japanese were tossed into a slit trench.

The platoon headed east then veered south along a narrow jungle trail that led through the Marine lines and into the rugged mountains. Twenty yards outside of the Marine perimeter, Lieutenant Pomper halted the column and ordered PFC Perelli to take the point.

Broken Wing looked over his shoulder at Jessie. "Missed it."

"Missed what?" Jessie asked as he wiped the barrel of the BAR with a small green rag he had soaked with Cosmoline oil.

"Did not think he would stay on the point so long."

"So long? Crap, we can't be thirty yards past our lines."

"Yep."

The march began again. It continued to rain. Two hours later the platoon of weary Marines cleared the lower ridges of the first series of mountains. Night was less than twenty minutes away when word to halt filtered back down the column. The men dropped off to the side of a narrow fern-covered trail. There they spent the night.

Jessie felt miserable. In fact, it seemed as if miserable was just another way to spell Bougainville. The night passed without incident, each man sitting and shivering in the never-ending rain. Some tried to keep warm by hugging themselves or breathing into their shirts or ponchos. The first gray shafts of morning light brought new hope that the rain would finally end, but it didn't.

The platoon broke camp and moved out without morning chow. They reached the bank of a wide jungle river. It took scouts three hours to find a place to wade across and another hour to find an overgrown trail.

The trail rose and dipped through dense jungle valleys and up steep mountain slopes. They marched until noon, and finally the word to halt for chow came as they reached the foot of a massive volcano. Somehow Perelli knew that the volcano was called Bagana, but no one cared. Jessie shoved down some cold hash with pork and beans. The word came down before he swallowed the last spoonful.

"Saddle up."

"Saddle up."

"Saddle up."

Broken Wing turned and grunted.

*"A-chi yeh-hes."*

"Wait a minute, Broken Wing. That doesn't make sense. Intestines can't itch."

The stone-faced Navajo stood up.

"Mine do."

"You know, Wing, I'm beginning to think you do have a sense of humor."

The long march started again. Jessie began to wonder just how far away from their own lines they were going. A thirty-man platoon could be trapped and surrounded in those mountains and never be heard from again. He tried to think of Kate as he trudged along the narrow mountain trail, but every thought of her brought with it a memory of Charlie Rose that made Jessie's stomach twist with remorse and his heart ache with guilt.

The platoon paused in a gorge beside a swift mountain stream. The trail led along the bank of the stream for a mile. There they found a ford that was flanked on both sides by high bluffs. The ford was a natural bridge of fallen trees and earth and slick rocks. On the other side the trail rose from the jungle canyon and across a spine of ridges, then down a steep gradient.

The trail rose again over the spine of another ridge that doglegged sharply to the left. At that point the narrow footpath became treacherous for twenty yards, with sheer drops into dark crevasses on both sides. After that the trail widened and sloped downhill through dark jungle. The men, weary to the point of collapse, seemed to become suddenly cautious, as if each sensed impending danger. Helmets along the trail began to drop and turn as the word passed quietly back.

"Village up ahead."

"Village up ahead."

Jessie looked over his shoulder and whispered at Oglethorpe. "Village up ahead."

He turned forward again. The old gunny was hustling back down the trail, sidestepping the men as he came. His eyes widened as he spotted Jessie. A swell of pride swept through Jessie that he found hard to conceal. O'Cleary stopped and squatted between Jessie and Broken Wing. He took a moment to catch his breath, then looked straight in Jessie's eyes.

"We got a vill up ahead. Scouts are checking it out. I don't like the looks of it."

"What's wrong, Gunny?" Jessie asked.

"Don't know. Maybe nothing. It looks deserted. Here's what I want. Now listen good! Back down the trail, where it takes the sharp turn along the peak of the ridge."

"Yeah," Jessie said.

"You and Broken Wing set up the BAR and don't be stupid! Set up on the trail past the dogleg so you can fire across the crevasse. You should be able to sweep that narrow ledge in case they're coming after us if we pull back."

"Right," Broken Wing muttered. His broad, rugged face showed no emotion. He actually seemed to grow calmer under pressure. Jessie found it irritating.

The gunny looked at Jessie. "You got it, Marine?"

"I understand." Jessie frowned.

"What's wrong, Slate?"

"Him." Jessie pointed at Wing with his thumb.

Wing's eyebrows lifted. "Me?"

"He acts like he's bored."

"Family quarrels later, gentlemen. Now listen up. Stay in that position for ten minutes—"

The sound of Lieutenant Pomper approaching stopped the gunny in midsentence.

Pomper squatted down beside the gunny. "This is unnecessary, Gunnery Sergeant," he said calmly.

"Well, Lieutenant, you might be right, but there was a time back in '27 when we thought we cornered old Sandino."

"This is not Nicaragua, Gunnery Sergeant O'Cleary."

"No, sir, it ain't. But it's jungle just the same."

"We're fighting the Japanese, Sergeant," Pomper said sarcastically.

"Yes, sir, I think I know that. I been killin' the little yellow scumbags since China."

Pomper straightened his spine and blinked. "I'll go along with you and your overly cautious nature, O'Cleary, but your insubordinate attitude just earned you a hearing before Lieutenant Colonel Roering the minute this long-range patrol is over."

"Aye, aye, Lieutenant."

Pomper glanced at Jessie, turned, and walked briskly toward the front of the column. A painful vision of Pomper kissing Kate filled Jessie with a sudden jealous rage. He spit toward the departing lieutenant.

"If he gets you busted, I'll kill him!"

Gunny held up his hand and waved. "Mark time, Marine. Ain't nobody gettin' busted. Back in the Old Corps Lieutenant Colonel Roering got to be known as Rip Roarin' Roering in the Fourth Marines."

"Why, Gunny?" Broken Wing asked.

The old salt winked slyly and grinned. "You ain't got enough time in grade to know that yet, Marines, but let's just say Roarin' Roering ain't about to bust one of the Old Corps on the word of some boy lawyer playing second lieutenant."

"That guy's a class-A—" Jessie began.

"At ease. Now listen up! If we run into trouble, we'll be high-steppin' back down this path, so don't go blastin' away at our own men. I'll make sure I'm the last one comin' down that trail and around that bend, and after me you shoot anything that moves! Clear?"

"Aye, aye, Gunny," Jessie said.

"And watch out for Nips comin' up on your rear."

Broken Wing gave a thumbs-up. "Semper fi, Gunny."

"You wait in that position for ten minutes, then bring up the rear."

Gunnery Sergeant O'Cleary stood up and rushed back to the front of the column. Jessie and Broken Wing made their way down the trail until they passed Lopez, the last man in the column. They continued on for another thirty yards until they reached the dogleg. Jessie led the way with the BAR on his hip. His heart felt as though it were about to push through his chest as they rounded the blind corner. Gigantic trees rose up from the canyon on the left side of the trail and towered over the narrow footpath. On the right side was a deep black crevasse. Jessie paused for a moment at the blind corner, then jumped out facing down the narrow path with the automatic rifle on his hip and ready to fire. He breathed a deep sigh of relief and looked back at Broken Wing.

"I was scared. I don't know what I would have done if a bunch of Japs were coming down that trail."

"Pull trigger," Broken Wing said without a smile.

Jessie smirked and looked around. He shrugged his shoulders. "Where do you think?"

Broken Wing glanced back nervously.

"Go on."

Broken Wing pointed at a rotting tree stump covered with moss and ferns ten yards up the trail. From there they could fire across the crevasse and sweep the trail leading to the village or turn around and fire in the other direction.

"Looks good," Jessie said.

They hustled over to the stump. There was barely enough room for the two of them to flatten out behind it. Jessie shoved the barrel of the Browning automatic rifle through the thick fern cover until only the tip of the muzzle showed. Broken Wing flattened out on Jessie's right and spread out a dozen twenty-round magazines of ammo for the BAR, along with a small rubber bottle of oil.

"Do not roll left," Broken Wing said with a glance over Jessie's back.

Jessie peeked over the ledge and grunted. "Wish you hadn't said that."

"How far down?"

Jessie took a second look and shrugged his shoulders. "Can't tell; it's black down there."

"If you fall off, do not scream. Give away our position."

Jessie frowned at Broken Wing but said nothing for a few moments.

"I'm worried about 'em coming up the trail behind us."

Broken Wing turned around to face the other way. "I'll watch our rear."

"Good idea."

Ten minutes passed like an hour. Broken Wing checked his watch, shifted onto his side, and nudged Jessie.

"That's ten."

Jessie rolled over and looked back at the Indian. "It might sound stupid, but I almost wanted the gunny to be right just to make that jackass Pomper look like the jerk that he is."

"That *is* stupid."

"Old Tom Mix would never take this abuse off no redskin."

Jessie pushed up to his elbows and knees, only to be shoved back onto his stomach by the butt end of Broken Wing's rifle. Movement coming up the trail from their rear, along the spine of the ridge, caught Jessie's eye. He stiffened as Broken Wing took aim at a five-man Japanese machine gun team twenty yards down the trail and closing fast. The khaki-clad Japanese wore laced-up leggings, and their faces were blackened. Automatic fire erupted from the direction of the village. The jungle rocked with exploding grenades. Suddenly it was clear. The Japs would strike at the village to drive the Marines back along the treacherous narrow path. A single machine gun, placed exactly where Jessie and Wing had put the BAR, could annihilate anyone retreating along the ridge and around the dogleg.

Broken Wing waited until the last possible moment. Ten yards away the lead Jap paused and stared straight at the two prone Marines. Broken Wing opened fire. The lead Jap flew backward. Jessie lifted the BAR from the fern cover, twirled around, and sprayed a twenty-round clip over the heads of the retreating Japanese. Broken Wing stood up and fired a single shot. One of the Japs stumbled forward onto the heels of another, causing them both to fall. Broken Wing fired again as the two Japs scrambled to their feet and disappeared over a ridge. He looked down at Jessie.

"Would have had 'em with a bow."

The sound of men running grabbed Jessie's attention. Lopez appeared on the trail coming from the village, looking over his shoulder as he ran. A moment later a squad of Marines sprinted from the jungle in single file. Two heavy machine guns opened fire from the direction of the village. The jungle rocked with a series of explosions as Lopez rounded the corner of the L-shaped trail and rushed past Jessie and Broken Wing.

"Gunny said to keep going all the way to the stream!" Lopez shouted as he ran past.

Another squad of Marines ran out of the dark green jungle and onto the narrow edge of the ridge. Each man darted around the corner and raced past the BAR team without a word. The shooting sounded closer. Bullets smacked through the leaves and whined off trees. Still another squad ran past.

"How many was that?" Jessie asked.

"Wait for Gunny."

Jessie aimed across the black crevasse at the point where the trail dropped down to the jungle village. He kept his finger away from the trigger, fearing he might squeeze off a round on a Marine instead of a Jap. Another series of grenade explosions shook the ground. Suddenly Doc Kuipers rushed out of the jungle with a wounded Marine over his shoulder in a fireman's carry.

"Get ready," Broken Wing said.

"As soon as I see the gunny."

Broken Wing nudged Jessie with his elbow. "There he is!"

Gunnery Sergeant O'Cleary ran out of the jungle, stopped, and threw a grenade back toward the village below, then turned and ran. A sharp explosion shook leaves from the towering trees. Doc Kuipers hustled past, breathing hard under the weight of the wounded Marine. A thin Japanese soldier sprinted out of the jungle onto the narrow trail in a full-out hunched-over run. Jessie squeezed off a ten-round burst. The skinny Japanese soldier dropped his rifle, staggered forward two steps, turned around, then fell onto his stomach. He crawled back into the jungle, leaving a wide trail of blood. Gunnery Sergeant O'Cleary hustled around the dogleg and ran five yards past Jessie and Broken Wing before he stopped and dropped to one knee. He gasped for air.

"You have to hold them until we get another position set up!"

"We'll hold, Gunny!" Jessie yelled.

"I'll send word back in a few minutes."

The gunny stood up and ran back down the trail that led over the spine of the three steep hills then down toward the ford that crossed the mountain stream.

Broken Wing gave a disgruntled moan, and Jessie knew a redskin wisecrack was on the way.

"*We.*"

"What?"

"We will hold them."

A maniacal scream echoed through the wet jungle mountains. Jessie gripped the BAR until all the blood was forced from his fingers. An eight-man squad of Japanese ran screaming onto the trail, firing straight ahead. Their bullets thudded harmlessly into the ground and trees. Jessie opened up across the crevasse with two accurate five-round bursts that swept the first three Japs from the crest of the ridge and over the other side.

"Ammo!" Jessie screamed as he ripped out the empty clip.

Broken Wing shoved in another clip and quickly squeezed oil into the end of the gas cylinder. Jessie rammed the stock of the Browning into his shoulder and opened fire again. Three more Japs dropped onto the trail. The last two leapt over the bodies of their comrades and kept coming. Jessie swept his fire after them until the BAR clicked as the magazine went empty. The two Japs rounded the corner of the L-shaped trail and fired from the hip as they came on. Broken Wing sent both Japs backward with an automatic burst from his Johnson rifle.

"Ammo!" Jessie shouted again, just as another group of Japanese moved onto the trail, screaming "Banzai."

Broken Wing shoved one clip into the BAR and grabbed a second to prepare for a quicker reload. The first two Japs paused for a moment to look around, as they weren't sure where their enemy was. Jessie squeezed the trigger and blew both of them into the ravine. The next two stopped and pitched grenades toward the Americans. Both grenades fell short of their mark and exploded harmlessly in the dark crevasse. Jessie raked the trail, and more of the enemy fell to the ground. The clip was empty, but there was hardly a break in the fire as Broken Wing yanked it out and shoved in the next one. Jessie pulled on the trigger and cut the last two Japanese down as they neared the corner of the L-shaped trail. Broken Wing pointed back at the jungle, where the trail dropped away toward the village below.

"There!"

A Japanese soldier had crawled out onto the narrow ledge that formed the trail, and just behind him two more crawled out, pushing a Nambu machine gun in front of them. Jessie opened fire. The enemy had no cover. Jessie's first round exploded the lead man's head like a broken watermelon. The other two scrambled back down the trail and into the cover of the jungle, leaving the machine gun and its tripod on the trail.

Broken Wing nudged Jessie. Jessie ceased fire. They both lay stiff, staring, not moving a muscle.

"Awful quiet," Broken Wing mumbled.

"Can't hear anything but this ringing in my ears."

"You can't hear that?"

The first sounds of many men chattering came from the village.

"They're regrouping, Wing." Jessie's voice cracked.

Broken Wing shifted onto his side to look back down the trail.

"See any of the platoon?" Jessie asked with his eyes glued on the dead Jap lying facedown beside the machine gun.

"Nope."

"How much ammo we got left?"

"Not much."

"Why don't you count the clips so we'll have some idea when we're about to die."

"Why you want to die?"

"I don't wanna die!"

"You hear that?"

"What?"

"Duck."

Broken Wing shoved his face into the ground and held on to his helmet. Jessie looked up as a high-pitched scream grew louder and closer. He flattened his face into the damp earth and covered his helmet with both hands. A ringing explosion high above cut the top of a huge tree in half.

"Mortars?" Jessie shouted.

"Jap 90s."

"Nineties?"

"That scream."

A moment later the rain-swept sky filled with the high-pitched screams of incoming mortar rounds. Most of the rounds sailed long, exploding in the canyon on the other side of the trail. A few struck the tops of the huge trees towering up over the trail, raining shrapnel on the jungle below. Then the mortar fire ceased. Jessie peeked out from under his helmet. Japanese soldiers ran onto the trail screaming like madmen.

"Fire!" Broken Wing shouted as he took aim and opened up on the lead man.

Jessie shoved the BAR into his shoulder and sent a twenty-round clip into the screaming Japs. Four of the charging Japanese were swept from the narrow ledge and into the canyon on the far side. The others paused, then retreated, grabbing the machine gun as they ran back to the safety of the jungle.

"Two clips left," Broken Wing said calmly.

"That's all?"

"I have no trouble counting up to two."

"I hate it when you're a wise guy!"

"Better put BAR on the slower cyclic rate."

Jessie pushed the change lever forward just aft of the trigger. "Maybe we should run for it. Even firing slow, we're in deep trouble."

Broken Wing put his finger on his lips. "Listen."

The noisy chatter of a large group of Japanese filtered from the village.

"They're getting ready," Jessie said.

"They probably moved around by now. They will try to get to us from the canyon side of the trail."

"Where's the gunny?"

Broken Wing looked back.

"Don't see anybody coming."

"If we don't take off soon, we're gonna die here."

"Yep."

Jessie stiffened. He stared and looked across the narrow

trail on his right. "Did you hear that?" The rustling sound of men moving through wet brush in the canyon below was faint, but there could be no doubt.

"Flanking us."

"Got any grenades?"

Broken Wing checked his cartridge belt.

"Got three."

"Three?"

"Your name Dewey?"

"Yeah, nickel face, give me a recount!"

"Three."

"I got two, but I'm gonna save one to put in your mouth."

"Toss over edge. Take off."

"Right," Jessie said. He pulled the pin on one grenade and held the spoon tight.

"Ready to sprint? Three hills, down to that ford that crosses the stream!"

Broken Wing pulled the pin on a grenade.

"One, two, three."

They tossed the grenades over the canyon side of the trail, scrambled to their feet, and ran. The explosions sounded muffled and far away as Jessie led the way back down the narrow footpath as fast as he could run. He could hear Broken Wing's boondockers plodding after him in the soggy earth. A scream of "Banzai" sent goose bumps up Jessie's spine. He tried to run faster, but the twenty-pound Browning automatic rifle seemed to weigh his feet to the ground, and he yearned for his little eight-pound Johnson.

"They swarmed our old position," Broken Wing shouted from behind Jessie.

Jessie glanced back over his shoulder as he reached the crest of the first hill. Khaki-clad Japanese with blackened faces stopped searching their old position and pointed toward the escaping Marines. Jessie cleared the crest of the first hill and started down the other side. The crack of Jap rifles and the whine of bullets overhead pushed his legs faster. Jungle on both sides of the narrow path grew more dense as they started up the second hill. The incline was steeper than the first, and the fear of the Japs catching up filled Jessie's system with adrenaline.

He looked back. "Are they coming?"

Broken Wing didn't answer. Jessie stopped and laid the

BAR down as they reached the crest of the second hill. He bent over, grabbed his knees, and gasped for breath.

"They're coming!" Broken Wing's shout sent a shock wave of panic through Jessie.

He grabbed the heavy Browning automatic and raced down the other side of the second hill. His lungs burned as he started the run up through the jungle covering the third hill. He could hear Broken Wing gasping for breath behind him. Each step came harder than the last until finally Jessie had to walk the last few feet to the top.

"Slate!"

Jessie looked up. Gunny O'Cleary, Perelli, and Lopez came toward him.

"Japs are coming up behind us, Gunny!"

"Move it, Broken Wing!" O'Cleary barked.

Broken Wing struggled forward up the path, his face wet with sweat and his eyes glazed with fatigue. He seemed unable to answer.

"Sounded like you guys had a shoot-out," Perelli said excitedly.

Jessie tried to answer, but his breath wouldn't come. His lungs burned, and every inch of his flesh tingled and itched. He nodded at Perelli and tried to force his legs to move up and over the crest of the final hill.

"Come on, Wing, move it! We got a perimeter set up on the other side of the stream."

"Are they in sight?" Jessie asked as he started down the steep gradient that led to the ford across the canyon stream.

"Not yet," someone answered from behind.

Five minutes later they were inside the perimeter. The Japs either had given up the chase or were biding their time before assaulting the Marine line later. Two hundred yards beyond the natural bridge, at the sloping foot of the charred and rock-strewn Bagana volcano, Jessie spotted the beautiful round shape of two camouflaged Marine helmets.

"Slate!" One of the helmets peeked over the edge of a shallow foxhole.

"Oglethorpe," Jessie said with a tired wave.

Jessie staggered past Oglethorpe and dropped to the ground. LaBeau stood up in a foxhole beside Oglethorpe and tossed Jessie a canteen.

"Good job, Slate."

"Thanks." Jessie set the BAR down and took a long drink.

"Charlie Rose would have been real proud of you."

Jessie sagged to the ground on his knees beside the BAR. Charlie Rose. His name awakened a flood of painful emotions that seemed to drain the last portion of energy from Jessie's body.

"You okay, Slate?" LaBeau's face was a mask of concern. Jessie nodded.

"You get hit?"

Jessie shook his head no.

Broken Wing and the others filed past them and stopped. Gunny O'Cleary knelt on one knee.

"How many did you see?"

"Big war party," Broken Wing said.

"We shot at least ten of 'em, Gunny," Jessie said quietly.

Gunny O'Cleary looked at Broken Wing. "That right?"

"Maybe more."

"We tried to hold out; we were down to two clips."

The old salt's battle-hardened eyes softened. He patted Jessie's helmet with his fist. "Outstanding."

"Who Doc Kuipers carry by us, Gunny?" Broken Wing asked.

"That young kid with the Johnson light."

"Yeah. Blaine from Colorado," LaBeau said.

"How bad?"

"Caught a round right through his hip and out his rear end. He'll live if we get him back to the field hospital."

Broken Wing jumped to his feet. His face turned pale. "You, you feel that?"

Oglethorpe snickered.

"I ain't kiddin! Ground moved!"

"This is quite accurate, Broken Wing," Oglethorpe said.

"What?" Jessie asked.

Oglethorpe held out his hand as if introducing the giant mountain that towered over them.

"Gentlemen, you are in the unique position of experiencing the power of a live volcano."

"Don't like unique position," Broken Wing muttered nervously.

Gunny O'Cleary laughed.

"Crap, boy! Dead's dead, and there ain't no better way to die than to die a Marine!"

"Die Marine, okay. Fry Marine, not good."

Gunny laughed and stood up. "You two did good. I'm putting you both in for corporal as of now."

"Thanks, Gunny," Jessie said.

"Me, too," Broken Wing said.

"You earned it. Now get that BAR set up over there." O'Cleary pointed to a spot ten yards on LaBeau's left beside two large charred stones.

"Aye, aye, Gunny," Broken Wing said.

"Who's on the other side of us in the next position?" Jessie asked.

"Scuttlemouth Perelli and Lopez," Chris said.

"Dig in and make sure you have a clear field of fire," Gunny said. "My guess is we ran into at least two companies of Nips. They'll probably try to pin us against the river and overrun us or else pick us off when we cross."

"Think that useless Yankee lieutenant will listen this time, Gunny?" LaBeau asked.

"Pomper still talking about busting you, Gunny?" Broken Wing asked with a sly grin.

"Yeah, bet that sucker's blowing wind over you being right," Jessie said.

Gunny O'Cleary frowned. "All right, let's stop flapping our jaws and get some oil on those weapons. Slate, you and Wing dig in." Gunny O'Cleary turned and walked back toward the CP.

Digging in the rain-soaked volcanic ash was relatively easy. The field of fire was better than most places on Bougainville since the jungle around Bagana had been burned away numerous times through the centuries. In some places the ground was still barren. They dug in deeper than usual, especially now that they knew the Japs had the big 90-mm mortars. Broken Wing rounded up five extra clips of ammo for the automatic rifle while Jessie fixed up a tasteless meal of pork and beans and three hardtack biscuits.

"Youz guys sent some Tojos to see their ancestors, I hear."

Jessie looked up to see Aldo Perelli squatting beside their foxhole, holding a paperback book out of the rain, close to his chest.

"It was tight, Perelli, real tight," Jessie said.

"That right, Wing?"

"Now I know how Custer felt."

Perelli handed Jessie the paperback. "Here."

"What's this for?"

"Your mom was a teacher, right? You can read, can't you?"

"Don't be a wise guy. What are you giving it to me for? You could get a lot for this."

Perelli shrugged and looked embarrassed. He moved his hands in small circles as if looking for the right words.

"Hey. It's sort of like saying thanks. We were in a real jam back there, and you two gave us time to get out."

Jessie and Broken Wing exchanged puzzled glances.

"Thanks, Perelli," Jessie said.

"Yes," Broken Wing said.

"Hey, it's nothin'," Perelli called as he walked back to his position.

Broken Wing held out his muddy hand, and Jessie handed him the book.

"That was really nice of old Perelli."

Broken Wing's eyebrows lifted. "Ellery Queen. Sounds like a queer," he said.

"It's a detective mystery, stupid. You want to read it first?"

"Detective? Perry Mason is the best."

"You like mystery books?"

"Like Perry Mason."

"Erle Stanley Gardner?"

Broken Wing gave a nod. "Books too much money. Cost two dollars!"

"You never stop surprising me, Wing. I never figured you for a reader."

"Two dollar could buy whole bottle of firewater. I'm thirsty."

"Did you know that some of those guys in the Third were issued little bottles of booze? Brandy, I think."

"Not right. I bet Mustache Smeller gives whiskey."

"Who's that?"

"Hitler."

"What do you call Mussolini?"

"Big Gourd Chin."

"And the Japs are Narrow Eyes?"

"I'm thirsty."

"So what's new? Give me the book. I want to read some before it gets dark."

Jessie grabbed the book as Corporal DiCicca approached.

"What's up, Phil?" Jessie asked.

Phil knelt down beside Broken Wing's half of the foxhole. "Make sure that your position is secure, cause we're staying put till Sam Hill finds a place to cross the river."

"How long will that be?"

"With twenty days of rain, who knows?"

The next day the platoon ran small squad-size patrols from the Bagana perimeter but never went out any farther than Torokina river canyon. That night they expected an attack, but it never came. The next morning began with something that no one in the First Platoon of the First Parachute Battalion had seen since landing on Bougainville: Blue sky. No rain. The sun blazed overhead in a hot, clear sky.

Jessie looked at his hands. They were wrinkled like wet prunes. Broken Wing stretched and yawned.

"Thirsty."

Jessie grinned. "Is that all you can say? I feel like Noah, man."

"Noah?"

"Yeah, you know, Noah and the ark after forty days and forty nights of rain."

"Forty days?"

"You know, in the Bible."

Broken Wing grunted and nodded thoughtfully. "I will read this book someday."

"Probably not a bad idea," Jessie said.

Broken Wing put a finger to his lips. "Listen."

The ominous sound of big naval guns rose like thunder from the sea.

"Hey, look up there!" Lopez shouted.

Jessie stared into the blue sky. The closing drone of fighter planes filled the air. Vapor trails crisscrossed the sky.

"Hey, there's three Nips on one of our guys!"

A silver P-51 Mustang dove low over Bagana to escape the tracer fire from two banana-yellow Japanese Zeroes while a third circled above. Suddenly yellow flame shot from the underbelly of the P-51. A piece of the American fighter plane exploded away from the fuselage. Bright sunlight glistened off the shiny piece of metal as it fluttered away from the plane. A squadron of black Marine Corsairs suddenly dropped out of the bright morning sun and upon the Japanese fighters. The two Zeroes chasing the American P-51 Mustang exploded in flames with the first pass by the diving Corsairs. The third Jap plane rolled, dived, and fled toward the east and the safety of Rabaul.

Broken Wing leaned against the wall of their foxhole. He followed the wounded American fighter with his eyes as the Mustang limped by low overhead, trailing black smoke.

"Think he will make it to Torokina Airstrip?"

A white flash of sunlight shot into the corner of Jessie's eye. He glanced up and to his right. A shimmering piece of the American fighter was hurtling out of the hot blue sky. Jessie followed the man-made meteor down until it clipped a branch near the top of a tall jungle tree about fifty yards outside the Marine perimeter. Jessie watched hypnotically as the broken branch dangled back and forth, held on the limb by a few strands of bark.

Then something else grabbed Jessie's attention, in another tree about thirty yards farther out. He stiffened, his eyes squinting to see more clearly. It was a man camouflaged in the foliage.

"Hit the deck! Sniper!"

Broken Wing flattened out just as a muzzle flashed from the tree. Broken Wing groaned. Jessie grabbed him by the collar and yanked him hard into the foxhole.

Broken Wing lifted his face from the dirt. His dark eyebrows were back to his hairline. He removed his helmet and showed Jessie a bullet crease on the top of the steel pot.

"You should see your face," Jessie said with a laugh.

"You saved my life."

Jessie laughed again and pretended to wipe sweat from his forehead. "You were a hair away from being scalped, Wing."

Broken Wing looked out at the jungle, then back at Jessie. "My child will have a father."

Jessie started to laugh, but something grave in the Indian's steadfast eyes stopped him. Jessie turned his attention and his aim back to the sniper.

The powerful BAR was probably the most accurate weapon in a Marine rifle platoon. It was highly effective up to five hundred yards. The Jap had no chance. Jessie shot five bursts of three rounds each halfway up the tall tree. A rifle tumbled to the ground.

"I got him!"

"Maybe," Broken Wing said, peering over the edge of their foxhole.

Corporal DiCicca slid in beside Jessie. "Good shooting. You got him."

"Better make sure," Broken Wing cautioned.

"Why?" Jessie asked.

"Snipers on the Canal played possum. Have two rifles. Get spotted, take fire, drop rifle from tree, and play dead."

Corporal DiCicca slapped Jessie on the shoulder. "Jessie, cover us. Me and Broken Wing are gonna check him out."

Ten minutes later Broken Wing and DiCicca ran crouching back into the perimeter. DiCicca signaled a thumbs-up to Jessie and headed for the CP.

Broken Wing stepped down into the foxhole and pulled a rectangular sheet of metal out of his shirt. It was a piece of the P-51. He cleaned it off, pulled out his K-bar, and began punching holes into the metal until he had two ten-inch strips cut out. Jessie sat silently watching the jungle beyond the perimeter as Broken Wing continued patiently working. No one spoke. A half hour later Jessie figured enough was enough.

"All right. When are you going to tell me what you're doing?"

"Psst!"

"Psst! Slate. Wing. Pass the word I got movement out here."

Jessie looked to his right. Chris LaBeau pointed toward the jungle ahead. Suddenly a shot rang out from the left flank of the perimeter. Then another burst of fire came from the right flank. Broken Wing shoved his metalwork into his pack and began laying out BAR clips on the edge of the foxhole. Jessie strained his eyes until they watered but could see nothing moving. Another burst of automatic fire shot from the left side of the perimeter. The sound of men moving through the jungle ahead stiffened Jessie's spine. The urge to shoot without a target was almost overwhelming, but Marine discipline came through, and fire control was maintained around the perimeter.

"Slate! Wing!" Oglethorpe shouted from the other side of LaBeau.

"Yo!"

"Pass the word. Sam found a place to cross. Saddle up."

Jessie turned to face the position on his left. "Perelli!"

"Yeah. I heard."

"Pass it on."

"Aye, aye, Corporal," Perelli said sarcastically.

Jessie and Broken Wing exchanged a quick smirk then glued their eyes back to the jungle ahead. Still no movement.

"Wing, we're coming in."

Jessie spun around as Corporal DiCicca and Gunnery Sergeant O'Cleary flattened themselves out behind the foxhole.

Gunny O'Cleary was breathing extra hard. The old salt's age was beginning to tell.

"Corporal DiCicca's squad is gonna set up a delaying action while the rest of the platoon wades across the Torokina," he said. "We're pulling back to the river. Sam Hill is leading us to a crossing point. When we get close, I'll give Phil the word. Clear?"

"Clear," Broken Wing said.

Jessie nodded. Gunny and Phil stood to a crouch and ran toward Perelli's position. A sniper round cracked from the green foliage beyond the perimeter and whined off a nearby rock.

Jessie aimed in the general direction. "Where's he at?"

"Can't see a thing," Broken Wing said.

Five minutes later the word to pull back echoed around the perimeter. One squad at a time moved to the trail and headed toward the river. Corporal DiCicca's squad was the last to move out.

Perelli and Lopez brought up the rear. Both men walked backward, waiting for the first sign that Japs were following. Forty yards farther on the jungle turned so thick that if the Japs were to attack the retreating platoon, it was obvious they would have to come down the trail. Word filtered back down the column to halt. A few moments later Lieutenant

Pomper made his way to the tail end. He squatted on one knee beside Corporal DiCicca. Sweat streamed down his flushed face. He looked nervous and spoke fast.

"The rest of the platoon is wading across. You have your orders. Now, hold 'em off until we reach the other side. Got it?"

"Aye, aye, sir."

"Good luck," Pomper said. He stood and hustled back to the front of the column at the river's edge.

Corporal DiCicca turned back to the anxious squad. "Well, you heard the man."

"Set up here?" Chris LaBeau asked with a disapproving frown.

Corporal DiCicca pointed back down the trail. "See that bend in the trail twenty yards back there? If we set up here, we should be able to pick 'em off when they come around the corner."

"What if they don't oblige us by staying on the trail?" Perelli asked sarcastically.

"Crap. Perelli! You think you could walk through that mess without hacking out every inch of it?"

Perelli shrugged his shoulders and rolled his eyes. "I might if—"

Perelli's words disappeared in a hail of gunfire as Broken Wing dropped to his stomach and opened fire on two Japanese soldiers in olive-drab uniforms walking casually around the corner Corporal DiCicca had pointed to.

The lead Jap fell onto one knee, dropped his rifle, and clutched at his left thigh. Then both men scrambled back around the blind corner of the trail.

"That's terrible shooting!" Jessie yelled as he dropped onto his stomach beside the prone Indian, who tightened the wing screws on the BAR's bipod legs and took aim.

Three Japs came screaming around the bend of the trail. The lead man fired from the hip, but his aim was high. A barrage of return fire blew the man back into the soldier behind him, knocking him down, too. The third charging Jap opened fire over his fallen comrades. His first shot brought an agonizing scream from behind Jessie. Jessie pulled on the trigger. A five-shot burst cut the man's legs from under him. He fell onto his face, writhing in pain. Jessie sent another five-round burst into the three Japanese twenty yards down

the trail. The middle soldier lifted himself onto his knees
and tried to take aim. Broken Wing opened fire. A bullet
exploded the man's face. He fell back.

"Phil's hit!" Perelli shouted.

Perelli and Lopez were kneeling beside Corporal Di-
Cicca. A sharp piece of white bone protruded through a rip
in Phil's blood-soaked trousers, just below his left hip.

"It's gonna take a couple of us to carry him!" Lopez's
voice cracked with strain.

"Go on!" Jessie shouted. "Get started before they try it
again."

Broken Wing opened fire. More Japanese soldiers were
charging single file around the bend in the trail. Jessie also
opened fire. The first man stumbled forward then fell dead.
The next jumped over him with a paralyzing scream. Two
rifles fired over Jessie, and the screaming Jap dropped so
close to Jessie that he could feel the thud vibrate the ground.
Broken Wing reloaded the BAR. The two Japs who remained standing paused ten yards away and drew back their
arms to throw. Jessie pulled on the trigger. The lead Jap let
go with his grenade and fell dead. His comrade stumbled
backward from a spattering of repeated hits then crumpled
among the bodies sprawled on the trail.

A ripping explosion rocked the jungle behind Jessie and
Broken Wing, covering them with dirt and debris. Jessie
touched the back of his neck. Something on it felt cold and
wet. He examined his hand. It was covered with blood that
was not his own. Men groaned behind him.

"We're hit."

"Get 'em back to the river! We'll hold 'em off! Go on!"
Jessie screamed. Broken Wing shoved another clip in the
BAR.

Jessie aimed directly at the bend in the trail. He had to
clench his teeth to stop them from chattering. Someone
grabbed his boot and shook it hard. It was Oglethorpe.

"We're hit. We're pulling back."

Suddenly Broken Wing began to fire single shots. A
charging Jap tumbled into the thick brush on the side of
the trail. A second enemy soldier tripped over a dead body
sprawled across the trail, then raised himself up on his knees
and threw a grenade. Jessie opened fire. The Jap fell forward
dead. The grenade thudded into the mud and brush just off

the trail on Broken Wing's right. Jessie and Broken Wing buried their faces in the dirt, covered their helmets with both arms, and waited. A deafening explosion blew a hole in the thick foliage to Broken Wing's right. Jessie pulled his face out of the dirt and immediately fired back down the trail, but there was no one alive to hit. Broken Wing groaned and made a gurgling noise. He lay facedown. Jessie shook him.

"Wing!"

"I'm hit," the Indian said quietly without looking up.

"Bad?"

"Yep."

"How bad?"

"Can't do squaw dance."

"Can you move?"

"Don't think so."

"You got to!"

Broken Wing lifted his face out of the dirt. He turned slowly toward Jessie until they were nearly nose to nose. "You go back. I hold 'em off."

"Don't be stupid."

"No time to argue, go on."

"Bullcrap! A little shrapnel never hurt anybody."

"Go, Jessie."

"Ain't going without you, so get moving."

"Don't think I can."

"You better or you're gonna get us both killed."

Broken Wing groaned as he rolled over onto his side. Blood from a gaping hole streamed between his fingers. He turned and began crawling back toward the river. A single Japanese soldier ran around the bend and flattened out behind the dead bodies. When he raised up to fire, Jessie squeezed the trigger until the firing pin of the BAR clicked against an empty chamber. The Jap rifleman's helmet and pieces of his skull had exploded into the air, and he had fallen facedown on the dead man he had hidden behind. Jessie stared at the top of the man's open skull. Gray brains and dark red blood oozed through black hair and bits of bone. Jessie shivered and belched up a mouthful of bile. He spit it out and fumbled for another clip of ammo. His fingers felt stiff. The only movement was that of a wounded Jap writhing in pain fifteen yards away. Jessie glanced back to check on Broken Wing's progress. The Indian lay motionless on his stomach.

"You ain't got time to lay around! Get movin'!"

Broken Wing's right arm reached forward, then went limp.

Jessie slapped against his cartridge belt with his left hand, searching for a grenade while he kept his right hand ready to fire. He pulled a grenade off his belt and pulled the pin, then squeezed the spoon and got to his feet. He walked backward until he nudged against Broken Wing's boots with his own.

"Get up!"

Broken Wing rolled onto one side and weakly lifted his hand toward Jessie's cartridge belt. Holding on to a canteen pouch, he tried to pull himself up but couldn't.

"Crap, Wing! Saddle up!" Jessie dropped the BAR on its bipod legs and grabbed Broken Wing under one arm. He lifted him to a sitting position.

"Ready, Wing? Here we go." He pulled Broken Wing to his feet and shoved his shoulder under the Indian's armpit.

"Jap," Broken Wing muttered as he pointed back down the trail.

Two Japs stepped around the bend; both crouched with bayonets fixed. Jessie flipped the grenade toward the surprised soldiers with an underhand throw. The Japanese shouted in alarm and rushed back as the grenade exploded among the bodies lying on the trail. Jessie spun the Indian around, bent down, and lifted him over his shoulder in a fireman's carry. Broken Wing moaned out loud. Jessie jogged toward the river. After ten yards the trail sloped downhill. Jessie picked up speed, but each bouncing step brought deep painful gasps from Broken Wing. Twenty-five yards later Jessie could see the sun glistening off water through the brush.

"River's up ahead," Jessie said, and grunted under the weight of Broken Wing's limp body.

He lowered his wounded friend to the edge of the steep, muddy riverbank, then glanced back up the trail. No sign of movement. Broken Wing's eyes were closed. "Can you walk or swim?"

"Yes."

"Here we go." Jessie slid down the muddy bank, dragging the Indian behind him as gently as he could.

Jessie shivered at the touch of the chilly black water. He pulled the Indian in behind him.

"I can touch the bottom. You stay on your back, and I'll float you across."

"Any Japs?" Broken Wing asked through gritted teeth.

"Not yet."

Jessie put an arm under Broken Wing's pack and tried to wade swiftly through the chest-deep river, but the downstream current nearly swept him off his feet.

"Come on! Move it!" Gunny O'Cleary barked from the other side.

Each step felt slower than the last. Jessie wanted to look back over his shoulder but forced himself not to. Visions of a Jap sniper taking aim at the back of his head sent a wave of panic through him. He struggled to move faster.

"Hurry, Marine." O'Cleary's voice sounded calm now.

Jessie looked ahead. He could see the helmets of the platoon. The men were taking up positions along the river's edge. Rifle barrels pushed through the thick jungle growth. Doc Kuiper and Gunnery Sergeant O'Cleary waded out into the river. He could hear the loud piercing crack of a Japanese rifle as it opened fire. A sharp pain screamed through Jessie's left lat muscle. He spun in the water as if he had been hit by a sledgehammer. He gained his balance and looked down. Blood floated to the top of the black water. His latissimus muscle burned, and his left arm felt numb and limp. The Marines opened fire with what sounded like every weapon in the platoon.

"Move it! Move it!" O'Cleary shouted as he reached a hand to Broken Wing. Jessie floated Broken Wing toward the gunny and clutched at a gaping hole in his own lat.

"You can make it!" Doc Kuipers yelled as he grabbed Jessie by his lapel and pulled him forward.

"I'm hit," Jessie mumbled.

A spray of automatic fire ripped by Doc Kuipers's right shoulder. Rows of tiny white geysers erupted from the black water. Another barrage of Marine fire silenced the Japanese machine gun as the four Marines clawed and pulled each other up the riverbank and into the safe cover of the dense jungle. Five minutes later Doc Kuipers shoved a hypo of

morphine into Broken Wing, then one into Jessie. He bandaged them enough to slow the bleeding, and the platoon immediately moved out. Corporal DiCicca and Broken Wing
were carried on makeshift stretchers made of two rifles and
a poncho. Jessie was able to walk along with Perelli, La-
Beau, and Benjamin Oglethorpe.

A half hour later the tired, bloody Marines waded into
the Torokina swamp and the outer perimeter of Marine
lines held by Third Division Marines. A baby-faced PFC
sitting beside one of the brand-new air-cooled .30-caliber
machine guns pointed at the platoon as they passed.

"Hey, that's those Para-Marines, ain't it?"

Another Marine looked and shook his head. "No way,
Mac. They wouldn't waste those guys on Bougainville."

Jessie felt a wave of pride swell up from within.

Just inside Marine lines the wounded were laid on ponchos until transportation back to the beach field hospital
could be brought up. The only available transportation was
a wooden sled towed behind one of the Seabees' small bulldozers, but the sled was already stacked up with dead Japs.

"Hey, listen, we got to get these wounded Marines back
to the field hospital!" Lieutenant Pomper shouted over the
rumbling engine of the bulldozer.

The shirtless driver shrugged. "I have to dump these
Tojos in the big slit trench back at the airstrip. That's where
we're burying all of 'em."

"Just dig a trench here and throw them in!"

He shrugged again and nodded. Ten minutes later, the
bulldozer pushed dirt over the Japanese corpses. A corpsman shoveled dirt onto the sled with his hands to cover the
slick left from the oozing bodies. The wounded Marines
were dragged back to the field hospital at Empress Augusta
Bay. A column of new replacements marching to the front
shouted friendly insults as they passed. Jessie tried to signal
a thumbs-up, but he was too tired. Someone was singing the
Para-Marine song. He closed his eyes and wondered how
badly the others were wounded.

# CHAPTER TEN

HE TRIED TO OPEN HIS EYES BUT COULDN'T. KATE'S
face surged forward from somewhere in his memory, and
he felt warm and content. She was standing next to something, a long box, an open coffin with a dead man in it. Charlie Rose. Jessie shook violently and sat up.

"Back down, Marine. You're okay now."

"Where's Charlie Rose?"

"Open your eyes, Marine."

Jessie opened his eyes. A gray-haired man stared down
at him. A young corpsman stood beside the older man.

"Where am I?" Jessie asked.

"I'm Dr. Reese. This is a field hospital."

"Still on Bougainville?"

The doctor glanced up at the roof of the tent. Rain pelted
it hard enough to split the canvas. He laughed.

"What do you think?"

"Why don't Bougainville sink?"

Reese laughed again. "You've been here a couple of days,
and you're doing fine. The bullet went clean through the
latissimus dorsi muscle. It didn't strike any vital organs or
bone, and there's no infection."

"How about the other guys, Doc? Broken Wing and Corporal DiCicca?"

Dr. Reese turned to the corpsman. "Broken Wing? Is that
the Indian Marine who keeps demanding to be put in this
tent?"

"Yes, sir."

Dr. Reese looked down at Jessie. "He'll be fine. Shrapnel

broke two ribs, and he lost a lot of blood, but he'll be all right."

"How about the others?"

"They all had shrapnel wounds, I believe. They're fine. A few weeks in bed. Corporal DiCicca was the most serious. We'll know more in a day or so."

"Keep me posted, Doc."

"I will. You rest and make sure you get some chow in that body real soon."

"Aye, aye, sir."

"Don't be moving that side of your body just yet."

"Yes, sir."


Four days later Jessie was feeling better, but it was still hard to stay awake.

"Jessie."

The big deep voice sounded familiar. Jessie blinked open his eyes and tried to shake away the morphine stupor. The sound of rain beating against the tent roof felt good. He blinked and rubbed his eyes, then winced with pain.

"Chaplain Parker?"

"Thank God you're okay, Jessie."

"Thanks, Chaplain."

The big man pulled an envelope from his trousers pocket. "I'll get right to the point, Jessie. The CO got a letter from your wife asking if you're okay. She's terribly worried. She says she hasn't heard a word from you since you were married." The big man scratched the back of his neck and frowned.

Jessie shrugged, but he felt the hurt again of remembering Charlie Rose, as he did every time he thought about his wedding.

"Why haven't you written?"

"I don't know."

"I think you do. And I'm paid to listen. It always helps to talk things out."

"I'm sorry. I just can't explain." Jessie stopped and sighed.

"Did you try praying, Jessie?"

"I've never been too much on religion, Chaplain. My dad

went to church a lot at one time, but something happened with the preacher, and after that he always taught me that religion was a waste of time."

The chaplain nodded sadly, "Yes, that can happen to people. It's unfortunate. They lose so much when that happens."

"Well, anyway, I promise I'll try to get a letter out soon."

"Yes, do. I hate to put it like this, Corporal, but that's an order from the CO."

"Yes, sir."

"I don't know if this has anything to do with our talk on Vella Lavella, Jessie, but then you were confused about forgiveness. Let me urge you to think about this: Once you've accepted Christ's forgiveness, forgiving yourself and others becomes a lot easier."

"I'll think about it, Chaplain."

"I laid some writing gear under your cot. I'll be back to check in on you. Just rest and try to get back some of your strength."

"Where's Broken Wing?"

"Here."

Jessie turned toward the cot on his left. Broken Wing removed a barracks cover from his face.

"Where'd you come from?"

"Took you long enough."

"Long enough for what?"

"To ask if I was at the great powwow in the sky."

"Keep him on his toes, Broken Wing," the chaplain said with a chuckle as he tossed Kate's letter onto Jessie's stomach and walked out of the tent.

"Letter from Tom-Toms?" Broken Wing asked.

"Will you quit with the tom-tom stuff?"

Jessie dropped the letter to the dirt floor beside his cot and closed his eyes.

"Hope you are not a very stupid man," Broken Wing said thoughtfully.

"Why do you care how stupid I am?"

"You saved my life. Gave my child a father."

Jessie turned his head and opened his eyes to look at Broken Wing. He flinched back when he found himself nose to nose with the Indian.

"God! I hate it when you do that!"

"Yes. You do."

"How do you guys get to be so sneaky?"

Broken Wing took Jessie's left hand and turned it palm up.

"What are you doing?" Jessie asked suspiciously.

Broken Wing pulled a K-bar knife out of a sheath on his pack beside his cot.

"What are you doing?"

"Owe you my life."

"So what?"

"We will be blood brothers."

The Indian quickly made a small cut above Jessie's wrist.

"You're crazy!" Jessie yanked his arm away.

Broken Wing put the knife to the same spot on his right arm and sliced open a small cut.

"No. Do not wipe away the blood," Broken Wing said as he grabbed Jessie's wrist and pressed the two cuts together.

"You've seen too many Tom Mix movies."

"Your blood is my blood, and my blood is your blood. We are brothers."

Jessie couldn't keep from grinning. He looked at their arms pressed together and then back at Broken Wing's stoic face.

"Thanks, buddy. I'm honored."

"Yes. Now I need your help."

"What?"

"Tonight."

"Tonight what?"

"Found two swabbies from PT boat out of Tulagi."

"And?"

"They got firewater."

"How?"

"Torpedo juice."

"What exactly is torpedo juice?"

"Fine stuff."

"Aqua Velva is fine stuff to you."

Broken Wing turned back to his cot and dragged his pack from underneath. He opened it and pulled out two silver bracelets. He handed one to Jessie.

"Here."

Jessie studied the Indian symbols carved in it.

"What is this for?"

"Yours."

"Mine?"

"Do not like it?"

"No, yes, I like it very much, but I guess I'm just surprised. Did you make this? It's beautiful."

"They match. Made from P-51 Mustang wind god threw into tree when you saved my life."

Jessie laughed. "That wasn't the wind god, ol' buddy. Looked more like a Jap Zeke to me."

"*Bi-so-dih a-chi.*"

"Pig intestines yourself. What's this writing on here, these symbols?"

"Says 'Honor the god of wind. And honor brothers of the god of wind.' "

Jessie sat up in his cot. "I can't believe you made a bracelet this nice out of that scrap metal.

"Family has made jewelry for many generations."

Jessie stared into the Indian's black eyes. "I'll wear it until I die, Broken Wing. Anyway, I always wanted a brother," he said with a grin.

"Can you man a shovel?"

"Do what?"

"Dig."

"Dig for what?"

"Need Jap souvenirs."

"Why?"

"Trade."

"For what?"

"Torpedo juice."

"Yeah, but trade with who, exactly?"

"Seabees."

"How'd they get booze?"

"PT boats from Tulagi."

"Yeah. So?"

"Boot," Broken Wing said, shaking his head in disgust.

"What do you mean, boot?"

"Open ears and grow wise."

"Boy, is it getting deep in here."

"Torpedoes from World War I."

"Yeah."

"They got alcohol in them. Strong alcohol."

Jessie dropped his head and sighed. "Why did I have to ask?"

"Drain alcohol through strainer. Mix with powdered grapefruit juice you can steal from the mess sergeant. Fine stuff. Best in South Pacific."

"Okay, I think I understand."

Broken Wing crossed his arms and got a satisfied look on his big rugged face. " 'Bout time."

"But look at the two of us, you maniac!"

"What?"

Jessie closed his eyes and took a deep breath. He would speak slowly and calmly, he decided. "We are wounded. We are both still weak. We are covered with stitches."

"Have to dig tomorrow morning."

"You are insane."

"Hospital ship picks us up in two nights."

"Really?"

"PT boats come in tomorrow night."

Jessie frowned. "Where are you planning on getting souvenirs?"

"I know where."

"Where?"

"You see. Tomorrow."

"I'm hurt, and I ain't going anywhere."

*"Cha-le-gai."*

"White cap? You mean sailor? You called me a squid!"

"White man loyalty."

"White man loyalty, what about it?"

"Fickle."

"That's a lie!"

"Good."

"I'm not going digging!"

"Bracelet fits well."

"You are not getting the bracelet back, and I am not digging."

Broken Wing looked up and shrugged at someone on the other side of Jessie's cot.

"You talk to him yet?"

Jessie twisted to see who was standing beside his cot. The pale, freckled face of Benjamin Oglethorpe stared down through his wire-rim glasses as if he were waiting for an important answer. He balanced himself on wooden crutches.

"Yes," Broken Wing said.

"Outstanding. Here is our operational blueprint."

"What?" Jessie asked.

"The plan."

"What plan?"

"The plan that I am at this moment trying to explain."

"You, Oglethorpe? You can't be part of something this stupid!"

Christopher LaBeau stepped up beside Oglethorpe. His head was wrapped in tight beige bandages. Perelli came up behind LaBeau. His arm was in a sling.

"You tell him yet?" LaBeau asked.

"You gotta be kidding me. You guys are as crazy as this fool Navajo!"

The big, handsome Cajun frowned. "I ain't had a drink or a woman in a long time, and if that don't make a man crazy, then let's blame this Yankee war."

"A woman I could almost understand, but I heard that torpedo juice can burn a hole right through your guts."

LaBeau and Oglethorpe exchanged puzzled glances then looked over at Broken Wing. Broken Wing shrugged.

"So what's your point?" LaBeau said.

Jessie groaned and pinched the bridge of his nose.

"And, Mr. Slate," Oglethorpe added, "one should not make light of the importance of female company."

"What?" Jessie asked dumbfounded.

"Yeah, Slate. Just because you got yourself a permanent honey."

"What have women got to do with this?"

LaBeau looked at Broken Wing. "I thought you told him what we're doing."

"Then you don't even know the big reason for all of this!" LaBeau said.

Jessie shook his head in confusion.

Broken Wing shrugged.

"You useless jarhead," Perelli said to Broken Wing.

"Your partner here is now the father of a ten-pound baby boy, who remains nameless," Oglethorpe said to Jessie.

"This is a celebration for the Wingman!" LaBeau exclaimed.

Jessie looked at Broken Wing and frowned. "Why am I the last to know?"

"Would have got around to it soon."

"Well, what's the boy's name?"

"No name."

"What do you mean no name?"

"Only the father can name."

"You mean the kid won't have a name till the war's over?"

"No. I have name for boy."

"What?" Jessie asked.

"You do? What is it?" Perelli asked.

"Yeah, you told us you didn't have one," LaBeau said.

"Change mind."

"Why?" Oglethorpe asked.

"Wife says in letter boy has many bowel movements."

"Yeah, so what? All babies do that," Jessie said.

*"Tsosie a-chi."*

LaBeau looked at Oglethorpe. "Well, you learned some of this Injun code. What's the name?"

"I knew it!" Jessie said with annoyance.

"I think it means small something," Oglethorpe said.

"It means 'Small Intestines'! This man is preoccupied with intestines," Jessie said.

"No way!" LaBeau bellowed.

Broken Wing searched the faces staring at him as if looking for some hint of approval, but he found none.

"Maybe Johnny Walking Skunk?"

"You can't do that to my nephew," Jessie said firmly.

"Your nephew?" Oglethorpe asked.

Jessie held out his arm to show the cut, which was still

bleeding just slightly. "Yes. Broken Wing and I are blood brothers."

"So?" Broken Wing grunted.

"So I refuse to be related to anyone named Small Intestines, and no Skunks. It would be embarrassing."

Broken Wing crossed his arms and seemed to pout.

"He's right, Broken Wing," Oglethorpe said.

Broken Wing grunted.

"If you let me name the kid, I'll help you get the booze," Jessie said.

"You name my kid, I name your kid."

"With your track record so far? Not a chance."

*"Tkal-kah-dineh-ih."*

"Fine with me. No booze."

"Name him," Broken Wing grunted through clenched teeth.

Jessie grinned victoriously as the others clapped their hands. He waited for the clapping to cease, then turned ceremoniously to Broken Wing, who was pouting again.

"Swift Eagle," Jessie announced proudly.

"Well, it's not Robert E. Lee, but it does have a southern charm to it," LaBeau said.

"Swift Eagle," Perelli said thoughtfully.

"Yes. Quite a moniker," Oglethorpe said.

"Thank you, thank you," Jessie said as if acknowledging their applause.

The pouting Indian's reaction was slow in coming, but finally Broken Wing closed one eye and glared at Jessie suspiciously, then nodded a reluctant yes. The others applauded.

"Good," Oglethorpe said. "Now that that is settled, we need to drink to the occasion!"

"Gung ho!" LaBeau said with a raised fist.

"You still haven't told me what any of this has to do with women," Jessie said.

Perelli howled and pretended to shiver. "Stand by to stand by, Marine."

"What have you clowns cooked up?" Jessie asked.

LaBeau, Perelli, and Oglethorpe squatted beside Jessie's cot as Broken Wing hunched forward to join their huddle.

Oglethorpe cleared his throat as if he were about to give a speech.

"Scuttlebutt is that the hospital ship USS *Trixi* will pick up all of the wounded in a couple of days."

"Yeah."

"They have women nurses on the *Trixi,* and the 'butt is they will make trades for anyone who can come up with some booze."

"Oh, no! Not again!"

"What do you mean not again?" LeBeau said accusingly.

"I mean I've heard this tune before. Did Perelli have anything to do with this scuttlebutt?"

"Without me youz guys would be living in a permanent blackout! And you wait till you have to come to me for a car after the war, Slate."

"He might be right, Slate," Oglethorpe warned. "You never know."

"All right. Let me hear the rest of it."

"That sounds a little more Semper fi," LaBeau mumbled.

"How do you expect to go souvenir hunting without some officer catching us?" Jessie asked.

"We're just gonna go dig up Jap stiffs," Chris said.

"Yes," Oglethorpe said, "it's actually not a matter that should concern anyone."

"Funny how officers always look at things differently than we do," Jessie said sarcastically.

"True," Oglethorpe said.

"So we need a detail," LaBeau said.

"Detail?"

Oglethorpe smiled as if the idea had been his. "Yes, of course. What Marine would question a work detail? Our entire life is a work detail."

"True," Jessie agreed unhappily.

"The plan is really quite ingenious."

"Your plan, no doubt, Oglethorpe."

"Of course. We have in the tent next door two badly wounded Japs receiving first aid. We have it on good authority that one of the Japs will join his ancestors very shortly."

"Real sad," Broken Wing said in a tone that was hard to read.

"With his demise will come the necessity for a burial," Oglethorpe continued.

"Yeah, he'll start stinking real quick," Perelli said thoughtfully.

"For a burial we need a burial detail."

"Almost every time," Jessie quipped.

"We are that burial detail. When we bring the expired Nip to his final resting place, we should be able to complete the first part of the plan."

"Where would that be?" Jessie asked.

"Here, I can show you better with a map." Oglethorpe sat down on a vacant cot on Jessie's right. Chris LaBeau sat beside him. Perelli remained standing. Oglethorpe began to draw a long rectangle in the dirt with the end of one of his crutches.

"All right, this is the airstrip. Over here, near the eastern tip, is the field hospital. Down at the other end of the strip are the big slit trenches where the bulldozers shoved all of the dead Japs in."

"This is stupid," Jessie said.

"Why?" Broken Wing asked.

"They were probably picked clean of souvenirs before they buried them."

Oglethorpe held up a finger. "Half correct," he said. "The fact is that Perelli got it straight from the Seabee that drove the bulldozer."

"Perelli's never been right in his whole life."

"Two Hamiltons! Put your money where your mouth is, Slate!"

"As I was saying," Oglethorpe continued, "the Japs killed during the landing were gathered up onto the sleds or just dragged to the hole and dumped in. Because the landing was still under considerable fire—"

"Yeah, Slate, they were catching air raids from Rabaul," Chris said.

"And a bunch of fire from Puruata, that island in the bay."

"I know, but—"

Oglethorpe held up his finger to stop Jessie in midcomplaint. "So, the Seabee bulldozer driver says that most of the first Jap bodies were not picked clean. He said he bull-dozed over swords, pistols, binoculars, and all kinds of valu-able memorabilia."

"Yeah, but since then we've killed hundreds of Japs."

"True, but the first ones are in a rather small area a few feet away from the newer kills."

Jessie made a face and shook as though he'd been hit by a chill. "Gosh, can you imagine the smell?"

LaBeau grinned and leaned closer until he was face to face with Jessie.

"I've been thinking about the smell of those nurses."

The next morning began like all mornings in the United States Marine Corps: a formation for the walking wounded. At 0500 in the morning, if harassed, wounded Marines had a tendency to be vocal and potentially dangerous. The Marine Corps has never cared, and on that morning all the walking wounded stood formation. Only rain excused one from formation, and that exception was for the purpose of keeping bandages dry. After formation was morning mess call, and although the food was pitiful by civilian standards, it was warm, which made it a rare item for frontline Marines.

After chow Jessie and Broken Wing sloshed their way back to their hospital tent and racked out. Jessie had confused dreams about Charlie Rose and Pomper and Kate and the baby.

Eventually, Broken Wing shook him awake. He opened his eyes and stared into the black eyes of an excited Indian.

"You ready?"

"Sometimes you look just like the Indian on the penny."

"White men all see alike."

Jessie blinked and considered the logic of Broken Wing's words. "You're a funny character."

"Told you. Funniest in family. You ready?"

"I don't believe we're doing this."

"One small problem," Broken Wing said.

"Just one?"

Oglethorpe appeared beside Broken Wing. Jessie sat up

in his cot and faced the two of them. Curious expressions
on their faces made him feel uneasy.

"Yes, Jessie, we do have one very small insignificant problem," Oglethorpe said. He sounded apologetic.

"What is it?"

"Well, it would appear that reports of the wounded Jap's
imminent death were just slightly exaggerated."

"Slightly?"

"Yes. It seems that he could last a little longer."

"How little?"

"Till somebody kills him," Broken Wing said calmly.

Jessie studied Broken Wing's stoic broad face. No one
spoke. Jessie finally put the question to Oglethorpe: "You
gonna kill him?"

Benjamin Oglethorpe's red eyebrows lifted high on his
freckled forehead. He turned to Broken Wing. "Hmmm.
Never considered that approach."

Broken Wing tilted his head and stared up at the roof of
the tent as if formulating a plan.

"Now wait a minute," Jessie said.

"Actually, Jessie, my original thought when this change
in plans occurred had not involved killing the Jap."

"My plan easier," Broken Wing mumbled.

"Our original thought was to replace one Jap body with
another."

"Another?"

"Sure."

"Whose?"

"We drew straws. You lost," Broken Wing said with a
shrug.

Twenty minutes later Jessie's shoulders sagged in resignation as he followed the others to the back of their tent, where
LaBeau had stored a "borrowed" stretcher. Jessie lay on the
stretcher. Perelli covered him with a stale-smelling poncho,
and the four Marines hobbled to the airstrip. Jessie couldn't
see, but the whining racket of a plane taking off told him
they were close. He could hear footsteps getting closer.

"Say! What are you Marines doing?"

"Burial detail, sir," Perelli answered quickly.

Jessie stiffened and held his breath.

"Burial detail. Good grief! You know I can't help thinking that the Marines are just a little too much, know what I mean?"

"No, sir."

"You men are those Para-Marines, aren't you?"

"Yes, sir," Perelli said.

"Yeah, I could tell by the boots. Well, if you ask me, Para-Marines or not, you don't send wounded men out on burial details!"

"Oh. Well . . ." Perelli stuttered.

"We volunteered, sir," Oglethorpe blurted.

"What do they feed you characters, anyway?"

"Bayonets, sir," Broken Wing said dryly.

The officer laughed. "Well, I'm glad you maniacs are on our side. Carry on."

"Aye, aye, sir."

Jessie breathed a sigh of relief as the guys started walking again.

"Say! Wait a minute there, Marines," the Navy officer called. Jessie held his breath again. Footsteps approached.

"You know, I haven't seen one of them yellow bellies up close yet, dead or alive."

"Oh, don't do that, Ensign," someone blurted out.

"Why not?"

"No face," Broken Wing said.

"Yeah, it's sickening, Ensign."

"Just awful, sir."

"Maggots!"

"Yes, sir, lots of maggots."

Suddenly the poncho was pulled away from Jessie's face. Jessie squinted from the sudden light.

The startled young ensign's brown eyes opened wide, and deep frown lines appeared across his forehead. Jessie forced a grin.

"This ain't no Jap!" the ensign yelled.

"And I'm not dead, either, sir," Jessie added.

"Set that man down!"

"Yes, sir."

"About-face!"

"Aye, aye, sir."

"Follow me! We'll see what your CO thinks about this!"

The limping march back through the mud to the field hospital felt long and quiet. The Marines all felt deep remorse at having been caught, along with the supreme embarrassment of being marched back to certain punishment by a Navy squid, of all God's creations. Though most Marines would grudgingly admit that the Navy did have a minor supporting role in helping the Marine Corps win the war and that God would probably even allow some of them into heaven, especially corpsmen, in the eyes of most leathernecks, a grave mistake had occurred somewhere along the last 167 years. Instead of the Marine Corps being under the Department of the Navy, it quite obviously should have been the other way around.

"You know, that looks like our men," LeBeau said, pointing toward the white-sand beach of Empress Augusta Bay.

"Well, here we are," Jessie said at just about the same moment.

The Navy ensign paused and looked back at his five wounded prisoners. "That's your outfit?"

"Yes, sir," Oglethorpe answered.

"Good. Let's see what your CO says about faking burial details."

Perelli wiped the sweat from his forehead. "Yes, sir. As long as Gunny O'Cleary don't hear."

"He'll be just the man I'm looking for, PFC," the Navy ensign said coldly. "You run up ahead and catch that column and find Gunnery Sergeant O'Cleary."

Perelli waited for the ensign to look away, then winked at Jessie and the others. "Aye, aye, Ensign."

Perelli and Gunny O'Cleary met the captives near the end of the column, which had stopped along the beach in front of the field hospital tents. The gunny looked tired. Mournful pouches underlined his battle-aged eyes, and Jessie wondered what kind of mood the old salt might be in.

"Morning, Ensign," O'Cleary said with a tired salute.

"Good morning, Gunnery Sergeant," the Navy ensign said with a sharp return salute as he halted the tiny column of prisoners.

"What have these eight balls done now?" Gunny O'Cleary asked harshly.

"I caught 'em faking a burial detail over near the airstrip. I'll just leave 'em here with you, Gunnery Sergeant. You can deliver whatever punishment you think appropriate."

"Aye, aye, sir. That I'll surely do."

They exchanged salutes, and the brash Navy ensign did an about-face and walked away with a smirk on his face that Jessie wanted to slap across the Pacific.

"Let's hear it," Gunny O'Cleary growled.

"We were trying to dig up some Jap souvenirs, Gunny," Jessie started.

"Yeah, that's all, Gunny," LaBeau interrupted.

"We had a deal with the Seabees, Gunny," Perelli said, waving his hands excitedly.

"Yeah, they were supposed to barter our Jap souvenirs to the Navy PT boat squids for some torpedo juice," Oglethorpe explained.

"Torpedo juice. Hmm. Been a while, ain't it?" O'Cleary mused.

"To celebrate my son," Broken Wing said proudly with a fist over his heart.

The old salt's eyes opened wide. "A boy!"

Broken Wing's chin lifted higher. He looked at Jessie for a moment, then back at the gunny. "Yes. Son named Swift Eagle."

A rush of pride sent goose bumps up Jessie's spine. He suddenly felt proud of the special bond between himself and the Navajo. The gunny allowed himself a grin, then his face turned solemn.

"Congratulations, Broken Wing. I'm happy for you. I hate to put a damper on things, but I got some bad news."

"Wait a minute, Gunny! You can't kick him out of Para-Marines just cuz he's married! He's gonna be a corporal!"

"You can't blame us for trying to celebrate the baby, Gunny," LaBeau pleaded.

The old salt shook his head and waved it off. "No, no, not that."

"What is it, then, Gunny?" Oglethorpe asked.

The gunny took a deep breath. The words seemed hard

coming. "We were the First Marine Parachute Regiment and the last."

"What do you mean?" LaBeau asked.

"They're breaking up the outfit, boys. Disbanding."

"What?"

"They can't!"

"No way!"

"That's impossible!"

"I feel the same way, believe me, men. In my twenty-six years of wearing the finest uniform on God's green earth I've been in some mighty fine lashups, but this is the best outfit of Marines that I ever served with."

"What are they doing with us?" LaBeau asked.

"That's why we're here on the beach. Scuttlebutt has us shippin' out for Pendleton."

"Pendleton!"

"Home!"

"Stateside!" Perelli shouted.

"But what then?" Jessie asked.

"Scuttlebutt has the parachutists as the core for a whole new division."

No one spoke for a few moments. The news had to sink in. Going home was a wonderful thought. But breaking up the Para-Marines? Jessie couldn't make himself accept it.

Broken Wing nudged Jessie, leaned close, and whispered. "Where's Gold Bar? Haven't seen *him* here."

"Yeah. You're right, buddy," Jessie said. "He hasn't been around. Gunny?"

"What?"

"Second Lieutenant Pomper. Do you know where he is?"

"He's gone, son."

"Gone where?"

The gunny shrugged. "He went to report me to Rip Roarin' Roering, just like he said. Haven't seen him since. I don't expect I will, either."

"Sorry to hear it," Jessie said with a broad smile.

The next morning the USS *Trixi* anchored in Empress Augusta Bay, and the wounded Marines were taken off Bougainville. It rained as the *Trixi* weighed anchor. A fitting end to the Bougainville campaign as far as most of the wounded were concerned. Three days into the voyage Corpsmen passed around the latest communique, which had been brought aboard via ropes and baskets from another ship in the convoy.

Aboard S.S. Meteor

January 29, 1944.

Press News.

**Pacific War Undated:** New damaging aerial blows to the Japanese in the Southwest Pacific were reported today as reports of barbaric treatment of the heroes of Bataan brought demands to "bomb Japan out of existence." In the mid-Pacific, bombardment of the Marshall Islands approached pre-invasion intensity. General MacArthur's communique reported between twenty-two and thirty more Nip fighters were brought down over Rabaul when dive-bombers and torpedo planes returned to the attack on New Britain Wednesday noon after being grounded for a day by bad weather. This makes 390 enemy planes listed as definitely or probably destroyed there this month as against sixty American, including four Wednesday. A destroyer and a gunboat were hit off Kavieng, New Ireland, 160 miles northwest of Rabaul. Mistreatment of American and British troops in Japanese war camps was announced in Washington and London, including the killing of thousands by beating, starvation, overwork, and neglect. From all quarters expressions of sheer rage grew more vocal by the hour as the full import of last night's Army/Navy disclosure sank in. For sheer bestiality, however, the official accounts don't approach some of the unpublishable stories of Japanese atrocities circulating among the fighting men of the patrols. An indication of the scope of future action in the Pacific came from Vice Admiral Adolphus Andrews who said every officer and man in the Navy Coast Guard and Marine Corps capable of sea duty would be needed.

**Moscow:** The people of liberated Leningrad rolled out of

bed and went to factories Friday after a night of wild joy
and singing and dancing in streets illuminated by brilliant
flares and rockets, Associated Press correspondent Eddy
Gilmore reported. Those in the city had not seen a spark
of light by night except that bursting from enemy shells
and bombing and burning homes for twenty-seven
months.

**London:** London newspapers played the success of American negro fighter pilots in Italy prominently on their
front pages Friday. Flying Warhawks, the negroes
bagged eight German planes south of Rome.

**Washington:** Enraged as never before America Friday
vowed merciless vengence on every one of the Japanese
who tortured and murdered the unforgettable heroes of
Bataan. Even the calm, judicial Secretary of State Cordell
Hull was moved to use words such as "demons" and
"fiendishness" as he gave the official promise that the
butchers of Nippon would be brought to account. Cries
of "hand the ax," "Mikado," and "bomb Japan out of
existence" roared out of Congress. No one knows yet exactly how many of the U.S. and Filipino troops were bru-
tally slain, but Palmer Hoyt, former Director of OWI,
Domestic Branch, declared that most of the fifty thousand who surrendered met their deaths from deadly heat,
thirst, starvation, and other forms of torture. Hoyt was
critical that the ghastly news was withheld from the public for two years.

**Allied Headquarters Algiers:** Allied land and air forces
have dealt the Nazis a crushing twin defeat in the battle
for Rome, smashing an enemy assault on the British
American bridgehead at a point twenty-one miles from
the Italian capital and destroying twenty-eight German
planes in furious sky fights over the landing beaches, the
allied command announced. The Nazi debacle in the air
and the repulsing of the heaviest enemy attack so far
against the week-old bridgehead came as German prisoners declared Adolf Hitler had ordered Germany's Tenth
Army to "stand or die" on the Cassino Front some eighty
miles from Rome.

**Guadalcanal:** A description of the Japanese fighter plane known as the Tojo was issued here. Fliers say it looks like the Army's P-47 Thunderbolt, that it's lighter than the P-47, the Navy Corsair, or Hellcat, and possibly less powerful, but very maneuverable. It has a radial air-cooled engine. The Tojo was first encountered in the South Pacific by Major Gregory Boyington, missing Marine ace.

**Ankara, Turkey:** The Japanese military attache in Bucharest has been arrested and jailed by Rumanian authorities on a charge of maintaining illicit radio communications with Moscow according to a report from Bucharest. The report said the Japanese diplomat attempted suicide when his residence was raided but was captured too quickly.

NOTICE                                          NOTICE

Please do not destroy this news sheet—Joe would like to read it also.

The long voyage back to Oakland, California, was filled with nearly as many conflicting emotions as the voyage over had been. Thoughts of Kate were never complete without the memory of Charlie Rose. Every thought of Charlie Rose came with a dull, painful ache in the pit of Jessie's stomach and the echo of Pomper's accusation on Vella Lavella. The miserable regret at not forcing Pomper to speak plainly about Kate grew until by the time the USS *Trixi* passed under the Golden Gate Bridge it dominated Jessie's thoughts. Four local high school bands along with a Marine band and hundreds of well-wishers greeted the wounded Marines. The walking wounded would get a thirty-day leave as soon as the processing at the Oak Knoll Naval Hospital was complete.

The wounded were driven to the hospital in ambulances and were immediately given full checkups by a staff of doctors that had been brought in from other nearby hospitals. Marines who were not seriously wounded were put in one large room that had probably been a cafeteria before the war. Broken Wing was two beds down on Jessie's left, and Oglethorpe was straight across the aisle. He wasn't sure where the others were yet.

His doctor finished giving him the once-over. "Corporal Slate, you have a good clean wound. No permanent damage.

We'll let it drain for a few more days, and you'll be fit for duty."

"Fit for duty?"

"That's right."

"Just what I wanted to hear, Doc," Jessie grumbled.

The tall thin doctor turned and motioned to a blond Marine major standing near the doorway of the big room with his barracks cover in one hand and a piece of yellow paper in the other. The solemn-looking major headed toward Jessie. Jessie's stomach tightened. He didn't like the look on the major's healthy Stateside face. This is something to do with not writing Kate, he thought. Maybe it's the baby. The major stopped at the foot of Jessie's bed as the thin doctor left for another patient.

"You are Corporal Jessie Slate, First Battalion, Second Platoon, First Parachute Regiment?"

"Yes, sir."

"You are from Logan County, West Virginia?"

"Yes, sir."

"Your mother is—"

"Jean."

The major looked at the yellow piece of paper in his hand and grimaced slightly. "I regret to inform you, Corporal Slate, that your mother died three weeks ago. She was apparently the passenger in an automobile that slid off an icy road into an embankment. On behalf of the commandant of the Marine Corps you have our deepest sympathy and the heartfelt thanks of a grateful nation."

Jessie sat up in his bed and stared straight ahead but saw nothing.

"If there is anything we can do to help you at this time, Corporal, please let me know. You will be released for leave as soon as your doctor says that you are well enough to travel. If you would like, I can arrange train passage home for you."

"Thanks," Jessie heard himself mumble.

Forty-eight hours later Jessie was handed his release from the hospital, a thirty-day pass, and new orders to report to Camp Pendleton at the end of that period. The ride to the train station in the major's staff car was quiet. Jessie wanted it that way. He didn't feel like making a lot of small talk with some Stateside Remington Raider driving around in his new Packard with the plush mohair seats.

"Here, Corporal. You have to read this before you board that train." The major pulled a long sheet of paper out of his olive-green briefcase and handed it to Jessie. Jessie began reading:

RESTRICTED

To:  All men returned from combat zones.

Subject:  Officers and enlisted personnel, contacts with publicity media.

1.  Since the activities of all men returned from combat zones are of great interest, particularly to hometown newspapers, radio stations, etc., all officers and enlisted personnel are instructed to contact the nearest public relations officer before committing themselves to cooperate with any and all publicity media.

2.  The public relations officer will clear your script or story for publicity media, but for your general guidance here are some things to guard against even in conversation:
   a.  No mention of specific battle stations.
   b.  Armament may be mentioned but not described; that is, you may say if you were serving at a gun, but do not comment on accuracy, timing, caliber, or location.
   c.  Specific enemy hits should not be told; it is permissible to refer to hits hereby and to estimate the caliber of the shell, but not details of damage done.
   d.  No mention of casualties shall be made beyond what already has been published, especially no mention of how men were lost or at what post.

3.  The following general rules should be observed:
   a.  Don't mention or discuss tactics, even of an action which took place months ago.

   b.   Don't discuss individual units, their designation, strength, or armament.

   c.   Give no hint of enemy effectiveness; why let the enemy find out something he may not know?

   d.   Discussion of the sources from which information about the enemy was obtained is absolutely prohibited.

   e.   Protect our friends by soft-pedaling your talk about natives aiding our side.

   f.   Avoid gory details, be tactful and avoid boastfulness, and exercise ordinary good taste in discussion of things which may be commonplace in battle but may prove offensive to civilians.

4.   If your hometown newspaper, press association, or other publicity media asks for your story, clear it FIRST through one of the following centrally located Marine Corps public relations offices, even if it has to be done at the expense of the media seeking such material!

NAMES AND ADDRESSES OF MARINE CORPS
PUBLIC RELATIONS OFFICES
New York—90 Church Street
Chicago—225 South Clark Street
Atlanta—50 Whitehall Street
San Francisco—Crocker 1st Nat'l Bank Bldg.
San Diego—Marine Corps Base
Washington—Marine Corps Headquarters
Philadelphia—1700 Sansom Street
Parris Island—Marine Barracks
New River—Marine Barracks, Camp Lejeune, N.C.

5.   In cities where there is no MC PRO, utilize the Navy PRO.

6.   Personnel who have been cited or decorated, or whose exploits have been widely publicized, have in the past been approached and in some cases exploited by persons offering to promote or manage public appearances and similar activities. All such officers and men are warned against entering into agreements of any kind with

promoters, managers, or agents. Arrangements for public appearances and similar activities should be cleared with the nearest public relations office.

Jessie finished reading and stuck the paper in with his orders. He glanced at the major. Funny, Jessie thought as they neared the Oakland County railway terminal. Just a year ago the mere sight of a major would have had him shaking in his winter greens, and now he felt near disdain for the man because he had seen no part of the war.

The train ride across the country was a heavy-hearted trip that seemed to take forever. When the train pulled into the Charleston terminal, a quarter of his leave was gone. It took a week of shuffling through paperwork to get his mother's things in order. Jessie was shocked to discover that his mother had had a life insurance policy worth $10,000. There were a few outstanding bills amounting to $2,500, and the cost of the burial, which Leefee had paid, had to be paid back, another $400. That left $7,100 for Jessie, the only beneficiary. It was the most money he had ever seen in his life. Nothing made sense anymore. All along Jessie had figured that for the first time in his mom's life she would have money, as the $10,000 GI insurance policy would be hers if he died. Life was so strange, so backward.

He signed the check over to Kate and put it in an envelope addressed to La Rue sans Issue in Nouméa. He wrote a small note explaining about his mom's death, then tore up the note and sent the check with no explanation.

# CHAPTER ELEVEN

Endless trainloads of men and combat materials for the Fifth Marine Division rolled down the winding spur of the Santa Fe Railroad and into Camp Pendleton. The rest came down Highway 101 on trucks and buses. Green recruits were trucked in from boot camps at Parris Island and San Diego. Marines were bused in from infantry training centers at Camps Elliott, Lejeune, and Pendleton itself. Some men were even transferred from ship detachments of the fleet. A load of officers and barracks men poured in from Quantico. The new Fifth Marine Division was now formed. The 26th and 27th Marine Regiments were organized, then the 13th Artillery.

The last to arrive were the veterans, hundreds of Marines who had survived earlier campaigns. They came straight from ships just back from the Pacific or from hospitals and sick leave or emergency leave, like Jessie. The 28th Marines were the last regiment of the division to be formed. Most of the First Parachute Regiment went into the 28th, but the majority of Jessie's old platoon ended up in the 26th. That was good news to the men. Some of the Para-Marines, however, were used as squad leaders and platoon leaders for green, untested troops.

Jessie climbed out of the back of a truck. The driver pointed at a large tent. "That's the First Platoon CP, Gyrene."

Jessie signaled a thumbs-up, threw his seabag over his shoulder, and pushed through the tent flap. He dropped the bag to the wood floor and snapped to attention. "Corporal Slate reporting for duty, sir."

A short, stout first lieutenant shoved a folder into a small filing cabinet and faced Jessie.

"At ease, Corporal." He exchanged Jessie's salute. "I'm Lieutenant Leonard. I've had a chance to look at your record. This is a brand-new outfit, Slate. We're going to need the leadership of proven veterans like yourself."

"Thank you, sir."

The tent flap opened behind Jessie.

"Just the man I wanted," Lieutenant Leonard said.

Jessie turned to see an old familiar face.

"What do you need, Lieutenant?" Gunnery Sergeant O'Cleary asked.

"Take Corporal Slate to his new squad."

"Aye, aye, sir."

"Follow me, Slate," O'Cleary said gruffly as he saluted, did an about-face, and pushed back through the tent flap.

Jessie threw his seabag over his shoulder, saluted, and hustled after the gunny.

"Hey, hold up, Gunny!"

Gunny O'Cleary kept moving. Twenty yards later Jessie jogged up beside him. The old salt kept his eyes straight ahead.

"How you been, Gunny?"

O'Cleary didn't answer. They walked quickly past rows of tents for another twenty yards, then Gunny O'Cleary stopped abruptly and pointed.

"That's your squad over there, second tent down. You'll basically take over DiCicca's old squad."

"Where's Phil?"

"They had to amputate his leg."

Jessie's shoulders sagged. He felt like someone had kicked the wind out of him.

"Move it, Slate. We got a lot of work." The gunny's tone was anything but friendly as he turned and headed back to the CP tent.

"How about Stukowski?"

"Yeah. Perelli. Lopez."

"Anybody else?"

"Get over there and get squared away, Marine," O'Cleary said gruffly as he walked away.

Jessie stood staring after him, wanting to speak, but it was clear that the gunny did not intend to listen. Jessie knew instinctively what was wrong: the gunny had found out he hadn't been in contact with Kate. "What could I say that would make any sense?" Jessie muttered. From then on if the gunny spoke, it was strictly business.

The training was rough like everything in the Corps. No one knew what the new division was headed for, but one thing was certain as the hot summer of 1944 wore on: the Fifth Marine Division was ready. On July 12 the 26th Marines had maneuvers canceled. They were brought back from the field, and on July 22 they shipped out from San Diego. That was the warning that every man had been waiting for. Time was short. Two weeks later the outfit sailed out in the middle of the night. Destination unknown.

"Slate."

A familiar nasal twang scratched at Jessie's ear. He rolled onto his side, being careful not to bump Broken Wing in the rack above him. Aldo Perelli stood in the cluttered narrow aisle of the forward compartment.

"Yeah, Perelli."

"I got the scuttlebutt."

"Figured you did. Where we going?"

"Guam."

"Guam?"

"Yeah. One combat team from the 26th was ordered into floating reserve for the First Provisional Marine Brigade."

"Where's Guam?" Jessie asked.

"What's a Guam?" Broken Wing mumbled from the top rack.

Oglethorpe leaned out from the top rack across the aisle. He pushed his glasses against the bridge of his thin nose.

"Though Guam may sound to the uninitiated like an exotic ingredient in a salad, it's actually an island in the South Pacific."

"It's Guam all right," Perelli said, shaking his head cockily.

"You're full of crap, Perelli," Lopez growled from the bottom rack.

"What's that? I try to keep you clowns informed."

"Jeezus, if you were ever right about anything, I'd re-up!"

"All right! Listen up, you eight balls," Sergeant Rim shouted from the front of the compartment.

"Bet we find out now," Jessie said quietly.

"First Platoon! Listen up!"

Gunny O'Cleary swaggered past Sergeant Rim and pulled his cigar from his mouth. His steel-blue eyes paused on Jessie, and his lips tightened.

"Hawaii," he said, still looking straight at Jessie, then turned and left.

The lead ships of the long gray convoy made their first landfall six days out from the San Diego channel. The sun was hot on deck as the Marines crowded the rail, aching for the first sign of Hawaii.

"Hey!" a sailor yelled, pointing off the bow. "There it is!"

Marines on deck yelped and howled like wounded dogs. Perelli elbowed Broken Wing.

"Two mountaintops! See 'em, Wing?"

"Yep."

"Those ain't just hills, Marine."

Jessie looked over his shoulder. Gunny O'Cleary stood behind them with his arms crossed, staring at the faraway peaks like a man seeing home for the first time in a long while.

"What are they, Gunny?" Lopez asked.

The old salt pulled the cigar from his mouth and exhaled smoke through his nose so slowly that it looked like the smoke was falling out. "Volcanoes. That one on the left is Mauna Kea, and the other one is Mauna Loa. God almighty never made a more beautiful place, Marine."

"Sounds to me like you got yerself a chick there, Gunny," Lopez said with one raised eyebrow and a big dumb smile.

The old man smiled, shoved his cigar between his teeth, and bit down. "A long time ago, son."

"Are the women nice, Gunny?" another Marine asked.

"Make even an old salt think about tying up the seabag."

"Makes my mouth water, Gunny," Lopez said.

Perelli jumped in front of the gunny like a man being prodded with a hot poker. "Liberty, Gunny?"

"Yeah, where's the nearest town, Gunny?" Lopez asked.

"Kamuela will be the only village."

Jessie started to speak but didn't.

The gunnery sergeant stepped up to the railing and gazed out at the warm blue Pacific. "I'll tell you characters right now that you got more work than play ahead of you."

"That means no liberty call, Gunny?" Perelli whined.

"You'll see Kamuela, Marine. Don't get your skivvies out of military alignment. It's part of the Great Parker Ranch. That's Camp Tarawa now."

"What's that vill like?"

"You mean the camp is a ranch?" Lopez asked.

"Biggest"—Gunny paused, removed his cigar, and rubbed his chin—"At ease on that; might be the second biggest cattle ranch in the world."

"And now it's called Camp Tarawa?"

"After Pearl Harbor the Army was based at the ranch. Looked like the Nips might invade for a while there."

"Where was the Corps, Gunny?" a boot named Turner asked.

O'Cleary turned a hard stare on Turner that made it clear that his question was stupid.

"Why'd you join the Marine Corps, Turner?"

Turner's brown eyes opened wide. He snapped to attention like a Parris Island recruit.

"I wanted to be the best, sir! A green amphibious killing machine that thrives on—"

"At ease. You are part of the finest fighting outfit in the history of the world, Marine. You are the most highly trained, best-equipped fighting man on Earth. The United States Marine Corps assaults and conquers the enemy. God forbid the day a Marine is satisfied with holding and defending!"

"That's why God invented the Army, right, Gunny?" Lopez quipped.

"Affirmative."

Jessie couldn't fight off a grin. He thought that the pride that came with being a Marine would diminish after boot camp, but it seemed to just keep growing. He was beginning to feel traveled and tested like the hardened vets he admired. The old gunny was a walking, talking piece of history.

"Last December the Second Marine Division was pulled off Tarawa and brought back to Parker Ranch for rest and regrouping," Gunny O'Cleary went on. "Tarawa cost us a lot of good Marines."

"Arizona papers said six hundred KIAs," Broken Wing said.

"I heard the water along the beach was red with Marine blood," Jessie added quietly.

"That's why the Second renamed the ranch Camp Tarawa—in honor of a lot of brave Marines. They took Tarawa at a cost, but it cost the Japs more, a lot more."

"What's Kamuela like, Gunny?" Perelli prodded.

"It ain't Diego, but it'll do. A few slop chutes, maybe a moving picture show, and a couple of places to get some local chow. The skipper says they got a USO canteen."

"Can't wait to see them dames in grass skirts," Perelli said.

The gunny put his cigar back in his mouth. "You'll see it all soon enough, Perelli." Gunny O'Cleary walked back to the hatchway and disappeared below deck.

Most of the men remained on deck, watching the distant mountains grow until the black lava peaks of Mauna Kea and Mauna Loa were towering over them. Off in the distance another giant cone called Haleakala stretched into the cloudless sky from the island of Maui like a pyramid to heaven. Most of the Marines had never seen the big island of the Hawaiian group, and a lot of the new Marines were seeing their first piece of soil that wasn't part of the good old USA. Even the veteran Marines on board who had already seen combat in the Pacific had usually gone by way of the Panama Canal, Samoa, New Zealand, and Australia.

A light ocean breeze rippled the fields of sugarcane that stretched from the ocean on up the sides of Mauna Kea and Mauna Loa. Black tentacles of hardened lava weaved through the jade-colored cane fields and into the deep blue ocean like roots from a charred stump.

When their transport finally neared Hilo anchorage, hundreds of people lined the waterfront under a fence of gently flowing palms. Behind them, the afternoon sun glistened off tin-roofed warehouses and big Quonset huts and stores.

Perelli threw his cigarette butt into the sea. "Crap!"

"What's wrong with you?" Jessie asked.

"I don't see no grass skirts," Perelli fumed.

Jessie wanted to laugh, but there was no laughter in him. The island only brought on thoughts of Kate. He loved her, he knew. But he hadn't done right by her. He wondered if it was too late to change that. How could he explain? He didn't understand his own mind anymore. Why did guilt turn his guts inside out with even a fleeting thought of what marrying Kate had cost? The Klaxon sounded, and Jessie jumped.

Broken Wing slapped him on the shoulder. "Calm down. This beach is secure."

Jessie looked at Broken Wing and forced a smile. "Is it?" The Klaxon sounded again.

"Now hear this! All Marines, prepare to disembark."

Parker Ranch was huge. The area now known as Camp Tarawa was 2,600 feet above sea level and about twelve miles from the nearest coastline. It was about sixty-five miles from Hilo in the north central part of Hawaii, and transporting a whole division to the place proved to be a major feat. Some were trucked up the steep twisting coastal highway, then overland to the ranch area. Some of the Marines were loaded into tiny railroad cars from the island's railroad system and pulled by strange-looking ancient engines.

The 28th Marines were convoyed up a steep dirt road that the Army had constructed and named Saddle Road. Truck engines strained with the climb, moving higher and higher through the black-gray lava fields of the two great volcanoes. Two hours into the trip the temperature began to drop. Jessie shivered. Perelli huddled around his rifle, facing Jessie on the opposite truck bench. Jessie frowned.

"I didn't think it got cold in Hawaii."

"We're not in Hawaii anymore, Slate. We're in the clouds now."

The road finally leveled out and then seemed to go downhill a way. The air again grew warmer as they came closer to the ranch, until soon sweat dripped down each man's face. Worn brakes began to squeal from the dust-covered trucks as the convoy rolled to a stop. Officers and noncoms began shouting up and down the convoy.

"Get out of those trucks! Move it, Marines! We don't got all day!" Sergeant Rim barked from the truck.

The men moved into a quick formation facing twenty rows of pyramidal tents that were quivering in the strong wind. The only permanent structures were administration buildings of wood and cane board and Quonset storerooms and galleys. Everything was covered with a thick coating of gray dust blown up from roads made of dirt and gravel.

Each squad was crammed for the night into a tent filled with dust-covered cots. The next morning, for some reason, Jessie didn't seem to hate the blaring of reveille as much as usual. He forced open one eye and then the other. Somewhere an angry voice cursed the Marine Corps as the tent city slowly rustled into consciousness.

A quick formation and march to the chow hall took an hour, and the sun still wasn't up. By 0650 the Marines found themselves sitting at attention on rows of leaky sandbags facing an outdoor movie screen that somebody had named the Roxy.

"Attention!"

The men stood as a red-faced Marine officer quick-stepped to the screen.

"As you were!" he barked, and the men sat back down.

"I am Colonel Perkins! Welcome to Camp Tarawa."

And so it began. More Marine Corps training. The only difference was that now Jessie was a squad leader, and if anything hit the fan, it blew his way. By 0600 the long daily march had started. They hiked across the flat lava-covered terrain behind the tent city, then up as the grade grew steeper and more rugged, finally ending fifteen miles later at the foot of Kohala. Camp Tarawa seemed to have every kind of terrain from lava-covered flatlands to thick wet jungle. It was big enough to run through the most complicated field problems while using tanks and artillery in various joint exercises.

After two weeks of full-dress military field problems, unit commanders began to stress new information about Jap island defenses as it came from battlefronts on Saipan, Tinian, and Guam and the bloody developments at Peleliu. Marines armed with rifles, carbines, BARs, bazookas, and flame-throwers worked together with mortar crews and machine gun crews and even the heavy weapons of artillery units. By the end of the second week the word "liberty" finally shot through the ranks. There wasn't a man who wasn't ready.

"Slate!"

Jessie looked up from his cot. The tent flap was pulled back, and the outline of the old gunny was clear against the setting sun.

"Yeah, Gunny?"

"Liberty call already went out. Why ain't you gone?"

"Don't feel like it."

"Come on, get out of the rack. You're going with me to the Kamuela USO club."

"No thanks, Gunny."

"I ain't askin', Corporal Slate," O'Cleary said gruffly. "Get your barracks cover and meet me at the HQ hut in five minutes. And look squared away." He shut the tent flap.

Jessie sat up and stared at the flap for a few seconds, wondering what had just happened.

The walk to the HQ Quonset hut produced enough unanswered questions to fill Jessie with dread. Daylight was nearly gone when the gunny came out with two liberty passes in hand. He looked at Jessie with a businesslike expression and started for a jeep parked near the guard shack at the front gate.

"What's up, Gunny?" Jessie asked hesitantly as they jumped in.

"You'll see."

Kamuela Village was mostly made up of grass huts and three or four colonial-style wood-frame houses. The Kamuela USO club was a pretty little farmhouse with a tin roof and a front porch complete with cane rocking chairs. Swing music blared through the open windows. Marines, beers in hand, crowded the front porch, trying to outmaneuver each other with the black-haired village girls.

Gunny O'Cleary parked the jeep against a row of rocks, painted white, lining the front yard of the club.

Jessie followed him up the dirt walkway. He felt like a little boy being marched to the shed. The gunny climbed the three steps to the porch and looked back as if making sure Jessie was behind him.

Jessie felt his face flush with anger. "You think I ran away?" he asked sarcastically.

Gunny O'Cleary turned and opened the screen door. The main door was propped open with a bullet-riddled Japanese steel helmet.

The wood floor was scarred by the shoes of a thousand jitterbugging Marines and soldiers who had passed through Camp Tarawa. A jukebox blared out "All God's Children Got Rhythm." There was a small stage area at the far end of the main room with the instruments of a missing swing band resting against chairs and the back wall. Clouds of gray cigarette smoke drifted up from cane-top tables cluttered with glasses and formed a blue cloud near the ceiling.

"O'Cleary! Over here!" a familiar voice called from Jessie's right. A sharp pang of anxiety shot through Jessie's stomach like the point of a spear.

Gunny O'Cleary paused and searched the crowded room, then waved and called out, "Sarge!"

Jeremiah Polk stood up and extended his left hand toward Gunny O'Cleary, but his gentle eyes were fixed on Jessie.

Jessie was stunned. He forced himself to speak. "Hello, Mr. Polk," he said quietly as the two old salts shook hands.

"How have you been, son?" Mr. Polk asked.

"Not too bad, sir. What are you doing in Hawaii?"

They shook hands and sat down staring at each other.

"You two talk, I'll get us a beer," Gunny O'Cleary said.

Jessie watched as the gunny pushed his way through the crowd of Marines until he reached the cane and plywood bar on the other side of the main room. Jeremiah cleared his throat and scratched at the empty shirtsleeve pinned across the front of his buffalo plaid shirt.

"Well, Jessie, I ain't much for flanking actions. I believe in 'fix bayonets and go straight ahead,' just like we did at Belleau Wood."

"Yes, sir."

"Between O'Cleary and me, we probably got more inside dope on the Corps than Commandant Holcomb himself."

"I don't doubt that, sir."

"Well, let's just say I called in a couple of old favors. You know why I'm here, boy?"

"Yes, sir."

"Why haven't you written?"

Jessie looked at Jeremiah. How could he possibly explain? Should he just tell him how Charlie Rose had died because he and Kate had been so eager to get married?

"No."

"What do you mean no?"

"I . . . I can't explain it, Mr. Polk. I know I'm wrong—"

"You're wrong, all right. Now, what are you gonna do about it?"

Jessie chewed at the inside of his mouth and searched anxiously for the right words, but there were no right words. He looked Jeremiah in the eye.

"I need to see her."

"You got that much right."

"We have to talk."

"Think you'd like to see your son, Marine?" Jeremiah asked in a tone riddled with disgust.

"Yes, sir, I do."

"Does your mother even know that she's a grandmother? We've written and gotten as little response from her as we have from you. You want this marriage annulled, boy?" Jeremiah snapped angrily.

"My mom died before I got home."

Jeremiah's eyes softened, and this time he was the one looking down at the tabletop searching for something to say. He shook his head slowly.

"Jessie. Why haven't you told us anything? I'm sorry, son. Forgive an old jarhead for not reconning the situation first."

"No, Mr. Polk, you have nothing to ask forgiveness for. I'm the scumbag here, and I wish I could explain, but I just can't. Not to anyone but Kate."

"Do you want to see Kate and your son?"

"You mean she's here? In Hawaii?"

"Yes. We used some of that money you sent to get here."

"Yes. I have to see her."

"I'll talk to O'Cleary about getting you a little leave time. You young people work this out between you, and I'll try to keep out of the way, but you need to know this. She's been hurt, and she's angry."

"Yes, sir. I don't blame her."

"Look, Jessie. I had a pretty strong suspicion that Kate was pregnant when you two were married. Has this problem got something to do with having to marry Kate?"

"I want to be married to Kate, sir." Jessie spoke clearly and deliberately.

"Gunnery Sergeant O'Cleary and me go back a long way, Jessie."

"Yes, sir."

"He tells me that you saved the lives of most of your squad on Bougainville. Says you're a whale of a Marine."

"Gunny said that?"

"He don't say what he don't mean. That's why I'm giving you the benefit of the doubt over this nonsense. But don't you let Kate and your boy down."

"I'll try not to, sir."

Jessie tried to imagine himself as a father, but it didn't seem real. He drank his beer and excused himself to let the old salts talk of old wars. He caught a ride back on a liberty truck and spent the night staring at the canvas ceiling, trying to find an answer, trying to forgive himself. The next day the 26th Marines began a regimental field exercise that lasted seventy-two hours. At the end of the long early morning march back to Tent City, Gunnery Sergeant O'Cleary handed Jessie a three-day pass before he had time to drop his pack.

"Seventy-two hours, Slate. Don't waste any of it."

"How do I reach her?"

"She will be waiting at Hilo Harbor at 1300 hours."

"What time is it now, Gunny?"

O'Cleary checked his watch. "You got time to swab down. The pineapple train leaves in about forty-five minutes."

"Thanks, Gunny."

"Move out."

Broken Wing, Oglethorpe, and Sam Hill didn't say anything as Jessie left. Their lack of questions told him that they must have already figured out what was happening.

Jessie hitched a ride in the back of a truck that was picking up supplies at the tiny mountaintop train depot. The cars were better suited for sugarcane than for passengers, and the curious little ancient engine that pulled the train down its narrow track did not fill Jessie or the other Marines aboard with confidence. The sixty-five-mile journey weaved through cane fields and spanned deep gorges. Twice they actually crossed over rainbows formed by plummeting waterfalls. Children would toss in various fruits and coconuts as the train passed, always shouting, "Welcome, Marine!" One young PFC caught a coconut just above the ear that nearly knocked him unconscious.

The top of the last mountain gave a full view of Hilo Harbor. Anxiety squeezed Jessie's stomach like a vise. Nothing he could say would make sense, he thought.

Marines began whistling and howling from the tiny open-air passenger cars. That could mean only one thing: women. Jessie leaned his head out to see for himself as the little train rolled into Hilo station. A stunning, tanned auburn-haired girl in a bright yellow sundress stood on the rickety station platform beside a small blue baby carriage. Jessie's heart fluttered with excitement. He had all but forgotten how beautiful she was.

"Hilo station!" the Hawaiian train conductor shouted, and clanged a bell with a piece of pipe.

Jessie grabbed his seabag and tossed it through the open-air window and onto the station platform.

"Kate!" he shouted, and waved as he climbed through the window.

"Jessie?" she called with a hesitant wave.

Jessie ran toward her with arms out. Kate stepped forward slowly. She began to cry. Jessie stopped in front of her. He moved to put his arms around her, then hesitated. "Can I hug you?"

Kate put her arms around his neck. He could feel her tears against his cheek. Jessie hugged her. Her waist felt small. Her skin smelled fresh.

"I love you, Kate."

"Jessie, oh, Jessie, are you sure?" She sobbed as she spoke. "We have so much to talk about."

Jessie began kissing away the tears that ran down her cheeks. The howls and whistles from onlooking Marines turned her tan face crimson. She smiled through the tears and looked up into Jessie's eyes longingly.

"I have a room at the Hilo Hotel."

"Let's go," Jessie blurted, twirled around, and ran back for his seabag.

"Want to meet your son first?"

Jessie stopped, picked up his seabag, and turned around slowly. Kate grinned and glanced toward the carriage. Jessie walked back to Kate and the baby carriage like a man with lead boots. He looked down into the carriage. A little bald sleeping child lay covered by a pale blue blanket.

"Mr. Slate, meet Mr. Slate."

Jessie looked at Kate, then back at the little face. He felt anxious. How could he tell Kate that he didn't know the baby's name, that he hadn't read any of her letters? He opened his mouth to speak but just stood gawking down at the little Mr. Slate. Kate put an arm around Jessie's waist and leaned her head against his chest.

"Isn't he beautiful?"

"We don't want him to look too pretty, honey. He'll be a silly-looking Marine."

Kate laughed politely. "You sound like Dad. He's already got the baby in Annapolis."

"Officer, huh? We'll have to think about that one."

"Dad sings him to sleep with the 'Marines' Hymn.'"

They laughed and embraced, and for the first time in as long a time as Jessie could remember, he felt at ease. Of course, he knew it couldn't last. Sooner or later, he'd have to give her some reason for his strange behavior.

He kissed Kate again, inhaled her perfume, and squeezed her until she groaned and finally pulled away from him.

"You seem different, Jessie. Older."

"I am, Kate."

"You've seen a lot of death." Kate sounded sympathetic, but there was something distant in her eyes.

"Do you still love me, Kate?"

"Let's go to our room."

The small anchorage town of Hilo had been growing since the attack on Pearl Harbor. It had become the second largest active port for the U.S. Navy, but even so it was still a very small town, and the Hilo was the only hotel. Kate led them down a narrow street behind the train station. She pointed toward the harbor.

"That's the hotel. See the tall greenish building?"

Jessie chuckled. "It's the only one above two stories. Guess that makes it the tall one."

They walked along silently for the next two blocks, the tension between them building as they neared the hotel. The front doors of the old building were propped open by a couple of cane chairs. Kate pushed the carriage into the lobby. Jessie followed. The lobby was light and airy, in the tradition of most South Pacific hotels, with big ceiling fans pushing down a steady breeze.

"Watch the baby. I'll get the key," Kate said.

A short gray-haired Hawaiian man put down a newspaper and stood up behind the counter. He smiled.

"You find husband?"

"Yes, thank you. Could I have the key to room 304?"

The Hawaiian turned and pulled a key off a hook on the wall behind him.

"You need baby-sitter," he said, "let me know. My wife will be very happy to watch baby."

"Thank you very much, that's extremely kind of you. I might take you up on it."

Kate picked the baby up gently and whispered to Jessie. "Can you carry the carriage up the stairs?"

Jessie nodded, picked up the carriage with his left arm while balancing his seabag over his right shoulder, and followed Kate up the creaking stairs. The room was small but clean, Jessie thought as he set the carriage down beside a queen-size bed. He could see Hilo Harbor crowded with massive ships, their guns pointed skyward, silhouetted by a golden sun sinking into an emerald sea.

"Five transports, six destroyers, one cruiser," Kate said. "I've had time to count."

Jessie turned to face Kate and found himself breathless. She was wearing only her garter belt and hose. Her yellow sundress lay around her feet. She stepped out of it and put her arms around his neck and kissed him. Her lips were soft and wet, and her grip around his neck was tight as she pressed against him with her breasts. She pulled back and looked at him, tears forming in her bright blue eyes.

"I've been so worried, Jessie. When you wouldn't write back, I thought you . . ." She put her face against Jessie's chest and cried.

"Don't cry, honey. I wanted to write. I wanted to."

"Why? Why didn't you answer any of my letters?"

"Things have happened that I just can't explain."

"Why didn't you tell me that you were wounded? Or that your mother had died?"

"I couldn't."

Kate pulled back and wiped at the tears streaming down her face. "What's wrong, Jessie? Don't you want to be married?"

"Kate, look, I've made some real stupid mistakes. I don't understand half of it myself."

Kate stared at him for a moment as if searching for something. She shook her head and fell against him, squeezing her arms around his waist.

"Please forgive me, Kate. I want you to know everything."

"Make love to me, Jessie. Tell me it's going to be all right."

Jessie closed his eyes and sighed aloud. "We'll be all right," he said softly.

She pulled him down onto the bed, and for a while all the guilt and fear and confusion disappeared. Their love was hard and furious, and their passion went on as if they both wanted it never to end. Finally they curled around each other like children holding tight to face the dark and slept.

After an hour the baby cried out from the carriage at the foot of the bed, and Kate sat up quickly. She leaned over Jessie and kissed him.

"Oh, Jessie, this is it. Now you can meet him!"

Jessie sat up grinning and kissed her, then she rushed over to tend to the baby.

"Get my robe hanging on the bedpost, honey," she said to her husband as she picked up the tiny baby and held him to her.

Jessie brought over the white terry cloth robe and placed it around Kate's shoulders.

"I can't see him," Jessie said.

"Turn on the light."

Jessie found a lamp beside the bed and flicked it on. The baby stopped crying and looked around the room.

"Gosh, he's really alert, isn't he?" Jessie said.

Kate held the baby out to him. "Here."

Jessie pulled back. "Oh, no. I've never held one before. I might drop him. You keep him."

Kate laughed. "He won't bite you." She put the baby into Jessie's arms and stepped back smiling.

Jessie stood stiffly.

Kate laughed. "I wish I had a camera! You have the most terrified expression I have ever seen on a Marine."

"Maybe you better take him back. He looks uncomfortable."

"Would you please quit calling Charles Rose Slate a him."

Jessie felt as though his heart had stopped. He stared at

Kate but wasn't seeing her. Her brows pinched together. Her beautiful face was a mask of stinging pain.

"Jessie? Are you . . . you didn't know our child's name." Kate's revelation sounded cold and distant.

She stepped forward, took the baby, and gave her husband a curious look.

"You received my letters, didn't you? You chose not to read them." Kate sounded out her words slowly, in total disbelief.

"You named him after Charlie Rose."

"I knew that he was your best friend."

"How did . . ."

"Broken Wing wrote me. How could you not read my letters? Didn't you even care about the birth of your own child?"

"It's not that. Kate . . . it's just that I can't think of the baby without also thinking that we paid for his life with somebody else's."

Kate burst into tears.

"Go away, Jessie!" she shouted, and laid the baby back down in the carriage.

"Kate I want you to know—"

"Go away!" Kate shouted, and slapped Jessie hard across the face.

The baby began screaming.

"Kate, you know I love you."

"I know nothing about you! I was an idiot to marry you!"

"Kate, you can't mean that."

"Get out!"

The baby screamed louder. Kate picked him back up and patted him on the back. Suddenly someone pounded hard on the wall.

"Hey! Keep it down in there! I'm trying to get some sleep in here!"

Jessie ran toward the wall that separated their apartment from the one next door. He kicked against it with his bare foot so hard that two small paintings fell from their hooks.

"Shut up and mind your own business, Mac!"

"Keep it down or I'll shut you up permanently!"

The baby screamed louder. Kate hugged him tighter and began pacing back and forth.

"Please listen to me, Kate."

"Why should I?"

"I love you, Kate."

"I don't think you love anything."

The baby screamed louder. Someone in the other room slammed the wall again.

"Jessie, please. Just take a walk until I can get the baby calm. I need time to think."

Jessie inhaled and sighed. He felt a tear run down his cheek. He started to plead again but didn't. He grabbed his clothes and got dressed, then walked to the door, opened it, and looked back.

"I love you, Kate."

She rocked back and forth kissing the baby, staring out the window.

"Please, Kate! You have to hear the whole story."

"I'll listen, but I'm promising nothing, Jessie."

"I don't blame you, Kate, but I love you and I love our baby. Please hear me out."

Kate continued to stare out the window. "Let me get the baby to sleep. Come back in an hour."

"All right, one hour. But please promise to listen to me."

"I'll listen, Jessie."

She sounded cold and distant. She continued to rock back and forth with her gaze fixed on Hilo Harbor.

Jessie took a step toward her. She shook her head no. He paused. The baby was quiet. Jessie backed through the door and slowly closed it behind him. His stomach twisted. He checked his watch: 2000 hours.

Jessie went down the stairs like a man in a daze. Memories of his mother and father mingled with memories of Charlie Rose.

"Excuse me," Jessie called to the Hawaiian gentleman behind the check-in counter.

"Yes, can I help you?" he said with a friendly smile.

"Is there a bar in the hotel?"

"No, but if you would like to go across the street to the Harbor Bar, you may have your drinks for half price if you tell them you are a guest here."

"Thanks." Jessie started for the door.

"They have their blackout curtains down. It's straight across the street."

"Thanks."

Twenty minutes later Jessie found himself in the crowded Harbor Bar staring into a mug of warm beer. He downed it in one long swallow.

"Barkeep! Another beer."

"Comin' up, Marine." A squat, bald middle-aged man with tattoos on both of his enormous forearms snatched up the empty mug, quickly filled it, and splashed it down in front of Jessie.

A new tune from Tommy Dorsey blared from the juke-box. Jessie glanced around the crowded, dimly lit bar. He checked his watch. Thirty minutes. He looked around the bar again. It was filled with sailors in their dress whites.

"Oh yeah!" a loud angry bellow rose over the chaotic drunken chatter.

"It'll take a lot more than one ship's worth of squids to do it!"

Jessie leaned out to see what the commotion was at the far end of the bar.

"You like chewin' without any teeth, jarhead?"

A big Marine stood up from his bar stool and faced three sailors. His broad shoulders and the back of his big head looked vaguely familiar, but the light was too dim to see clearly.

Suddenly the big Marine decked one of the swabbies with a straight left. Before the swabbie hit the deck of the bar, three other sailors jumped the big Marine. Jessie looked back at his mug of beer, moaned out loud, and gritted his teeth.

"Crap!" he shouted.

The bar erupted in drunken howls and shouts as a crowd of sailors cheered on their pals. Jessie threw back the rest of his beer, slammed the mug down, stood up, and shouted as loud as his lungs would allow.

"Semper fi!"

He ran toward the fight at the end of the bar, bowling over two sailors along the way. Then he crashed through a ring of Navy men watching the four participants punching and wrestling on the floor.

The big Marine was on top of one sailor, punching him in the face with both fists while two other sailors were doing the same to the back and side of his head.

Jessie grabbed the nearest attacker by the back of his shirt, pulled him up, and hit him square in the nose as hard as he could. Blood squirted from the sailor's nose as he fell onto his back.

Jessie threw a wild swing at the other sailor, hitting him hard above the ear, then something cracked loudly against the top of Jessie's head. A sharp pain shot down the back of his neck, and he fell forward onto the back of the big Marine, then rolled to the sandy, beer-covered plank floor. Jessie pushed himself to his knees and faced the big Marine, who was still sitting on top of the unconscious sailor. Jessie shook his head to clear the cobwebs and blinked his eyes clear as he focused in on the big, round angry red face of Duffy Johnson.

"You!" Jessie shouted. A surge of anger shot through him. Jessie threw a grazing punch at the sneering, sweaty face. An instant later the two of them were rolling over the unconscious sailors in a pool of beer, sand, and blood. Screaming cheers erupted from the sailor-packed bar.

"Shore patrol!" someone shouted above the howling crowd.

"No! Don't stop it!"

"Let the jarheads kill each other!"

"No, we need 'em to kill Japs!"

"Break it up!"

"Atttttennnshun!" a low, angry voice shouted, and the bar grew silent. Johnson rolled over on top of Jessie and drew back his fist. The blur of a blackjack cracked against the side of Johnson's head. Jessie quickly threw a punch that helped roll the big ox off him. A stinging pain smacked through Jessie's right ear. The world went black.

Five hours later, Jessie sat shivering in the cold morning air of a brig overlooking Hilo anchorage. He stared out to sea as the first streaks of sunlight pushed through early morning rain clouds. A lump the size of a small egg throbbed against his right ear. His uniform was wet and stained with beer, dirt, and dried blood. He felt horrible, but even the physical pain could not keep his mind off his mental anguish. In his heart he knew that he had lost Kate. The sound of a guard walking by lifted Jessie's eyes.

"Hey, Marine!" Jessie called.

Jessie stood up and walked to the barbed wire, where the guard had stopped and lowered his rifle.

"What do you want, Mac?"

"Look, buddy, I have to get word back to my wife at the Hilo Hotel to let her know where I am."

"You're dumb out of luck, Mac."

"Look, I'll pay ya!"

"Yeah, Semper fi, Mac," the guard said with a chuckle.

"No, really, Marine! This is life or death to me."

"Look, I'd like to help ya, pal, but—"

"Please, you have to help me. My wife is there waiting with my baby. I have to get word to her!"

The guard scrunched up his face and looked hard at Jessie. He put his rifle back over his shoulder and shook his head.

"All right, Mac, I'll see what I can do when the OD comes out. What's the broad's, I mean, what's your wife's name?"

"Kate. Mrs. Kate Slate. Mrs. Slate, room 304, Hilo Hotel."

"What do you want us to tell her?"

"Just tell her what happened and where I am. By the way, where am I?"

"Camp POW."

"POW?"

The guard pointed toward the far side of the forty-square-foot barbed wire enclosure. "Yeah, this is where we relocated all of the Japs that lived here before the yellow bellies hit Pearl."

Jessie looked. A row of barracks were surrounded by tall barbed wire with machine gun bunkers every twenty to thirty yards around the camp.

"Am I the only prisoner?" Jessie asked

"Yeah, for now."

"What happened to the other guy? And the three squids we were fighting?"

"They all got released while you were sleeping it off."

"Released?"

"Well, released to their respective outfits. Your outfit didn't send anyone down here to get you yet."

"Great. Just great."

Jessie slumped back down to the ground and put his head

between his knees. If he couldn't get word to Kate, it was over. She would never believe him again. How could she? Jessie wanted to pray for help, but who to? He looked at his bracelet and the wind god symbols Broken Wing had carved on it.

"Maybe I should pray to the wind god," he mumbled to himself, and didn't know whether to laugh or cry. He thought of Duffy Johnson until the grinding of his teeth made the lump behind his ear ache. Killing Johnson was the only pleasant thought he could muster. He thought of the baby. Charlie Rose Slate. The name and the memory would haunt him until he died. He knew that. He deserved such pain, he thought. There could be no forgetting and there could be no forgiveness for running out on his friend. Jessie put his head between his knees again. Maybe I'll buy it on the next beach, he thought. Kate and the baby would get the $10,000 GI insurance. They'd be better off without him. Jessie blew out a sigh that brought his soul lower than it had ever been. He closed his eyes and tried to keep his mind quiet.

"Hey, Marine."

Jessie opened his eyes. The sun was overhead.

"Hey, reveille, Marine!"

Jessie uncurled out of a fetal position on the ground. His body ached. He focused in on the Marine guard standing on the other side of the barbed wire stockade. He scrambled to his feet and ran to the wire.

"Did you get word to her?"

The guard's face told him the story before he said a word. "No. Sorry, Mac."

Jessie's chin dropped to his chest.

"The OD called up the place, and the manager said that she checked out early this morning."

Jessie looked up at the long-faced guard. "Did she leave a message?"

"Nope."

Jessie's shoulders sagged under the most overwhelming grief he had ever known. Numb with despair, he slumped down in the dusty compound and stared out at the ocean. Three hours later two MPs in a jeep showed up to escort him back to Camp Tarawa. They drove along the coastal road, then up into the scenic mountains and overland to the ranch. The road was unusually jammed with Marine convoys. The two MPs said very little during the drive, and that was fine with Jessie. The last thing he wanted was conversation. Just when he thought he might make the whole trip without having to speak, the MP in the passenger seat looked back over his shoulder.

"You picked a good time to go to the brig, Marine."

"Yeah, why's that?"

"See all of these trucks going by? Well it ain't no division picnic. Scuttlebutt has it that the Fifth got its island."

Jessie sat up straight in the back of the jeep. "You know where?"

"No, heard a lot of guesses, though."

The driver glanced back over his shoulder. "I heard Rabaul or Yap Island."

"How soon?" Jessie asked.

"I don't know, but they started loading up some of the heavy stuff three days ago."

"I ain't sittin' in no brig while my guys hit a beach!"

"You ain't got to worry about that, Mac," the driver said with a chuckle. "You'd have to shoot a two-star in the balls to get out of this boat ride."

The hot Hawaiian sun had mellowed into a cool red ball by the time they drove through the main gate and stopped in front of the guard shack.

A face that was nearly as red as the sun but was neither cool nor mellow stared out of the guard shack window.

"Slate!" Gunny O'Cleary barked through the open window like an angry DI.

"Yes, sir, Gunny."

"Get out of that jeep!"

Jessie climbed out of the jeep as the gunny came out of the guard shack.

"Follow me!" O'Cleary walked around to the back of the guard shack with Jessie right behind. He stopped, did a sharp about-face, and glared hard at Jessie.

"I went out of my way to get you that three-day pass, Marine. I did not do it just for you. You married an outstanding girl. The daughter of a great Marine."

"Gunny I—"

"Shut up! You hear me clear, mister. You pull some Army crap on that girl and baby, and I'm gonna put my boot up your rear end so far you'll spit-shine my boondockers with your tonsils!"

Jessie found himself standing stiffly at attention.

"Well?" Gunny shouted.

"Sir."

"I wanna hear it!"

Jessie looked at the ground, then brought his eyes up to meet Gunny O'Cleary's.

"Kate got upset when she realized I didn't know the baby's name, that I hadn't been reading her letters."

O'Cleary turned and kicked at a pile of lava dust. "You didn't know your own son's name?"

"I know, Gunny," Jessie went on. "I know how it must sound, but—"

"You stupid jackass, you know how it sounds." O'Cleary growled and spit at the ground.

"I went downstairs to let things cool off. The baby was crying, and Kate wanted me to go away for an hour."

"I can't imagine why! Can you, Slate?"

Jessie's face flushed with frustration. "Look, Gunny, you can't say anything to me that I haven't already said to myself, but something happened."

"How'd you end up in the brig?"

"I went to the bar across the street to wait out the hour. I was gonna tell Kate everything and try to make things right. Then these three squids jumped this Marine in the bar; and I couldn't just sit there and not help!"

The gunny's angry face seemed to soften just a bit. "Three squids?"

Jessie nodded. O'Cleary frowned.

"On one leatherneck?"

"Me and him were the only Marines in the whole place."

The gunny smacked his lips and grunted as if his position were uncomfortable.

"Well." O'Cleary paused. He scratched at his chin and looked at the ground. "Let's say I understand how these squids attacked your fist with their faces. How is it that in the report I got, it was you and another Marine going at it?"

"After I jumped in, I saw who it was that I was helping."

"Who?"

Johnnie M. Clark

"Johnson. Duffy Johnson."

"That big jackass?"

"I just had to hit him, Gunny!"

"Good God, son! You get yourself in more crap than any Marine I ever saw."

"I know."

"You tell me the truth, mister. Do you love Kate and that baby?"

"More than life itself, Gunny."

The old salt shook his head and scratched the back of his neck.

"Well, son, I'm inclined to believe you, but I sure don't know why."

"I'd die for her, Gunny! I—"

"All right, all right. At ease."

"What can I do, Gunny? She'll never believe me now."

"That could be, Slate. And now there's a new problem."

"What's that, Gunny?"

"We're weighing anchor."

# CHAPTER TWELVE

On January 4, 1945, the Fifth Marine Division command post officially closed down at Camp Tarawa. The new division command post opened for business aboard the USS *Cecil.* The long gray convoy of steel settled below the horizon and two days later reached Pearl Harbor. It seemed that every available inch of docking area was taken by what most of the men thought was the entire Pacific fleet. Every tiny inlet was occupied by gray steel carriers, battlewagons, cruisers, or destroyers. The power of America had never been so evident. Every Marine aboard, from the old China hands to the newest boot recruits, was filled with awe. Scuttlebutt had the entire Fourth Marine Division on one group of transports docked at Pearl. On January 21 the Fifth Division moved out of Pearl on LSTs, LSMs, and three transport divisions. Scuttlebutt Perelli had most of the 26th convinced that the invasion was on, but as usual Perelli was wrong. They were only making practice beach landings on Kahoolawe Island about sixty miles from Pearl. The practice landings went on for three days before the Fifth returned to Pearl.

On January 27, the morning arrived with a flurry of harbor activity that sent a chill of expectancy through the troops. Soon a convoy formed and steamed into the Pacific, and every man aboard every ship sensed that this was it. Two days out of Pearl Harbor, Sergeant Rim entered the forward hold.

"First Platoon! Listen up!"

"Something's up," Broken Wing mumbled from the cot above Jessie.

"Why?" Oglethorpe asked from below Jessie.

"Rim's horseshoe is red."

Broken Wing was right. Rim's shrapnel scar was prominent. Something was up.

"I want the First Platoon on deck, on the fantail, in five minutes! Move it!" Sergeant Rim bellowed.

Broken Wing was obviously right. Groups of Marines huddled together with officers and sergeants in galleys, on bows and fantails, on upper deck gun platforms, in holds and wardrooms. From the looks of it the men of the First Platoon were the last ones getting the word, Jessie thought as they reached the fantail.

"Hurry up and gather around!" Gunnery Sergeant O'Cleary barked as the men staggered into the area.

"What's up, Gunny?" Lopez asked.

"Listen up. I want you to keep your big mouths shut until it's time to ask questions." The gunny turned and nodded to Lieutenant Leonard.

Lieutenant Leonard stood up and pointed to a rubber and plaster relief model of a strange-looking island.

"G-2 put this together for us to study. It's a model of our target island. Just call it Island X."

"Looks like a pork chop with a breast on the end," Lopez called out.

"All right, call it Island Pork Chop."

"Shut up, Lopez!" Sergeant Rim snapped. "Get your mind on business."

Lopez whispered something to Perelli, who said nothing but stared at the model of Island X like a man seeing a ghost. Lopez elbowed Perelli in the ribs.

"Come on, scuttlebreath, you look like that broad you had in Honolulu."

Perelli's expression didn't change throughout the forty-five-minute briefing. The briefing was useless to the average Marine. It did give some idea of what the division's part in the overall operation would be, but each man already knew his job: killing Japs one at a time. The overall scheme wouldn't matter a nickel when the landing ramp hit the soft lava sand of Island X.

On February 5 the convoy reached Eniwetok. The blackened tree stumps and litter from an old battle were spread among a small community of Quonset huts. The ships refueled and two days later steamed back out to the open sea. By February 11 the convoy reached Saipan. It must have been an ugly sight to the Marines from the Fourth Division, who had conquered Saipan and Tinian the previous June and July. Many a good friend was buried there. There was a one-day invasion rehearsal off the coast of Tinian.

It was a four-day trip to Island X, or so the scuttlebutt said, and it didn't take a genius to figure out that the farther north the convoy sailed, the closer to Japan it got. When the convoy left Saipan, it headed north. A day out of Saipan a destroyer nosed up beside the troop transport. Bags of mail were roped across from the destroyer, to the cheers of the men on deck. Soon the Marines were shouted below to the troop compartments for mail dispersal. No one complained.

Sergeant Rim entered the First Platoon compartment with a rare smile on his scarred face. The smile did not seem to suit him. He looked like a guard dog showing his teeth.

"What are you so happy about, Sarge?" Stukowski asked as he dealt out a hand of pinochle to Perelli.

"That new doll that I ordered for the gunny's kid came in."

"Oh, yeah?" Lopez asked.

"Looks good, too."

"Got the print dress with the embroidery?"

"Yep, and that hat, too."

"Wow! Good score, Sarge," Perelli said with a thumbs-up.

"Has he seen it yet?" Broken Wing asked.

"Yeah. I gave him and the padre their mail first, so when I saw that I got the package, I opened it up for him."

"How'd he like it?" Jessie asked.

Sergeant Rim gave a thumbs-up, then paused and pointed at Jessie. "Oh, yeah, Slate. Lieutenant Leonard and the gunny want to see you right away in the lieutenant's quarters."

"Me?"

"You."

"Why?"

"What'd you do now, Slate?" Lopez prodded.

"Yeah, Slate, you been on another treasure hunt? Find

a new map?" Perelli asked loudly enough for the platoon to hear.

The guys started howling and laughing as Jessie stood to leave the compartment. He pointed at Aldo Perelli.

"I should have made you eat that last map, Perelli."

"Move out, Slate," Sergeant Rim said as he tossed a letter toward Oglethorpe.

"Aye, aye, Sarge," Jessie said.

The lieutenant's quarters were in officer country, amidships. Jessie removed his cover and slapped his hand hard three times above the cabin door, as was customary for Marines.

"Advance," Lieutenant Leonard shouted.

Jessie opened the door and stood at attention inside. "Corporal Slate reporting, sir."

"At ease, Corporal."

Jessie relaxed and looked around the tiny cabin. Gunny O'Cleary stood puffing on his cigar, staring solemnly out a porthole behind the lieutenant, who stood behind a small metal desk, studying Jessie curiously.

"Is something wrong, Lieutenant?"

Gunny O'Cleary turned away from the porthole. He removed his cigar, closed his mouth tight, and pinched his brow. Jessie's stomach twisted.

"It's not good news, Slate."

"Look, Corporal," Lieutenant Leonard began, then paused.

Gunny O'Cleary cleared his throat. "There's no easy way to break something like this to a man, so I'll just drop the ramp, son. Kate wrote me a letter—"

"Wrote *you!* Why hasn't she written me?" Jessie demanded.

"As you were, Marine," O'Cleary said sternly.

"Yes, sir."

"Because of the contents of the letter, I thought it appropriate to contact the lieutenant."

Fear gripped at Jessie's insides as he stepped forward. "Charlie? Is anything wrong with the baby?"

The lieutenant's stern face softened as he shook his head and waved his hand at Jessie. "No, no, no, Slate. The baby is fine."

"It's Kate, Jessie," O'Cleary said.

"Kate? Is she all right?"

"Yes. She's fine, or at least her health is fine. She has filed for a divorce. She thought it might be easier on you if the news came by way of me."

Jessie's shoulders sagged. His stomach churned wildly and felt as though it were shrinking. For an instant he feared that he would vomit.

"Maybe you better sit down, Corporal," Lieutenant Leonard said as he moved around the metal desk with a folding wooden chair.

Jessie felt for the chair like a blind man and slumped into it. He stared blankly straight ahead and saw nothing. He could hear the gunny speaking but didn't listen. He tried to visualize Kate's face, but the pain made it impossible. He blinked and realized that he was crying.

". . . so she's asking that you make this easy on all concerned by not contesting the divorce. She wishes you all the best and says right here that 'You can feel free to write or visit Charlie Rose in the future if you wish,' etc., etc. You can read it for yourself." Gunny O'Cleary laid the letter on the desk.

"Thank you," Jessie mumbled. He stood up and looked down at the letter.

The tinny-sounding intercom crackled with static. Jessie's eyes popped open.

"Reveille. Reveille. Now hear this! All officers report to the wardroom."

Broken Wing poked Jessie in the back from the cot below. "This is it."

"Who says?"

"Nobody."

"What's the old scuttlemouth have to say?" Jessie asked as he rolled out of the rack.

"Yeah, Perelli," Lopez grumbled from the other side of the narrow aisle. "Why so quiet?"

"Ah, shut up," Perelli said quietly. Broken Wing looked at Jessie and shrugged.

Stukowski leaned through the compartment hatch.

"What are you doing up so soon, Stu?" LaBeau asked through a yawn.

Stukowski's face looked pale and serious even in the dim light. "They're serving steak and eggs in the galley."

The morning chatter faded into silence. Broken Wing nudged Jessie in the back.

"Told you so."

The galley was alive with nervous chatter. Marines joked and laughed to relieve the tension. Jessie peered down at his traditional steak and eggs.

"Go on, Slate, dig in!" somebody said with a deep laugh.

Lopez looked up from cutting into his steak. "Yeah, fatten the lambs for the slaughter!"

Benjamin Oglethorpe touched his lips with a paper napkin and pushed his glasses back up on his nose. "You know, it is odd how the Corps makes us get haircuts and clean up our uniforms before we hit a beach."

"Got to look squared away in the casket, jerk!" Lopez shouted.

"Drop it, Lopez," LaBeau said with a frown.

"All right, then, let's talk women. Nothing better to talk about for your last meal."

Perelli dropped his knife and fork to his plate. "Look, fellas. I ain't makin' it off this island." His voice cracked. Beads of sweat covered his forehead, and he looked greasier than normal.

"Don't talk like that, Perelli," Jessie said.

"Yeah, you know better than that," LaBeau scoffed.

"I'm serious."

Lopez flipped a piece of egg at Perelli. "Shut up, Perelli! We'll all probably buy it, and you'll go home and have twelve kids!"

The men at the table laughed, but the laughs didn't sound genuine.

"Yeah, youz should know," Perelli said, forcing a nervous grin.

"Course I do. You'll be the richest lemon dealer in Jersey."

"Enough of that garbage. Let's talk about women!"

So for the final meal, as the men so aptly dubbed it, they changed the subject to women, and at the end of the meal Broken Wing tugged Jessie's sleeve as they filed out of the galley.

"Let's run up on deck and see."

"Lead the way."

The sun wasn't up. The only sound was the swish of water around the ship as it slipped through the black ocean. Men moved quietly around the forward deck. Others lined the starboard rail, pointing and staring through field glasses. Jessie followed Broken Wing to the crowded starboard rail and squeezed in between other Marines.

Suddenly a blinding yellow flash illuminated the black water like lightning. A thunderous roar followed, and Wing jumped. He looked at Jessie accusingly. "Didn't that scare you?"

Jessie forced a tight-lipped grin. "I don't care enough to be scared anymore."

The Indian's rugged face did not change, but his piercing black eyes softened with concern.

A moment later the big guns of hundreds of gray ships opened fire. The dark sky was streaked with red lines as glowing shells rained on the black island. White flashes erupted from the gray shape of a mountain now illuminated by constant explosions, so many explosions that even the dark shoreline of the enemy island was visible. The ocean itself seemed to vibrate from the cannonading. The flapping of a hundred trouser legs in the long line of Marines standing along the rail rose and fell with each gushing concussion wave from the shoreline explosions. Clouds of sulfurous-smelling gunpowder hovered around the giant cruisers and battlewagons as their huge guns roared salvo after salvo into the island. The powerful unleashed violence was hypnotic. Most of the Marines watching seemed unable to speak.

The first shafts of sunlight were already revealing the full scale of the incredible armada amassed against Island X. Jessie wondered how long he had been watching. Broken Wing nudged him and pointed at another troop transport about two hundred yards off the port bow. A sailor was leaning over the rail waving a signal flag at the small boats pulling alongside the big troopship, and green-clad Marines struggled down the rope nets, each man overloaded with the gear of war. Timing for the drop from the rope to the landing craft was a matter of life and death as the Pacific waves rose and fell and the small boats crashed against the steel sides of the big ship.

"We better get below. We will get word soon."

Jessie looked at the Indian's dark eyes. They beamed with the same fear and adrenaline and excitement that were finally beginning to race through his own system.

"Wing, look." Jessie pointed at the shoreline.

American dive-bombers were working the island over in wave after wave. Fighter planes strafed the dark sandy beaches with thousands of fiery tracers. A flight of B-24 Liberators droned in over the black mountain that towered over the island. Its slopes erupted in smoke and flame as each bomber unloaded its payload. Soon the entire mountain was hidden with dust clouds kicked up by thousands of pounds of TNT.

Broken Wing tugged on Jessie's sleeve. "Better get below."

Half an hour later the ship's intercom crackled with the first official word about the landing.

"Now hear this. The first wave is ashore."

A few weak cheers went up. From somewhere in the troop compartment a group of Marines started humming "Don't Sit Under the Apple Tree."

About an hour later the intercom crackled again.

"Now hear this. The second wave is ashore. Resistance heavy. Red Beach One is in Marine hands."

Christopher LaBeau sat on the deck checking the pins on his grenades. He looked up with a frown. "I thought we were going in on the first wave."

"Yeah, well, don't knock it," Perelli snapped nervously.

"All right, you eight balls, let's get on deck!" Sergeant Rim shouted from the compartment hatchway.

Jessie's heart fluttered. He grabbed up the heavy BAR and looked at Broken Wing.

"You look like a fawn seeing the arrow," Wing said.

"That's pretty good. Now, that really sounds like an Indian."

"I *am* an Indian."

"Yep," Jessie said as he filed out of the troop compartment.

The smell of gunpowder was strong on deck. The concussion of bombs reverberated across the water. The ship was a flurry of activity.

The bosun's whistle screeched over the intercom.

"Prepare to disembark!"

The Marines formed lines facing the starboard rail as the ship's crew tossed over the rope nets. One group after another climbed over the rail and down the nets into the waiting landing craft. One landing craft would fill up and pull away from the troopship, and another would motor up like a taxi to a curb. Then the small landing craft would join an ever-growing number of small boats that circled astern of the troopship. Jessie stepped up to the rail with Broken Wing, Lopez, Benjamin Oglethorpe, Perelli, and LaBeau. On the far right of the men facing the rail was Gunny O'Cleary. He leaned over the rail and gave a wave, then faced the Marines with a thumbs-up.

"Here's your ride, Marines. Gung ho!"

Jessie stepped over the rail and started down. Some of the men howled enthusiastically, but most were silent. Jessie grabbed hold of the rope strand going horizontally, and the boot of the man above crushed his fingers. Jessie released his grip and quickly grabbed a vertical rope. He looked down as he neared the rising and falling landing craft and timed his step to the bobbing deck of the boat. Quickly the boat was packed with the First Platoon. The motor rumbled, and the landing craft pulled away from the troopship. Twenty minutes later the circling landing craft seemed to slow its engines as the Navy coxswain swung the boat around and headed toward the shore. At that moment the gunny bellowed from the front of the landing craft.

"Keep your head below the gunwale!"

Suddenly the Navy coxswain gave the landing craft full throttle.

A flight of American fighter planes whipped by low overhead. It was a comforting sight. The rumble of the boat's engine was so loud that Jessie could no longer hear the shelling. The platoon crouched below the level of the gunwale, exchanging glances but not speaking. It was as if there was nothing left to say. A couple of men began to pray. Then, as if on cue, a majority of the platoon bowed their heads. Jessie found that he wanted to pray with them but didn't know how or even know what to pray for. He wasn't even sure that he wanted to live. Then he remembered big Chaplain Parker telling him how: no other name. Jessie lowered his head and mumbled quietly, "Jesus Christ. Please forgive me for being a sap. Please take care of Kate and baby Charlie." He looked around at the faces nearest him and wondered how many of them would live through this. He peeked up over the gunwale. Another landing craft sped past, returning from the beach to pick up more men from the transport, shooting a spray of white water in its wake. Jessie glanced down. His hands were shaking. He squatted down, trying to remember the honeymoon cottage in New Caledonia and Kate standing in the front yard. Coral and sand scratched the landing craft. Suddenly the boat lurched to a stop with its nose high in the air. Bullets whined off the steel hull.

"This is it!"

The ramp dropped with a thump and a splash. The platoon ran off, three men abreast. Jessie waited his turn, standing to a crouch, inching forward. A cracking explosion sent a wave of salt water over the port side of the landing craft. Jessie spit water from his mouth as he sprinted forward down the ramp. Dead Marines littered the shoreline, some rolling to and fro in the wash of the breakers. His boot sank into the soft black volcanic ash of Island X, and his sprint turned into a slow jog under the weight of his seventy pounds of gear. Twenty yards off the beach a steep ridge of ash and sand formed a fifteen- to twenty-foot wall that ran the length of the beach. A wounded Marine lay at the water's edge waving the newcomers on. His face was painted with camouflage, and Jessie knew the man had been part of the first wave. Beside him lay a young ghostly-looking corpse, his face white with antiflash burn cream. Along the top of the seawall Marines flattened out with rifles aiming at targets on the other side that no one could see. No one seemed to be firing. The whoosh of incoming artillery sent every Marine diving for cover.

Jessie dived into the steep wall of ash. An incoming round hit at the water's edge ten yards from the retreating landing craft. The ground shook from the ear-splitting explosion. Coral and shrapnel thudded nearby. Jessie pulled his face out of the ash and looked up at Broken Wing. The Indian's face was gray.

"They got us pinpointed!"

"See that guy waving us on?" Broken Wing asked.

"Yeah."

"His face was painted up like a ghost!"

"Yeah. He was on the first wave."

"Yes. He is still lying there."

Lieutenant Leonard ran up the beach shouting, "Get off the beach! Move out!"

"Move it!"

"Saddle up!"

Wing looked solemnly at Jessie, "Good luck, my brother."

"If I don't make it, tell Kate . . ." Jessie paused and wondered what words would make any difference to Kate now.

Broken Wing's black eyes opened wide like those of a madman.

"YEEEE!" He screamed out a bone-chilling war cry into Jessie's face. Jessie's eyes were shocked open with adrenaline, and he joined in the scream.

"YEEEE!"

They stood and rushed over the wall. The bodies of four Marines lay facedown on the other side. Jessie rushed past and tried not to look but couldn't help himself. Rifles were sticking in the sand beside each man. Twenty yards beyond the four dead men a burning APC sent black smoke billowing into the hazy sky. Another dead Marine lay beside the APC, and beside him a corpsman worked feverishly on a screaming bloody Marine with no arms. The platoon pushed forward through the sucking ashen terrain. The screech of a Jap 90-mm sounded close.

Lieutenant Leonard turned and shouted, "Take cover!"

Jessie and Broken Wing dived for a small bomb crater as the first 90 screamed into the ground nearby. The muffled explosion covered them with sand. An instant later another hit even closer. Jessie held on to his helmet and waited for the pain that he knew would follow. Suddenly explosions rippled around the platoon like giant popcorn going off. Thirty seconds later the barrage stopped. Men lifted their faces from the earth slowly and looked around. Someone was crying in between loud gasps for air. Another man moaned quietly nearby.

"Corpsman!"

"Corpsman!"

"Move out!"

"Saddle up!"

Jessie glanced around to see who was hit. A Marine was writhing in pain on the ground fifteen yards away. Private Turner was kneeling beside him. Jessie ran over and kicked Turner in the rear end.

"Leave the wounded, boot! You're a killer, not a nurse!"

"Aye, aye, Corporal!"

Jessie turned away. Gunnery Sergeant O'Cleary gave an approving nod and signaled a thumbs-up. A sudden rush of pride sent a stream of goose bumps down Jessie's arm.

"Move it, Marines! You ain't back on the block with your gal!" O'Cleary shouted.

Jessie sprinted forward. The terrain was flat and open. The platoon moved forward another forty yards, stopped, and hit the dirt. A minute later Lieutenant Leonard stood up and started shouting and pointing men into positions.

"Dig in! Make it deep! You're probably here for the night!"

The digging was close to useless. Broken Wing and Jessie took turns trying to shovel out a hole in the soft sand, but for every shovelful tossed out of the hole another would cave in from the sides.

The platoon set up a line of defense and settled in for the night. The expected counterattack never came. No one slept. Heavy pounding from American cruisers and destroyers continued all night, mixing in with the racket of Jap mortars and coastal guns. The drone of enemy planes circling over the American fleet pulled all eyes upward. Suddenly the night erupted with thousands of streaking tracer rounds from AA guns ashore and the guns on the ships. One ship exploded in flames, then a plane burst into yellow fire and flamed into the ocean. It was quickly followed by a second. And so it went off and on again, one light show after another until daybreak finally came.

Jessie had barely shoved down a can of breakfast when the dreaded word was shouted through the platoon.

"Saddle up!"

"Move out!"

The platoon had moved forward another hundred yards across the flat lava-covered terrain when the word came back to halt and dig in. There they sat for the next twenty-four hours, watching and listening to the battle raging all around the island. Island X. The big black volcanic mountain that dominated the island's terrain seemed to be the focal point of most of the second day's activity. The Japs could obviously pinpoint their artillery fire from the top of the mountain, and anyone who controlled it could control most of the movement on the island. The big guns of the American fleet rained shells on the mountain all day and deep into the night. It seemed impossible that anyone could live through it. Again, no one slept for fear that he might never open his eyes again.

The third morning was greeted by the barking orders of Gunny O'Cleary.

"Saddle up! You can't live forever! Let's go kill some rice-balls!"

Jessie flipped the last piece of his hardtack biscuit over his shoulder and shook his head. "You know, Wing, I love that guy!"

"Yes."

"That's all you have to say?"

"Yes."

"Think we'll see any Japs today?"

"Yes."

"That's all you have to say?"

"Yes."

"Saddle up!"

The platoon moved ahead single file. Somebody said that the 27th Marines were somewhere up ahead, but no one had seen them yet. They moved forward through a battered Jap airstrip called 0-2 on the map. Pieces of blown-apart Jap bombers lay scattered about. A group of Navy corpsmen and doctors worked on wounded men in an earthen Jap revetment that was intended to shelter enemy planes. Three hundred yards farther on the point man of the platoon reached a long steep embankment of dirt, ash, and sand that looked at least twenty feet high. The embankment lined both sides of another abandoned airstrip. The wreckage of Jap planes littered the northeastern end of the strip. A smaller airstrip crisscrossed the larger one, forming a narrow X shape. Both strips were pockmarked with huge craters from American bombing. Pieces of Jap planes ringed the strip. Every fifty to seventy yards along the larger strip the Japs had constructed revetments to protect parked planes from bombing. Each revetment was surrounded by twenty-foot walls of earth and ash. The platoon rushed forward and flattened out against the dirt wall protecting the airstrip.

"All right! Over the top!" someone shouted.

Jessie was first to reach the top. A shrill whistle filled the air, then went silent with a whooshing sound like air escaping from a punctured tire. A shattering crack blew Jessie over the embankment and down the other side into a revetment. He tried to open his eyes but couldn't. He shook his head, and the weight of something heavy kept his neck from moving. He tried to push himself off his stomach, but something held him down.

"I got you, Jessie!" Broken Wing's call sounded far away.

Jessie felt someone tugging on his boots. He couldn't breathe. He gagged and tried to spit, but his face was under ash.

"Hurry up! Grab that leg," someone said, but the voices sounded faint.

Suddenly Jessie felt the strong pull of hands on his boots. He tried to open his eyes again. Light. The burnt taste of blood and ash filled his mouth. He spit and felt something flap against his chin. He moved to wipe ash from his eyes, but his right arm started shaking as if in a wild muscle spasm. He felt a hand wipe debris from his face. He opened one eye. Broken Wing grinned at him.

"Corpsman!" someone shouted.

A moment later a freckle-faced corpsman knelt down and shoved two sulfa pills into Jessie's mouth. He sprinkled some kind of powder on Jessie's upper lip. It burned.

The corpsman scrunched up his face. "That lip's a mess." He searched through his bag for gauze.

"Grow mustache," Broken Wing said with a scoffing motion.

"Hey, Corpsman! How was the lieutenant?" Sergeant Rim shouted from somewhere behind Jessie.

The corpsman grimaced as he looked away from tending to Jessie's lip. "Nothing I could do, Sarge. He got it right in the forehead."

"Get up! Let's move out!"

"Move it, Wing! You ain't no doctor!"

Broken Wing stood up and looked down at Jessie. "You okay?"

"You ain't going anywhere without me, you stupid Injun." Jessie shoved the corpsman's hand away and struggled to his feet.

"You better stay put, Marine! You're losing a lot of blood."

"Here. Just wrap something around my head to keep the lip from flapping," Jessie said.

"What? You're crazy!"

"No. Just like this," Jessie said. He demonstrated by pretending to wrap a bandage under his nose and around the back of his head, but when he reached back, his hand felt something wet and sticky. It was blood. Jessie took off his helmet. There was a nickel-sized hole through the front.

"Hey! Am I hit in the head?"

"Sit down, Marine."

The corpsman gave Jessie a gentle push on the chest. Jessie slumped back. He could feel blood streaming down his forehead and more blood dripping down the back of his neck. A sharp pain shot through his temples. He touched a deep hole in his forehead at the hairline. A rush of fear overwhelmed him. He wanted to cry out but didn't. He looked up at Broken Wing.

"Wing."

"Yes."

"Am I dying?"

"Don't think so."

"Don't think so? Is that all you can say? You useless sister to a swab jockey!"

"You okay. Dying people are more quiet."

"Move out!" Gunny O'Cleary shouted.

The corpsman put his face close to Jessie's and shouted. "Now, shut up and let me work!" He pressed a square bandage over Jessie's mouth and upper lip.

"Where's our doc? Doc Kuipers?" Jessie mumbled through the bandage.

"He didn't make it."

"Oh, no. His poor mom."

The platoon filed past, each mumbling a good-bye of sorts or offering a thumbs-up as he passed. They crossed the airstrip and climbed over the ash embankment there. Five min-

utes after the last man had disappeared over the top, a hail
of gunfire erupted from the other side.

The corpsman looked toward the gunfire. "Good luck."

"Thanks, Doc," Jessie mumbled. His lip felt huge.

"This should do you till you get to the rear."

The corpsman finished wrapping a bandage around Jessie's head. He stood up with his medical bag. "Stay right
here until they come by and bring you back to an aid station."

"Right."

The corpsman turned and hurried across the airstrip, up
the embankment, and out of sight. Jessie sat still, trying not
to think about the pain in his head or the blazing sun.

Forty minutes later no one had yet come for him. He
touched a bandage and looked at his hand. Blood was beginning to soak through. Jessie looked around the abandoned
airstrip. He wondered if he was bleeding to death, and a
wave of panic seized him. He crawled back up the embankment. From there he could see back toward the beach for
nearly a hundred yards. There was no movement. He tried
to remember how far back the aid station at the first airstrip
was. He half climbed and half rolled down the other side
of the wall of ash, struggled to his feet, and began to stagger
back toward the first airstrip. He guessed the distance to be
about two hundred yards, maybe three hundred.

He stumbled and crawled until he could go no farther.
He then collapsed into a shell hole and watched as American fighter planes wove a protective web of vapor trails in
the blue sky above. The explosions sounded more distant
now. He closed his eyes, then jerked suddenly and sat up
in a cold sweat. He looked around. No one in sight. He
crawled out of the shell hole and staggered to his feet again.
He wondered how long he had been walking. It felt as
though it had gone on for days. His vision was blurry. Up
ahead he thought he caught a movement. He walked faster.
He could see the airstrip. The remains of Jap planes were
scattered around the fringe of the runway. A faraway whistle was getting closer with frightening speed. Jessie dropped
facedown in the dirt. Incoming shells went silent, then
whooshed by low overhead. The ground shook as a series
of blasts erupted from the airstrip. Then silence.

Jessie lifted his face out of the dirt. Black smoke billowed from the revetment that had housed the aid station. A direct hit. He moved toward the remains slowly. Inside he found two dead men, one of whom was headless. Pieces of human bodies were scattered around the ash walls, mixed with parts of canvas stretchers and boots and bones. No one was alive. Jessie stood staring for a while. He tried to pull his eyes away but couldn't. An American P-38 Lightning ripped by low overhead. Jessie gazed after it and wished he were up there, where it was clean.

An hour later he reached the twenty-foot dunes that past storms had built up all around Island X's shoreline. The rumble of diesel engines sounded close. Jessie scrambled up and over a dune. Spread out in neat rows along the water's edge were about thirty Marines on stretchers. Corpsmen moved from stretcher to stretcher checking wounds, then turning and shouting orders to Marines rushing off the ramps of three beached landing craft.

"Over here! This man's ready to board!"

Jessie stumbled down the steep dune and onto the soft sand of the beach. A big corpsman stood up from tending to a man on a stretcher. Jessie slumped to his knees and gave a weak wave.

"Hey, Mac! Can you give me a hand?" Jessie called with his last ration of strength, closed his eyes, and fell onto his side.

A ripping explosion vibrated the ground. Jessie tried to open his eyes. The left eye was glued shut by a thick scab of dried blood. Through his right eye the sky looked hazy. Waves breaking against the shore pushed cool ocean water under his canvas stretcher. His back was wet. Eight-inch guns from a Navy cruiser belched out an ear-splitting salvo of shells overhead. Jessie struggled to sit up. Next to him, an IV bottle had been hung on a Garand rifle stuck in the sand by its bayonet. A needle was taped to his right arm. He glanced left. A long row of wounded and dead Marines lay along the beach. Some of the dead were covered with ponchos; others were not.

"Slate!"

A wounded Marine sat up amid the long row of bodies. "Rim?"

Jessie winced and felt his lip. The bandage was gone, and

a large piece of his top lip was flapping against his bottom one. Sergeant Rim rolled onto his side and pushed himself to his knees with great effort. He had a bloody bandage around his left thigh and neck. He got to his feet and limped over to Jessie.

"Glad you made it, Slate."

The look on the old bulldog was as pleasant as Jessie had ever witnessed.

"What happened, Sarge? Any of the other guys here?"

Sergeant Rim's expression turned cold. "Yeah. Most of 'em are here. Under ponchos."

"What happened?"

"We walked about three hundred yards after we left you at the second airstrip. Got hit by everything. Gunny went down right away."

"Dead?" Jessie stiffened with fear.

"I don't know. They already took him out to the hospital ship. You don't look too good, Slate. You better lay back down."

"Who else? Broken Wing?"

"Think he got hit, but I'm not sure. Lieutenant Leonard's dead."

Jessie dropped back onto the stretcher.

"Me and LaBeau and a couple of others jumped into a bomb crater for cover, and a Jap popped out of a hole and tossed in a grenade. Lopez jumped on it. How do you figure a guy like that?"

"God, I hope Gunny and Wing made it."

"Old Gunny will make it. People been trying to kill him from France to China and ain't done it yet!"

"I don't feel so good, Sarge. You think I'm dying?"

"Corpsman! You lay still. You're gonna be around for the next war, Marine."

"Think so, Sarge? Maybe."

"Sure you will, boy. Be hard to find another war this good, though. . . ." Sergeant Rim's voice faded away.

Kate's lovely face was surrounded by her long auburn hair. She smiled and looked down at the baby and kissed his little fat cheek. He could hear someone crying; it sounded far off. Kate's face began to sway gently back and forth.

"Easy with the boom, sailor!"

Jessie opened his eyes. They stung with salt water. A light drizzle beat against his face. He moved to wipe the rain from his eyes to clear his vision. His arms wouldn't move. He shook his head and strained to free himself, but he was strapped down.

"All right. Bring him in a little faster," someone shouted from below.

Jessie lifted his head to look around. He was on a stretcher, and he was off the ground. A landing craft bobbed beneath him in rough sea swells. He looked to his left. The giant steel rusting hull of a large ship was close enough to spit at. He looked up again into the gray rainy sky. The boom of a crane hovered above, lifting Jessie's stretcher higher and higher.

"That's it. Swing him aboard."

The crane swung the stretcher over the deck of the big ship and lowered it gently. Two sailors in blue dungarees unhooked the ropes and shouted. "All clear!"

They picked up the stretcher, one on each end, and started to walk.

"Hey, where am I?" Jessie asked.

"Transport ship that's been converted into a hospital ship," said a round-faced sailor carrying the foot end of Jessie's stretcher.

"Am I gonna make it?"

"We got the best doctors in America on this ship, Marine. You're gonna be fine."

Jessie closed his eyes and fell into a black dreamless sleep. When he opened his eyes again, a bright light made him squint. Something was tugging on his right foot. He lifted his head. A white-clad corpsman was cutting away his boondockers. Someone pushed against his chest.

"Lay still, Marine. Corporal Slate, is it?"

Jessie looked up into the eyes of a man wearing a surgical mask and cap. "Yes, sir."

"How do you feel?"

"Top of the world, Doc," Jessie said gruffly.

The doctor chuckled as he prepared a syringe. "You shy of needles?"

"Hate 'em."

"Turn the other way so I can get a good angle on this head wound for a second."

Jessie looked to his left and winced at the expected pain. An arm hung down limply from a table beside him. Two doctors worked over the man. On his wrist dangled a silver bracelet. Jessie tried to sit up.

"Wing? Wing!"

A strong hand on Jessie's chest shoved him back down.

"Don't move, you idiot! Want this needle in the eye?"

"Wing! Broken Wing! It's me, Jessie!" he said, though his words were slurred almost unrecognizably.

"Hurry up with that sedative!"

"Doc, that's my buddy. Is he okay?"

"We're doing everything we can."

"Ouch! What is that, a square needle?" Jessie yelled.

"Shut up and close your eyes."

"How bad is he, Doc?"

"Shut up, Marine. That flap you're working used to be a mouth, and if you want it to resemble one again, you'll stow away the rest of your questions till I'm finished!"

Jessie tried to argue, but he could hear his words begin to slur. A heavy fog seemed to float down over him until even the pain was sort of gray and dull.

"You ready for some chow yet, Gyrene?"

Jessie opened his eyes. The most painful throb he had ever experienced pounded against his temple and forehead. He winced.

"Easy does it, now. You feel like some chicken soup?"

Jessie focused in on the broad face of a corpsman standing beside him.

"Yeah," Jessie mumbled through his bandaged and swollen mouth.

"I got you a straw here. See if you can sip up some of this broth."

Jessie nodded. It was easier than speaking. He tried to lift himself up as the corpsman shoved a second pillow under his shoulders.

"There. That should help you get to it."

Jessie reached for the straw with his right hand. The arm and hand worked. Jessie stared at his hand as he worked his fingers to make sure.

"The arm's okay now, Marine. Doc says that head wound just made it spaz out for a while or something like that."

Jessie looked at his hand again. The silver bracelet stared back.

"Wing. My buddy, Broken Wing!"

"Stay calm, now. You don't want to rip out those stitches."

Jessie grabbed the arm of the corpsman and pulled him closer, staring him coldly in the eye.

"I have to know if he's okay."

The corpsman frowned, then nodded in understanding. "I'll find out."

"He was in the operating room right next to me."

"I'll find out. Now shut up. Your mouth is starting to bleed, and you're going to rip out those stitches."

"His name is Corporal Broken Wing."

"I'll be back the moment I find out something."

"And can you requisition something to write home with?"

The corpsman nodded and left through an open hatchway. Jessie looked around the room. It was filled with wounded Marines. It must have been officers' quarters, Jessie thought, as the cots were hung in two tiers rather than five, the way the poor enlisted slobs' beds were. The thunderous booms of naval bombardment vibrated the room. Jessie looked to his left. Two Marines sat at a card table, playing rummy. One man's face was bandaged so completely that only small holes for the nose, mouth, and eyes were visible. The other man looked okay except for a cast on his right leg.

"Say, Mac," Jessie called.

The man with the cast on his leg looked at Jessie. "Yeah."

"Where are we?"

" 'Bout a quarter mile off of Iwo."

"Iwo?"

"Yeah. Iwo Jima. That's the name of that black turd out there that we been dying for."

"Quarter mile? We're still that close?"

"Look out of that porthole. You can still see the show."

"Corporal Slate?"

Jessie turned, then winced in pain. His lip began to drip blood down his chin.

"Don't try to speak. I'm Jim Engleman, the ship's chaplain."

"I can speak okay. Just can't laugh."

The chaplain smiled. He was a handsome character who looked a little like an older version of Cary Grant.

"Anything I can do, Corporal?"

"Yes, sir. I have to know if my buddy is okay—Corporal Broken Wing. He's with the 26th. He was in the operating room. And Gunnery Sergeant O'Cleary."

"You lie back now. I'll find them."

Jessie dreamed about Kate and his baby boy. He dreamed about home. Memories of his mom, her soft face against his. Memories of his dad stepping off a train in his dress greens with a seabag over his right shoulder and a leather bag stuffed full with the most beautiful marbles Jessie had ever seen.

Someone nudged him. Two hours had gone by.

"Corporal." It was the chaplain.

Jessie opened his eyes. Everything hurt.

The chaplain looked pensive.

"Broken Wing?"

"Yes. I found him."

Jessie sat up quickly. A shooting pain in the back of his head closed both eyes and forced him to groan.

"Corporal Slate, you should stay flat."

"No, Chaplain. How is he?"

"He told me to give you a message. Hope I can pronounce it. He said, 'A-chi yeh-hes.' Does that sound right?"

Jessie laughed, and for a very brief moment the world was right again.

"What's it mean?"

Jessie smiled. "His intestines itch."

The chaplain's face remained pensive.

"What about Gunny O'Cleary?" Jessie asked him.

The chaplain shook his head nervously.

"Where is he?" Jessie asked.

"The next room over. He won't last long."

"What?" Jessie asked.

Jessie headed for the hatchway.

"Slate, you're still bleeding."

"I'm okay, Chaplain. Take me to the gunny."

Jessie followed the hesitant chaplain down a narrow passageway and into another room much like the one Jessie was staying in. Chaplain Engleman looked around for the corpsman, but the two who were in the room were busy working on another wounded man. Chaplain Engleman pointed to a regular hospital bed near the starboard bulkhead, just beneath an open porthole.

"He's over there."

Jessie followed the chaplain. Gunnery Sergeant O'Cleary's eyes were open and glazed over. The pillow under his bandaged head was soaked with blood, which seemed to be draining from his ear.

"Gunny, I brought a friend to see you," Chaplain Engleman said quietly.

"Good," the gunny said. His lips were dry and cracked, and his voice was raspy.

"Gunny, it's me, Slate."

"Slate," he said weakly.

"How do you feel, Gunny?"

The old man coughed, and blood ran down the corner of his mouth. He smiled.

"Slate."

Jessie held the old salt's callused hand. It felt cold.

"Right, here, Gunny."

"Got a doll for Kate. Get it to her."

"Aye, aye, Gunny."

"People don't always forgive mistakes, Slate."

"Yes, sir."

"Hard to forgive yourself, ain't it, boy?"

Jessie wiped away another tear. "Yes, sir."

"Jesus is the only help. Don't take as long as I did in figuring that out, son."

"You're gonna be okay, Gunny."

O'Cleary gasped for a breath. "No better way to die than like a Marine."

"You're okay, Gunny. You're the Old Corps."

"I'm fine, son. Chaplain?"

"Right here, Sergeant."

"Read it again will you?"

Chaplain Engleman opened his Bible.

Be it known unto you all, and to all the people of Israel, that by the name of Jesus Christ of Nazareth, whom ye crucified, whom God raised from the dead,

even by him doth this man stand here before you
whole.

This is the stone which was set at nought of you
builders, which is become the head of the corner.

Neither is there salvation in any other: for there is
none other name under heaven given among men,
whereby we must be saved.


"Hey! Look at this!" someone shouted.

"They're putting up Old Glory on Suribachi."

Jessie looked toward the shouting Marines. He released
the gunny's hand and moved over to an open porthole. Tiny
figures struggled to straighten an American flag on the big
black volcano that dominated the pork-chop-shaped island.
A surge of pride swept through Jessie. He turned back to
Gunny O'Cleary.

The old salt had landed on another beach.

# GLOSSARY

**03**—Springfield rifle

**782 Gear**—Marine Corps equipment issued to every Marine

**AK-47**—A Russian assault rifle

**ARVN**—Abbreviation for Army of the Republic of Vietnam

**AWOL**—Absent without leave

**B-40 Rocket**—A communist antitank rocket

**BAR**—Browning automatic rifle

**Betty**—Japanese light bomber

**blouse**—Marine dress jacket or coat

**body bags**—Plastic zipper-bags for corpses

**boondockers**—Marine field shoes

**boondocks**—Rough terrain; jungle

**boot**—Slang for a new recruit undergoing basic training

**bulkhead**—Protective wall; used by Marines to describe the walls of every structure from a barracks wall to the inner walls of a tank

**bush**—The outer field areas and jungle where infantry units operate

**C-130**—A cargo plane used to transport men and supplies

**C-141 Starlifter**—A large jet transport

**C-4**—Plastic explosive

**C-47**—WWII cargo planes

**C-rats**—C-rations or prepackaged military meals eaten in the field

**Charlie**—Slang for "the enemy"

**Chi-Com**—Chinese communists

**Chinook**—CH-46 troop helicopter

**choppers**—Helicopters

**chow**—Food

**claymores**—Mines packed with plastique and rigged to spray hundreds of steel pellets

**click**—One kilometer, sometimes spelled klick

**Cobber**—New Zealand word for buddy

**com shack**—Communications building

**concertina wire**—Barbed wire that is rolled out along the ground to hinder the progress of enemy troops

**Corsair**—American single-engine fighter plane

**CP**—Command Post

**cruise**—One tour of duty

**deck**—The floor; also ground

**dee dee maw or didi mau len**—To run quickly

**deuce-and-a-half**—A heavy transport truck used for carrying men and supplies

**DI**—Drill Instructor

**dinks**—Slang for an Oriental person, especially in reference to the enemy

**ditty bag**—Small bag for carrying personal articles

**Dogface or Doggie**—Any U.S. Army personnel

**earbanger**—One who fawns on another for personal gain; a brownnoser

**flak jacket**—A vest worn to protect the chest area from shrapnel or bullets

**frags**—Slang for fragmentation grenades

**Freedom Bird**—Slang for the flight that took a soldier home after his tour

**friendlies**—Friendly Vietnamese

**Frogs**—Slang name for French soldiers dating back to WWI

**galley**—Kitchen aboard ship

**GE-Dunk Shop**—PX aboard ship; Marines use the term for most PXs

**gear**—Marine Corps equipment

**gooks**—Slang for an Oriental person, especially in reference to the enemy

**grunt**—Slang for any combat soldier fighting in Vietnam

**gung ho**—Chinese saying that means "to work together"; later changed to describe an overzealous person

**Gyrene**—Slang for Marine

**hatchway or hatch**—Any kind of door, including a tank hatch or helicopter hatch

**Head**—Any kind of toilet in any location

**Ho Chi Minh Trail**—The main supply route running south from North Vietnam through Laos and Cambodia

**hooches**—Slang for any form of a dwelling place

**HQ**—Headquarters

**Hueys**—Helicopters used extensively in Vietnam

**humping**—Slang for marching with a heavy load through the bush

**I Corp Tactical Zone**—The northern five provinces of South Vietnam, called "Marineland" by some

**III Corp**—The military region around Saigon

**junk on the gunk**—Marine Corps gear laid out on a rack for inspection

**K-bar**—A Marine Corps survival knife

**KIA**—Killed in action

**LAAW**—Light antiarmor weapon

**lashup**—Outfit, unit

**LCI**—Landing Craft Infantry; length 15 feet; can carry over 200 infantrymen

**LCM**—Landing Craft Mechanized; length 50 feet; can transport 1200 men, one medium tank, or 30 tons of cargo

**LSM**—Landing Ship Medium; length 203 feet, carries a dozen tanks, vehicles, and cargos of men

**LST**—Landing Ship Tank; ocean-going ship that carries smaller craft topside, plus numerous tanks, vehicles, guns, and cargo within her tunnel-like hold

**LZ**—Landing zone

**M14**—An automatic weapon used in Vietnam by American ground forces

**M16**—Standard automatic weapon used by American ground forces

**M60**—A machine gun used by American units

**M79**—A 40-mm grenade launcher

**Maggie's drawers**—A complete miss on the rifle range

**mark-time**—To march in time

**medevac**—A term for medically evacuating the wounded by chopper or plane

**MOS**—Military Occupational Specialty

**mustang**—An enlisted man who wins a commission

**NAMBU**—Japanese machine gun

**NVA**—North Vietnamese Army

**P-51 Mustang**—American fighter plane

**PBY**—Seaplane; a Patrol bomber

**PFC**—Private First Class

**piece**—weapon

**pogey bait**—Candy

**pogue**—A derogatory term for rear-area personnel

**POW**—Prisoner Of War

**PT Boat**—Motor Torpedo Boat whose primary mission is to attack surface vessels with torpedoes, rockets, or guns

**punji sticks**—Sharpened stakes used to impale men

**PX**—Post Exchange

**R & R**—Rest and Relaxation

**Raiders**—Elite Marine force trained for action behind enemy lines

**rear echelon pull**—Anyone who is behind you in battle; usually used by front-line Marines to sarcastically describe anyone who was not a front-line marine

**RPG**—Rocket-propelled grenade

**sack**—Marine Corp bed, also called rack or bunk; could be used to described an actual bed or the mud you're sleeping in

**Sally**—Twin-engine Japanese bomber

**salt**—A term used to describe a man who has been in the Corps a long time or in combat for a significant amount of time

**sappers**—Viet Cong infiltrators whose job it was to detonate explosive charges within American positions

**satchel charges**—Explosive packs carried by VC sappers

**scuttlebutt**—Drinking fountain; also rumors often started at the drinking fountain

**seabag**—Marine khaki barracks bag used to carry nearly everything a Marine owns

**search and destroy**—American ground sweeps to locate and destroy the enemy and his supplies

**short-timer**—Someone whose tour in Vietnam is almost completed

**slop chute**—Any place that serves alcohol in any form

**smoke grenade**—A grenade that releases colored smoke used for signaling

**survey**—Turning in used equipment for new gear; also used to describe a man being discharged, "surveyed out of the Corps"

**swab jockey**—Also swabby, or squid; any sailor of any rank

**TBY**—Portable military radio

**Tet**—The Chinese New Year

**The Island**—Could mean any island, but usually meant Guadalcanal

**The Eagle Craps**—Payday

**The Great War**—World War I

**The Slot**—Partially sheltered sea route between the Southern Solomons and the Bismarcks

**Tiger beer/33 beer**—Vietnamese beers

**Tojo**—General Hideki Tojo, Prime Minister of Japan

**Top or Top Sergeant**—First Sergeant; highly respected rank

**tracer**—A bullet with a phosphorous coating designed to burn and provide a visual indication of a bullet's trajectory

**VC**—Viet Cong

**Viet Cong**—The local communist militias fighting in South Vietnam

**Web-gear**—Canvas suspenders and belt used to carry the infantryman's gear

**WIA**—Wounded in action

**Willie-Peter**—White phosphorous round

**Zeke**—Japanese fighter-bomber larger than a "Zero"

**Zero**—Single-engine Japanese fighter plane; light, fast, and maneuverable

# ABOUT THE AUTHOR

Johnnie M. Clark joined the Marines at seventeen and served with the famous 5th Marine Regiment as a machine gunner during the 1968 Tet Offensive, during which he was wounded three times.

He returned to graduate from St. Petersburg (Florida) Junior College. He is a Master Instructor of Tae Kwon Do and is now a free-lance writer.

His other books are SEMPER FIDELIS and GUNS UP! Now in its twelfth printing, GUNS UP! is required reading in a number of high school and college history courses.

In researching THE OLD CORPS, Johnnie Clark tracked down all the old Para-Marines he could find. He worked closely with artist Michael Herring on the cover painting for this book, which will now hang in the Marine Corps Museum in San Diego.

new man," Swafe asked loudly enough for the platoon to hear.